Praise for
bestselling aut

"An amazing, breathtaking and vastly entertaining family saga, filled with twists and unexpected turns, cowboy fiction at its best."
—*Books and Spoons* on *The Last Rodeo*

"With a great combination of drama and romance, plus a huge twist, this might be the best one in the [Blue River Ranch] series. *Roughshod Justice* has it all."
—*RT Book Reviews*

"Fossen certainly knows how to write a hot cowboy, and when she turns her focus to Dylan Granger… crank up the air-conditioning!"
—*RT Book Reviews* on *Lone Star Blues*

"Overall, this romance is a little sweet and a little salty—and a lot sexy!"
—*RT Book Reviews* on *Texas-Sized Trouble*

"This is much more than a romance."
—*RT Book Reviews* on *Branded as Trouble*

"Nicky and Garrett have sizzling chemistry!"
—*RT Book Reviews* on *No Getting Over a Cowboy*

"Clear off space on your keeper shelf, Fossen has arrived."
—*New York Times* bestselling author Lori Wilde

"Delores Fossen takes you on a wild Texas ride with a hot cowboy."
—*New York Times* bestselling author B.J. Daniels

To see the complete list of titles available from Delores Fossen, please visit www.deloresfossen.com.

DELORES FOSSEN

HOT TEXAS
Sunrise

HQN™

Recycling programs for this product may not exist in your area.

ISBN-13: 978-1-335-04105-0

Hot Texas Sunrise

Copyright © 2019 by Delores Fossen

www.HQNBooks.com

Printed in U.S.A.

HOT TEXAS
Sunrise

CHAPTER ONE

DEPUTY JUDD LARAMIE glanced up at the sign that dangled and squeaked from a wrought-iron hinge mounted over the door of the bar.

The Angry Angus.

Well, that's what it was supposed to be, anyway, but someone had slapped some black paint over the second *g*, making it the Angry Anus.

Judd was betting a variation of "hold my beer and watch this" had been a factor in the vandalism. Of course, this was a bar so it didn't require any of his cop skills to figure out that one.

Despite the closed sign, Judd opened the door that was meant to mimic one from an old barn. Rustic with crisscrossed boards. It, too, squeaked, and he stepped in, the cool air from the AC immediately spilling over him. It felt good, considering the afternoon April temps were in the high nineties and still expected to climb.

The place smelled like a bar. That was the first thing he noticed. The clash of wine, beer and limes. There was a chalkboard sign on the shiplap wall right next to the door. Stupid Sh*t Men Say was scrawled out in cursive letters.

And, yes, it had the asterisk instead of the *i*.

Beneath that were comments and examples. Some were also in cursive, some in print, and one was so illegible that he again suspected large amounts of alcohol had been involved.

Tell your tits to quit staring at my eyes.

Whoa, you've put on a few pounds, haven't you?

Think you can get your friend's number for me?

He had to study the last one a bit because of the drunken scrawl, but Judd was pretty sure that it said: "You're only three feet away from having the best sex of your life."

Sh*t indeed.

Sometimes, there wasn't much good he could say about his gender.

Judd let go of the door so that it swung shut behind him, and he glanced around at the rest of the place. Black-and-white cowhide seats with white-washed floors. Hay bales, saddles and other tack were big in the decor. But the focal points, if you could call them that, were the life-size plastic cows and steers. There was one in every corner and a pair on each side of the bar, and they looked downright spooky with their blank, wide-eyed gazes.

The furnishings were obviously "Western,"

meant to go along with the name when the second *g* hadn't been blacked out. But there were enough glass-and-silver whatnots and doodads throughout to make it look trendy.

It definitely wasn't a bar that would have been a fit in Coldwater, where he lived, but then that applied to a lot of places. The small Texas ranching town might be only forty miles from this bar in San Antonio, but they were worlds apart.

"We're closed," someone called out, and Judd spotted the bald sumo-sized guy wiping some glasses behind the bar—which was also simulated black-and-white cowhide. He spared Judd a glance but didn't give him a chance to respond before he added, "You here about the cowboy stripper's job?"

Since he'd been a cop for over a decade, and was fully dressed, Judd hadn't thought he could be surprised by any question tossed at him, but he'd never heard that one before. However, he was wearing cowboy clothes because he was one. Part-time, anyway.

Judd tapped the badge clipped to his belt. "I'm Deputy Judd Laramie."

The guy shrugged, kept on wiping. "If you're here about the job, the auditions are by the mechanical bull." He tipped his head toward the back of the building. "You'd better hurry, though, 'cause they're almost done."

Judd considered another badge tap. Considered, too, adding "You here about the stripper's job?" to the Stupid Sh*t Men Say board, but a direct question was the way to go here.

"Where's Cleo Delaney?" Judd asked, making sure he sounded more cop than cowboy. Sometimes that laid-back drawl worked, but instinct told him the "good ol' boy" approach would be lost on…Tiny.

Yep, that was according to the name tag he was wearing.

This time, Judd's repeated question and tone earned him more than a mere glance from the bartender, and he actually stopped his glass-wiping duties to look at Judd. "We got all the right permits," Tiny volunteered, adding some growl to his tone. "What you want with the boss lady?"

There was a dull ache throbbing in Judd's right temple, but he resisted the urge to try to rub it away. "What I want is to talk to her. I don't care about permits or auditions. Where is she?"

Tiny narrowed his eyes, probably trying to look like a badass, but Judd was better at it than he was. They played an eyeball game of chicken for a few seconds before Tiny tipped his head again. "Back there."

In the same direction as the cowboy stripper auditions. Of course.

So that's where Judd headed, and with each step he cursed Cleo. Cursed himself, too, for not trying to call her back so that maybe he could have cleared this up without driving all this way. Or seeing her.

Sometimes, blasts from the past could eat a hole in him. And even though Cleo had been somewhat of a bright spot, a hole was still a hole, and it'd taken him a long time to climb out of the last one.

Still…here he was. Intrigued, curious and hoping this visit didn't undo him. Putting the pieces back together was a bitch he didn't want riding him again.

"Judd, it's me, Cleo," the voice mail had said. "Cleo Delaney," she'd added as if he might not recognize her voice.

He would have had an easier time not recognizing his own hand.

She'd chuckled in the voice mail then, and repeated his name—twice. It was the kind of repeat a person would do when they were trying to figure out how or what to say, except Cleo had said it in that whispery sigh voice of hers. A voice that reminded him of things that could be put on the Stupid Sh*t Men Say board.

"Look, Judd, I need to talk to you," Cleo had finally said, "and it's not something I want to get into over the phone. Call me when you get a chance so we can set up a meet."

He hadn't called. Instead, Judd had gotten in his truck and driven first to her apartment. When no one had answered the door, he'd looked up the address of the bar—the one she'd emailed him about shortly after she'd told him she'd bought the place. That'd been three months earlier, with the subject header of "Catching up." It went with her other emails over the past ten years or so of "Just saying hello" and "Long time, no see." Phone calls and voice mails were rare. So rare that it'd spurred him to come to her right away.

By the time Judd reached the hall at the back of the building, he heard the music. "Save a Horse (Ride a Cowboy)." There was also the occasional male whoop and yee-haw, and Judd followed those sounds into a large room that might have been used for private parties. There were tables that circled a stage with a mechanical bull, where three men were dancing.

Cowboys.

And Judd used that term loosely.

They were wearing boots, cowboy hats and small swatches of denim fabric that covered their crotches. There was so much oil slathered on their bodies that Judd was surprised it wasn't dripping onto the stage floor.

He spotted Cleo right off. She was seated with a blonde woman at a table at the front of the room, and both had their attention fixed on the greasy cowboys who were gyrating and grinding to the song.

"Uh, cowboy on the right, something fell out of your G-string during that last kick," Cleo called out.

"Cowboy on the right" quickly shoved what appeared to be a wad of cotton back into the swatch. Considering the other things that could have come tumbling out, Judd decided that had been the best option of what he'd just witnessed.

Not wanting to interrupt the audition, Judd leaned against the wall, waited. And watched. Not the cowboys but Cleo. She was typing something on a tablet and didn't look especially into the entertainment. Unlike the blonde. She was doing some whooping and yee-hawing of her own. Despite Cleo's indifference, though, she lasted through the entire song before she stood.

And Judd felt *it* when he got a look at more than just the side of her face.

That punch of heat below the belt, and he didn't have any cotton padding to stave it off. However, he did have common sense—some days, anyway…and this was one of those days. Just in case that common sense was about to lapse, he slipped his hand in his pocket and slid his fingers over the bronze sobriety coin.

One year.

Not nearly enough time to forget that whole pit-of-despair shit. Nowhere near enough to risk dragging someone into that pit with him.

The blonde noticed Judd first, and she gave Cleo an elbow nudge that sent Cleo turning to look at him. The smile was instant. Ditto for her starting toward him.

He'd always thought she looked a little like a fairy. Delicate and petite with her curly brunette hair tumbling around her face and onto her shoulders. But looks could be deceiving. Cleo was tough, strong.

And happy.

Somehow, the shit upbringing they'd had in foster care hadn't rid her of those rose-colored glasses.

The years had settled nicely on her, giving her a

few more curves that he had no trouble seeing because of the slim dress she was wearing. What was missing was the riot of bright clothes she usually wore. Today, it was just the sedate blue dress with a thin silver chain around her neck.

"You came," Cleo said, and she drew him into her arms for a hug. A friendly one that didn't have a trace of heat on her part.

When she pulled back, she was still smiling, and that smile made it all the way into her sweet-tea-colored eyes. Eyes that looked a little tired. Still, Judd didn't have to wonder if she was happy to see him.

She was.

However, the nervous way she clamped onto her bottom lip confirmed that something was up. Maybe something wrong with the bar. Or, hell, maybe she wanted him to beat up some guy who was bugging her, as he'd done when Cleo and he were fifteen.

Their gazes held for a moment until the blonde cleared her throat. "I'm guessing he's not here for the audition?" she asked. "Because if he is, he's hired."

Cleo blinked in surprise and then laughed. "No. He's a friend. This is Judd Laramie."

The woman grinned, got out of her seat and walked toward them. "Ah. Judd the Stud. Cleo mentioned you," she added before she stuck out her hand for him to shake. "I'm Daisy Gunderson." She seemed ready to add something else, but then her eyes landed on his badge. "I own the Angry Angus, but Cleo runs the place."

Judd looked at Cleo for her to clarify that "stud" mention, or why she'd told him three months ago that she'd bought the bar, but before Cleo could say anything, one of the oiled cowboys waved his arms around, trying to get their attention. It was the one who'd lost his crotch stuffing.

"Uh, hate to interrupt," oiled guy said, "but I've got to get to work. You need to see any more dance moves? I can do another squat hip grind if you want. It's my signature move."

"No," Cleo answered, glancing at each of the stage trio. "You've all got the job. Only because no one else auditioned," she added under her breath to Judd and then raised her voice when she continued with the cowboys. "Just make sure everything stays tucked away beneath the G-strings."

Cleo turned to Daisy. "Could you do the contracts and give them the time and date they'll be needed for the Wainwright bachelorette party?"

"Sure. And I put copies of that catering order on your desk." Daisy seemed to have another clam-up moment, and she glanced at the badge again. "I'll sign it after you've had a look at it."

When Daisy walked away to chat with the cowboys, Cleo motioned for Judd to follow her into a hall that threaded off the party room. She also dodged his gaze.

"This is an interesting place," he commented.

"I'm going to pretend you mean that as a compliment." There was amusement in her voice. "Yes, it's cheesy, but there are some fresh plans in the works.

A new name, new decor. Less trendy, more intimate. In the meantime, bachelorette parties with cowboy strippers pay the bills."

"Why'd you decide to manage a bar?" he asked.

Cleo shrugged. "I'd been looking at other possibilities. A coffee shop. Maybe even a bookstore with a wine bar. But this was such a good deal that I couldn't pass it up."

All of this sounded like a reasonable explanation, but there was something in her voice that made Judd believe she was having second thoughts about whether or not she should have passed it up.

"Are you going to add a Shit Women Say board?" he added.

Cleo threw him a glance and a smile from over her shoulder. "There's one in the men's bathroom. But, yes, I'm considering moving it out front. The customers seem to like venting with chalk."

She kept up the gaze avoidance until she ushered him into an office. There was cowhide here, too, on the pair of chairs, and there was a large plastic Angus bull shoved into the corner. It was on its butt, its stiff legs jutting out, as if the bull was at attention.

Judd skimmed his gaze around the rest of the room. A cop's habit. And his attention immediately landed on the framed photo on the bookcase behind the desk.

A photo of Cleo, Judd and his brothers, Kace, Nico and Callen.

Cleo was in the center, grinning, as was Nico.

Kace was looking pleased, too, since it was his eigh-
teenth birthday. Callen and Judd sported their usual
"pissed off at the world" expressions. Judd was sure
he still sported his often, though Callen was smiling more these days.

Cleo closed the door, went behind the desk and
finally looked at him. "Sorry about the 'Judd the
Stud' thing, but I called you that after I broke up
with that Realtor I'd been dating and was whining
to Daisy about there not being any good men. The
rhyme just sort of rolled off my tongue, and I didn't
expect her to remember it."

"A rhyme," he muttered. It was stupid to feel any
kind of pride over being called a stud, but that brainless part of him behind his zipper seemed to like it.
"Good thing my name isn't Rick or the rhyme might
not have been so flattering."

She smiled again, and because "brainless" had
gotten in on this, Judd wanted to say something else
to put that light back on her face. He might do it,
too, after he got a few more explanations, and one
he needed was about the bar itself. The other was
about why she'd called him. Judd just made a circling motion with his finger for her to start talking.

For such a simple gesture, Cleo immediately understood what he wanted. She blew out a breath,
motioned for him to sit down. "I bought the bar, but
it's in Daisy's name."

He gave that a few seconds of thought and figured it out. "Because of your criminal record. You

thought you might have trouble getting a liquor license."

She nodded, smiled. "Are you going to arrest me?"

Judd studied her and sank down into one of the chairs. "No. But I'm not sure you needed to do things this way. You were arrested for stealing a car when you were barely sixteen. That's a juvie record and doesn't usually have any weight once you're an adult."

"I was arrested again when I was eighteen," she confessed. "I helped someone get out of a bad situation when she was trying to get away from a guy who was whaling on her. I was charged with breaking and entering after I picked the locks on his apartment so she could get her things. I didn't do any jail time for it, only got probation, but I didn't want to take any chances that it would interfere with the liquor license."

Judd got that. Didn't like it much, though, because she was bending the law. "You trust Daisy?"

"Absolutely. We've been friends for years now, and she spent time in the system, too."

The system. Such sterile little words that always made Judd's stomach tighten into a rock-hard knot.

"Daisy didn't have it as bad as we did," Cleo went on, and she immediately waved off that answer with a gesture of her hand and another smile. "Thanks for coming." She paused. "Are you okay?"

Okay was a little word, too, but it could open a

big-assed conversation that he didn't want to have so he settled for a nod.

"When I called Buck, he mentioned that you'd had a bad time a while back," Cleo added.

Now his gut tightened for a different reason. Buck was Buck McCall, the last foster father Judd and his brothers had had after a long string of foster dickheads and assholes. The same applied to Cleo, since she'd landed under the care of Buck, and his then wife, about the same time as Judd. Buck was decent, as solid as they came.

And apparently he was also a blabbermouth.

"I'm fine," Judd said once he got his jaw unclenched. When he got back to Coldwater, he'd be having a chat with Buck about keeping private shit private.

"Don't be mad at Buck." Cleo obviously noticed the jaw reaction. She fluttered her fingers toward the photo. "He remembers how close we were, and he didn't get into specifics. He only said you had been through a rough patch. Your brother Nico also mentioned it. Again, no specifics."

Judd had no intention of filling her in on those particulars, but he got a nasty flashback of himself falling down drunk. Literally. He'd ended up at the bottom of his porch steps.

"You talk to Buck and Nico often?" he asked, wondering if that's why she'd left that voice mail. Buck was recovering from cancer treatments. Also, he was no spring chicken, and it didn't take a cop's eye to see that the man hadn't been looking his best.

Too pale, and just the day before, Judd had walked in on him napping. Buck wasn't a napper.

"Nico and I talk every now and then," Cleo explained, "and he's stopped by a couple of times to see me."

Well, Nico sure knew how to keep a secret because he hadn't mentioned a word of it. Apparently, Judd would be chatting with his little brother…after he'd dealt with Buck.

"As for Buck," Cleo went on, "I try to call him at least every other month, and I visit him when I can." Cleo finally sat, then picked up an ink pen and fidgeted with it.

Nerves, Judd knew. And he waited for her to voice the same concern Judd had for their foster father's health. Since Buck was recovering from cancer, the concern was justified.

Still fidgeting, Cleo glanced at the picture. "You and I go back a long way. Seventeen years. *Friends*," she added, as if testing that word to see if he agreed with the label.

Not quite friends. More than that. Then less, once she'd been moved to another foster home shortly after that picture on her bookshelf had been taken. Judd had stayed in Coldwater with his brothers and Buck, while Cleo had been placed with a family in San Antonio only days after Buck's wife, Anita, had been killed in a car wreck. The system hadn't thought it appropriate for a teenage girl to be living in the house with four teenage boys and a foster father when there was no female around.

"Remember the night I left you a note on your bed and asked you to do me a big favor?" The smile she flashed him was laced with nerves now, too.

"Sex," he provided. "You wanted me to rid you of your virginity." And she'd done that with a "check yes or no" box with the question "You want to get lucky tonight?"

"You obliged me," she said.

Judd lifted his shoulder. "I was sixteen. It didn't take any arm twisting. I checked that 'yes' box pretty damn fast." He paused, studied her. "You didn't ask me here to have sex with you, did you?"

He knew the answer to that was "no." Cleo and he hadn't had sex in seventeen years, not since she'd moved to San Antonio. Still, it took her several long moments to confirm his "no" by voicing one of her own.

She looked him straight in the eyes. "You remember how bad it could be in the system."

Yeah, he remembered. Still had nightmares about it, but he settled for a nod. One that accompanied what Judd was certain was a confused look. Why the hell was Cleo digging up this old dirt and memories?

"I need you to go somewhere with me," she said, standing. She scribbled a note and put it in the center of her desk. It said, "Daisy, I'll be back soon."

Judd looked up from the note and stared at her. "Go where?"

She opened her mouth. Closed it. Opened it again and repeated the process until she took hold of his arm, pulling him up from the chair. "Please, just come with me."

"What's this about?" Judd demanded.

"Another favor." With her grip tightening, she led him out the door. "A big one."

CHAPTER TWO

WHEN UNDER STRESS—like now—Cleo liked to play a little mind game that she called BS, as in "best scenario." The rules of BS were simple. She mentally skirted past all the bad and unfortunate things that could happen until she reached the one that was good and fortunate.

In this case, she might have to settle for fair to middling.

"What's this about?" Judd repeated, and even though he pushed off the grip she had on his arm, he continued to follow her out the back exit and to her car. What he didn't do was get in after Cleo used her keypad to unlock the passenger-side door for him.

She considered what to say and how to say it and decided she'd been right that showing him was the only way. If she spelled it out now without Judd seeing the situation firsthand, he was going to tell her a flat "no" instead of the fair to middling response that she hoped he'd give after some serious thought.

"Remember when you beat up Simon Peterson because he was harassing me?" she asked.

Judd's dark right eyebrow winged up over his equally dark eye. Actually, a couple of things were dark about him. Midnight black hair, deep brown eyes and a skin tone that she'd heard Buck say was a legacy from Judd's Apache grandmother. His expression was dark, too. Always had been, with some serious intensity thrown in. In a nutshell, Judd was tall, dark and dangerous-looking, but Cleo knew his touch could be incredibly gentle. That's why she'd gone to his bed seventeen years ago.

That's why she'd wanted him here now.

Not for his gentle foreplay, though. But because he was the perfect package for what she had in mind. Of course, Judd wasn't going to see it that way.

"I'm not going to beat up Simon Peterson for you again," Judd growled. "He's a preacher now and has six kids."

Apparently, Simon had come a long way from the time he'd grabbed her boob. Then when she'd put Simon in his place by yelling at him, he'd made it his teenage life's mission to harass her. That had included flicking globs of spit-filled gum in her hair, tripping her and shoving her into a mop bucket that the janitor had left out. Cleo wasn't especially proud to have come to Judd for help with that, but Simon had outsized her by eight inches and a hundred pounds.

Those were the days before she'd learned a good kick to the balls was the great equalizer.

"Just please get in the car," she begged. "This won't take long."

She held her breath, waiting, and mercy, the man did indeed make her wait. It was probably only the risk of heat stroke that had Judd finally sliding into her car. Before he could change his mind, she put on her seat belt and drove out of the parking lot—fast.

With Judd staring at her.

"If this is about Buck," he grumbled, "just give it to me straight. Did his cancer return?"

"It's not about Buck." And she wanted to assure Judd that Buck was in good health, but even when she played the BS game, the best she could do was that everything was *possibly* all right when it came to their former foster father. "The last time I spoke to him, he did mention that he was going back in for a regular checkup. Did he?"

Judd lifted his shoulder in that casual shrug that was as easy as the smoky drawl of his voice. "If he did, he's not talking to me about it. He just said he was *fine*," Judd said, emphasizing the last word.

Cleo wondered if Judd knew that was the exact word he himself had used when she'd asked how he was. Probably not. She hadn't believed it any more than Buck's *fine*. And that troubled her a lot.

Maybe what she was going to ask Judd to do would be too much for him. She knew about his drinking problem. Buck had mentioned it. She'd heard gossip. Plus, five or so years ago when she'd stopped by Buck's on Christmas Eve, she'd also decided to say hello to Judd, who lived in a house on Buck's ranch. When Judd hadn't answered her knock, she'd peeked in the window and had seen him passed out on the sofa, an empty bottle of whiskey next to him on the floor.

The devil you know.

As bad as the whiskey devil was, she knew from what Judd had muttered in his nightmares that he often battled with far worse demons. Both those demons and the booze could drag him down, but Buck had assured her that Judd was now clean and sober.

Those clean and sober eyes were now drilling into her. "I don't like surprises," he reminded her.

She nodded. "And I'm not being secretive to piss you off. It's just a picture is going to be worth a thousand words." Cleo paused. "And then I can ask you for that huge favor."

He continued to study her. "Is the favor legal?"

Since the BS answer to that was "possibly," Cleo just stayed quiet and took the turn into the Pleasant Park neighborhood. Years ago, when it'd been in its prime, it had deserved that name, but it certainly didn't now. It was a long street of run-down houses, trash, gang graffiti and abandoned cars.

When she pulled to a stop behind one of the cars spray-painted with anatomically impossible sexual suggestions, Judd slid his hand over the weapon in his shoulder holster. "This isn't my jurisdiction, and I'd rather not have to shoot anyone."

"Shooting won't be necessary." She hoped.

Steeling herself, Cleo went to the door of the small wood-frame house with its blistered blue paint and rust-scabbed iron porch railings. Since what was once a doorbell was dangling from what had once been its mount, she knocked. Waited.

Prayed.

And knocked again.

Her heart was doing a pitter pat, and not in a good way, then the door was opened by a pint-size *cowboy* wearing just a pair of tighty-whities, boots and a hat. He was eating a red Popsicle that had melted down his arms and onto his belly. A little gray kitten pranced and coiled around his legs.

"Aunt Cleo!" he squealed, and launched himself, Popsicle and all, to hug her legs. She scooped him up, kissed him on the cheek and made a mental note to take her dress to the dry cleaners.

Judd didn't say a word, not verbally, anyway, but he knew she didn't have any siblings. "This is Leo."

"Little Leo," he corrected, and he held up five fingers of his left hand to indicate his age, something he was proud of since he'd only held that age-five distinction for a week.

One very long, very shitty week.

Yet, Little Leo still managed a smile—and an immediate interest in Judd. Leo eyed Judd's face, his cowboy clothes, his gun and then his badge before he started squirming for Cleo to put him down. The moment his feet were back on the floor, Leo took off running away from them.

"Beck!" the boy yelled as he ran, his cowboy boots clomping on the floor.

"His big brother," Cleo explained to Judd. "Beckham will probably think you're here to arrest him."

"Did Beckham do something to warrant an arrest?" Judd sounded very much like the cop that he was.

On the BS test, the answer to that was another "possibly" so Cleo kept quiet and stepped inside.

The place was a cluttered mess, just as it had been the other times Cleo had visited, and the TV was blaring with a talk show where people were yelling about the paternity of a baby being held by a crying woman. Everything smelled of booze, piss and other things she didn't want to identify.

"What the hell's going on here?" Judd demanded, still using his cop's voice.

She closed the door to stop the loss of the meager amount of cool air from the AC. "Yesterday, I went to the funeral of a dear friend, Miranda Morrelli. Cancer," she added.

Cleo blinked back the tears that she swore she wouldn't spill. There'd already been enough tears, and now it was time to woman up and try to do the right thing for her friend.

"Little Leo is her son," Cleo went on. "He's named after me," she said, hoping it would tell Judd just how close Miranda and she had been. No way could she say it with words right now because those tears would just leak out and her throat would close up from the grief.

Like his tone, Judd's gaze was all cop as it slid around the room. "What the hell is going on here?" he repeated.

Cleo tried to give him a quick summary before his patience wore out. "Miranda died only three weeks after her diagnosis. She got a very aggressive form of cancer, and there wasn't time for her to finalize giving me custody of the boys. That's how they ended up here with Miranda's *mother*."

And speaking of the devil, Miranda's mother, Lavinia Mercer, staggered from the kitchen and into the living room, a can of beer in one hand, a cigarette in the other. She was wearing a flimsy gown, with no bra. Cleo had no trouble determining that because the woman's boobs sagged practically to her belly button, and they flopped when she walked.

Lavinia's bloodshot eyes immediately narrowed when they landed on Cleo. "You're not welcome here," Lavinia spat out. "I don't want no hoity-toity bitch looking down on me." Since Lavinia tripped and fell onto the couch, Cleo had no choice but to look down on the crone.

"I came to see the boys," Cleo said. "To make sure they're okay."

"They're fine. Now get the pissing hell out of here." Lavinia's scowl got harder when she looked at Judd. "Get out and take your cop friend with you."

"Not until I see the boys." Cleo took Judd's hand, leading him to the hall. Lavinia continued to shout at them, but Cleo was hoping the woman was too drunk to get up and follow them.

Thankfully, Judd didn't three-peat his question about what the hell was going on, but Cleo did some silent cursing when she stepped into the small bedroom. Little Leo was there, his Popsicle still dripping while he watched Beckham try to pry open the paint-stuck window.

Isaac, the third brother, was on the bed, playing a video game. He only spared Cleo and Judd a blank glance.

"He's not here to arrest you." Cleo hurried to Beckham, and even though the fifteen-year-old towered over her, she still spun him around to face her. Beckham might have been the size of a man, but that face was all boy, and she immediately saw the grief, anger and fear.

Feelings that Cleo was experiencing herself.

With some more steeling up, Cleo hooked her arm around Beckham's shoulders and, with a little force, turned him toward Judd. "This is Beckham, and that's Isaac. You've already met Little Leo. Guys, this is Judd Laramie, an old friend of mine."

All three pairs of eyes went to Judd. Suspicious eyes except for Leo, who held out his Popsicle to Judd to offer him a lick. Judd declined with a head shake before he did another of those cop sweeps around the room.

"We need to talk," Judd told her. No cop's voice this time. It was more of a pissed-off warning.

"I want you out of here!" Lavinia yelled again, and Cleo looked out the door at the woman to make sure she wasn't coming in their direction. She wasn't. Lavinia was still on the couch and flailing around like a turtle that had been tipped over on its back.

Cleo shut the boys' bedroom door and looked at Judd. "Miranda's husband died in a construction accident when Leo was just a baby. They have no kin, other than Lavinia, that is. Yesterday she showed up at the funeral with her biker boyfriend and his buddies, who blocked me from taking the boys. I spent yesterday afternoon and this morning trying to reason with her and to get the local cops to intercede and give me temporary custody."

Judd studied her face. "I'm guessing they said no or the boys wouldn't be here. *I* wouldn't be here," he added. The face-studying continued a moment more. "You want me to go to the locals and continue reasoning with them, badge to badge?"

"It might be too late for that." Cleo dragged in a long breath. "For reasons known only to her, Lavinia clearly hates me."

Judd didn't disagree with her about that. "She's not fit to raise kids."

That was an understatement. She stared Judd straight in the eyes for this next part. "Lavinia doesn't want the kids, and she's going to put them in foster care." She gave him some time to let that settle in.

It didn't settle well.

The muscles in Judd's jaw went to work, stirring and tightening, and the old emotion drew his mouth into a grimace. Emotion that she hoped would swing in the right direction so he would help her.

"I talked to Child Protective Services, and they don't think I'm a candidate to be a foster parent. Because of the police record, and because I work at a bar," she added under her breath. "I figure I have a day or two at most before the boys are taken, and you know as well as I do that they probably won't end up together."

Yes, Judd would know all about that firsthand since his brothers and he had often been separated as they'd been moved from one home to another. Judd hadn't told her all the details, but Cleo knew enough.

"Buck said he would help," Cleo went on. "But he's sixty-nine, closing in on seventy, and with his health problems, he's out as a fostering candidate as far as CPS is concerned."

Which was too bad because Buck had been a top-notch foster father and would have been great with the boys.

"You talked to Buck about this?" Judd snapped.

She nodded. "And Rosy." Buck's bride of only four months. "They said I could use their house for the boys since my place isn't big enough." Cleo took another deep breath and spelled the rest out for him. "I'm tapped out financially and can't buy a bigger place. And no, I'm not asking you for money," she added.

Cleo left it at that for more of that sinking-in time. It didn't take long.

This time there was a different emotion that flared in his eyes. "You want me to foster them."

Bingo. But since Judd clearly wasn't on board with that, she spelled out some of the details. "The boys and I can live at Buck's, and I can commute to work. Buck will help me, and you won't have to do a thing except legally be listed as their foster parent. No way would CPS turn down a cop with a spotless record."

She hoped.

While she was hoping, Cleo wished Judd's jaw would relax a bit. And that he would stop with the head shaking. "There's gotta be somebody else who can do this. One of my brothers could…"

She gave him a flat look as he trailed off, and he was no doubt mentally going through why that wouldn't work. Because of his business, Callen spent a lot of time in Dallas. The youngest Laramie brother, Nico, had a police record that was even more splotched than Cleo's. The oldest, Kace, was the sheriff of Coldwater and would never agree to a shade this gray when it came to the law. In fact, Kace would likely report her to CPS for what she was trying to do.

"Someone else then," Judd amended. "A friend of yours. Daisy could do it."

Now she was the one shaking her head. "Daisy's a single mom of a two-year-old. A very cute but very active little girl named Mandy Rose. Despite Daisy having her hands full with her daughter, she's going to put in more hours at the bar so I can do this. All I need is your signature on the CPS paperwork, and you'll be their foster parent in name only."

They stood there, eyes locked, while Lavinia shouted out slurred obscenities and Leo tattled that Beckham was trying to get out the window again. Definitely not an ideal environment for thinking.

Judd didn't say anything. He took something

from his pocket and showed it to her. It was one of those token coins that AA handed out. Judging from his expression, he thought this would come as a complete surprise to her.

"I know you're a recovering alcoholic," Cleo said. "But there's nothing about that on any record. No arrests for it, no mention of it anywhere on the internet. That gives you a clean slate as far as CPS is concerned."

"I'm an alcoholic," he declared. "I'll figure out some other way to help you, but I'm sorry, Cleo. I can't do this."

And with that, Judd turned and tore her heart to pieces by walking out.

CHAPTER THREE

"I WASN'T FLASHING NOBODY," Gopher Tate protested. It wasn't his first protest, either. He'd been saying variations of that since Judd had cuffed him and put him in his truck to take the man two blocks up to the Coldwater Police Station.

Judd didn't bother to point out that Gopher had been wearing only a pair of tighty-whities and a ribbon beneath his raincoat—a raincoat he was wearing despite there not being a chance of a single raindrop in the scalding-hot forecast. Of course, the coat was just the tip of the iceberg here. That red ribbon was as good as a smoking gun. Gopher had taped it on the front of his underwear as if the contents beneath were some kind of present.

Too bad Gopher had decided to do his flashing just as Judd had been driving by. If Judd hadn't been right there, someone would have called it in, and another deputy would have responded. Then Judd wouldn't have had to take the time away from the calls he'd been making on his entire drive back from San Antonio.

"I just didn't have any clean clothes, that's all," Gopher went on. "And I needed to run to the Quik

Stop for some cigs. How was I to know a gust of wind was gonna catch my coat and flip it open?"

Judd also didn't point out that the coat flipping had happened in front of two female customers who'd been coming out of the Quik Stop. Nor did he point out that there were no gusts of wind and that Gopher had been arrested eleven other times for flashing women all over town.

While he drove to the station, Judd glanced at his phone to make sure he hadn't missed any calls. He hadn't. His screen was blank, something that would have normally pleased him.

But not this afternoon.

He wanted some answers on the feelers he'd put out on the Morrelli kids. Heck, he wouldn't have even minded seeing a call from Cleo. One where she'd left him a scathing voice mail because he hadn't done her that favor. No voice mail, though, scathing or otherwise.

Of course, maybe Cleo hadn't reached the point where she could even yell. He'd obviously taken the wind from her sails, along with robbing her of her breath because she hadn't said a single word to him when she'd driven him back to his truck that he'd left parked at her bar.

"All I need is your signature on the CPS paperwork, and you'll be their foster parent in name only," Cleo had said.

She'd made it sound simple, but he'd be lying by

signing those papers. Bending the law, and "in name only" wouldn't last the first time there was a hitch.

And there would be hitches.

Three kids would be a big-assed handful. There'd almost certainly be times when Cleo needed help, especially since she had no experience raising kids. With the boys living only a stone's throw from him, Judd knew that Buck and Cleo would look to him for that help. Buck's continuing health problems—yes, the health problems that Buck hadn't gotten around to discussing with him—would mean Judd would get sucked into something that he couldn't handle. Hell, there were times when he couldn't handle his own life.

Too many times.

Rosy, Buck's wife, had no doubt assured Cleo that she would help, too. And she would. But Judd knew the woman was sick with worry over Buck. It had only been four months since he'd been diagnosed with lung cancer and then gone through chemo and radiation. While the doctors thought they'd gotten all the cancer, it would be months or longer before Buck got an all clear.

"You can't make me believe you've never had your raincoat come open at the wrong time," Gopher complained.

"Believe it," Judd retorted, and he tuned the man out as he led him into the police station.

The dispatcher, Ginger Marlow, who was Gopher's cousin several times removed, sighed and rolled her eyes when she saw them. Eyes that the woman had "adorned" with what appeared to be a vat of green sparkly makeup. Judd supposed it was coordinated with the tower of flame-red hair that she'd swirled on top of her head. She had a quick smile, a flirty wink and, Judd suspected, a dirty mind since her gaze always wandered in the direction of his crotch.

"Why is it that only ugly geezers flash their junk?" Ginger complained.

"That's a question for the ages," Judd replied, and kept moving.

He got the man in lockup and headed back to his desk to do the paperwork on the arrest. For all the good it'd do. Gopher would get some jail time, some community service, probably even mandatory counseling, and then in about six months he'd do it all over again. Of course, by then it'd be winter and maybe the threat of his balls freezing off would have him delaying the next incident until spring.

Judd's desk was in the squad room, along with three others that belonged to his fellow deputies. Kace was the only one with an actual office. Such that it was. Coldwater wasn't exactly a hotbed of crime so there was no door on Kace's office and a large window allowed anyone to look right in. Judd could see his brother doing some paperwork, as well.

"What color was the ribbon on Gopher's junk?" Deputy Liberty Cassaine called out from her desk. No eye gunk for her. She was as plain and unadorned as a sheet of recycled printer paper, and she never glanced at his crotch.

"Red," Judd answered without looking in her direction. He immediately heard groans from the two other deputies and a satisfied "pay up" from Liberty. Apparently, there'd been a bet involved.

Judd stared at his laptop, silently cursed. His mind was a mess. A tangle of raw guilt and flashbacks. Being in that filthy house, knowing those boys needed help, had sent the past crashing into him like a fully loaded Mack truck. Too damn many memories of the beatings, the hunger and the fear. Other more recent memories of what'd happened at another house.

Those two jolts combined also brought back the gnawing hunger for a drink.

His drug of choice was whiskey, straight and from the bottle. No adornments for him. He hated the taste. Hated the searing burn it caused in the pit of his stomach, but without it, it was hard to squash down the darkness that choked him.

He could feel that dark hole eating through him again so he yanked out his phone and called his primary "feeler," Sergeant Darrell Boyd at San Antonio PD. Judd had worked with the man for two years when they'd both been on the force in Austin. Before things had gone to hell in a handbasket and Judd had transferred to Coldwater to work for Kace. Darrell had also ended up transferring—to San Antonio—so Judd suspected that "hell in a handbasket mess" that had happened there had also made it impossible for Darrell to stay at Austin PD.

Thankfully, Darrell had agreed to keep the call and request Judd had made earlier as a personal favor and not make it official. Also thankfully, he answered after just a couple of rings.

"It's not the news you'll want to hear," Darrell said without a greeting. "After we talked, I drove straight out to the house. You're right about CPS not allowing the kids to stay there for long even if the grandmother wanted them. She doesn't. What a piece of shit in the global gene pool."

Judd made a sound of agreement, but "piece of shit" was too mild of a term.

"I had a look around," Darrell continued, "and from what I can tell, the kids aren't in immediate danger. Then I talked to CPS—off the record. I spoke with a friend there who used to be on the force. When she checked the house, the piece-of-shit grandmother was sober. So, my friend told me they're leaving the boys there tonight with the hopes they can find a place where all three of the kids can go together first thing in the morning." He paused. "CPS thought you'd be interested in taking the boys."

"Cleo Delaney told them that," Judd spat out.

"Actually, it was Buck McCall who mentioned it to my friend in CPS who then mentioned it to me. In the last couple of days, your former foster father's been active in trying to find placement for the kids."

Active. That was an interesting word. *Sneaky* was another word Judd had for it, and he suspected that's why Buck wasn't answering his phone. He didn't want Judd calling him out on that sneakiness.

But Judd rethought that.

Buck of all people knew him. Knew what he'd been going through, and that meant Buck knew that Judd wasn't the right person to do this.

"The boys have been through a rough time, losing their mom, but I can understand why you wouldn't want to take on fostering them. Especially the oldest one," Darrell added. "He's fifteen and already got a two-count juvie record. One for assault and another for evading arrest after he ran from a uniform who suspected him of truancy. That kid's got trouble written all over him."

No, he had "acting out" written all over him. Judd had done the same—he just hadn't gotten caught.

"What are the odds that CPS will be able to keep the boys together?" Judd asked, though he already knew the answer.

"Slim to none. You know how this works. The little kid is cute, and the middle one does okay in school so somebody will want to take them. The older kid keeps threatening to run away. Not sure what they'll do with him."

Drag him into custody and keep dragging him with the threat of juvie lockup. Judd knew something about that, as well.

"Too bad Buck's too sick to take them," Darrell

remarked. "Or that your friend Cleo fell so short in her background check. My friend at CPS mentioned her, too. Both Buck and Cleo seem to want the kids."

Yeah, too bad, and it sucked about Cleo's record. Either of them would have been better suited to this than Judd would.

"Sorry the news wasn't better, but if anything changes, I'll give you a holler," Darrell assured him, and he ended the call.

Judd put his phone away, and tried to do the same thing to his emotions, then turned back to the laptop to start the paperwork on Gopher. He got two words into the report before he stood and kicked his trash can. It turned out not to be a very satisfying outlet for anger since there was no trash in it. The mesh metal can just made a clanging sound as it bounced and rolled across the floor.

His fellow deputies wisely didn't say anything about it, but Kace did. His brother came out of his office and looked at the can. Then at Judd.

"A bad mood or are you testing the durability of office equipment?" Kace asked.

Judd gave him a glare that could have frozen every sweaty armpit in El Paso in August.

"Bad mood," Kace concluded. He calmly picked up the trash can, put it in its usual place and then sank down onto the chair next to Judd's desk. "I got the message you left, telling me that you were taking an early lunch so you could go see Cleo. What'd she want?"

"A favor," Judd grumbled and downed the rest of an old, cold cup of coffee.

Kace stared at him. "Sex?"

Judd cursed him and cursed himself for telling Kace about what had gone on between Cleo and him all those years ago. "No," he managed to say once he got his teeth unclenched. "Something bigger. *Much bigger.*"

"This is about Buck, isn't it?" Kace's forehead bunched up. "You know, because he's still looking a little shaky."

Judd wasn't surprised that Kace had noticed that, but he wondered if Buck knew his secret health problems were in no way a secret. "Not about Buck. Cleo wanted me to help her foster some kids."

Now it was Kace who ground out some profanity. "Sheez, did Cleo think your onetime roll in the sack bound you two together or something? That it obligated you to do whatever she wanted, including raising some kids?"

Judd nearly explained that Cleo's favor didn't involve kid raising. Not in her mind, anyway. But Kace's opinion of Cleo would lower even more if Judd mentioned the whole part about her bending the law.

"She's just trying to do the right thing for a friend who died," Judd insisted. "I've made some calls to see if I can find her some help."

Kace studied him a moment. "Then you're doing all you can. I'm sure Cleo appreciates that," he added before he gave him a friendly slap on the arm, got up and went back to his office.

Yeah, right. Cleo was probably cursing him, and there's no way she would believe he was doing all he could.

His phone rang, and Judd answered it right away when he saw Darrell's name on the screen. Maybe this time the cop would have good news.

"I just got a call from the Morrelli boys' grandmother," Darrell said, his words rushing out. "I'm heading over there now because she's claiming the boys ran away."

Hell. Definitely not good news.

"I'll look for them," Darrell went on, "but if you want to keep this unofficial, then you should get over here. If I haven't found them soon, I'll need to report this. I can't keep it off the books for long."

"Shit," Judd growled, and he repeated it a few more times as he jabbed the end-call button on his phone and stood. "I've got to run an errand," he said to exactly no one. "I'll do the paperwork on Gopher when I get back."

Judd didn't wait around for questions—especially any from Kace. He went out and started for his truck, but then remembered he was low on gas. He didn't want to take the time to fill up so he took one of the cruisers and started the drive back to San Antonio. He also used his Bluetooth connection to call Cleo.

No answer.

He left her a message and tried Buck next. Judd struck out there, too, and was forced to leave another message. Judd didn't have the number for the Angry Angus but used his Bluetooth to find it, and he cursed some more when he got the answering machine to tell him the hours of the place. He left a third message, cursed again and kept on driving.

With his hands aching from the grip he had on the steering wheel, Judd was more than three-quarters of the way there when his phone finally rang. He hit the answer button and heard Buck.

"Are the boys still missing?" Buck asked. His voice was just naturally unruffled, as was the man himself, but there was still a tinge of worry to it.

"As far as I know. A cop friend of mine is out looking for them." Judd paused only long enough to rein in his temper enough so he could try to have a conversation that didn't lead to a shouting match. Of course, it wouldn't actually be a match since Judd would be the only one shouting. "Why didn't you tell me about Cleo's plan?"

"Wasn't my place to tell. It was her idea."

"And it was a stupid one," Judd snapped.

Buck made a sound that could have meant anything, and even though Judd couldn't see him, he highly suspected the man had shrugged. "I told her you wouldn't go for it, but you could probably tell she was desperate."

That took some of the fire out of Judd's temper. Cleo had indeed been desperate, but he wasn't going to let Buck off the hook just yet. "You should have talked her out of it."

"I'll bet *you* weren't able to talk her out of it," Buck said. There was some "touché" in his tone now.

"I told her no. That's how I handled it."

"Of course you did." Buck's voice was back to calm now. "I didn't expect you to agree to it because like you said, it was stupid."

It was. But it still made Judd feel like shit.

"You need me to go to San Antonio to help you look for the boys?" Buck asked.

Judd thought of the man's too-pale face. "No. I'm almost there. Thanks, though. I'll let you know when they're found."

He ended the call and focused on the turns to get him to the neighborhood. Judd didn't have an address, but he had a general idea of the place, and he wove his way through the streets, trying to settle the knots in his stomach. Hard to do, though, because this wasn't a safe place for kids.

Since he'd done the whole teenage runaway thing many times in his life, Judd tapped into the mindset. If Beckham had half a brain, he'd stay off the sidewalks, so Judd focused on the alleys and greenbelts, and he tried to calculate just how far three kids could get in the hour or more that'd passed.

Not far.

Unless they'd managed to get a ride. But since

that definitely wasn't helping the knots, Judd pushed the possibility aside.

He stopped to read a text from Darrell, who said he was searching the south area of the neighborhood, so Judd focused on the north. After driving around for a good fifteen minutes with no sign of them, he headed back to Lavinia's. Not because he hoped the woman would be able to tell him anything, but he wanted to start the search from the beginning point.

And that's when he felt the tingle go down his spine.

He pulled to a stop behind the graffiti-covered car, got out and started walking. Instead of checking alleys, though, Judd looked in the vehicles. Some were missing tires and almost all had some broken windows. He checked each one, not just on Lavinia's street, but the next one, too.

Judd found them four blocks over.

The two older boys were hunkered down in the back seat with Little Leo sacked out between them. He was dressed but still sported the Popsicle stains on his mouth, and the gray kitten was snuggled against him. The middle one, Isaac, didn't even glance up at Judd. He just kept his attention on his phone even though the screen was blank. Beckham gave him a glare sharper than broken glass.

Judd gave him a mean look, too. One that softened considerably when he saw the red mark on Beckham's cheek. Judd knew the markings of a hard slap when he saw it. And that's when he noticed the fingerprint bruises not only on Beckham's wrist and neck, but also on Little Leo's arm and on his cheek.

"We're not going back there," Beckham snarled. He slid his hand protectively over his sleeping brother.

It took Judd a moment, several of them, to rein in his rage—and the memories. He didn't want that rage to work its way into his voice. "No. You're not going back there. Because you're coming with me."

CHAPTER FOUR

JUDD FORCED HIMSELF to keep a cool head. He needed to think like a cop now and not let anything from his own past play into this. But needing to do something didn't necessarily mean making it happen.

The anger rolled through him.

Sonofabitch. He was thirty-three years old, but seeing those boys had made him feel like a kid again. A kid who had been beat to hell and pushed around. Just as they had been.

"Are you arresting Popsicle, too?" Little Leo asked from the back seat of the cruiser.

Judd had to fight through the haze from the anger and try to figure out what the heck the kid meant. Little Leo helped with that when he lifted up the kitten and announced, "His name's Popsicle."

Most people probably would have smiled at the cutesy name, but Judd wasn't most people. However, he could do something to ease the troubled look on the kid's face.

"I'm not arresting any of you," Judd assured him.

Glancing in the rearview mirror, Judd got skeptical stares from all of them, including the cat. It was reasonable for them to think an arrest was imminent, he supposed, since they were in a cruiser while he sped toward Coldwater.

"I'd rather go to jail than back to that house," Beckham snarled.

Judd got that, and he would do whatever it took to make sure the kids didn't go back with their bitch of a grandmother.

He glanced at his phone, which was on the passenger seat. Still nothing from Cleo, even though he had left her several messages to let her know what was going on. However, there was a voice mail from Darrell. One that Judd didn't intend to listen to right now.

Shortly after Judd had found the boys, he'd texted Darrell to let him know that he was taking them into temporary custody for their own safety. He didn't want Darrell challenging that, not until Judd could figure out how to handle this, and handling it meant having a chat with Cleo since she was the one who'd gotten him into this mess.

Judd was regretting the second text he'd sent— the one to Buck. Buck definitely hadn't been high on his list of people to contact, but Judd had messaged him after striking out with Cleo; Rosy; Buck's daughter, Shelby; and Judd's brother Callen. When none had answered, Judd had gone with Buck, to let him know what was going on.

"Where are you taking us?" Beckham, again, and his voice still sounded suspicious.

Judd pointed to the sign for the Coldwater Hospital as he pulled into the spot reserved for emergency vehicles by the side entrance. He saw the immediate argument on Beckham's face and knew what he was about to tell him wasn't going to improve that look.

"I need to document proof of what Lavinia did to you." Judd turned in the seat so he could make eye contact. "Pictures of the bruises," he clarified. "Legally, it's how I'll stop her from trying to get custody of you."

Best not to mention the nonlegal ways, but if Judd had to hide the kids, he would. He respected the badge, but there were times when the law wasn't justice. Giving the kids back to that bitch damn sure wouldn't be justice.

"We gotta see a doctor?" Isaac asked. For the first time since this ordeal had started, Judd saw emotion in the boy's eyes, and it wasn't a good emotion. Fear, maybe even terror. Perhaps because of what his mom had gone through.

Judd wanted to assure him that it would be a nice doctor, but that probably wouldn't put a dent in the boy's fear. Best just to get this over with as fast as he could, and then… Judd was still working out what would happen afterward.

He sent a quick text to Dr. Audrey Holcomb to let her know they had arrived. Audrey was an old friend, and while she didn't exactly owe him any favors, she hadn't questioned him when he'd called her as he'd been driving out of San Antonio. She would examine the boys, get the pictures and they'd take things from there.

Judd waited until Audrey came out of the hospital before he stepped from the cruiser. "Thanks. I appreciate this," he told her.

She was a tall, attractive blonde, and she nodded before giving him a long look. And, yes, it was somewhat heated since Audrey was interested in him. That was the big reason Judd normally steered clear of her. Even if he had been attracted to her, too, which he wasn't, she would end up hurt by getting involved with him. He'd already been the cause of enough people getting hurt and didn't want to add her to his weighed-down conscience.

However, it was her doctor's eyes that combed over Judd now. Silently asking him if he was okay. Since Audrey was one of the few people who knew he was an alcoholic, he gave her a nod to let her know he was fine. It was bullshit. He wasn't okay. But what was happening now wasn't going to send him running for a bottle.

He hoped.

Audrey smiled when she turned her attention to the boys. The smile was BS, too, because it had to punch her in the gut to see those bruises. Still, she stayed calm and friendly. It wasn't enough, though, to get the boys to voluntarily get out of the cruiser. Judd had to help with that.

"This is Little Leo," Judd told Audrey as he helped the boy from the vehicle.

"And Popsicle," Little Leo announced. "He's gotta come with me, okay, or he'll get scared."

"Of course he can come." Audrey ran a soothing

hand over the kitten's head. "I'm Dr. Holcomb, and I can make sure Popsicle's okay, too."

"Isaac," Judd continued, bringing him out next. The boy had gone back to looking at his blank phone screen. "And this is Beckham." Who was sticking with his badass attitude and "mad at the world" glare.

"This way," Audrey instructed, leading them into the hospital and straight into her office. Thankfully, the waiting area was empty. Probably Audrey's doing, and that meant Judd had something else to thank her for.

The moment they stepped in, Judd felt some relief when he spotted Buck and Rosy. Relief, quickly followed by concern. Buck still looked weak. Correction—he *was* weak, and now he was here in the middle of this.

Rosy and Buck stood, and Judd noticed they were holding hands and still looking very much like newlyweds. Which they were since they'd only been married four months now.

"I didn't get your message untíl I checked my phone after doing errands, and I didn't want to call you back while you were driving," Rosy said. "So we just came here to wait for you."

Even though she was in her late seventies, she was a sturdy woman who always managed a smile. Even now. And unlike Audrey's, it wasn't BS despite the bruises she no doubt saw on the kids. Rosy, who was true to her name, just had a way of filtering out the bad even when it was staring her right in the face.

Buck didn't filter. His green eyes watered a little as he looked at the boys—he would have taken them in a heartbeat if it hadn't been for his own health and age.

"Are you Santa?" Little Leo asked.

Maybe the boy had wondered that because Rosy and Buck were both wearing red and had white hair. The question caused Rosy to laugh, and she gave Little Leo a hug that didn't make the boy move away from her. But Isaac and Beckham did. They didn't give Rosy a chance to get her hugging hands on them. They didn't know how gentle she could be.

"This is Miss Rosy and Mr. Buck," Judd said, continuing the introductions.

Judd opened his mouth to add that Mr. Buck had been his foster father, but that label had always fallen short. Buck had been his father, period. The only one who'd ever lived up to that title. Too bad that for all of Buck's good heart, he hadn't been able to erase the fifteen crap years that Judd had had before the system had finally given him and his brothers a break and placed them with Buck.

"Why don't you wait out here while I take the boys into the exam room?" Audrey asked Judd, and she added in a whisper, "They might tell me things they wouldn't say in front of you."

Good point, especially since it was obvious that Beckham didn't trust him one bit. Of course, he likely didn't trust Audrey, either, but she'd do her job and get the pictures and medical reports that Judd needed.

He considered warning Audrey that the boys might try to escape, but Judd went to the source for that. He aimed a hard look at Beckham. "Don't run, and I mean it. Trust me when I say that you don't want to piss me off."

Judd had no idea if that would be effective enough, but just in case his message hadn't gotten through he wouldn't move far from the examining room where Audrey took the boys.

"Have either of you heard from Cleo?" Judd asked the moment Audrey had closed the door.

"Earlier today but not in the last couple of hours," Buck answered.

"We've been trying to reach her," Rosy piped in, letting Judd know that Buck had filled her in on what was happening. "You don't think something bad happened to her, do you?"

Damn it. Judd hadn't even considered that, but he wouldn't have put it past Cleo to go storming into Lavinia's house, demanding to know where the boys were. Lavinia was capable of violence. Judd had seen proof of that. But from all appearances, the woman had used her hands to leave those marks. No weapons. Maybe she'd tried to use her hands on Cleo, too.

That had Judd taking out his phone again to call Cleo. The concern went all the way to his bones when it went straight to voice mail. He left her another message, ending it with a demand of "call me, damn it."

Even though Judd didn't want to ask for another favor, he texted Darrell to have him check Lavinia's house to make sure Cleo wasn't there.

"Are you okay?" Buck asked.

Judd nearly laughed. Nearly. Leave it to Buck to be concerned about him when he'd just seen three kids with injuries or when Cleo's safety was in doubt. Of course, Buck had a knack for seeing what was below the surface.

"I'm fine," Judd said, continuing the lie. It wasn't getting easier, and he doubted he was fooling anyone. "I'm not so sure about the boys, though. Their grandmother did that to them," he spat out.

That caused Rosy to throw her arms around him, her attempt to hug it out. Judd let her try that while he kept his attention on Buck. His stomach dropped when he didn't see a whole lot of hope on the man's face.

"Callen and Shelby are eloping," Buck announced when Rosy finally let go of Judd. "That's why they didn't answer your call. They're on a plane to Vegas right about now."

Judd cursed under his breath even though he figured the language would earn him an arm swat from Rosy. It did. Not a surprise since she'd been trying to clean up his foul mouth for the past eighteen years. Even before Rosy had married Buck, she'd been the housekeeper and cook at the ranch and had helped Buck raise the foster kids who came and went.

Actually, the elopement wasn't a surprise, either. His brother and Shelby were crazy in love and had dropped some hints about not wanting a big wedding to-do.

But the timing sucked.

Callen, along with being a stinking rich cattle broker, also had contacts in Child Protective Services. And, as Buck's daughter, Shelby had plenty of experience dealing with foster kids. Judd could have used their help.

"I could call them and ask them to postpone the wedding," Buck offered.

Judd nixed that with a head shake. Callen had been through as much shit as he had and deserved some happiness. Shelby, too, since she had been helping care for Buck and his ranch during his recovery.

"Nico should be back from the rodeo in a day or two," Rosy pointed out. "Maybe he'll be able to help. Nico's moving his office into the building that Callen bought on Main Street."

Judd wasn't sure what kind of help Nico, his womanizing kid brother, could offer even if he did seem to be turning over a new leaf by building his livestock contractor business. But even if Nico had been good as gold, Judd didn't have a day or two. He needed to work out something now.

"Will you get in a lot of trouble because you took the boys?" Buck asked.

"Not as much as their grandmother when CPS

sees the bruises she left on them." But, yeah, there was the possibility of trouble for Judd, too.

Because he didn't want Buck to stay on his feet, Judd eased the man into one of the chairs. Rosy sat on one side of him, and Judd the other. While they waited, the silence came, and Judd was finally able to clear his head enough to think.

He'd need to call Kace. Not only because his brother might be able to help suss out what to do about the kids, but also because Kace was his boss. Judd had bolted out of the police station when he'd gotten Darrell's call about the boys running away. Kace could get someone to fill in for him at work in case this dragged on longer than Judd wanted.

Of course, it had already dragged on too long.

"I'm going to get us some Cokes and snacks," Rosy volunteered, giving Judd's hand a pat. "The boys might like a treat when Audrey's finished with them."

Yeah, but treats weren't going to fix their problems. Well, except for maybe Little Leo. He didn't seem to be too affected by this.

"This is bringing back the old stuff, isn't it?" Buck said after Rosy had left.

"Some." Judd settled for the one-word reply because he knew he wouldn't be able to pull off a flat-out denial.

Buck made a weary sound of agreement. "The past has a way of keeping right on your heels."

It did. It was nipping right at him now.

Suddenly, his mind was no longer clear, but was

instead filled with too many memories of other bruises. And worse. So much worse. It had started with Judd's own junkie of a mother. Neglect more than actual beatings. That'd been followed by a string of foster homes. Some okay, some that had left him with flashbacks and nightmares.

The worst nightmare, though, was that the abuse hadn't been just limited to him. Callen had been severely injured, and Nico had nearly been killed. Nearly been beaten to death by a man named Avis Odell, and because Judd and Kace had been in a different home at that time, they hadn't been around to protect them.

"Avis Odell," he muttered under his breath.

The man would always be a sore spot. No. Worse than that. A jab to the heart. Avis was an unrepentant sonofabitch who was on his way back to jail. This time not for the beatings he'd given Callen and Nico when they'd been kids, but because he'd recently tried to extort money from Callen. And because Judd had goaded Avis into a fight and then had him charged with assaulting a police officer.

Avis deserved to be in jail. Hell, he deserved worse, but Judd hated that those old memories and all that pain could still twist away at him like this.

It was his brothers' nearly being killed that had brought them to Buck's. The system had finally moved Callen and Nico, and shortly afterward, Buck had petitioned to get Kace and Judd, too. Buck had saved them, but as good as he'd been, Buck hadn't managed to cool down this fireball of bad memories that Judd figured would stay with him for a lifetime.

The door opened, pulling Judd out of his thoughts, but it wasn't the door to the examining room. Cleo came rushing in from the waiting area.

"Are the boys okay?" she blurted out before he could say anything.

It took Judd a moment to get his jaw unclenched. "They're in with the doctor now." He tipped his head to the door. "They're bruised up some."

The color drained from Cleo's face, and she would have bolted into the exam room if Judd hadn't stepped in front of her. "Just give them a few more minutes. I want pictures and a report of the abuse."

"Abuse," she repeated. Cleo made a strangled, distressed sound, followed by tears, and she went right into Buck's arms when he reached for her. "God, I'm sorry," Cleo murmured. "So sorry."

"This wasn't your fault." Buck, being Buck, stroked the back of her head as if she was still one of his kids who'd come in with a scraped knee.

It was true—this wasn't her fault—but Judd wasn't going to let her off the hook just yet. "I tried to call you. *Four times*," Judd said with emphasis.

She nodded and dabbed at tears as she lifted her head off Buck's shoulder. "Isaac called to tell me that Lavinia had hit Little Leo and that they were running away. I drove there as fast as I could, but they were already gone. Lavinia wouldn't tell me where they were, and…we got into a tussle, I guess you could call it. I dropped my phone, and it broke."

Well, as explanations went, it wasn't a bad one, and Judd immediately found himself checking Cleo for bruises. And he soon found some on her left wrist.

"Did you put any marks on Lavinia?" he asked, already dreading the report he was going to have to write about this. A report that damn sure better not lead to Cleo's arrest.

Cleo followed his gaze to her wrist and shook her head. "Once I realized the boys weren't there, I left." She paused. "I wanted to slap her. God, did I want to do that, but I knew it wouldn't do the kids any good."

No. It wouldn't have. "I want your wrist photographed, too," he said. "You'll need all the ammunition you can get to make sure Lavinia never sees those boys again."

Cleo's gaze met his, she nodded, then muttered, "Thank you." She added, "You found them," as if relieved and talking to herself.

"And they're safe for now," Judd pointed out. "But we need to talk about what happens next."

Again, she nodded, but Judd wasn't optimistic about the head shake that quickly followed. Maybe that meant she didn't have a clue about the "next" part, but if so she didn't get a chance to voice that because Audrey opened the door of the examining room. Cleo went rushing in before anyone could stop her.

The boys did some rushing, too. Little Leo and

Isaac both hurried to Cleo, letting her gather them in her arms.

"Aunt Cleo," Little Leo squealed. Not a distressed kind of greeting but one of a truly happy child.

The kitten was on the floor, but it also got in on the Cleo welcome. Popsicle went to her and started coiling around her legs. Beckham was the only one who stayed back, but Cleo soon put a stop to that. She took hold of him in sort of a gentle reverse choke hold and pulled him into the group hug.

Keeping an eye on them, Audrey came out and walked to Judd. "I'll email you the photos," she said, her voice low enough so the boys wouldn't hear. "Both Leo and Beckham have other bruises beneath their shirts. They wouldn't talk about how they got them, though."

So, they weren't ratting out their grandmother. Judd would see what he could do about that. "I'll question them. I need to do a report, too."

Audrey nodded. "Cover yourself on this because I'm guessing the courts will get involved." Her gaze drifted back to Cleo. Judd was pretty sure that Audrey remembered Cleo and him hooking up when they were teenagers. Pretty sure that Audrey didn't like that, either. "She'll be taking them, I assume?"

Judd was still trying to figure out how to answer that when Buck spoke. "No. Cleo can't take them, not legally."

Buck didn't exactly turn his concerned expression in Judd's direction, but Judd figured Buck was waiting for him to speak up. But he couldn't. Not the way Buck or Cleo wanted him to do, anyway.

"I'll make some calls," Judd finally said. "I'll work out a temporary placement for them."

Of course, that was the exact moment that Cleo and the boys came out of the examining room, and they had obviously heard him because they looked at him as if he'd broken some kind of big-assed rule and betrayed them.

"No," Buck murmured on a heavy sigh. "These boys have been through enough. Both of you have, too." He glanced at Cleo, then Judd. "As soon as you've had pictures taken of your bruises, we're all going to my ranch."

CHAPTER FIVE

"WHAT'S MY *RANCH*?" Little Leo asked. "Is it where Santa and his girlfriend live?"

While Cleo was considering how to answer that without putting a damper on the boy's jovial expectations, Little Leo just kept on.

"Because if Santa lives there with his girlfriend, they might got reindeer and presents," he said. "And elves."

"There won't be stupid presents." Beckham's voice was stern, more grumpy parent than brother. "No reindeer or elves, either. It'll be just a stupid house."

Harsh, but she hadn't expected Beckham to be a little ray of sunshine. "It's a big house," Cleo said, "and there'll be horses."

"Will the horses be stupid?" Leo immediately asked.

"Some of them," Judd muttered, his tone very similar to Beckham's.

Yet another ray of sunshine.

Rarely did Cleo have to remind herself to smile, but she was having to do that now. And she played a mental round of her BS game. In the best scenario, the boys would love Buck, Rosy and the ranch. Lavinia would back off, and they'd all live happily-ever-after.

And that sounded more like actual bull crap than best scenario. She knew it. So did Isaac and Beckham. They were in the back seat of Judd's cruiser, watching her like a hawk, looking for any signs that going to Buck's might not be a good idea.

If they looked closely enough, they would see that it wasn't.

Even though she'd planned on the kids staying at Buck's, Cleo darn sure hadn't wanted things to go down this way. With Buck recovering from cancer, he didn't need this kind of stress, and he could end up being on the wrong side of the law for harboring the kids. Ironic since the boys would be safe here. Cleo had no idea, though, just how long that would last, but she kept smiling, anyway.

Maybe that made her the stupid one.

Judd definitely wasn't in a smiling mind-set as he drove the kids and her toward Buck's, where she hoped Leo wouldn't be disappointed when he saw no trace of Santa. Ahead of them on the country road, Buck and Rosy were in their truck, but Rosy continued to glance back at them. There was caution, too, on the woman's normally cheery face.

"Will she come here after us?" Beckham asked after he tapped Cleo on the shoulder to get her attention. Now his tone had some caution in it as well, but it was coated thick with anger.

Cleo didn't have to ask who the "she" was in

Beckham's question. Lavinia. And even though Isaac didn't say anything, he was looking at her, clearly waiting for the answer. Little Leo was playing with his kitten.

"Maybe," Cleo admitted. She turned to face him so he could see the determination in her eyes. "But if she does, I won't let her take you."

Judd didn't voice or grunt any kind of agreement, but the fact that he was driving them to Buck's hopefully meant that he would back her up on this. Temporarily, anyway. Judd certainly wasn't jumping to say that he would be the boys' foster father, even in name only.

Since it wouldn't take them long to get to Buck's, Cleo got started on something she did know how to fix. The work schedule at the bar. She texted Daisy to tell her what was going on and asked her to call in some part-time help to cover the night shift. It was only a Band-Aid fix since Cleo couldn't afford to hire anyone to fill in for her full-time, but it would take care of the here and now.

Because kitten poop was also part of that here and now—or soon would be—Cleo located the number of the local grocery store, connected with the store owner, Will Myers, and asked him to have someone deliver litter supplies and cat food to the ranch. She'd need him to send boys' clothes, too, if Rosy and Buck didn't have some on hand. From what she could tell, the boys hadn't carried much with them when they'd run away from Lavinia's, and Cleo wasn't about to contact the woman and ask her to hand over their things.

Just as Cleo finished her own call, Judd's phone rang, and while he glanced at the screen, he let the call go to voice mail. "Darrell," he relayed to her.

That was the San Antonio cop who'd helped look for the boys. He could be calling to demand the boys' return or to drop some other bad news that Cleo was certain she wouldn't want to hear.

Somehow, she kept smiling.

The smile became genuine, though, when they turned into the driveway to Buck's ranch. Time hadn't exactly stood still here, but it was close. The large two-story house that'd once been white was now yellow, and there was another barn. A red one. Other than that and the spruced-up porch on the log cabin where Judd lived, everything was as it had been when she had lived here as one of Buck's kids.

Her attention lingered on the cabin a moment. On the memories there. Smile-worthy ones because that's where Judd and she had sneaked off to on the night of her de-virgining. Judging from the way Judd scowled at it, it didn't hold the same fond memories for him as it did for her.

By the time Judd had parked the cruiser, Rosy and Buck were already out of his truck, and Rosy came their way. Her cautious expression was still there but so was her usual welcome.

"Come on in," Rosy told them, helping Little Leo out and sliding her hand around him. "You're in luck because there's nobody else staying here. That means you'll each get your own rooms."

"We want to stay together," Beckham mumbled.

"Oh." Rosy blinked but quickly recovered. "Okay. One of the rooms has four bunk beds and its own bath so you can use that one."

Rosy looked at Cleo to get her approval, and Cleo nodded. But Cleo would tell the woman later that there was an asterisk on her nod. Beckham might want them all in the same room just to keep an eye on his younger brothers, but it would also make it easier for him to run off with them again. Cleo wasn't sure how to convince Beckham not to do that, but she needed to try.

Judd stayed on the porch to make a call. Maybe to Darrell. Cleo would be making her own call—to Kace, to ask for his help. But for now she followed Buck, Rosy and the boys inside.

Cleo immediately got another rush of the past when she glanced around the living room. Again, only a few changes here, including the stuffed armadillo on the entry table that immediately caught Little Leo's eye. He grinned just as Popsicle hissed at it. Cleo went with the kitten's opinion on this because the armadillo wasn't just stuffed. It was one of Rosy's taxidermic critters.

"That's Billy," Rosy proudly announced, running her hand over the armadillo's head. "Isn't he handsome?"

"Yeah," Leo confirmed with what sounded to be a little awe.

"I have a shop, Much Ado About Stuffing," Rosy went on, "and when Billy met his...end, I made sure he would stay handsome forever."

Concerned about the topic of conversation, Cleo studied each of the boys to see how they were handling this. Isaac was back to staring at his phone screen, and Beckham was rolling his eyes. "Stupid," Beckham groaned.

Well, she supposed that was better than a reaction from the boys saying it was morbid, or Cleo's personal favorite—creepy.

Cleo shifted her attention, continuing her sweeping glance around the room, and her smile brightened when she saw a framed photo on the mantel of her with the Laramie brothers.

"Good times," Buck said to her. Looking much too tired and pale, he sank down onto the sofa as Rosy led the boys upstairs. Cleo was about to go with them, but Buck motioned for her to sit next to him. "Rosy will show them the room and then bring them back down." He paused only long enough for a labored breath before he added, "We need to talk."

"I'm sorry," Cleo blurted out as she sat. "I didn't want to involve you like this."

He shook his head, gave a weary sigh. "I don't see as how you had a choice." It was the right thing to say even if it didn't fix things. "Besides, Judd's the one who brought them here. That's a good sign."

If only. "Not really. He said no when I asked him to sign the foster papers. And judging from his expression, he'll stand firm on that no."

Buck made a "maybe" sound. "Part of me wants to give him an out by calling Shelby and Callen home from their honeymoon. They'd come and they'd agree to work with you on this plan for you to foster the boys."

Yes, Shelby and Callen would, but Cleo didn't want to go that route unless there was no other choice. "I want to talk to Kace. He might be willing to become their foster in name only." A risk because of that whole "letter of the law" thing. "If that doesn't work, then I can possibly have my business partner do it. Her place isn't big enough, but maybe she could move here temporarily until we get something better worked out."

Though Cleo had no idea how she would manage to move Daisy and her baby to Coldwater without completely busting her budget.

Buck touched the bruises on her wrist. "Work out something better than their grandmother."

"Definitely. Of course, the bar isn't set very high there for finding something better. Plus, she doesn't actually want them. She was going to put them in foster care, anyway, so as long as it's not my name on the documents, I think Lavinia will back off."

At best that might be wishful thinking, but there was enough gloom and doom hovering over her without adding the possibility of an abusive bat-shit crazy relative to the mix.

"Remember when you came here?" Buck asked.

There was so much whirling around in Cleo's mind that it took her a moment to calm her thoughts.

Which had likely been the reason Buck had asked. He'd always had a knack for nerve-settling. "Yes. You were very kind to me."

He lifted his shoulder. "It's easy to be kind to someone like you."

She gave him a considering look. "Clearly, you and Lavinia have a different notion about that."

Buck smiled, bobbed his head. Paused. "You weren't broken. You were just in need of a place to thrive."

Now she winced because there'd been nose-diving along with that thriving. "I'd been arrested for stealing a car just weeks before I came here."

"Running," he acknowledged. "Something that Beckham and you have in common."

"I didn't have it as bad as they did. They're orphans, caught up in a bad situation. I had folks. Well, a dad, anyway." Her mom had cut out around the time she'd started kindergarten. And her dad just hadn't wanted her once she'd started acting out and getting into trouble. "It stung some when he signed over his parental rights and put me in the system, but in hindsight he did us all a favor."

In that wise way of his, Buck just stayed quiet and let her continue. It was yet another layer in his nerve-settling skill set.

"I don't hear from my father, but that's okay," she went on. "He rebuilt his life with a new wife. New kids, too."

In the interest of staving off the gloom and its pity partner, the doom, she wouldn't mention the last time she'd called him. It'd been about a decade ago, and he'd calmly asked her never to call him again. Of course, Buck likely knew that in a good dad–ESP kind of way.

The front door opened, and while slipping his phone in his jeans pocket, Judd came back in. Cleo immediately got to her feet, trying to steel herself since it didn't look as if Judd was going to give her much to smile about.

"Where are the boys?" Judd asked.

Cleo fluttered her fingers to the stairs. "With Rosy. She's getting them settled in their room." She thought she detected a smidge of relief that meant Judd likely had something to say that he didn't want the boys to hear.

"Darrell and I called in every favor we could, and for now the boys are in my protective custody."

He muttered some profanity under his breath to let her know that this had not been his first choice of solutions. But it was music to Cleo's ears. "That definitely won't go on my Stupid Shit Men Say board," she said, gushing. "It's wonderful, Judd. Thank you."

She wanted to throw her arms around him and hug him. Heck, she wanted to kiss him, but then that had nothing to do with her gratitude.

"Don't thank me. You don't have long to find another way to fix this," Judd went on. "Darrell's lieutenant will almost certainly question this and will want CPS brought in immediately."

Oh. Immediately didn't sound good at all. "How much time?" she asked.

"A day, maybe two at the most."

So, not much, but it was still breathing room, and she'd take it. "Thank you," she repeated.

Judd didn't look any more comfortable with her double thanks than he had with the protective-custody arrangement. "I've got some things to do," he mumbled when Rosy and the boys started down the stairs, and without even sparing Cleo another glance, Judd turned and walked out.

Cleo made sure she was smiling again when she faced the boys.

"I got the stupid bed on the top," Little Leo announced, and since he was grinning, he obviously approved of that.

Beckham, however, wasn't anywhere close to grinning, and she had no doubts—none—that the "stupid" adjective had been his.

"Will you stay, too?" Isaac asked.

Cleo glanced at Buck to make sure that was okay, and she gave Isaac a nod after Buck gave her one. "But I think I'll look for a nonstupid bed," she joked. But only Little Leo and Rosy laughed.

"I was going to show the boys around," Rosy said. "Thought they might like to meet the horses."

"And the chickens," Leo insisted.

Rosy patted his head. "And the chickens."

"I'll take them out," Buck offered. "I could use some fresh air."

Rosy didn't seem certain about that at all. Neither was Cleo, since Buck still looked a little weak and pale. But she didn't object when Buck led the boys through the kitchen and out the back door. However, both Rosy and Cleo went to the window to keep watch.

"Thank you for doing this," Cleo told the woman. "I know it's a lot to ask."

"The boys need help." Rosy's attention drifted from Buck and the kids to Judd's cabin. It was only slightly more than a stone's throw away.

And there was Judd.

He, too, was at a window, his gaze on Buck. He was talking to someone on the phone, and like Rosy, there was plenty of concern on his face. Plenty of hotness, too. He looked very much like the cowboy who could have hands-down won that audition for the bachelorette party.

"Still a little gaga over him, aren't you?" Rosy said.

Cleo nearly attempted some kind of denial, but what was the point? Rosy didn't need Buck's ESP to figure that out. "Judd the Stud," Cleo remarked, causing Rosy to hoot with laughter.

"Good one. He does get plenty of attention from the women around here. Including women who aren't exactly free to give that attention, if you know what I mean."

Cleo did indeed know what Rosy meant. Judd had those incredible Laramie looks, and even with his eternally broody mood, that wouldn't deter lustful glances and attempts to snag him.

"Dr. Audrey Holcomb," Cleo said as she watched Buck lead the boys into the barn. Leo was skipping along. Isaac, quietly following. And Beckham was giving Judd a run for the "broody mood" crown. "Either she's already snagged Judd or would like to do that."

Rosy made a sound of agreement, lifted her shoulder. "I think she's more the 'liking to do that' sort. I can't say for a hundred percent sure, but Judd doesn't make it a habit of bringing women here to his bed."

Ironic, since that's exactly where Cleo had landed when they'd been sixteen. In that bed on rumpled sheets and with the hottest guy in Texas ridding her of her virginity. She suspected that plenty of women regretted their choice of first lovers, but no regrets for her.

She was betting, though, that Judd didn't feel the same way.

Judd likely felt that old intimacy between them had come back to bite him in the butt. And that meant Cleo owed him big-time. And a whole boat-load of thank-yous wasn't going to do it. She needed to show her gratitude by working out a solution for the boys that didn't involve him.

"This has really shaken Judd, you know," Rosy went on. "Might not seem that way to most folks, but you and I can see it just fine."

Yes, Cleo could indeed see it. She didn't know all the details of what'd happened to Judd before he'd come to Buck's, but she'd heard enough to know that he'd likely been on the receiving end of much more abuse than the boys had. It was the reason that Judd drank.

Correction: it was the reason he was an alcoholic.

"We'll need to keep an eye on him to make sure this doesn't set him back," Rosy quietly added.

Oh, God. That fired a fresh blast of worry through Cleo. "How long has he been sober?"

"Not long enough."

Well, crap. Cleo shut her eyes a moment and groaned. She darn sure hadn't brought this to Judd to have it undo the progress he'd made.

When Judd finished his call and stepped away from his window, Cleo figured it was a good time for them to talk. Too bad she didn't have options that would take him out of the picture that he didn't want to be in, but she could run some possibilities by him.

And be certain that Judd wasn't about to take a drink that he might feel he needed.

"I'll be right back," Cleo told Rosy. She didn't expect this to be a long conversation. In fact, it might not even happen at all. Judd could be so riled that he might not speak to her.

Cleo hurried out and across the yard to Judd's front porch. She was ready to knock, but the door was already open. The screen door was shut, but she could still see into the cabin, and since it was one big room, she had no trouble spotting Judd.

Naked.

Well, almost. He was shirtless, bootless and his

jeans were unzipped. Cleo felt the quick zing of heat that left her "less," too. Breathless. Mindless.

And suddenly wanting another taste of Judd Laramie.

Again, because of the small space, Judd immediately saw her, and while he didn't actually huff, that's what it looked as if he wanted to do.

"I was about to shower and go back to work," he said.

That should have been her cue to go, but her feet had seemingly adhered to the porch. "I came over to thank you," she said. "And check on you. And maybe go over some possible fixes for the boys."

Along with feet-to-floor adhesion, she'd obviously contracted a severe case of babbling.

It didn't help that the nearly naked Judd was standing right next to the bed where she'd made her sexual debut with him. Because it'd been pitch-dark that night, she certainly hadn't seen as much of him then as she was seeing now. The man certainly had a filled-out, toned body. Probably a result of the ranch work and the bench and weights in the corner of the room.

Judd kept his hands on the waist of his jeans—it was the stance of someone waiting for her to leave so he could finish stripping down. When she didn't leave, Judd blew out a long breath and walked toward her.

Because he hadn't zipped back up, the flap of his jeans shifted and moved, giving her the answer to a burning question. Boxers, not briefs. Judging from the flat look he gave her, he had no burning questions about her.

He pushed open the screen door, holding it in place with his shoulder and thereby blocking the doorway. The stance also put him very close to her. Oh, mercy. He smelled all man, and that wasn't in a "you need a shower" manly kind of way. It was more like musky, leathery foreplay to her suddenly aroused body.

"I need to put in a couple of hours at work," he said. "Then we can talk about the boys."

Cleo nodded and balled her hands into fists to stop herself from reaching out and touching him. She wasn't a teenager anymore and could certainly put her hormones in check before Judd figured out she was lusting over him.

Too late.

When their gazes connected and held, she could tell that he'd already seen it. No flat look now but a heated one that he obviously wasn't happy about. Since it had already become a seriously big gorilla in the room, Cleo just went with it.

She tipped her head to the bed and made a pinching motion with her fingers. "That's the site of my first butt-cheek pinching. Your butt cheek," she said to clarify and hoped it would lighten the mood. "It was a fantasy of mine."

Well, he sure didn't smile. But he did zip up his jeans as if concerned she might have another go at him. "I remember. It was an odd fantasy."

Cleo shrugged. "I think it got all tied up with the

realization that a really good butt pinch would have required you to be naked."

"Still…" he said as if he wasn't convinced that it was the best of fantasies.

"Oh, I had others, but I figured I'd sprung enough on you." She paused, then asked, "Do you regret it happened?"

"The butt pinch or the sex?" Judd countered so fast that it made her laugh. And she was so playing with fire here. She knew it. He knew it. Heck, his butt cheek knew it, too.

"I don't regret either," she admitted. "You were good." Which, of course, was a weak and puny description. He'd been incredible. Just a little awkwardness and a whole lot of the stuff that'd made it incredible. "Do you recall what you said to me that night after you brought me here?"

Obviously he didn't because Judd just gave her a blank stare. "I said I'd be gentle with you?"

She could tell that was a guess. A wrong one, but it was a solid effort. And he had indeed been gentle. Well, until she hadn't wanted him to be, but Judd had sussed out when to make the switch and go harder and faster for the finish line.

"You said that was your first pinch on the butt and that you'd never forget it," Cleo said.

He shook his head, grimaced a little. "Obviously, I needed to work on my silver-tongue skills."

"Oh, you did just fine, tongue included."

Their gazes continued to hold and the heat kept on spiking until they heard the sound of the approaching car. No. Not a car, Cleo quickly realized. A motorcycle. And, once she turned around, she saw two riders sitting on it.

Judd spat out some profanity and hurried back into the cabin. Obviously, he wasn't happy about these visitors, and Cleo soon joined him in the unhappy camp when the beefy guy stopped the motorcycle and got off. So did the woman who'd been riding behind him.

Lavinia.

She yanked off the helmet that she'd been wearing and stormed straight toward Cleo.

CHAPTER SIX

JUDD DIDN'T LIKE the idea of facing down trouble when he was half-dressed, but that's what he got for hanging around in the doorway and half-assed flirting with Cleo. Now he was going to have to pay for that by being barefoot while he confronted a woman who for damn certain hadn't come here to pinch his butt.

She was here to bust his balls.

He pulled on his shirt, the one with his badge attached, as he hurried back outside. Still barefoot. Just in the nick of time, too. Cleo was already off the porch and in the yard, and she was right in Lavinia's rage-tightened face.

Lavinia was even less dressed than Judd because she, too, was barefoot and was wearing the same housedress/nightgown garb that she'd had on earlier. So, she'd likely come in a hurry.

But she hadn't come alone.

The woman had brought her Harley-riding backup with her. A big guy in a stained wifebeater shirt and orange—yes, orange—leather pants was making his way across the yard. Obviously, he wasn't moving as fast as Lavinia because he was moseying a good ten feet behind her. Fat that had perhaps once been muscles jiggled and swayed in his belly and thighs, and the motion made Judd wonder if there was enough friction to light a fire.

"You had no right to take my grandkids, you bitch," Lavinia yelled at Cleo.

Judd glanced around to make sure the boys weren't hearing any of this, and he groaned when he saw Little Leo come running out of the barn. Buck, Beckham and Isaac were right behind him, and thankfully Buck caught onto Leo and herded them all back inside.

Partly inside, anyway.

Isaac and Leo went with Buck, but Beckham stayed in the barn doorway. Watching, listening and seething.

Cleo made a strange sound. A growl and shudder combined, probably because she was having to suppress a whole bunch of anger and cusswords that she wanted to aim at this hellhound dingbat.

"I've got two words for you, Lavinia," Cleo said, her voice an angry whisper. She made another of those sounds. "Support bra. Buy one and use it or you'll end up bitch-slapping yourself with one of your own boobs."

Clearly, Lavinia hadn't been ready for that particular insult, and she hesitated as if trying to figure out how to respond to it. She also glanced down at the sagging body parts in question and perhaps realized that it was hard to argue with the truth. Even when the truth had nothing to do with anything else that was going on.

Lavinia's head did an indignant wobble that she probably didn't know made her look like a strutting rooster. It also set her boobs to swinging. "Yeah, so what? I don't need hoity-toity fashion advice from the likes of a bar owner. I'm here to take my grand-kids."

"No, you're not," Cleo growled. "I won't let you take them."

"You and what army?" Lavinia challenged.

"This army." Judd tapped his badge and moved between the women.

In hindsight, that probably hadn't been his wis-est move because Lavinia spun around, causing her boobs to smack into his chest. Judd nearly told her that he could arrest her for assaulting a police of-ficer, but he'd be too embarrassed to write "boob assault" in a report. Obviously, Lavinia had more than her breasts as potential weapons. She'd used her hand and put some muscle behind it when she'd left those marks on Cleo and the boys.

Lavinia balled up her fist, and she volleyed her attention between Cleo and Judd, as she obviously tried to decide which of them to slug.

"Hit either one of us if you want to spend the night in jail," Judd warned her, and he shot a glare at the guy just in case he was going to get in on this. However, the man just shrugged, causing more of him to wobble.

"Say, you got any beer?" the man asked. "Long ride, and I'm thirsty. Vinia said there'd be beer."

Judd's glare got significantly worse, and the man merely shrugged again.

"I want my grandsons!" Lavinia howled. She aimed her nicotine-stained index finger at Cleo. "She had no right to take them, and I know they're here. I remember Miranda talking about this place and how much Cleo just loved it here."

Judd was surprised the woman could piece all of that together. Heck, he was surprised she'd managed to get out of her own house. She reeked of stale beer and cigarette smoke, and was obviously not a fan of good dental hygiene.

"Cleo didn't take them," Judd told her. "I did, after they ran away from you. Now they're in my protective custody."

"Protective custody?" she howled. "What the fuck is that?"

Cleo took a step toward her, getting back in Lavinia's face again. "Watch your language. The boys can hear you."

Lavinia opened her mouth, no doubt to spew some harsher profanity, but Judd gave her a look that stopped her in her verbal tracks. And he knew he was good at it, too.

"Protective custody is what I have and you don't," Judd warned her. "It means you can't take the boys because you assaulted them."

"I didn't do nothing of the sort." Again, it was a howl. The woman only seemed to have one volume level on her voice. "Is that what they told you? Because if so, it's a bald-faced lie."

"Then how'd they get the bruises?" Cleo demanded.

Lavinia hesitated. "They did it to each other. Boys fight, and they get bruises when they fight."

Cleo's groan was just as loud as Lavinia's voice, and Cleo held up her wrist for the woman to see. "They got them the same way I got these. Remember, Lavinia, or do I need to refresh your memory?"

"Vinia, I'm ready for that beer now," her companion complained.

"Not now, Otto." Lavinia went with another head wobble in response to Cleo. "You did that to yourself to get me in trouble," she said smugly.

"I don't need to do anything to get you in trouble," Cleo stormed. "You managed to do that all by yourself."

Judd was about to hurry this along so he could get Lavinia and her beer-requesting friend out of there, but he wasn't able to launch into a "get lost" order before he heard a sound he didn't especially want to hear.

A police siren.

He glanced at Buck's house and saw Rosy in the window. She had her phone pressed to her ear, and since she didn't especially seem surprised by the cruiser coming in hot, it meant she'd called for it.

The sound got Otto hurrying back toward his motorcycle, proving that he could indeed move faster than a snail and without starting thigh fires. He motioned for Lavinia to join him. Not a casual, "come here" gesture, either. It was frantic, causing his arms to flap like pterodactyl wings.

Judd was betting the man had a sheet. One that maybe he could use to make sure Lavinia never came back here with him again. First, though, he was going to have to explain to Kace what the heck was going on.

Kace killed the sirens and pulled to a stop behind the motorcycle, causing the guy to groan and shake his head. Lavinia didn't go into retreat mode, though. She whirled around, clomping her way to the cruiser.

His brother got out, but he wasn't alone. Deputy Liberty Cassaine was with him, and that let Judd know that Kace had come expecting trouble.

"You'd better be here to arrest them for kidnapping," Lavinia said, flinging her hand back at Judd and Cleo.

Kace made a sweeping glance at all of them, then at the house and the barn, where Beckham was still watching. Judd wasn't sure how much Rosy had told Kace, but his brother seemed to have a quick understanding of what was going on. Of course, Kace usually did.

"I'm Sheriff Kace Laramie. And you are?" he asked Lavinia.

"I'm Lavinia Mercer, and I'm here to get my grandbabies." She spat out the word *grandbabies* like milk past its expiration date. "They stole them from me." She aimed an accusing finger at Judd and Cleo.

Kace ignored the finger jab and barely spared the woman a glance before he shifted toward Otto. "And you are?"

It was so obvious that the man didn't want to give even that bit of info, but Kace didn't back down with his cop stare. "Otto Burrell," the guy finally mumbled.

"Run them," Kace told Liberty, who went back to the cruiser. Kace turned toward Judd. "These two people are trespassing?" Kace asked.

"Yes!" Cleo answered before Judd had the chance. "And she assaulted her grandchildren."

That set off a profanity-laced howl of protest and counteraccusations from Lavinia. More groans and gaze-dodging from Otto.

"SAPD's investigating the assault charges, and for now the kids are in my protective custody," Judd told his brother and hoped Kace could hear over Lavinia's rantings. "But if she doesn't shut up, I'll arrest both of them for trespassing and disturbing the peace."

As expected, that caused Lavinia to aim her fresh tirade at Judd.

"Uh, Vinia," the man said as he started up the motorcycle, which, of course, only added to the noise. "I gotta go. Like now."

Kace cut through the loud spew by aiming his stare at the woman. "Ms. Mercer, you've got five seconds to leave or I haul you in." And with that, Kace started counting. "Five, four..."

Lavinia might not have had a clue about suitable undergarments for breast support, but she realized when a cop meant business. "I'm coming back with a lawyer," she said, hurrying to get on the motorcycle. "So help me, I'll have your badge."

However, the woman's threat was somewhat diminished by the farting noise the motorcycle's exhaust made as Otto sped away. Lavinia obviously hadn't been prepared for the jolt of speed because her body jerked back and her arms and legs went flailing. Judd hoped she didn't fall off because he didn't want to have to deal with any injuries right now.

"Rosy, it's okay," Kace called out to the woman who was now in the doorway. He gave her a quick wave.

"No sheet on the woman," Liberty called out to Kace. "You'll probably want to sit down and have coffee, though, while you read Otto's. It's multiple pages. Apparently, he has a thing for urinating in public."

Considering his beer requests, Judd supposed that made sense. Lavinia probably hadn't considered that bringing an ex-con with her would hurt her argument for getting the boys. An argument that she wouldn't have won no matter what.

Now Judd would have to explain that to Kace, too.

Since he was still barefoot, Judd motioned for

Kace to follow him to his cabin. Along the way, he buttoned his shirt and hoped that Kace didn't misinterpret his clothing issues as his carrying on with Cleo. But one glance back at his brother, and Judd got confirmation that Kace did indeed believe that. Great. Now Kace would think that lust and sex were playing a part in this mess.

They weren't.

But Judd wasn't going to convince anybody, not even himself, that the lust wasn't there.

"Rosy said there was a dispute," Kace said as Cleo, Judd and he went into the cabin. "The grandmother bruised up the kids, they ran away, you found them and brought them here."

It was a good summary, void of emotion. In other words, Kace was speaking like a cop.

Judd went straight to his bedroom area, sat on the bed and pulled on his boots. "SAPD put the boys in my protective custody."

"For how long?" Kace asked.

Judd had to shake his head, but the answer was… not long. In fact, someone in SAPD was likely already starting the paperwork to undo it.

Cleo shook her head, too. "I can't let the boys go back to living with that woman."

Kace helped himself to a Coke from Judd's fridge and had several gulps while he studied them. "Any reason you didn't come to me with this before you ended up with a motorcycle thug and a shrieking woman in the driveway?"

Again, it was a good summary, but he doubted

Kace would consider his response a good one. "I was trying to handle it myself," Judd said, just as Cleo blurted out, "I asked Judd to foster the boys, as a favor to me."

Kace nodded, considered and had another sip of the Coke while he propped his shoulder against the fridge. "No parents involved in this?"

Cleo shook her head again. "Both are dead. But I was close friends with the boys' mother, and before she died, she asked me to raise them. I can't legally do that because I have a police record. And, no, it's not for urinating in public."

"Breaking and entering when you were eighteen," Kace stated. "I had Liberty run you on the way over." He stayed quiet a moment before he shifted his attention back to Judd. "I take it you turned Cleo down? On fostering the boys," he added.

Yeah, Kace was aware of the lust problem.

"I did turn her down," Judd admitted.

"I asked him to be a foster in name only," Cleo confessed. "In other words, I wanted him to bend the law."

The silence came, and it lasted for some long moments before Kace spoke. "Buck and Rosy are in on this?" he asked.

Cleo nodded. "They were going to let me use the house because my apartment isn't big enough. I'll buy a place, eventually. And I have a sitter lined up who can be here when I'm not, and I'll commute to work."

Kace stared at her from over his Coke can.

"You're willing to spend more than the next decade or so raising these kids?"

"Yes, I am," Cleo said without hesitation. "I owe that to their mother. The oldest, Beckham, and I have talked about this. He's fifteen, and when he turns eighteen, he'll petition the courts for custody of his brothers. I'd still continue to be with them, but that would let Judd legally off the hook."

"Three years," Kace muttered. "That's a long time for Judd to be a foster father on paper."

The breath that Cleo released sounded as if she'd been holding it forever. "It is. I knew it was a huge favor to ask and don't blame him for refusing." She sighed. "I just need a fix for this, Kace. A fix that keeps those children away from their turd-head of a grandmother." Cleo shook her head and blinked back tears. "She doesn't even want them and will put them in foster care first chance she gets."

Even though Judd had heard Cleo say that multiple times, it still made his chest tighten. Kace didn't say anything, but Judd figured he was having the same reaction. It was impossible to forget what they'd gone through.

"The boys likely wouldn't be able to stay together in foster care," Cleo went on. "Beckham has a juvie record." She stopped and gave her bottom lip a quick nibble. "So, are you going to arrest me for trying to get around the law?"

Again, Kace paused. "No." Then he huffed, "Actually, I'm going to help you."

That got Judd's attention. Cleo's, too, because

she took several cautious steps toward Kace. "Help me how?" she asked.

"Let me look over the boys' case file, and then I'll contact CPS," Kace explained. "I'll ask them to sign over custody to me."

THIS WAS A GOOD THING, Judd reminded himself as he stood in the hall of the second floor of Buck's house and watched Cleo putting the kids to bed in the bunk-bed room. A *really* good thing. Kace had stepped up to the plate and would help Cleo go through with her plan to raise the boys.

Judd couldn't even argue with the plan itself. The boys needed someone to take care of them, someone who would keep them together, someone who would love them, and Cleo was going to do all of that.

With Kace's help.

Too bad it made Judd feel like shit.

He knew what it was like to be in foster care and separated from his brothers. He knew what it was like to have no one give a damn. But he was also well aware of his limitations. Flashbacks and memories could send him straight back to the bottle, and if that happened, it wouldn't do anybody any good.

Judd shoved his hand in his pocket to touch the sobriety coin that he always carried with him. It was a reminder that feeling like shit was better than *being* shit—which was what would happen if he went back to drinking.

"How long do we get to stay in this stupid place?" Little Leo asked, grinning as Cleo shadowed him up the ladder to the top bunk. Once he was on the bed, she lifted the side railing that would stop him from falling out.

"A while," she answered. "And it's not stupid. I even slept in these beds a time or two before I got the room down the hall."

"It's stupid," Beckham complained.

He was already on the lower bunk and was wearing the devil-red pj's that Rosy had given him. The color wasn't just red. They actually had devils on them, making Judd wonder if Rosy was typecasting or if she'd just bought them because they'd been on sale. Probably the latter considering the other pj's that she'd given to Isaac had aliens on them and Leo's had dancing doughnuts.

"What about Popsicle?" Leo asked as he peered down at the kitten, who was sacked out on the bottom bunk of the other bed. "Is he gonna come up here and sleep with me?"

"No, he'll be fine where he is," Cleo assured him, "and this way he can get to his litter box if he needs it. And speaking of *needing it*, remember the bathroom's just across the hall, but if you have to use it in the night, call out for me to help you down the ladder."

"I'll help him," Beckham snarled. "But if *she* comes back again, we're not staying here," he added, still snarling. "And I'll punch her in her stupid ugly face."

Judd nearly made a sound of agreement about the punching before he caught himself. Best not to encourage Beckham to commit violence even when that person, Lavinia, deserved it.

"Will Miss Rosy lock the door so Grandma Lavinia can't get in?" Isaac asked. The kid didn't have the defiant tone like his older brother. Just the opposite. Isaac sounded scared. And that hit Judd even harder than the defiance did.

It had the same effect on Cleo.

Judd saw her swallow hard, and he heard the long breath she dragged in as if to steady herself. "Yes, the door will be locked, but your grandmother won't be coming back tonight," she said. "Remember, Sheriff Laramie said he was going to get some papers to make sure she stayed away."

A restraining order. Kace was indeed doing that, probably right now at this very moment, but Judd knew that a piece of paper rarely made idiots act smarter. That's why he'd be keeping watch tonight to make sure Lavinia and Otto didn't return to the ranch. Judd was almost hoping that Otto would come back so he'd have somewhere to aim this dangerous energy boiling inside him. He couldn't hit a woman, but Otto was fair game.

Cleo tucked in Isaac and Leo, giving them both cheek kisses, but Beckham turned away when she leaned down to him. "I'm giving you a good-night kiss in my mind. Five of them." She smiled, winked at him, then leaned down and whispered something to him that Judd didn't catch. Whatever it was had Beckham shrugging and maybe even relaxing a little.

Cleo gave all three boys and Popsicle a final check, turned off the lights and closed the door as she stepped out into the hall. She motioned for him to follow her to the stairs, no doubt so that she'd be out of earshot from the boys, and she let out another of those long breaths.

"I don't think they'll run," she whispered, "but just in case, I'm bunking in a sleeping bag outside their door." She pushed her hair from her face and glanced around. "Kace isn't back yet."

Judd shook his head. "A restraining order can take time." Plus, the ever organized Kace was probably making other calls, other arrangements. "What did you tell Beckham?"

"That the chickens would chase and peck him if he went out at night. He knows it's not true, that I was just trying to lighten him up some, but maybe part of him will believe it so he'll stay put. They all need a good night's sleep."

"So do you," he pointed out, but Judd figured "good" and "sleep" weren't going to happen with her bunking on the floor. "I can take a shift up here watching the boys if that'll help."

A tiny smile tugged at her mouth—a reminder that she had a mouth that interested him.

Yeah, even at a time like this.

That didn't help with the shitty feeling. Here they were in the middle of an upheaval, and he was going horndog with his thoughts.

"No offense, but you look even more exhausted than I do." Cleo patted his arm but didn't immediately pull back her hand. It stayed there while their gazes connected.

"Yeah, even at a time like this." But this time, Judd said it aloud. The only saving grace was that Cleo likely didn't have a clue what he meant.

But she did. The tugging smile let him know that. "It's okay. I'll be so busy running back and forth between here and the bar that the old heat won't get us into trouble. Trust me, I'll be too tired to go sneaking into your bed and asking you if you want to get lucky tonight."

Good thing. Because as good as sex with Cleo would feel right now, it would only add another layer to his crappy mood. It would give him something else to regret.

They both stepped back when they heard the footsteps on the stairs. Kace. And his brother was carrying a rolled-up sleeping bag.

"Rosy asked me to bring this up," Kace said. "Are the boys asleep?"

"Leo and Isaac might be." Cleo took the sleeping bag from him. "But I suspect Beckham is wide-awake and trying to figure out how many more things he can call stupid."

Kace did something that Judd rarely saw him do. He smiled. It didn't last, though, and he scrubbed his hand over his face. "I've got good news and not so good. The restraining order against Lavinia is done, but she says she'll challenge it."

"She might, if she stays sober long enough," Cleo

said, and then she winced a little. Probably because she thought she'd offended Judd. She hadn't.

Kace nodded as if that'd been the answer he'd expected. "As for custody, the best I could do was temporary, and I suspect Lavinia will challenge that, too."

Yes, as much as the woman hated Cleo, she would. "It takes money to hire lawyers to go up against even a temporary custody order," Judd reminded Cleo.

Kace made a sound of agreement. "That'll count against Lavinia and so will the assault charges I want filed against her. That means I need one of the deputies to question the boys. Not Judd or me, though, because I don't want proper procedure called into question here."

Cleo groaned. Then nodded. "I'll speak to the boys in the morning to let them know what's to happen. FYI, I tried to get them to talk about the bruises, but they wouldn't."

Probably because they were traumatized and scared. Being questioned by a cop wouldn't ease that any, but Cleo would hopefully be able to make them understand that this would be the way to stop their grandmother.

"One more thing," Kace said a moment later. "CPS will be out to check on the boys and their living arrangements."

Cleo touched her fingers to her lips for a moment. "You'll have to lie about being their foster parent."

Kace quickly shook his head. "No. I won't lie. I won't break the law."

Judd's stomach suddenly felt tight as a fist. This was the reason Cleo hadn't gone to Kace in the first place, the reason she'd asked him to do this.

"My house isn't big enough for all of us," Kace continued before Judd could say anything. "But I just talked to Buck, and we came up with a solution." His brother looked at Cleo now. "You and I will move in here together."

CHAPTER SEVEN

"GATHERING STUPID EGGS is fun," Leo announced as he came through the back door and into the kitchen.

Cleo sighed and looked up from her laptop where she was doing the payroll for the bar. Obviously, she needed to have another chat with Beckham about dubbing anything and everything *stupid*. Then she needed to chat with Leo about mimicking his big brother.

She should chat with Judd, too.

Cleo hadn't missed the troubled expression on Judd's face when Kace had laid out his plan for custody—a plan that involved Kace and her both moving in with Buck, Rosy and the boys. Since Cleo had planned on doing that—temporarily, anyway—it wasn't a big deal.

However, it'd seemed pretty big to Judd. Maybe because Judd was worried about Kace getting in legal hot water. Or maybe it was personal. Because of the sizzling chemistry between Judd and her, this temporary move would put her very close to his cabin. And to him.

"See?" Leo said, showing the contents of the basket to both Cleo and Rosy. There were indeed four eggs in the basket, and it didn't seem to dampen Leo's enthusiasm that two were broken.

Despite the 50-percent-yield rate of the egg gathering, Rosy smiled. "Good job." She took the basket from him, ignoring that the egg-white goo was seeping from the bottom. "You can put a gold star on the chore chart, and you can have a 'get out of jail free' card."

To a casual observer, that might not have sounded like a big deal. Maybe it even sounded menacing with the jail reference, but with stars came rewards. Like ice cream and movies. And a "get out of jail free" card could be ponied up to clean the slate of a minor or semiminor infraction, like missing chores or being late on homework. It could also be used to get extra dessert or treats.

Leo was enthusiastic about the star and card part, too, and he ran to the fridge, taking first a card and then a small foil star from the envelope that had been taped there. He stuck the card in his pocket to go along with the other one that was there. He applied far more spit than required to the tiny star when he quadruple-licked it and stuck it next to his name and the three other stars that were already there.

Considering that this was his first day using the chore chart, the boy had that star-sticking down pat, and he immediately pointed to another possibility. "Can I do this one?" he asked Rosy.

"Mucking the stalls," she said, reading the card. "We should probably save that one for Isaac or Beckham since they're a little taller and stronger.

You know, you only have to do two chores a day on a nonschool day and one on a school day, right?"

He nodded. "But doing stupid chores is fun."

Cleo sighed again, saved her work on the laptop and went to the boy. She stooped down and took hold of his shoulders. "*Stupid* might not be the best word to use for something that's fun." She gave that more thought. "Actually, *stupid* might not be a good word to use at all. If you say it when you're at school, the other kids might not take it the right way."

"School?" Leo beamed at that, too, making her wonder how Lavinia could have put that bruise on that precious little face. She'd never been around a happier kid.

"Yes. I'm going by the elementary school this morning. I have an appointment to talk to the principal so Isaac and you can go there." And then she'd do the same at the high school for Beckham.

It wouldn't be an easy transfer, and Cleo was anticipating some balking and general complaining from Beckham. There'd hardly be time for the boys to settle into their classes before school would end in six weeks, and considering everything they'd been through, there could be adjustment problems. Still, she couldn't hold them back until fall. They needed to finish out the year so they wouldn't have to repeat the grade.

"I'm going to try to sign them up for some after-school stuff, too," Cleo told Rosy. "But I need to work that out with the sitter."

"We got a sitter?" Leo asked, but he didn't wait for the answer.

When he heard the front door open and Kace called out, "It's just me," Leo hurried in that direction.

Cleo followed him and spotted Kace coming in with two boxes. Not a surprise since this was his third trip to bring in some of his things, but this time he wasn't alone. Liberty, his deputy, was with him, and Cleo knew why. Liberty was here to question the boys about their bruises.

"I can help," Leo volunteered, but both of Kace's boxes were way too big for the boy to handle.

"You can unpack them for me," Kace said without missing a beat, and he headed for the stairs with Leo trailing along behind him. "Cleo, can you round up Isaac and Beckham for Liberty?"

"I'll do that," Rosy volunteered, calling out from the kitchen. "They're in the barn with Buck."

"Daddy Kace," Liberty muttered under her breath after Kace was out of earshot. "Someday you can tell me how you talked him into doing this."

"I will after I figure it out myself. This is well beyond a favor, and I can never repay him for it," Cleo admitted. Kace was disrupting his life for what could be months since it might take that long for a permanent placement with CPS. "I just hope this doesn't cause any trouble for him."

Liberty shrugged. "He seems okay with it. Better than Judd is, anyway."

That got Cleo's attention, but since she didn't

know exactly how to ask why Judd wasn't okay, she just stayed quiet and waited for Liberty to continue.

"He came into work in a pisser of a mood," Liberty finally said. "And I heard him call his sponsor." She stopped, her eyes widening. "God, I probably shouldn't have said anything about that. I mean, in case you don't know."

Sponsor as in Alcoholics Anonymous.

"Yes, I know," Cleo admitted, but she wanted to groan. She hadn't intended for any of this to send Judd into a tailspin, but just being around the boys could bring back the old memories that had caused him to turn to a bottle in the first place.

"Please don't tell Judd that I mentioned it," Liberty stressed.

"I won't." Cleo paused. "Was it bad? Was Judd upset when he spoke to his sponsor?"

"Don't know. I'd popped into the alley to make a private phone call, and he was already there, talking to her. I could tell it was his sponsor by the things he was saying. I cleared my throat to let him know I was there, and he cursed and walked farther up the sidewalk."

So, definitely upset. Cleo had already added a "chat with Judd" to her to-do list. She could even mention her concern in a vague sort of way to Kace so he could also keep an eye on him.

"The anniversary of Judd's transfer from Austin PD is coming up," Liberty went on. "So, maybe his pisser mood doesn't have anything to do with the boys."

Cleo supposed Liberty had added that to make her feel better and take her out of the blame loop, but it only served as a reminder that Judd maybe had other demons. Ones that had led to his transfer to Coldwater.

"Say, what exactly did happen with Judd when he was in Austin?" Liberty asked.

The direct question threw Cleo for a moment. "I don't have a clue. I figured you knew."

Liberty shook her head. "Never mentioned a word about it. One day Kace just came in and said Judd would be transferring here as a deputy. It was so sudden that I figured it must have been something bad."

Well, if it was, Cleo hadn't been in that particular info loop, and she doubted it was a loop that Judd would just invite her into. He didn't like sharing his baggage—baggage that played into every part of his life—with anyone.

She hadn't been smart to try to rope him into fostering the boys.

Cleo heard the sound of the approaching vehicle just as Rosy came in with Beckham and Isaac. Clearly, Beckham wasn't happy about being corralled into the house, but then he likely hadn't been happy about being in the barn with Buck, either. Cleo made another mental note to contact a counselor not just for him, but for Isaac and Leo, too.

"Boys, this is Deputy Liberty Cassaine," Cleo said. "And this is Beckham and Isaac."

Cleo didn't have to explain what the deputy

wanted. She had already explained to them that they'd need to talk to someone from the police station and that it couldn't be Kace or Judd.

"Buck said you could use his office for your visit," Rosy told Liberty.

Liberty smiled and motioned toward Beckham. "Sorry, but I gotta talk to all three of you separately."

Beckham grumbled about that, of course, as Liberty led him away, and Isaac dropped down onto the sofa to wait his turn.

Since the front door was still open, Cleo saw the white sedan that stopped in front of the house. It was the sitter, Lissy Tate, and Cleo released the breath that she'd automatically held. Even though she doubted Lavinia would make a return visit anytime soon, Cleo had braced herself for that outside possibility.

Lissy had come highly recommended as a sitter, and Cleo tried not to be skeptical of those recommendations as the woman stepped from her car. Lissy looked more like a matronly librarian in her prim gray calf-length dress, white sweater and pearls. There wasn't a strand of her brown hair out of place, and as Lissy got closer, Cleo thought she knew why. There was the thick odor of Aqua Net hairspray swimming off her.

"Miss Delaney," Lissy greeted, her voice as prim and proper as her outfit.

The boys were going to eat her alive.

"Call me Cleo." She waited for Lissy to make the

same offer for first-name use, but when she didn't, Cleo went with "Miss Tate."

Lissy nodded. "I know what you're thinking, but I'm not anything like him."

Color her clueless, but Cleo had no idea what the woman meant. "Excuse me?"

Lissy's mouth tightened a little. "Gopher Tate is my uncle, and everybody thinks because he's a pervert flasher that I'm cut from the same cloth. I assure you that I'm not."

Cleo paused, gave her a firm nod. "Well, that's good to know."

"Lissy," Rosy called out, coming to the door to greet her. She pulled Lissy into a hug, causing Cleo to relax just a little. If Rosy thought this woman was huggable, then maybe she would work out for the boys.

And speaking of boys, Cleo heard Beckham snap out a very loud "no" through the door to Buck's office.

"Rosy, could you show Lissy around and introduce her to Isaac and Leo?" Cleo asked. "I need to check on Beckham." She glanced at the time and huffed. "After that, I have to go to the schools and then to work for a couple of hours."

Of course, those two things were only going to happen if these next ten minutes went okay.

"Just go ahead and do what you have to do," Rosy insisted. "Lissy and I will take care of things around here."

Cleo might have hesitated, wondering if that was

true, if she hadn't heard Beckham growl out an-other "no."

Since she didn't want him to do anything to add to his juvie record, Cleo left Lissy in Rosy's hands, went to the office and knocked. It surprised her when Beckham answered the door, but it didn't take her long to realize that he'd done that because he had been about to storm out. He would have con-tinued the storming, too, if Cleo hadn't sidestepped in front of him. Not just once but several times until it looked as if they were dancing.

"I don't want to talk about this," Beckham snarled, aiming a hard glance over his shoulder at Liberty.

"Of course you don't," Cleo readily agreed, caus-ing Beckham to give her a suspicious stare. "No one wants to talk about bad things. Well, maybe some people do, but they have that whole 'wallowing in pity' thing going on." She looked him straight in the eyes, and when he tried to dodge her gaze, she caught onto his chin. "In your case, though, you need to talk about it to stop Lavinia from getting away with a crime."

Beckham went still and quit trying to dance around her. His forehead bunched up for only a couple of seconds while he obviously considered that, and then—bam!—the surly teenage expres-sion returned.

"She'll get away with it," Beckham declared. "People like her never pay."

"Never is such a long time, and she will pay. But

only if you help the cops. Yes, I know helping them goes against the grain for you, but do this for Leo and Isaac."

Cleo knew she got him with that last handful of words. No way would Beckham do this for himself, but he would for his little brothers. Still, Beckham stayed put and didn't turn back toward the deputy.

"You've been arrested before." Beckham lowered his voice to a whisper. "And you still trust the cops?"

"I trust these cops," Cleo answered without hesitation.

Beckham shoved his hands into his pockets and looked down at the floor as soon as Cleo let go of his chin. "Stay," he said.

Cleo tried not to look floored by that. Beckham wasn't one who reached out to anybody, including her. "Of course." And Cleo gave Liberty a pleading look not to object when she went back into the office with Beckham and shut the door.

Liberty was seated on the small leather sofa, a recorder in her lap, and the deputy announced Cleo's arrival so that it would be on the official record. Beckham went closer, but he didn't sit.

"All right," Beckham said after a long pause. Then, he repeated it as if to steady himself. "Can I call her a bitch?" he asked Cleo. "Because I'm not going to call her my grandmother."

"How about witch?" Cleo suggested as a compromise. In this case, the *B* word applied, but she didn't want to encourage Beckham to curse.

Beckham nodded. "All right," he agreed. "The

witch got mad when the kitten scratched her. I mean, it's just a kitten, and it was swatting at the bottom of her gown. It smells like piss," he added. "Her gown. She smells like piss."

Since Cleo had detected the same aroma on the woman, she had to agree.

"The piss witch," Beckham went on, clearly trying to give some edge to Lavinia's new name, "got mad and said she was going to kill the cat. She started chasing it around with a skillet. Leo thought it was a stupid game, but when he went to scoop up the cat, the piss witch grabbed him by the arm, and she slapped him. I don't mean like a little tap, either. She hit him hard enough to knock him on the floor."

Oh, God. Cleo had thought she'd been ready to hear this, but she clearly wasn't. Her breath got trapped somewhere between her lungs and her throat. Everything inside her tightened and throbbed.

"The piss witch was going to hit Leo again," Beckham continued, "but I pushed her. Not hard enough. I should have pushed her harder." A muscle in his jaw flickered. "She came after me and hit me here with the skillet." He motioned toward his left arm, then his side. "I managed to knock the skillet out of her hand, and that's when she slapped me."

Obviously, Liberty was affected by this because she swallowed hard. "What about the bruises on your neck?" she asked. "How did you get those?"

Beckham took his time answering. "When she slapped me, Leo caught onto her leg, to try to pull her back, I think. He was crying then…and the kid almost never cries. But he was wailing loud enough that the piss witch tried to kick him. I reached down to move Leo out of the way, and that's when she grabbed me by the throat. I shoved her again. That time it was hard enough to make her fall. I took Leo, found Isaac and got us out of there."

Cleo clamped her teeth over her bottom lip to stop it from trembling. It didn't help. And worse, she was on the verge of crying. She could feel the tears sting her eyes and anger churned inside her. She wished that she'd punched the piss witch in her face.

"Isaac didn't see any of this so don't push him on it," Beckham told the deputy. "And Leo…well, don't push him, either."

Cleo laid a very unsteady hand on Beckham's shoulder. "I'm sorry," she whispered, and before she totally lost it, she turned to Liberty. "I know this is a big favor, but do you think you can wait to talk to Isaac and Leo? I want to be with them for that, but I have to get to the school for my meeting with the principal."

"Sure." Liberty turned off the recorder and stood. "This should be enough to back up the restraining order. Along with Audrey's report. Dr. Holcomb," she said to clarify. "It's a good report. She really went all out to say that she believed every word the boys had told her and that the grandmother shouldn't be allowed to see them."

Cleo would thank Audrey for that, and she didn't care if Judd was Audrey's motivation for her all-out report. Right now, Cleo would take anything that would help the boys.

"I didn't hit the piss witch," Beckham added when Cleo turned to him. "Mom always said I shouldn't hit a girl or woman." His voice caught, and Cleo could tell by the way he was blinking hard that the tears were threatening.

She blinked back her own tears, hugged him despite his going stiff and got out of there fast. Thankfully, there was no one in the living room, but she could hear Rosy and Lissy in the kitchen.

"I'm leaving for my meeting at the school," Cleo called out, and she hurried off before anyone could see her.

She still had an hour before the appointment and with the school only five minutes away, she would get there in plenty of time—time that she would need to sit in the parking lot and settle her jangled nerves.

The moment she was in her car, she took off, and she made it to the end of the driveway before the eye-blinking quit working. The tears spilled down her cheeks. Cleo wouldn't have minded that so much, but the tears also blurred her vision so she pulled off to the side and just cried it out.

Cleo hated what the boys had gone through. Hated that she hadn't been able to stop it. And hated just as much that she might not be able to stop it from happening again. All those bruises. And Beckham's words kept repeating in her head.

She hit him hard enough to knock him on the floor.

If Miranda had been watching that from heaven, then it must have broken her heart. It was doing the same to Cleo. Miranda had loved those kids with everything she had, and the fact that their future was so uncertain made the cancer and her dying even more painful.

And the grief over losing her.

Miranda had tried to help with the grief by leaving each of the boys a letter, but she hadn't managed to finalize the paperwork to give Cleo custody. The lawyer had still been in the process of writing that all out. Cleo still might be able to use that, though, to show intent, that it had been a dying woman's wish that her children not be left in the care of their grandmother.

Cleo dug through her purse to come up with a handful of tissues, but as soon as she wiped away tears, more came. She wasn't a crier, but there'd been so much stored-up emotion inside her that she supposed it had to come out. At least it hadn't happened in front of the boys.

Cleo's head snapped up and she sputtered out a garbled sound of surprise when someone tapped on her window.

Judd was there on the other side of the glass.

She hadn't heard him come up, probably because her ears were plugged up from the crying, but with a glance over her shoulder, she saw his truck now parked behind her. No one else was inside it, thank goodness.

Cleo quickly did more tear-wiping as she lowered the window, and she considered telling him that she had a severe allergy attack. One look at his face, though, and after hearing the heavy sigh that left his mouth, she doubted anyone could manage that good of a lie.

He went to the passenger side of her car and got in. She steeled herself for the questions she figured he would ask, but he stayed silent. Well, verbally silent, anyway. Those cop's eyes were steady on her.

"I lost it when I heard Beckham telling Liberty about Lavinia hitting them," she confessed.

He just nodded in that calm, effortless way of his that let her know he'd already suspected as much. "Is there anything I can do?"

She shook her head. "No, I'd just about finished. Crying sucks," she added and then groaned when she checked her face in the mirror. Cleo took out her compact from her purse, but she doubted some puffs of powder were going to help this.

"Liberty said Beckham's statement and Audrey's report should be enough to back up the restraining order," she added.

He made a sound that could have meant anything and just kept staring at her.

"You know, that look you're giving me feels like a truth serum," she said. "You really don't want me to start spilling all, do you?"

Judd stayed quiet, maybe considering her question. Considering, too, that her spilling might involve talking about this heat that was still between them. Heat that sizzled when her eyes cleared enough to actually see him.

He looked away from her.

Obviously, he wasn't in a spilling or hearing a spilling kind of mood. Too bad because a quick discussion of sizzle, followed by some flirting, might have washed away her dark film of thoughts.

"How are you?" Cleo asked, but what she really wanted to know was why he'd felt the need to call his sponsor.

His mouth tightened enough to let her know he didn't want to discuss it, but it did get his gaze back on her. A long, lingering, smoldering gaze. Though Cleo had to admit that the smoldering part might be her own overly active imagination.

Or not.

Judd said a single word of really bad profanity, grabbed her shoulders and dragged her to him. His mouth was on hers before Cleo could even make a sound. It turned out, though, that no sound was necessary because she got a full, head-on slam of the heat. And this time it wasn't just simmering around them. It rolled through her from head to toe.

Now she made a sound, one of pleasure, and the years vanished. It was as if they'd picked up where they'd left off seventeen years ago, when he'd been scorching her like this in his bed.

His taste. Yes. That was the same. Maybe with

a manlier edge to it, but it was unmistakably Judd. Unmistakably incredible.

Cleo felt herself moving right into the kiss. Right into Judd, too. Unfortunately, the gearshift was in the way, but she still managed some more body-to-body contact when she slid against him and into his arms.

Judd deepened the kiss, and she let him. In fact, Cleo was reasonably sure that she would have let him do pretty much anything. Yep, he'd heated her up just that much.

Apparently, though, he hadn't made himself as mindless and needy as he had her because he pulled back, cursed again and resumed his cop's stare. Though she did think his eyes were a little blurry.

They sat there, gazes connected, breaths gusting. Waiting. Since Cleo figured her gusty breaths weren't enough to allow her to speak, she just waited for Judd to say something memorable.

"Shit," he growled.

Okay, so maybe not memorable in the way she'd wanted. Definitely not romantic. But it was such a *Judd* reaction that it made her smile. Then laugh.

She leaned in, nipped his bottom lip with her teeth. "Don't worry, Judd. I'll be gentle with you."

CHAPTER EIGHT

JUDD DOUBTED HIS mood could get any worse, but
he figured Gopher was testing that theory when he
saw the man loitering outside the Lightning Bug
Inn. Gopher must have gotten a glimmer of the bad
mood because his eyes widened when Judd's cruiser
squealed to a stop and Judd barreled out.

Judd aimed both a glare and his index finger at
Gopher. "If you want your junk to stay where junk
belongs, then you'll keep that coat closed and get
the hell home—*now!*"

Gopher didn't even try to come up with some
lame excuse as to why he was there. He just took
off running, and Judd had never seen him move
that fast. Didn't know he could, and the speed told
Judd that the man clearly had some common sense
left if he knew better than to tangle with him. Too
bad, though, that Gopher had shown that escaping
wisdom now because it might have appeased Judd's
temper some to arrest his sorry flashing butt.

I'll be gentle with you.

Those were the words that had been going
through Judd's head for the past two days, and while
Cleo had meant it as a joke, it wasn't giving Judd any

fun and merriment. Just the opposite. That handful of words, coupled with the kiss, had left him in a bad-mood muddle.

He'd been a damn fool to kiss Cleo.

Because there was no way it was just a kiss. It was a Pandora's box to a whole bunch of other stuff. Stuff that neither Cleo nor he had time for. She didn't need to carry on with him right now, what with her hands full with the boys. Plus, if Cleo and he did land in bed, she would likely wonder why he'd shirked fostering when he hadn't shirked lust. He was already feeling shitty about turning down the foster request without adding another heap of guilt to it.

Judd again mentally went through the logic of why there'd be no sex with Cleo, and he hoped this time it stuck. He wasn't holding out hope about that, though. It'd been two days since that kiss in her car, and his mouth and the rest of his body were still burning for her.

At least he hadn't made the foolery even worse by kissing her again. Or coaxing her into the back seat of her car. Somehow, he'd managed to get out of her car and leave. Not easily. Because it'd been difficult to walk with a hard-on, but he'd managed to put some distance between them.

Judd had continued to keep that distance, too, though that was more because of Cleo's busy schedule than any planned avoidance on his part. With her trying to settle the boys in their new home and going back and forth between the ranch and the bar, there hadn't been time for other car kisses and sex jokes.

He got back in his cruiser to head to the station, where he would face more paperwork—something he'd spent the morning doing, and then dropped off that paperwork at the courthouse. Normally, it was something Kace would have taken care of, but he was working from Buck's ranch today so he could be there when the social worker showed up.

Judd suspected his brother was feeling some nerves about that visit from CPS because it was a necessary step in maintaining temporary custody, but unfortunately Judd wasn't going to be able to help out Kace in that area. Kace was the person of record for the boys' custody, which meant he was the one who was going to have to answer the questions and pass any kind of inspection or test CPS would have for him. It especially wouldn't be easy because the fostering was a partial lie.

Judd parked at the station and was heading in just as his phone rang. He practically jumped out of his skin, and that's when he admitted to himself that he, too, was wired about the CPS visit. But it wasn't Kace's name on the screen.

It was Callen's.

"I just got off the phone with Buck," Callen snapped the moment that Judd answered. "Why didn't you call me and tell me about Cleo needing help?"

"Hello to you, too," Judd growled. "And the reason I didn't call you was because you eloped and are on your honeymoon."

"I would have wanted to know. Shelby, too," Callen insisted, and in the background, Judd heard Shelby voice her strong agreement. "We're packing now to head home."

"No need. It's all under control." And Judd hoped that was true. "Kace has temporarily moved into Buck's, and he did the paperwork to foster the boys."

"Yes, but Buck said CPS might not go along with that," Callen argued. "If Shelby and I are there, we can step in if CPS has questions about Kace being able to handle this. We want CPS to know that Kace has backup if he needs it."

"We can help," Shelby added. "We *want* to help."

Hell. Talk about adding yet more to his guilt trip. Judd felt as if he was the only person in Coldwater who hadn't stepped up to the plate on this.

"Buck told us what the boys have been through," Callen went on, and he muttered some profanity. "I'm guessing Cleo's arranged for them to see a counselor, but if not, I can help with that."

Judd didn't know about the counselor, which for some reason heaped on more guilt. He should know something like that and could have maybe gotten the info from Cleo if he hadn't spent their time together kissing her.

"You'd have to ask Cleo about that," Judd said.

"I will. Shelby and I should be home in a couple of hours."

Judd didn't even try to talk Callen out of it, and

heck, maybe Cleo and Kace did need them. Three kids were a lot to manage, and with Cleo and Kace both having full-time jobs, they might welcome having the extra help.

And yeah, that led to even more guilt.

Judd hadn't even had time to put his phone away before it rang again, and this time it was Kace's name on the screen so Judd answered it right away.

"I have a problem," Kace said, and it immediately snagged Judd's attention because his brother was whispering. "I just got a call from Principal Winslow at the high school, and he said Beckham left without permission. It's his study-hall period, but he's still not allowed to leave campus."

Damn it. Not another runaway attempt. "What about Leo and Isaac? Are they with Beckham?"

"No. I checked the elementary school, and they're both in class."

Well, that was something at least, but that didn't mean Beckham didn't have plans to collect his brothers and run off again.

"Did something happen to piss Beckham off?" Judd asked.

"Nothing that I know about, but it's possible something went on at school." Kace was still whispering. "I can't go looking for him because the social worker is here, and I can't ask Cleo to do it because she's at work. I'd rather not involve Buck, either, but if you can't—"

"I'll go." Judd didn't want more to add to his guilt pile. "How long has Beckham been missing?"

"According to Principal Winslow, less than an hour."

Good. Then he couldn't have gotten far. Well, unless someone had given him a ride, but Judd wasn't going to jump on that worst-case scenario just yet.

"The principal agreed to keep this quiet as a favor to me," Kace went on. "I don't need this getting back to the social worker."

No. They already had enough strikes against them.

"I'll let you know when I find him," Judd assured his brother, and he ended the call.

Judd sent a quick text to Ginger, the dispatcher, and he kept it vague. He just told her that he'd gotten tied up with something and left it at that.

In hopes of keeping this off the gossip's radar, he didn't use the cruiser, but instead got in his truck and started the drive to the high school. It wasn't far, but then nothing in Coldwater was. Judd was there in only a couple of minutes, and he drove around the parking lot and grounds looking for any sign of the boy.

Nothing.

He wasn't even sure if Beckham knew the back road to get to the elementary school, but that's the way Judd took. There were plenty of trees on the narrow rural road, which meant plenty of places to duck and hide. But he was thinking Beckham wasn't in that mind-set. Speed would be his priority. And since he wasn't one to leave his brothers behind,

Beckham would likely have gotten to their school as fast as possible.

Judd cursed and had to slam on his brakes when he spotted the longhorn in the middle of the road, one that he instantly recognized. It belonged to the librarian, Esther Benton. For some reason, the darn thing was always breaking fence and wandering off, and it never responded to a honked horn. Though that was what Judd tried. Other than giving Judd a disinterested glance, it didn't budge an inch.

Hoping that no one speeding would slam into his truck, Judd got out to give the longhorn a swat on the butt with his hat.

And that's when he saw Beckham.

If the boy was actually hiding, he was doing a lousy job of it. He was in plain sight, leaning against a tree, his backpack slung over one shoulder. He had a pair of binoculars and was using them to look into the clearing just ahead, at the elementary school playground.

"Who sent you to look for me?" Beckham immediately snarled.

"Kace."

Beckham shook his head and mumbled something Judd didn't catch. Probably some curse words.

"It's not a good day for you to pull a stunt like this," Judd told him. He took out his phone and texted Kace to let him know that he'd found the boy. "The social worker's at the ranch doing an inspection."

Beckham didn't say anything about that, and definitely didn't apologize, but he did start walking toward the truck. "I didn't want any kids picking on Leo so I borrowed these binoculars from the tack room in the barn."

Judd gave the longhorn another swat, finally getting it to move, and he went back to his truck, meeting Beckham's gaze over the top of it. "Has somebody been picking on Leo?" And Judd had to tamp down his sudden urge to go to the school and put the fear of God into anyone giving the kid any trouble.

"Isaac said he saw some boys making fun of Leo," Beckham added. "They called him a mutt that nobody wanted and that's why he had to move to Mr. Buck's house and be a foster kid."

Then, yeah. "Fear of God" time. The anger snapped through him like a bullwhip. "Get in the truck. I'm going to the school."

Beckham's eyes widened, as if he was surprised by Judd's reaction. "You're not going to arrest a kid, are you?"

No, but he could put a stop to any bullying. "Did Isaac give you the names of who was picking on Leo?" Judd asked once they were both in the truck.

"He said they call one of them Smelly. Sound familiar?"

It did indeed. "One of the Smelton brats. Their dad, Arnie Smelton, works on one of the local ranches and has five kids, maybe six. All of them are dumber than rocks and as mean as snakes. I've already hauled in the oldest one a couple of times for fighting and creating a public nuisance."

Which was probably more than he should have shared with Beckham, but he'd learn it soon enough. There weren't a lot of secrets in a small town like Coldwater.

"You'll let me handle this," Judd added to Beckham. "That means no more leaving the campus to keep watch."

Beckham studied him. "You seem pretty pissed off. You're not going to start a fight, are you?"

"No." But he wished he could do that before this anger festered. "I'll just have a quick word with the principal, take you back to school and then I'll talk to Arnie."

Beckham nodded, and now Judd was the one who was surprised. He hadn't figured on Beckham letting him deal with this.

And maybe Beckham wouldn't.

Judd knew some of what was going on in the boy's head, and Beckham probably wasn't just going to trust him with something like protecting his little brother.

"Will you tell Cleo about this?" Beckham asked.

"Yeah, if Kace doesn't tell her first."

Beckham huffed, probably because he thought this was going to earn him lectures from not only the principal, but also Kace and Cleo. Heck, maybe Buck, too.

Judd pulled into the parking lot of the elementary school and found a spot right next to the playground.

It had a wire fence around it, but he could still see the kids through it. No sign of Isaac or Leo, though.

"I'm worried about Cleo," Beckham said out of the blue.

Judd practically snapped toward him. "Why?"

Beckham lifted his shoulder. "She likes you a lot. I can tell. She's really smart but not when it comes to men."

Judd didn't know if Beckham had just insulted Cleo or him. Since he wasn't sure whether to ask about the liking part or not-smart part, Judd just stayed quiet and kept watch of the playground.

"Right around the time Mom got really sick, I heard her talking with Cleo about some man who was bothering her. Bothering Cleo, not Mom," Beckham added, to clarify. "Mom told her she needed to quit hooking up with guys with issues." He frowned. "What exactly is an *issue*, anyway?"

"It could be a lot of things." But Judd figured he was the walking, talking definition of one. Hopefully, though, this issue-laden turd who had bothered Cleo was now out of the picture.

"Is this guy still around?" Judd asked.

"Don't think so. Like I said, Cleo's hung up on you now."

Judd frowned and was about to dole out reasons why that wasn't true. But then he remembered the kiss again. So, maybe there was a small amount of being hung up. That was even more reason to keep some emotional distance between Cleo and him.

"Wait here while I run in and have that word with the principal," Judd said, opening his truck door.

"If you know what me and my brothers have been through, then you know I can't take them back to the piss witch," Beckham announced before Judd could leave.

"Agreed." Judd was about to launch into an explanation of why that wouldn't happen, but Beckham continued.

"And you know they'll end up trying to put the three of us in separate homes. No one will want to take me because of the juvie shit."

"Stuff, not shit," Judd automatically amended.

"Stuff," Beckham repeated in the same tone he'd used with the profanity. "I need to be with my brothers if something bad goes down."

Judd found it hard to argue with that. If he'd been with Callen and Nico, they wouldn't have nearly been killed. It was a lot of emotional weight on his shoulders, and Beckham was feeling that weight, too.

Beckham looked him straight in the eyes. "If the temp custody thing with Kace doesn't work out, then I want you to hide Isaac and Leo. Hide them some place where they won't be hurt."

Judd groaned and shook his head, but Beckham caught onto his arm.

"Promise me you'll do it, and I won't run," Beckham insisted. He blinked hard, as if fighting tears. "In fact, I'll do anything you ask. Just swear to me that you won't let someone take them."

Judd knew what he should say—that he couldn't make a promise like that. But that wasn't what came out of his mouth. "I swear," he agreed.

And he meant it.

CHAPTER NINE

CLEO SIGHED WHEN she saw the sign for her bar. Someone had blacked out the *g* again so that it read Angry Anus. This was the third time, and while she figured the security cam would have captured the vandal with the fourth-grade sense of humor, it would take time to ID the person and then file charges.

Time that Cleo didn't have.

"I was going to call and tell you," Daisy said. She was standing in the bar's doorway, looking up at the sign. "But I figured it could wait."

Yes, it could wait, and it wasn't going to distract her or spoil her mood. Cleo had too much to do, what with catching up on paperwork and the meetings for the final details on not one but two bachelorette parties. She needed to stay positive. Also needed to keep her mind off the visit from the social worker that Kace should be having at this very moment.

"Maybe we should just keep the name," Daisy suggested. "Angry Anus is kind of catchy and it has an 'in your face' attitude that could hit the right note. We could even come up with bar snacks to complement it. Cow-pie sliders. Backside dip." She frowned. "Or not."

Cleo was going for the "or not" on the snacks because she didn't think customers would appreciate eating anything that reminded them of that particular part of the cow anatomy, but she might keep the name only to prevent her from having to report future vandalism and pay the painter to fix the sign. Again.

Daisy squinted one eye while she studied Cleo as they went inside. "You look—" Daisy made a humming sound of contemplation "—stressed."

"That's because I am." But the moment Cleo admitted it, she wished she hadn't. Voicing it wouldn't help, and it only added worry lines to Daisy's forehead.

"That's too bad," Daisy concluded. "I mean, I figured the boys would be causing you to worry, but I was hoping Judd the Stud would help with that."

Oh, he had. That magical kiss had indeed helped, but it had then given Cleo the mother lode of erotic dreams. Like poorly named bar food, that wasn't a good thing. Not when she didn't have an outlet to cool the heat from the dreams. Judd was avoiding her, she was certain of that, and even if he hadn't been, it wasn't as if she'd had time for any heat-cooling.

Cleo stopped in the entry and had a look around. Even though it'd only been two days since she'd been here, it was still the longest she'd been away from the place since she'd bought it. She wished that she felt centered here, instead of worrying because she wasn't with the boys. She was certain that she'd have to find some kind of balance for that. After all, generations of parents before her had worked and raised children and so could she.

"The cows are gone," Cleo said after another glance around, and this time she didn't have to think about forcing a smile.

Daisy smiled, too. "Tiny and some of his buds moved them into the back alley for trash pickup. We took out the one in your office, too."

Cleo's smile widened while she continued to look around. There'd been some new additions to the Stupid Sh*t Men Say board.

Labor can't hurt THAT bad.

I know a good way to burn off the calories in that wine.

The next one she recognized from a recent text she'd gotten, one that Cleo had shared with Daisy, who'd no doubt then chalked it on the board for everyone to see.

You stay madder about things than my last girlfriend.

The final entry was "I figured since you took this long to get dressed that you'd look hotter than you do."

Apparently, men and the stupid things they were saying would continue to keep the customers entertained.

"It was packed last night," Daisy continued, following Cleo when she headed for her office. "But we had it covered. The new waitress is working out."

There it was again. A hit of happy-centeredness quickly followed by worry because she hadn't been there. "I really appreciate all the extra hours you're putting in," Cleo told her. "How's Mandy Rose?"

"Good. My mom's helping out. What about the boys? How are they adjusting at the ranch?"

Cleo would have given Daisy a glossed-over version of an answer, but when she went into her office, the first thing she saw was a naked cowboy butt. The sight was enough to stop conversation but not in a "fan yourself and go all hot" kind of way. Though as butts went, it was impressive. She just couldn't figure out why it was in her office.

"Isn't that the best ass you've ever seen?" someone asked.

Cleo spotted the asker, Tiffany Wainwright, and her maid of honor, Monica Sanders, who were both ogling the cowboy, who thankfully wasn't completely nude. He was shirtless and wearing no jeans or underwear, but he did have on a Stetson, boots and chaps. On closer inspection, Cleo noticed that the chaps had a strategically placed leather flap over the cowboy's crotch.

"It's impressive," Cleo agreed. She glanced at

Daisy for an explanation of what was going on, but Daisy just shrugged.

"I must have been in the back when they came in," Daisy said.

"She was." That from Tiffany, who was now running her hand over the cowboy's right butt cheek while she glanced up at Cleo.

"The bartender said you'd be in any minute so we brought Harry back here. Tiffany and I wanted you to see him so you could put him on stage for the bachelorette party."

As if responding to a cue, Harry began to jiggle his butt, but since he had very tight muscles there, it was more of a jerk than a jiggle.

"Best ass ever," Monica declared.

Well, he was significantly better-looking than the guys she'd hired, but Cleo wondered if the bride's familiarity with Harry's butt was going to cause some problems. Not with some potential hanky-panky between the two—though judging from the way she was stroking him, that was a strong possibility— but because stroking him like that in front of other guests might lead to some legal trouble.

"I've already hired the crew for that," Cleo explained to the bride, "and you approved the contracts so I won't be able to just cut them. Maybe Harry could do a private show for Monica and you before the start of the actual party? Perhaps at your house, or Monica's?"

Tiffany's eyes brightened, and both women nodded. Then Tiffany frowned and nibbled on her lip. "But if anyone else asks, Harry is just one of the dancers for the party. Okay?"

Now it was Cleo's turn to nod. Oh, yes. There'd be hanky and probably quite a bit of panky, but since it wouldn't be happening under the roof of the Angry Angus, Cleo didn't care.

"Now, I just need you to go over the final menu for the party food," Cleo said, taking out the forms. "And I'll need the last payment." She got out the contract for that as well, but before Tiffany could even get her hand off Harry's butt, Cleo's phone rang.

"It's Judd," Cleo whispered to Daisy, and she excused herself to go into the hall for some privacy. Harry must have taken that as a cue, too, because he went into the "butt cheek jerk" mode.

"Is everything okay?" Cleo asked. She shut the door but not before Harry let out a loud "yee-haw," followed by Monica and Tiffany's equally loud giggles.

"More cowboy auditions?" Judd said.

"Something like that. How'd the visit from the social worker go?"

His hesitation caused even more jangling of her nerves. "Kace won't know anything for a day or two until he gets the report. The social worker is concerned about how he's going to 'adequately foster' the boys with his work schedule, but other than that, Kace thinks it went okay."

That didn't cause her to feel much relief. "But?"

She heard the deep breath that Judd took. "Beckham left school without permission. He's okay," Judd quickly added. "I found him near the elementary school, where he was keeping an eye on Isaac and Leo. He was worried that Leo had been getting picked on, and he wanted to make sure the kids didn't call Leo a mutt again."

That automatically put some knots in her muscles. "I'll get there as soon as I can."

"No need. It's all under control. I took Beckham back to school and smoothed things over with the principal. Beckham only got a warning this time."

This time. Which meant if he did it again, which he likely would, there'd be trouble. Trouble that none of them needed with a social worker who was worried about whether Kace could pull off this parenting thing.

"What about Leo being picked on?" she persisted.

"I handled that."

She waited for even a smidge more of an explanation, but when Judd didn't give her one, she pushed. "Handled it how?"

"I didn't beat up or arrest anyone," he muttered, adding a huff. "I talked with the principal and then had a chat with Arnie Smelton about keeping reins on that idiot spawn of his. It was his youngest dimwit piece-of-shit who was bullying Leo."

She had no problem hearing the anger in Judd's voice, and while part of her—the adult part—

thought that maybe she should mention that it wasn't good to call a child an idiot spawn/dimwit piece-of-shit, Cleo wanted to call the kid something worse for bullying Leo.

"You're sure I don't need to come to Coldwater?" Cleo asked.

"No. I'll follow the bus from school back to the ranch, and if there's any further stupidity from the dimwit, Isaac will give me a sign. Then, I'll stop the bus and take care of it."

Cleo had mixed feelings about that, too. Judd didn't have the gentlest approach when it came to conflict resolution. Plus, if he'd already found Beckham, talked to two principals and dealt with Arnie Smelton, then he'd taken a lot of time off from work. Too much time, considering this wasn't even his problem. Heck, it wasn't Kace's problem, though he had also spent a good chunk of the day dealing with the social worker and the boys.

Sighing, she checked the time and calculated that she needed at least two solid hours just to deal with the critical paperwork and make sure there was enough staff to cover the bar. Then she'd head back to the ranch and see for herself that everything was as okay as it could be. After the boys were in bed, she could maybe come back to the bar and tackle some more projects.

"If you get me the name of Leo's bus driver, I'll call him or her," Cleo said. "And I'll have a heart-to-heart talk to let him or her know what a tough time Leo's going through."

Judd made a skeptical "good luck with that" sound. "I'll be in touch," he said and ended the call.

Cleo was about to go back in her office when she saw a man coming up the hall toward her. It was rare for just the sight of someone to get her hackles up, but that was what happened now.

Because the man was Lavinia's biker friend, Otto.

Tiny, the bartender, was right behind him, and that's the only reason Cleo didn't immediately call the cops. Tiny was nearly twice Otto's size and would toss the man out on his leather-clad butt if he gave Cleo any trouble. But Cleo didn't want to stand behind Tiny's wide girth. She wanted to set some things straight on her own.

"You're not welcome here," Cleo told Otto. "And if you don't leave right now, you'll be getting a restraining order, too."

Otto nodded as if expecting her to say that, but he gave an uneasy glance over his shoulder at Tiny, who was making a low growling sound. Tiny's eyes were narrowed to angry slits.

"I won't stay long," Otto assured her. He was wearing the same stained shirt and leather pants that he'd had on when Lavinia and he had paid a visit to the ranch. "Say, did you know your sign is messed up?" The corner of his mouth lifted as he hiked his thumb in that direction. "Guess somebody thought it'd be funny to have a bar named after a cow's butthole."

Apparently Otto thought it was funny as well, because his mouth lift turned into a full smile that lasted until he noticed her expression. Cleo wasn't smiling.

"Anyway, this is a real nice place," he went on. "Wasn't sure what it'd be 'cause Lavinia said it was a boner bar. A tit tavern," he added as if that clarified things. "Strip club," he explained even more.

"It's not." And her crisp denial would have been a whole lot more effective if at that moment Daisy hadn't opened the door to reveal a perfectly framed view of Harry's butt. Yes, Monica and Tiffany were still touching it.

"Oh," Daisy said when her attention landed on Otto and Tiny. "Is everything okay?"

"Yes." Cleo tried to sound reassuring, but it was hard to manage with her jaw clenched. "Just give me a minute, okay?"

"Sure." Daisy shot Otto an uncertain look before she went back in and shut the door.

"Lavinia told me lots of stuff, more than this being a boner bar," Otto went on. "Not sure if it was all true, but she said you'd brainwashed her daughter and that you were a skank." He paused. "She used a different word than *skank* that I figure I shouldn't repeat." He gave Tiny another uneasy glance.

Cleo suspected she knew the word, or rather the words, that Lavinia had used to describe her, but she'd yet to figure out why the woman hated her so much. Maybe Lavinia did believe the brainwashing because Miranda had cut ties with her, and Lavinia perhaps thought Cleo was responsible for that.

She hadn't been.

Lavinia's own bad behavior was the reason for the rift between mother and daughter. And it'd been a long time coming since Miranda had said she'd endured a lifetime of bad behavior from Lavinia.

"I'm real sorry about all the fuss Lavinia caused and the names she called you and this place," Otto continued.

"Are you also sorry about the bruises she put on her grandsons?" Cleo snapped.

Otto's next nod was even faster than his first one. "Lavinia didn't say nothing about that when she asked me to give her a ride."

When Cleo felt the sharp pain in her hand, she realized she had such a hard grip on her phone that she was surprised it hadn't shattered. She forced her fingers to relax. "Well, now that you know, my advice would be not to give her more rides."

"I won't be. Me and Lavinia have had sort of a falling-out." Otto shook his head and plowed his sausage-sized fingers through his stringy hair. "That's the reason I came here. To warn you about Lavinia. She's madder than a pissed-on possum."

"I'm going to assume that's pretty mad," Cleo muttered.

"Yeah," he replied. "Mad and mean. I gotta say,

that's not a good mix. She worked herself up about you taking the boys, and I think she's gonna do something to get back at you."

Cleo huffed. "I can handle whatever Lavinia dishes out."

He nodded. "Yeah, but she wasn't talking about going after you. She plans to go after your fella."

Everything inside Cleo went still. "My fella?"

"The deputy," Otto confirmed. "You might want to tell him to watch his back 'cause Lavinia's got her pissed-on possum eyes set on messing him over."

CHAPTER TEN

"HEY, HOT HUNKY COWBOY," the woman called out.

Judd groaned because he instantly recognized the voice, and it was someone he didn't want to see. The day had already been hellishly long, and this particular visitor wasn't going to improve things.

He soon spotted Mercy Marlow leaning against his truck. Barring blindness, it would be impossible to miss her in her gold spandex bodysuit and the tower of unnaturally red hair piled on her head. She grinned around the drag she took off her cigarette and blew the smoke out the side of her pursed pink lips.

She had "porn star" written all over her. Literally. It was printed across the top of her bodysuit that looked ready to explode from the pressure of her breasts—which were also massively unnatural.

Since Judd had run a background check on her, he knew Mercy Marlow was her real name, but now that she was fifty-three, her porn-star days were over. However, along with her income as a phone-sex operator, she also taught acting classes for wannabe porn stars.

She wasn't a typical AA sponsor.

But she was a solid one, having overcome her own alcohol demons to stay ten years sober. And even at times like this, with this unexpected visit, Judd had never considered requesting someone else.

Mercy would bust his balls when he needed it and always answer his calls no matter what time of day or night. In his own way he loved her. Well, as much as anyone could love a foulmouthed, chain-smoking former porn star.

"What did one eye say to the other?" Mercy asked, but she didn't wait for him to give her a blank stare, groan or attempt a lame answer for a lame joke. She just went for the punch line, as she usually did. "Between you and me, something smells."

She hooted with laughter, slapping her hand on her thigh so loud that they drew the attention of folks passing by on the sidewalk. He didn't even want to speculate about what people would think of her. Or who they thought she was.

"We didn't have an appointment," Judd said, ignoring the attempted joke. He'd learned it was best not to encourage Mercy when it came to her incredibly bad sense of humor.

"Nope. It's not until day after tomorrow," Mercy said. She dropped her cigarette and crushed it with the toe of her stiletto. "But I got a hot date tomorrow night with my main man these days. A former wrestler who's hung like a horse and can move like a jackhammer. I figure I'd be too nookied out to meet with you."

Judd huffed. "Mercy, remember when we talked

about you sharing too much? Well, you just shared too much."

She laughed as if that was a fine joke, and followed him around to the driver's side of his truck. Mercy studied him. "Just checking on my favorite cowboy." She laid a hand on his arm. "How are you, Judd?"

Mercy's tone changed. It softened. And despite the thick gobs of mascara she was wearing, she managed to make direct eye contact without her lashes sticking together.

He didn't lie to her. Couldn't. Mercy had seen him at his worst, when he'd been coming off a three-day bender. She'd held his head when he'd puked. Like taking Cleo's virginity, that had created a bond between them, and it was there whether Judd wanted it or not.

"I've been under some pressure," he said. "But I'm handling it."

Her sliver-thin, unnaturally red eyebrow rose. "No burning yen to climb back in the bottle?"

"The *yen*'s always there," Judd admitted.

"What about the burning part?" She winked at him.

He didn't think it was a good sign that the first thing he thought of when it came to burning was Cleo. But there it was. The woman had been his burning source for years and apparently continued to be.

"You need a nookie night," Mercy declared when he didn't say anything. "And no, I'm not offering.

You need a nubile young woman who'll lick you in places you've never been licked."

Since he didn't want to encourage that kind of advice, he just gave Mercy a blank stare that caused her to hoot again. "Never underestimate the power of a good licker," she added.

"Or of a short conversation," he countered. "I need to get home and check on some things. Text me, and we'll work out another time for a meeting."

"Will do," she said, but she kept her hand on his arm. "You haven't even had to use our safe words or the distraction object since we last talked?"

"No." And Judd hoped that would be the end of this particular part of the conversation.

It wasn't.

"Good. You do remember what the words are, don't you?" Mercy asked. "It's dick inches," she disclosed before he could spell out—*again*—that he wasn't sure he needed safe/code words. Or if he did, he wanted ones that didn't take a swipe at his gender. Because according to Mercy, dick inches referred to grossly overestimating the length or size of something—as in a man claiming he had more inches than he actually did.

The "distraction" that Mercy had come up with was almost as bad. Instead of thinking about or visualizing a bottle of whiskey, she had insisted he come up with an actual object that he could hold. A stupid one. She'd suggested everything from cock rings to edible underwear. When Judd had nixed those, Mercy had instead gotten something from

Rosy's taxidermy shop. No way would anyone think the dead stuffed thing was cute.

She gave his hand a pat. "Use the words if you need them to draw you out of a dark mood and then call or text me. Don't pull a reverse dick inch and make something smaller than it is. If it troubles you, it's not small."

That was the reason she was still his sponsor. She cared about him, and nothing she'd just said was lip service.

Mercy turned and headed for her car, but then she stopped and looked at him. "Say, why don't men like to go down on comedians?" Again, she didn't wait for him to guess the punch line. "Because they taste funny."

The woman was howling with laughter as she got into her car. Judd frowned, wondering how she could be so profound in one breath and in the next have such bad taste in what she considered humor.

Ignoring the folks who were still milling around, Judd got in his truck and headed for the ranch. He steeled himself for whatever he would face there, but he knew at least the boys had gotten home all right, because as he'd told Cleo, he followed the bus home. No incidents. However, it was only 6:00 p.m., and there were still several hours when something could crop up.

Something that wouldn't be his concern.

That reminder didn't help with steeling himself. After all, he had turned down Cleo's fostering request, and now she was probably wondering why the heck he was doing things like following a bus, hunting down Beckham and chatting with principals. Those had taken far more time and effort than merely signing foster papers. Still, refusing had been the right thing to do. And he was almost certain of that.

Almost.

One certainty that didn't have an *almost* attached to it was Mercy's suggestion of him having a nookie night. He thought having a woman in his bed might help his mood. Not Cleo, though. Despite the heat between them, being with her would complicate things. Too many strings attached.

He frowned. Because when he pictured a woman in his bed, it was Cleo. An image he needed to shed fast. The shedding turned out to be a lot easier than he'd thought when he saw all the vehicles parked in front of Buck's house. Four trucks and Cleo's car. Hell. He hoped nothing else had gone wrong.

Judd parked and breathed a little easier when he saw Leo in between his cabin and the house. The boy was grinning and holding something that was dangling from his hand.

A green snake.

Judd glanced around to make sure Leo wasn't out here on his own, and he soon spotted a surly-looking Beckham peering out from the barn. Isaac was peering, too, from the loft.

"His name is Wiggles, and I'm gonna keep him," Leo said. "He can sleep in my bed."

Judd hated to burst his grinning bubble, but he

shook his head. "Have you ever heard Miss Rosy scream?"

Leo stayed quiet a moment, considering that. "Nope."

"Then if you want to keep it that way, don't bring the snake in the house. Sorry, buddy, but he'll have to live in the barn."

Leo gave that some thought, too. "You're sure?"

"Trust me on this. My brother Nico brought a snake inside when he was close to Isaac's age, and Rosy's screams are still echoing in my head."

Leo's face bunched up, and he sighed. "Okay. You got more than one brother named Nico?"

"No. Why?"

"'Cause that's who's inside. Nico said he's gonna be watching me some and giving me riding lessons."

Judd frowned again. Nico was the irresponsible Laramie brother, and that didn't sound like something he would offer. Besides, Nico was rarely around because he was on the rodeo circuit and often away on business trips.

"Has anybody gone over the rules with you about snakes?" Judd asked the boy.

Leo nodded. "Mr. Buck said I could only get close to the green ones, but to stay away from the other colors. I gotta stay away from the ones that rattle, hiss or look mean."

Good advice. Obviously, Buck was doing right by the kids.

While Leo took Wiggles to the barn, Judd went inside Buck's to find out what was going on. And he soon discovered that what was going on was some kind of meeting.

Buck, Rosy, Kace, Shelby, Callen and, yes, Nico, were all at the kitchen table. So were Cleo and Kace's best friend, Wyatt Cutler, who owned a ranch near Shelby and Callen's. Everyone had coffee or some other kind of drink, and there was a huge plate of cookies in the center of the table. Shelby was tapping out something on a laptop. The others had pencils, colored pens and hard copies of what appeared to be spreadsheets.

All of them spared him a glance, some muttered hellos, but they continued what they were doing.

Judd moved closer, looking at the stuff that was scattered on the table. There was a plastic sandwich bag of gold stars, which was probably slated to be taped to the fridge next to the chore chart, and also a stack of "get out of jail free" cards. Not the hand-printed ones that'd been around when he was a foster. These were printed with a little armadillo on them.

"Aren't those the cutest things? Thought we could use some new ones," Rosy explained. "That's my Billy."

Yes, it was. Billy, the armadillo, that'd been roadkill before Rosy had given him the taxidermic treatment. *Cute* wasn't the word Judd would use, but Rosy must have been proud as punch because she handed out one to everyone at the table.

"I can take Wednesday and Friday mornings to see the boys off to school," Shelby said, tucking her card in her pocket. "That way, Cleo can go into work early on those days."

"Thanks. I'll need it. I'm getting behind," Cleo answered as Shelby typed that into the laptop.

The others added it to their spreadsheets, and that's when Judd realized they were working out a schedule. A very detailed one that appeared to include every hour of every day that the boys would actually be on the ranch. When one of them wasn't on the schedule, the sitter, Lissy Tate, was.

"Then I'll take Tuesday evenings." That from Wyatt. "It'll give Kace a break and time to catch up on work."

Sounds of agreement went around the table.

"Put me in for Monday and Tuesday afternoons for the next four weeks," Nico volunteered. "I'll fix my schedule so I can be here when the boys get home from school. Then I might have to shift the days."

More sounds of agreement, and Judd moved closer to look at Cleo's spreadsheet. Buck, Rosy, Cleo, Kace, Callen, Shelby, Wyatt and even Cleo's business partner, Daisy, were on the schedule.

Judd wasn't.

There was a list of backup names at the bottom, an assortment of Buck and Rosy's friends. His name was there, but someone had put a line through it.

"So, that's it," Shelby declared. "I think we have it all covered." She gave Kace a high five and Callen a kiss—one that was hot enough to remind everyone that they were newlyweds.

"I can never thank all of you enough." Cleo got to her feet and went around the table, giving hugs to everyone. Including Kace. It took her a while to work her way to Judd. No hug for him, but she smiled and whispered, "Thanks so much for what you did today."

For some reason her thanks riled Judd. Actually, the spreadsheet riled him, too. And the easy way everyone seemed to be accepting the extra heapings of work that would be added to their weekly routines. But what riled him the most was that he hadn't even been penciled in anywhere on the damn schedule.

"We need to talk," Judd said to Cleo at the exact moment she said to him, "We need to talk."

Okay, that was a little easier than he thought it would be to get Cleo away from the others. "Excuse us for a minute," Cleo told the group, and Judd and she went out the back door and into the yard.

"Aunt Cleo, wanna see my new pet?" Leo called out.

"It's a snake," Judd mumbled, and that halted the big smile that was forming on Cleo's face. "Not poisonous," he assured her. "But still a snake."

"Uh, I need to talk to Mr. Judd right now, but maybe I'll come out and see it soon." She shifted her attention to Isaac, who was now by the chicken coop and in hearing distance. That's probably why Cleo took Judd by the arm and led him around the corner to his front porch.

"Otto came to see me at the bar this afternoon," she blurted out, keeping her voice low.

Good thing the boys couldn't hear him because Judd cursed. "What the hell did that sonofabitch want?" He looked at her face and wrists to make sure there weren't any bruises.

"He didn't hurt me," she said when she followed his gaze. "He came to warn me that Lavinia was as mad as a 'pissed-on possum' and that she was going to try to do something to get back at you."

Judd huffed, and his hands went on his hips. "Do what exactly?"

"Otto didn't have specifics." On a heavy breath, she pushed her hair from her face. "Judd, I'm so sorry about involving you in this. I'll do whatever I can to get her to aim her venom at me, not you."

He was still simmering from the other stuff, and that only added to it. "I can take care of myself, especially from the likes of Lavinia."

Cleo smiled, but he could tell she had to try really hard to eke one out. "If you get in a fight with her, be careful of her loose, swinging breasts."

That was worth him mustering up his own smile. "You could have put me on the schedule, you know," he said. But it seemed to be the day for them to talk at the same time because Cleo asked, "What did you want to speak to me about?"

"Oh," they both answered in unison.

It was Judd who continued. "Beckham said something about a guy giving you some trouble."

She blinked, then groaned softly. "Harmon Hawthorne, someone I used to date, but we broke up months ago. Why would Beckham tell you about him?"

"It just came up in conversation." Best not to mention that Beckham thought Cleo wasn't very smart when it came to men. "What kind of trouble did he give you?"

"Nothing recent. Like I said, we broke up. But afterward, he'd call and text me. A lot. That's when Daisy started the Stupid Shit Men Say board. A lot of the first entries came from Harmon. One of the more recent ones, too."

"When's the last time he contacted you?" And Judd was well aware that he sounded like a cop with a smidge of jealousy.

She glanced away from him. "It's been a couple of days."

"*Days?* And what did this clown say?"

"Nothing that screams red flags. His ego just can't seem to accept that I'm not the woman of his dreams. And I don't mean that as some kind of cliché. Harmon claims that he dreamed about me before we ever met and that he spent years looking for me."

Whatever Judd had been expecting her to say, that wasn't it. Hell, that was creepy.

"He believes we have this whole soul-mate thing going on," she added. "And that I'll accept it when I see all the signs."

"*Signs?*" Judd persisted.

She huffed. "Dumb ones. Again, that apparently came to him in the dream." She waved it off and switched topics. "As for the schedule, I didn't want to bother you." She paused. "While we were in the family meeting, Kace got a text from Liberty, who said you were meeting with a woman in the parking lot. Liberty thought you looked more intense than usual when you were talking to her."

Shit on a stick. That hadn't taken long at all. Nor did it take him long to connect the dots with what had been the thought process that'd gone on in the meeting. They'd decided not to put his name on the schedule because they thought the pressure of being around the boys had sent him running to Mercy.

"The woman Liberty saw was my sponsor who came to check on me and reschedule our regular meeting. I'm fine," he growled, but his tone was so rough and mean that he repeated it in a much calmer voice.

Cleo stared at him, blew out a massive breath and smiled. This time there was no mustering involved. "Thank God. I was just so worried after this hellish day. And that kiss. I thought when Liberty said you looked intense that maybe the pressure had gotten to you."

Hell. That made him sound like a wuss, but the truth was going to sound even wussier. "It's not pressure that triggers the problem. Present-day hellish is fine. It's the old stuff that gets to me."

She moved closer, no trace of a smile now, and she put her hand on the front of his shirt, flattening her palm over his heart. "Promise me that you'll come to me if it starts to get bad."

It was a generous offer, and one that he hated she felt the need to make. "You can't fix this."

A small part of her smile returned. "Maybe not, but after that kiss in my car, I think I know a way to distract you. Hard to drink if your mouth is on mine."

A certain part of his body tuned into every word she was saying. Tuned in, latched on and galloped with way too much interest.

Her hand wasn't exactly touching a hot spot for him, but it suddenly felt that way when her fingers moved a little, and her index fingers touched his shirt button. She made slow circling motions while her eyes stayed on him.

"I've seen your schedule," he said. "You don't have time for kissing or sex."

"I could work you in on Tuesday morning at nine fifteen."

Judd laughed before he could stop himself, and he caught onto her hand to stop the touching torture. Or so he told himself. But he didn't let go of her hand, which would make it very easy to pull her into his cabin, back her against the door and nail her.

Maybe it was a sign from the gods that nailing should be the last thing on his mind because Judd heard someone on Buck's front porch. Wyatt, Shelby and Callen came out of the house, and only then did Judd let go of Cleo.

"I need to say goodbye and thank them again," Cleo said, but she took something from her pocket and handed it to him.

One of the new "get out of jail free" cards.

"Anytime you're up for a distraction, just leave this on my bed," she said, then flashed him a siren's smile, gave him a harlot's kiss and hurried off his porch.

Judd looked at the card. Then at her. And he felt the slow burn go from the single stupid part of him and spread throughout his body.

Well, hell.

CHAPTER ELEVEN

A TEXT MESSAGE popped up on Judd's phone screen: you need a nookie night. It was from Mercy, of course, and while it wasn't exactly a new sentiment from his sponsor, he had to wonder about the timing. The text had come only a few hours after his latest encounter with Cleo. Maybe Mercy had some form of ESP, or else he was giving off some kind of cosmic vibe. Or it could be Mercy just thought about his sex life entirely too much.

That had to be it, Judd decided.

Of course, he was doing plenty of thinking about it, too, thanks to the chest touching from Cleo and the card she'd given him. Get out of jail free. Right. The small rectangular piece of paper was an invitation to some Texas-sized trouble.

Judd put the card in his shirt pocket and was ready to call it a night when there was a knock at the door. He got an automatic jolt of heat when he considered that it could be Cleo, returning to up the ante on her offer. But the heat vanished when Judd opened the door and he saw that it was Nico.

His brother was smiling in a "been there, done that" way that only he and a cocky Greek god could have managed. Without an invitation, Nico strolled right in, went to Judd's fridge and got himself a Coke.

"Make yourself at home," Judd mumbled.

"Thanks," Nico said so easily that it made Judd want to glare. It wasn't that he disliked his brother, but Nico wasn't the sort to pay casual visits—even if everything about him and his body language was nothing but casual.

"Kind of late for a visit, isn't it?" Judd checked the time—10:30 p.m. For the night owl Nico, this was probably early, especially for a Friday night.

"Saw your light on so I knew you were up." Nico sat on the sofa, stretching his legs out in front of him in his usual lounging pose. "I heard through the grapevine that Avis Odell went to trial for those charges filed against him a couple of months ago."

Charges that'd stemmed from Avis trying to extort money from Callen and then assaulting Judd. That had all been part of the man's scheme to get Callen to pay him blackmail money in exchange for not spreading rumors smeared with truth about the Laramie brothers' shitty past.

And just like that Judd's annoyance was replaced by a gut punch of old memories.

When Nico was eleven, Avis had been living with the woman who was fostering Nico and Callen, and Avis had beaten them to the point that Nico had nearly died. Avis hadn't spent nearly enough time in jail for that.

Of course, a lifetime wouldn't have been enough as far as Judd was concerned.

"Avis got a five-year sentence for this latest round of charges," Nico said.

Unlike Judd, there didn't appear to be a lot of emotion in Nico's voice, and Judd didn't think it was an act, either. For reasons Judd couldn't understand, Nico had somehow managed to push aside the past and make it not matter.

It mattered to Judd.

Hell, it ate away at him any chance it got. No matter what he did, the memories stormed hot and raw at him.

"I didn't bring all of this up to piss you off," Nico went on. "I thought…hoped it'd help for you to know that he's behind bars."

"It helps you?" Judd countered.

Nico shrugged. "Avis Odell isn't the monkey on my back." He paused, gave a Greek-god smile. Maybe Nico was waiting for Judd to pour out his guts, but that wasn't going to happen. Talking about shit didn't make it go away.

Nico made a "suit yourself" sound. "So, what's going on between Cleo and you?" he asked.

Now, Judd did glare. He didn't like this topic of conversation any more than talking about Avis Odell. "Nothing. And even if there was, it wouldn't be any of your business."

Nico had a long sip of the Coke. "A lie and a snarl. The second one is your specialty, but you don't usually lie."

Well, sonofabitch. "What is this? Some kind of intervention?"

"More or less," Nico admitted. "I really like Cleo, but she doesn't always make the wisest choices when it comes to men." He looked straight at Judd. "You're not a wise choice. Not now, anyway. Not with all that she's got going on. But she's obviously not see- ing it that way. She wants you, brother, and since I like her—in a sisterly friend kind of way—it'd be good if she got what she wanted."

Judd's stunned silence lasted a little longer than he thought it would, and during those long moments, Nico continued to lounge and sip his Coke. "How the hell would you know about Cleo's wise choices?" Judd asked.

Nico lifted his shoulder. "I've stayed in touch with Cleo, and I know about a guy who was giv- ing her some trouble. A dick who'd leave her like a thousand messages and then come crying to her when she didn't answer."

This had to be Harmon Hawthorne, and Judd made a mental note to follow up on the background check he'd already ordered on him. If Nico thought the guy was a dick, then he probably was. His baby brother had a lot of faults, but being a bad judge of people wasn't one of them.

Which was why the "wise choice" comment about him should have bothered Judd. It didn't, be- cause it was true.

"Cleo doesn't need me or my excess baggage," Judd admitted.

"No, but she wants it. She wants you," Nico amended. "And don't bother denying it because I saw the proof when she gave you her 'get out of jail free' card."

Judd gave him a blank stare. "Why would that card have anything to do with wanting me?"

Nico gave him a blank stare right back, and at the moment his was apparently better than Judd's because Judd was the first to glance away. Then he cursed.

"I don't want there to be gossip about Cleo and me," Judd explained. "It could get back to CPS and the social worker. I know that Kace is the legal foster parent, but both Cleo and I are on the grounds. It might cause trouble."

"And it might solve some things," Nico countered.

Judd had to go back to his blank stare because he didn't think his brother was talking about Judd having sex with Cleo to ease up his sexual frustration.

"I was at the Gray Mare for lunch," Nico went on, "and I heard some talk that Cleo and Kace might be getting together."

"What?" Judd snapped.

"Getting together as in for the sake of the boys. Marriage, building a family together, et cetera. Donny Ray says he's never seen Kace so wrapped up in something this personal. Well, not since Kace got married way back when."

It took Judd a couple of moments to wrap his mind around everything Nico had just said, and he reminded himself to consider the source. Not Nico but Donny Ray, who was a bartender with the IQ of a piece of shit. An IQ so low that he couldn't have come up with any of this on his own. Well, other than the part about Kace getting married way back when. Kace had indeed gotten married over a decade ago and then gotten divorced shortly thereafter. And it'd definitely wrapped him up for a while.

"Kace and Cleo aren't getting together," Judd said once he got his teeth unclenched.

"No, because Kace doesn't want her and Cleo wants you. But if the gossips believe they're getting together, then there'll be talk about them having sex under the same roof as the boys. Cleo's police record will come up."

Judd didn't have any trouble seeing where that would lead. CPS could give Kace a black mark if he was carrying on with someone like Cleo.

"I know Cleo needs to be nearby so she can keep an eye on the boys." Nico stood, finished off his Coke.

"She's looking for a house she can rent," Judd pointed out.

Nico nodded. "But in the meantime, she shouldn't be living under the same roof as Kace. My advice is to move her in here with you and go ahead and have sex with her. Good sex gives off a vibe, and the gossips will pick up on it." His brother flashed a quick grin. "Plus, it's fun. Might as well use that card Cleo gave you."

With that, Nico strolled out as if he hadn't just

shaken Judd to the core. What the hell kind of logic was that?

And why was Judd considering taking it?

At least the answer to the second question was easy. He was considering it because sex with Cleo was something he wanted to do, but that didn't mean it was right. But there was nothing sensible about moving Cleo in here with him. Well, except for staving off gossip that Judd wasn't even sure needed staving off.

His temper was rolling through him when his phone rang, and he jabbed the answer button when he saw Darrell's name on the screen.

"Harmon Hawthorne," Judd said right off. "Did you get anything on him?"

"Probably no more than you got. Trust-fund baby who co-owns a real-estate business with his mother. Is he connected to what's going on with your brother fostering the boys?"

"Indirectly." Judd huffed, then added, "He's just some jerk who's been bothering Cleo. Sorry if I wasted your time with him."

"I didn't spend long on it when nothing popped. No restraining orders, no arrests. Nada. The guy's squeaky-clean."

No, he wasn't, but the crap he'd pulled with Cleo didn't leave the kind of paper trail that cops looked at unless Harmon escalated things and started stalking her.

"I'm calling about Lavinia," Darrell said, snapping Judd's attention back to him. "She's been talking to a reporter, Crawford Banning, and she's convinced him to start digging into your official record. Maybe your personal stuff, too."

Hearing that didn't soothe any of Judd's temper. "The reporter's an idiot if he doesn't see, or smell, Lavinia for what she is."

"I agree, but idiots are all over the place, and judging from the way Banning's pressing, he could have a grudge against cops. I've heard through the grapevine that he's had a couple of run-ins with the law, and he might be looking for some payback. Just wanted you to know what he was doing in case something came up."

Meaning Judd's drinking problem. There was nothing about it on his official records, but that didn't mean it couldn't be dug up. *Easily* dug up. Lots of people likely knew about his fondness for the bottle.

"Say, have you ever just thought about telling everybody why you transferred from Austin to Coldwater?" Darrell asked.

"No." Judd likely wouldn't have added more to that even if Cleo hadn't caught his attention. She stepped onto the back porch of Buck's house, and his mouth went dry just looking at her.

Man, why did she have to be so damn beautiful? And why was the porch light spilling on her so that it allowed him to see every inch of her curves beneath the pale yellow dress she was wearing?

"Judd?" Darrell said. "You still there?"

"Sure." He was about to force himself to tune

back into their conversation, but then Cleo turned in his direction, their gazes connected and she smiled.

She started toward the cabin.

"I have to go," Judd told Darrell. "I'll call you back."

Judd put his phone away, but he didn't budge from his spot by the window. He needed to think this through, because if he went to the door and opened it...

He went to the door and opened it before he even allowed himself to finish that thought.

Cleo was already right there, stepping onto his porch. Still smiling. Looking good enough to eat. So, that's what he did. As soon as she reached the door, he hooked his arm around her, pulled her in and kissed her.

It wasn't relief that went through him. The exact opposite. It was a hot tangle of doubt, pleasure and realization that he was making a big-assed mistake. But since the mistake was already a certainty, Judd went ahead and made it worth his while by shutting the door and making things a whole lot hotter.

He deepened the kiss, catching the sound of pleasure that she made, and hauled her closer to him. He probably needed to let her catch her breath, or at least give her a chance to voice any objection she might have to this.

However, he doubted an objection was going to come because Cleo slid her arms around him and did some hauling of her own by dragging him against her body. Chest to breasts, as well as the alignment of other parts that gave him a reminder of the curves he'd admired when she'd been on the porch.

His tongue slid against hers. Tasting. And slipping right into that cauldron of fire that she was causing.

There was no coming back from this, Judd knew. No way to pull away and just pretend this hadn't happened. Nope. This was crossing the line. A really good one. One that got even better when he slid his hand between them and rubbed his fingers over her nipple. It wasn't hard to find since it had tightened and puckered against the front of her dress.

"Good use of your 'get out of jail free' card," she said when he finally broke the kiss. Cleo gulped in some air, causing her chest to heave. It also caused her nipple to press even harder against his hand.

"Oh, I'm not finished. That card has a ways to go before it's used up."

She laughed, like smoke, silk and sex, and she caught onto the back of his neck to pull him down for another kiss. Judd just slid right into it. And upped the touching.

His hand went lower this time, past her stomach and between her legs. There was a lot of clothing between them, but it was still effective because Cleo called him a dirty name and squirmed against him. So, Judd touched her again, and he planted some kisses on her neck.

"You remembered," she said.

Her voice was mostly breath, but Judd still managed to hear her. However, it took him a moment to realize what she was talking about. She liked having her neck kissed. When they'd made out as teenagers, it had been the spot that had taken her from smoke, silk and sex to "do me now." Judd was surprised and a little disgusted with himself that he hadn't remembered that sooner.

Cleo rolled her head to the side, giving him the access he needed to kiss that very sensitive spot for her. And he used his teeth, causing her to do the same. She bit his shoulder and then went after his sensitive spot.

She slid her hand over the front of his jeans. Since his hand was still in that same place on her, there was some bumping and jockeying for position, but that only made things better.

The urgency came. Man, did it. A fireball of heat came blasting through him and notched them up to the level just above foreplay. It was time to get naked, and Judd would have almost certainly started taking off his clothes if he hadn't felt Cleo stiffen.

"Damn it," she groaned.

All in all, that was not something he'd wanted to hear her say, and he was about to assure her that he had a lock on the door and condoms in his night-stand. But when he looked at her, he could see that Cleo no longer seemed to have that urgency to get naked. Judd followed her gaze to the side window and soon saw why.

Beckham.

The boy was on the back porch, and he was defi-nitely skulking. Not a surprise since it was well past his bedtime, and he shouldn't be out and about. His gaze was firing around the yard, and he had a backpack slung over his shoulder. After more of those fired gazes, he hurried down the steps, moving fast until he was out of sight.

"He's running away," Cleo grumbled.

She threw open the front door and hurried out into the night.

Judd was right behind her.

CHAPTER TWELVE

CLEO WOULD HAVE stormed right toward Beckham and latched onto him if Judd hadn't latched onto her first and held her back.

"Just watch and see what he's going to do," Judd whispered.

She didn't want to watch. Cleo wanted to catch up with Beckham and have a "come to Jesus" moment about him doing something this stupid. She and plenty of others had rearranged their lives and schedules so that he'd have a decent place to live, and this was how he repaid them?

Worse, he was leaving his little brothers behind.

Cleo stayed on the porch, only because of Judd's firm grip and repeated order of "watch him." And she did indeed watch as Beckham cut across the backyard and headed toward the barn.

"That's not his backpack," Cleo muttered more to herself than Judd. It was an old battered one that she was pretty sure she'd seen in the supply closet in the upstairs hall. If he was running away, why hadn't he just taken his own? Or both? That way, he could have carried more stuff.

"You think he's going to try to take a horse?" she whispered to Judd.

Judd shook his head and moved in front of her, and the moment Beckham disappeared into the barn, Judd finally stepped off the porch. *Quietly.* He was definitely in his lawman's mind-set right now. A cop on the trail of a would-be runaway.

This was not how she'd intended to be spending her night when she'd gone over to Judd's. And if she hadn't spotted Beckham when she did, Judd and she would have almost certainly been in bed by now. That reminder only made her feel even more frustrated because if she hadn't been making out with Judd, she might have seen Beckham sooner and talked things out with him. Now the confrontation was more likely to be an angry one.

Then she heard talking.

As Judd and she got closer, she could hear the boy's voice and realized he was on the phone with someone. They moved to the side of the barn door and listened.

"Just look around for a place I can go if it comes down to that," Beckham said to whoever was on the other end of the line. "And don't say anything about it to your folks." He paused. "No. They won't help. They'd just call somebody and report me."

So, not running. Not yet. But making plans to do that.

Beckham was apparently also making other plans because he went into the tack room, and when he came out, he no longer had the backpack.

"Just look," Beckham repeated, this time his voice filled with frustration. "I don't have anybody else I can ask."

"Yes, you do," Cleo blurted out. "You can ask me."

In hindsight, she probably should have gone about this in a more subtle way because it caused Beckham to curse. He immediately shoved his phone in his pocket, and she could practically see him trying to come up with a lie that would explain all of this away.

"What are you two doing out here?" Beckham snapped, and he eyed them with more than just mere suspicion. The eyeing and tone smacked of an accusation. "Are you bringing her here to make out or sleep with her?" he asked Judd.

Cleo huffed, ready to chew him out for even asking such a thing, but she backed down. It would have been hard to be indignant, considering they had indeed been making out just moments earlier.

"That's the best you can do?" Judd challenged. "You're caught putting together plans for running away, and you think a question like that is going to let you off the hook? Trust me, it won't."

Beckham's eyes narrowed. Now he was the one huffing. He even kicked at a clump of hay. All posturing so he could delay answering something that he clearly didn't want to answer.

"I think you owe Cleo the truth, don't you?" Judd insisted, but his voice wasn't cop now. It was firm, but gentle.

"I didn't do anything wrong," Beckham snarled. "I just need to be ready in case something goes wrong. I need to be able to get Isaac and Leo out of here if the social worker tries to take us and put us somewhere we can't be together."

Judd went closer. "You had me promise that I wouldn't let that happen. My words not good enough for you?"

"Say what?" Cleo went closer, too, and she looked at Judd. "What promise? When?"

Judd's gaze stayed on Beckham's, and it was Beckham who finally huffed again and then answered. "I'm not letting Isaac and Leo go back to the piss witch."

"Lavinia," Judd amended.

"Judd said he wouldn't let that happen," Beckham added to her.

Well, heck. Cleo had told the boys the same darn thing. Apparently, Beckham hadn't believed her because he'd clearly gone to Judd for a backup promise. Or maybe Beckham thought Judd's was the primary one.

"I swore I wouldn't let Lavinia get Isaac and Leo," Judd went on, "and in turn you promised me that you wouldn't run."

"I'm not running!" Beckham practically yelled, but the fit of temper was a flash in the pan because it cooled as quickly as it'd come. "This is just a backup plan."

"And what about the person you were talking to

on the phone?" Judd persisted. "Is he or she part of this plan?"

Beckham nodded. "It was a friend. A friend I don't want to get in trouble so I'm not going to give you his name."

Cleo sighed. Beckham didn't have a lot of friends so it wasn't hard to figure this out. "Mason Daughtry. They're close," she informed Judd. "Beckham spent some nights with Mason when Miranda first got sick." She turned to Beckham again. "You asked Mason to look for a backup place for you to go?"

Beckham nodded.

"And the backpack?" Cleo asked.

Beckham did some more hay kicking before he answered. "Just a few supplies. Snacks. A little cash. Some cat food," he said in a grumble. "I know I need more money, and that's why I want to get a job."

Cleo could have told him all the logistical reasons why it was a bad idea to try to run away from a rural area that didn't have any form of public transportation. Any snacks in a backpack would quickly get eaten up. The money, too. Plus, the odds were slim that Mason would even find them a hiding place.

But Beckham wouldn't want to hear logistics.

"How much money do you figure you'll need?" Judd asked.

Beckham lifted his shoulder. "As much as I can earn."

Judd nodded, made a sound to indicate he was considering the teen's answer. "Okay, I'll give you a job. But there are rules."

Even after Judd tacked on that last part, Cleo was shaking her head. She didn't want to make it easier for Beckham to do something stupid. Maybe even dangerous.

"I have two horses," Judd went on. "You can tend to them for me, and I'll pay you ten bucks an hour. But the rules are that it can't interfere with your schoolwork or the other chores you do for Rosy and Buck."

"I don't think this is a good idea," she whispered to Judd. It was an angry whisper.

"It's what Buck did for me when I first came here." Judd kept his attention on Beckham when he spoke. "I didn't know him. Definitely didn't trust him. And I wanted to be able to get Callen and Nico out of here if things got bad."

It surprised Cleo that she had forgotten those days, but yes, Judd hadn't been very trustful. Actually, he still wasn't. But he hadn't actually shared any escape plans with her.

"Oh, and FYI, the tack room is a dumb place to hide backup supplies," Judd told the boy. "Buck's always in and out of there. Best to put it in the hayloft up in the far right corner."

Beckham nodded, but the movement had a lot of uncertainty in it. "Why are you helping me?"

Judd shrugged. "To heck if I know. So far, you've been a pain in the butt. But maybe you remind me of myself. I was a pain in the butt, too."

"Yes, that's what Miss Rosy said," Beckham muttered under his breath. "You won't tell them about my backup plans?"

"Oh, I'm sure they already know them," Judd quickly assured him. "They've fostered dozens of kids over the decades, and I figure they're past the point of a kid doing something they've never seen before."

Maybe it was Judd's frank way of spelling it out that had Beckham's shoulders and chin lowering. "I just need to be able to fix things," he said. "Like my mom used to do."

Cleo saw it then. Beckham blinking hard and fighting back tears. Dang it. Of course, her own eyes had to get in on that, and she went to Beckham, pulling him into her arms. He went stiff again, but he didn't try to wiggle away.

"I miss her," he whispered. "God, I miss Mom so much."

That cranked up the likelihood that the blinking would fail to hold back the tears that would soon start spilling down her cheeks.

"I miss her, too," Cleo said despite the thick lump that had formed in her throat. Nothing, maybe not even time, was going to fix that, but Cleo thought of something that might help.

Cleo pulled back so she could look Beckham in the eyes. "Shortly after your mom got sick, she wrote you and your brothers letters that she wanted me to give you on your birthdays. Maybe it would help if you had your letter now?"

"Letters," he repeated. Dried his eyes with the back of his hand. "What do they say?"

She had to shake her head. "I didn't read them." In fact, she hadn't even known Miranda was going to write them, and it was probably best not to mention that Miranda hadn't given them to her until just a couple of days before she died. "But I have them in my room here at the ranch if you'd like me to get yours now."

When Beckham gave her a quick "yes," Cleo glanced at Judd to make sure he would stay with the boy until she got back. She didn't think Beckham would try to run, but Cleo also didn't think it was a good idea for him to be alone right now. Judd gave her a nod so she hurried back to the house.

"Everything okay?" Kace asked as soon as she stepped inside the kitchen.

Since the room was pitch-black, and she hadn't been expecting anyone, Cleo made a garbled sound of surprise blended with some PG-rated profanity. Kace was at the window, looking out at the barn.

"I think we have everything under control," Cleo said. "He wasn't running away but making plans for a possible future run." She paused. "You knew Beckham had left the house?"

"Big-brother ears." Kace tapped his own.

It was a reminder that he'd likely had to apply those ears to his own brothers and the troubled pasts they'd brought with them to the ranch. Those ears that might have picked up on other things, too.

"Uh, did you know about Judd and me?" she asked.

"Tonight or when you were teenagers?" Kace countered without hesitating.

Cleo didn't wince. After all, if she was woman enough to invite herself to a man's bed, then…okay, she still winced. "Both."

"Both," Kace answered.

Obviously, Cleo wasn't as sneaky as she'd thought she was.

"Normally, Judd just sleeps around," Kace went on. "One-night stands, that sort of thing." He looked at her. "You wouldn't be a one-night stand, Cleo."

"I sort of was before," she muttered.

"Only because you were moved to another foster home. This time it wouldn't be a one-night bang with you two practically already on top of each other."

She thought Kace meant that as Judd and her living in the same general area and not literally. "Are you trying to say you'd disapprove of me having sex with Judd?"

"I'm just saying go into it with your eyes wide-open. I don't want anything to happen to send him over the edge."

Well, no pressure there, and it took care of any lingering heat that was left over from the kissing session she'd just had with Judd. With her mood quickly sinking, she went upstairs, got the letter and then went back outside toward the barn. She hadn't intentionally planned to go in stealth, but Judd and

Beckham obviously didn't see or hear her because they continued to talk as she approached.

"If you hurt Cleo, I'm going to be really pissed off at you," Beckham said. She had no idea what had started this particular conversation.

"If I hurt her, I'll be pissed off at myself."

Apparently, this was the night for a potential pissing off. And for conversations about Judd and her. But she did like Judd's answer and smiled a little before she remembered Kace's warning. The smile came back when she took just one look at Judd the Stud, and the sizzle started up again.

If it was just the issue of her getting hurt, she would go for another round of kissing—that would easily lead to sex. However, Kace had put some doubts in her head—not about her state of mind but Judd's.

She cleared her throat to let Judd and Beckham know she was there, and they pivoted toward her as if they'd been caught with both hands in a cookie jar. Cleo tried to put on a blank expression, which was impossible to do because it wasn't just the overheard conversation she was dealing with, but what she was holding in her hand, too.

Cleo gave the letter to Beckham, and he studied it as if trying to figure out what to do with it. "You'll give Leo and Isaac theirs?" he asked.

"If you want. But I'd rather wait for their birthdays. They might need a lift since it'll be their first birthdays without their mom."

With his attention still on the envelope, Beckham nodded, tucked the letter in his shirt pocket and headed back toward the house. He definitely didn't offer to open it then and there. Something she understood. Reading his mother's last words was probably something better done in private. Though Cleo was worried about him. Beckham was already dealing with a mountain of emotions, and a letter from the grave might not help.

"I'll keep an eye on him," she muttered, and then Cleo turned back to Judd to launch into a discussion about sex.

Cleo wished she had worked up a "check yes or no" box as she'd done when she was sixteen. But even if she had, there wouldn't have been time for a single check because her phone rang, and she saw Daisy's name on the screen. Cleo immediately got a bad feeling about this.

That feeling was soon confirmed the moment she heard Daisy's frazzled voice.

"Cleo," Daisy greeted. "I really hate to bother you on your night off, but there's been some trouble."

Cleo immediately thought of the bachelorette party that should have been over by now, but maybe the bride's fiancé had caught her fondling Harry's butt. If so, things could have gotten ugly.

"You need to get to the bar right away," Daisy added. "Because the cops are here."

CHAPTER THIRTEEN

THE TROUBLE WAS COWS.

Despite it being after midnight, Judd had no problem seeing that the moment Cleo and he pulled to a stop just up the street from the Angry Angus. Except it was back to Anus again. It was hard to notice the sign, though, when there were so many other things to capture his attention.

The dozen or so plastic cows that had once been inside the bar were now on the sidewalk and street.

Not all in one piece, either. From the looks of it, they'd been chopped, hacked and hit, leaving bovine parts scattered all around. The vandal—or rather *vandals*, since he doubted one person could have done shit like this—had enhanced the parts by splattering what appeared to be gobs of thick red paint over them.

It looked like a scene from a horror movie. Or a frat party gone bad.

Judd had to hand it to Cleo. She didn't curse or get upset as she sat in the passenger seat of his truck and stared at the carnage. Just in case, though, he gave her arm a little jiggle to make sure she wasn't in shock.

"When things look bleak, I play a game with my-self," Cleo said. "It's called BS, as in best scenario." She stayed quiet a moment, probably trying to come up with something that would fit that particular bill. "The cows look better here than they did inside, and I might get some publicity for the bar out of this."

Leave it to Cleo to make him smile. Of course, maybe that was going to be the norm for the night since the two uniforms seemed to be fighting back amused expressions. They were in the doorway of the bar, talking to Daisy. No smile for her. Just plenty of puzzlement.

Judd got out when Cleo did, and after he took a whiff of the air, he realized the red gobs weren't paint after all. Cherry Jell-O was his guess. That smacked of a kids' prank, but as much of the glop as there was, it would have cost twenty bucks or more for the stuff. He supposed some kids would be willing to dole out that much, but a can of spray paint would have been cheaper.

His phone dinged with a text message. "Kace," Judd said after glancing at the screen, and Cleo im-mediately leaned in to read it.

Beckham's in bed. Will keep an eye on him to make sure he doesn't leave again, Kace had texted.

Now, Cleo sighed, and Judd knew why. When she'd asked Kace to be a foster parent, she hadn't planned on shackling him with this much respon-sibility. Especially since Kace had to be at work in the morning. But maybe this kind of "emergency" wouldn't come up very often.

The moment Daisy saw her boss walking up the sidewalk, she started toward her. "Sorry to make you drive out here this time of night," Daisy whispered. The woman had boxes tucked under each arm. "But I didn't want to sign the cops' report until you had a chance to look at it."

Cleo gave her a pat on the arm and walked closer to the uniforms. "I'm guessing someone found the cows in the alley, dragged them out here and did this?" Cleo asked the cops.

"We're hoping that's what happened," one of them said. "They're mechanical. Did you know that?"

"Yes, but it's only to make their mouths move," Cleo said. "And to make mooing sounds. We didn't turn them on when they were in the bar because it sounded more like farts than moos."

The cop actually jotted that down.

"The mechanical movement wouldn't have allowed them to walk out here," Cleo added, and she said it with a straight face, too.

"No, but they freaked out some kids," the uniform explained. According to his name tag, he was Sanchez. "Witnesses said they saw and heard some kids yelling and running so maybe they got scared and…beat up the cows." His lips twitched as he fought back a laugh, and Judd couldn't blame him. If he'd gotten this call, he would have had trouble not seeing the humor in it, too, and he rarely saw humor in anything.

"You on the force?" the other uniform, Davidson, asked when his attention shifted to Judd.

Judd nodded. "Deputy Judd Laramie, Coldwater PD." He tipped his head to the security camera. "Did you get anything from that?"

Sanchez and Davidson both shook their heads, and it was Sanchez who continued. "Somebody smeared it up good with Jell-O, but they started with a spray of Extra Creamy Dreamy whipped cream."

"And the camera didn't pick up who did that?" Cleo persisted.

"No. The vandal stayed to the side, just out of camera range. All you can see is a gloved hand holding a party-sized can of Extra Creamy Dreamy."

So, the person had been aware of where to stand, and that likely meant this wasn't his or her first time here. The glove could have been worn so there wouldn't be fingerprints, but it was possible the whipped-cream sprayer believed that Cleo would recognize whose bare hand had disabled the camera.

"Like I said, we got witnesses," Sanchez went on. "Some said they heard a ruckus in the alley. Some heard kids running and yelling. But nobody saw how the cows got here."

"Were there customers still inside?" Cleo asked.

"Just a few." That from Daisy. "Some stragglers from the bachelorette party. Harry, Monica and Tiffany." Daisy rolled her eyes. "They said they didn't see or hear anything."

"Uh, we had to give the cowboy a warning," Sanchez explained. "He can't be out here on a public sidewalk with his butt exposed like that."

Judd recalled the strippers Cleo had been auditioning when he'd visited her here, and yeah, an exposed butt would have violated a few laws. Maybe Cleo wouldn't get dragged into that. Especially since the cows were going to be enough of a problem. No witnesses and a camera that'd been tampered with meant reports and maybe even an insurance claim.

"Tiffany, Monica and Harry are gone now," Daisy assured Cleo.

Good. Judd doubted she was going to want to deal with that tonight.

"Are we free to get this cleaned up?" Cleo asked the officers. "Or will we need to wait until you've collected evidence?"

"Nothing left to collect," Sanchez said. "We've got pictures. All we need is the owner's signature." And he passed a clipboard with a form on it to Daisy since the bar was in her name. She made eye contact with Cleo before she signed it.

"I've already called my brother and Tiny to come out and do cleanup," Daisy said. She took a large box of trash bags from beneath her arm and set it on the sidewalk. Next to it, she put down the other box she'd been carrying. Latex gloves. "They're bringing friends and should be here soon."

"Thank you for everything," Cleo told her. "Go ahead back home. I'll wait until they get here, and then I'll lock up."

"I can stay." Daisy sighed as she eyed the mess.

"No," Cleo insisted. "Go home to Mandy Rose."

Daisy must have been wiped out because she jumped at the offer. Brushing a kiss on Cleo's cheek, the woman went back inside, got her purse and then left.

Cleo took some pictures of the cow parts with her phone. Then she set her own purse on the floor just inside the door, put on a pair of gloves and grabbed one of the garbage bags. Judd was about to tell her that she should wait for an actual cleaning crew, but he figured this was something she needed to do. She still wasn't as pissed as the average person would have been, but there had to be some anger simmering there.

To deal with his own simmering, Judd grabbed one of the bags, and together they started picking up cow parts.

"I could probably give this to someone who could use it for Halloween decorations," she said but then made a face when a globule of the red gelatin slid off a Hereford's severed head and splatted onto her shoe.

He would have preferred to dump it on the lawn of the person who'd done this. Or ram it up their ass. Especially if that ass belonged to Lavinia. Judd was about to broach the subject of the piss witch being a possible suspect, but Cleo spoke before he could.

"I've been playing BS with you," she said.

It took Judd a moment to realize she meant the best-scenario game. At least he hoped that's what she meant.

Cleo had a grip on a hacked-off hoof still attached to a partial hind leg when she turned to him. "Kace thinks it would be a bad idea for us to bang."

"Bang?" Judd asked, making a mental note to have a chat with his brother about keeping his mouth shut.

"His word, not mine. Kace has a way with flowery, romantic language." She flashed him a smile.

"So does Beckham," Judd said, remembering the conversations he'd had with the boy. "His favorite word is any form of piss."

Her smiled widened, but she might as well have doused him with sexual gasoline and lit a match. Instant fire. Inconvenient, too, since they were out on a sidewalk. But that didn't stop Judd from moving toward her and brushing his mouth over hers.

The hoof she was holding smacked against the partial Angus hindquarter in his hand.

Not the most romantic place—around the plastic-cow carnage—but it was still satisfying. And stupid. Because, after all, Kace could be right about his banging Cleo being a bad idea. It was even more reason to guard his heart. However, heart-guarding didn't take sex with Cleo off the table. He could have both.

And Judd was *almost* certain he could pull that off.

"You cause parts of me to flutter when you do that," she said, her voice breathy now. She shoved the hoof into the garbage bag and picked up another head. This time it was a Holstein. "The best parts," she added with a chuckle.

Yeah, he could pull this off, and Judd would have kissed her again if he hadn't heard the footsteps. Seconds later, Judd spotted the massive bartender and five other guys walking toward them.

There were lots of "holy shits" and "WTFs" grumbled as they approached, but one of the guys, a skinny blond, said, "Cool." It didn't surprise Judd when that one asked Cleo if he could keep the stuff.

Tiny picked up the box of garbage bags, pulled one out and handed the box to the others. "You think that loser dickhead ex of yours made this mess?" he asked Cleo.

"Harmon?" Cleo said, as if testing out that theory. But she shook her head. "He's never done anything like this."

Tiny huffed, and coming from a guy his size, it was a gust of breath big enough to blow out the candles on a senior citizen's birthday cake. "You blocked his number on your cell, but he still fills your work phone with messages. I've seen him parked out front watching the place, probably waiting for you to come out."

Now Judd huffed. And cursed. "This guy's a stalker."

"Yeah," Tiny readily agreed. "My granny would call him smitten, but I prefer the term dick-wad."

Judd liked that term, as well. "Did you happen to see him around here tonight?"

Tiny shook his head. "But I had the early shift and left at six. The cows were still in the alley then. I know because I saw them when I took out some trash." He glanced around. "How the hell did he get all of this out here without somebody noticing?"

That was something Judd wanted to know. "Where does Harmon live?" he asked Cleo. "Because I want to have a chat with him."

Judd figured Cleo would try to nix that, but there was fire in her eyes when she shoved the Holstein head into the trash bag and handed it to Tiny. "I'll show you the way, but if Harmon's ass needs kicking, I'll be the one to do it."

He admired her attitude, but Judd had no intention of letting her assault Harmon and have her on the wrong side of the law. If Harmon had indeed done this, Judd would make sure he paid, the legal way. With an arrest, a restraining order and money for cleanup. Of course, Judd would get in his face first and give the guy a whole lot of grief.

Cleo pulled off the gloves, dumping them into a trash bag, and she got her purse so she could follow Judd back to his truck. When Judd drove off, she started giving him directions.

Judd went through what he knew about the guy. Harmon was rich and had claimed to have dreamed about Cleo before he met her. No criminal record but plenty of nutjobs had clean records.

"Has Harmon ever been violent with you?" Judd asked.

"No," she snapped, but she must have realized it was best not to take her anger out on him, so she repeated it in a softer, calmer voice. "For him, it's more about ego. He's a dick-inch kind of guy."

Judd frowned and gave her a puzzled glance. Apparently, Cleo and Mercy shared some vocabulary words.

"You know, he exaggerates things," she explained. "Instead of saying he's down about our breakup, he'll say his heart is crushed. He never has just a single sleepless night but rather has dozens of them. And according to him, it's my fault. If I'd just get back with him, everything would be fine. Except he wouldn't say it was just fine—he would call it picture-perfect."

Maybe Judd wouldn't be able to stick to the legal way after all. "What a tool. Why the hell were you ever with him?"

"Because he was nice. At first. And he didn't tell me about the whole dream thing he'd had about me until after we were involved. But after Miranda got sick, I didn't have time to spend with him, and he resented it. That's when the dick-inch stuff started coming up. I got tired of it and broke things off."

But Harmon clearly hadn't gotten the message about the breakup. Judd would make sure he understood it tonight.

"Kace said you mainly have one-nighters," Cleo mumbled. "Smart. That's how you avoid the Harmons of the world."

She'd continued so fast after throwing out the "one-nighter" revelation that Judd didn't have time to say anything until after she'd finished. Now he said, "What?"

Cleo looked at him, shrugged and told him to

take a turn onto another street. "I guess you don't like Kace talking to me about your sex life," she commented.

"No, I don't." And he was going to bring that up, too, when he had a discussion with Kace.

"He's your brother. He's worried about you. Nico is as well, and I'm guessing that's why he paid you a visit earlier."

Well, hell. Apparently, nothing about his life was private. "Did Nico happen to talk to you about staying at my place?" Judd asked, only because he was certain that Nico had already chatted about this with Cleo.

Judd was wrong about that, though.

"What?" Cleo said. "No. What?" she repeated.

Judd took in a long breath, sorry that he'd even gotten into this. "Nico had a stupid idea that it'd look better with the social worker if you weren't staying in the house with Kace and the boys. He thought if you were at my place, then you could still keep an eye on things without raising suspicion from CPS."

She certainly didn't jump on confirming that the idea was stupid. Judging from her expression, she was actually testing out whether or not it would work. But then she shook her head.

"That would definitely take you out of your one-night-stand comfort zone," she concluded. Before Judd could figure out how to respond, she motioned to a modern two-story house just ahead. "There's Harmon's place. His car's in the driveway so he should be here."

Good. Best to deal with this now. Judd's "chatting to" and "clearing up" list was growing, and he wanted to get Harmon off of it.

Cleo and he got out of his truck, but before they even reached the front door, it opened, and a beefy, brown-haired guy came out onto the porch.

"Cleo," he said on a rise of breath. The kind of rise that meant he was surprised to see her. Happy, too, because he started grinning. The grin wavered significantly, though, when his gaze landed on Judd, but it was barely a glance before he turned his attention back to Cleo.

Harmon lifted his nose, sniffing. "Cleo, you smell good. Is that a new perfume?"

"It's Jell-O and Extra Creamy Dreamy," Judd explained.

"I know who you are." Harmon's mouth tightened, and his eyes went to slits. "Cleo, why do both of you smell like Jell-O and Extra Creamy Dreamy?"

Judd had no trouble picking up on the jealous undertones. Mr. Dick-inches probably thought those were sex aids.

"Why are you here, Deputy Judd David Laramie?" Harmon demanded before Judd could speak.

Judd had no trouble picking up on that tone, either. Harmon wanted to let him know that he'd been doing some internet searches on him and therefore knew his middle name.

"I'm here to ask you questions, Harmon Caspian Hawthorne," Judd growled back. "What the hell kind of name is Caspian, anyway?"

Harmon looked down the long length of his nose at Judd, and Cleo stepped between them before Harmon had a comeback for that. "Judd's with me," Cleo snapped. "There was some trouble at the bar tonight, and I wondered if you had anything to do with it."

Harmon pulled back his shoulders, and he volleyed his gaze between Judd and her. "If you mean the calls I made to you, that's not trouble. I have a right to call you. I *need* to call you, Cleo," he added. "It makes me insane when I can't hear your voice. My thoughts spin in my head, my heart nearly pounds out of my chest and I can't breathe. It's like I'm dying."

Yeah, so maybe this was the rare instance where dick inches did indeed apply. "Did it make you crazy enough to vandalize the bar?" Judd demanded, and because he was feeling especially mean, he tapped his badge.

"Vandalize? Vandalize! Vandalize!" By the third time Harmon had said it, his voice had some shrill to it.

"Vandalize," Cleo flatly repeated. "Someone chopped up a whole bunch of assorted plastic cows, globbed red Jell-O and Extra Creamy Dreamy on them, and dumped them in front of the bar."

Clearly, from his blank stare, Harmon appeared to be waiting for a punch line. What he didn't appear to be was guilty. "You mean the cows you had inside the bar?" he asked after a long pause.

She nodded. "But I'd had them moved to the alley by the dumpster."

This time when Harmon's mouth tightened, it didn't seem to be from being pissed off or jealous of Judd. "Why the hell would someone do that?"

Judd suspected that would be the most asked question when it came to the incident. "When's the last time you were at the bar?" Judd asked.

The mouth tightening turned mean again. "None of your beeswax. Like I said, I know who you are, and you don't have jurisdiction here."

Cleo huffed, rolled her eyes. "When's the last time you were at the bar?" she snapped.

Judging from his long silence, it wasn't a question that Harmon wanted to answer, but Cleo's persistent stare made it clear she wasn't leaving until she learned the truth.

"I was there a couple of hours ago," Harmon finally said, "but I didn't see any cows." Another pause. "Does this have something to do with the woman who was lurking in the alley?"

"What woman?" Judd and Cleo said in unison.

Harmon gave Judd a persnickety glance and settled his attention on Cleo. "She was probably in her sixties, long stringy dark brown hair. She was standing in the alley, leaning against the wall and smoking a cigarette."

Judd groaned. He already had a strong notion of who that might be even before Harmon added the clincher. "The woman obviously didn't believe in wearing a bra because her tits were hanging pretty darn low."

"Lavinia." Judd and Cleo said that at the same time, too.

"Come on," Judd told Cleo. "Let's go have a chat with her."

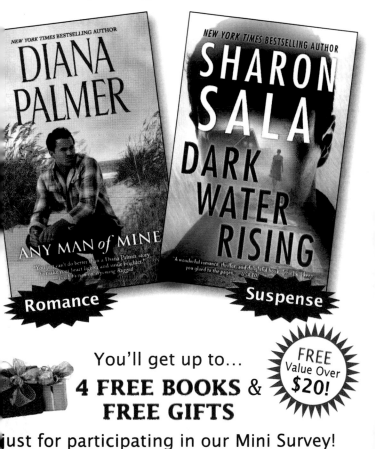

Get Up To 4 Free Books!

Dear Reader,

IT'S A FACT: if you answer 4 quick questions, we'll send you 4 FREE REWARDS from each series you try!

Try **Essential Suspense** featuring spine-tingling suspense and psychological thrillers with many written by today's best-selling authors.

Try **Essential Romance** featuring compelling romance stories with many written by today's best-selling authors.

Or **TRY BOTH!**

I'm not kidding you. As a leading publisher of women's fiction, we value your opinions… and your time. That's why we are prepared to reward you handsomely for completing our mini-survey. In fact, we have 4 Free Rewards for you, including 2 free books and 2 free gifts from each series you try!

Thank you for participating in our survey,

Pam Powers

To get your 4 FREE REWARDS:
Complete the survey below and return the insert today to receive up to 4 FREE BOOKS and FREE GIFTS guaranteed!

"4 for 4" MINI-SURVEY

1 Is reading one of your favorite hobbies?
☐ YES ☐ NO

2 Do you prefer to read instead of watch TV?
☐ YES ☐ NO

3 Do you read newspapers and magazines?
☐ YES ☐ NO

4 Do you enjoy trying new book series with FREE BOOKS?
☐ YES ☐ NO

Please send me my Free Rewards, consisting of **2 Free Books from each series I select** and **Free Mystery Gifts**. I understand that I am under no obligation to buy anything, as explained on the back of this card.

❏ **Essential Suspense** (191/391 MDL GNQK)
❏ **Essential Romance** (194/394 MDL GNQK)
❏ **Try Both** (191/391/194/394 MDL GNQV)

FIRST NAME	LAST NAME

ADDRESS

APT.#	CITY

STATE/PROV.	ZIP/POSTAL CODE

READER SERVICE—Here's how it works:

CHAPTER FOURTEEN

Lavinia.

Cleo was trying hard to keep the woman off her mind, but even with the Saturday-morning kid chaos going on around her, it was hard to do. Lavinia hadn't been home when Judd and she had gone to question her. Ditto for when the cops had paid Lavinia a visit. So for now, they still had no answers about whether she had anything to do with the plastic-cow carnage.

Judd was trying to fix that. He'd gone into work early so he could make some calls—not just to find Lavinia, but Otto as well, since the man might have info about the vandalism and Lavinia's whereabouts. That and Judd's regular duties would likely keep him busy. Maybe busy enough that he wouldn't think about what'd gone on before they'd gotten the call from Daisy about the cows.

She rethought that.

There wasn't enough busyness in the world to make her forget it, and she suspected it was the same for Judd. They had little willpower when it came to each other, so sex would almost certainly happen in their near future. Really great sex. And then they could deal with whatever gloom and doom Kace was predicting.

Sitting next to Cleo at the kitchen counter, Leo drew her attention back to him when he bashed a big brown egg against the side of the glass bowl. No part of the egg landed inside with the rest of the blueberry-muffin mix, which was probably a good thing. Cleo doubted the shell crunch would be very appetizing.

"Sorry," Leo said, and he reached for another egg that he likely would have attempted to bash, but Isaac took it from him. Isaac cracked it as if he was a trained chef.

"Miss Rosy taught me." Isaac's voice was quiet, and he looked both pleased with himself and embarrassed at the same time.

"Isaac's a big help when it comes to cooking," Rosy confirmed as Isaac cleaned up the egg mess Leo had made.

Cleo already had an inkling of that since Isaac's chore chart had a line of gold stars when it came to anything to do with the kitchen. Apparently he'd found his niche, so Cleo passed him the bowl to finish. He took it across the kitchen to the counter nearest the stove, and Leo trailed along behind him.

"There's no saving the Hereford, but you know, I could probably work some taxidermic magic on the Angus and the Holstein," Rosy muttered while she flipped through the pictures of the vandalism on Cleo's phone.

God, no. That was Cleo's first reaction, but

she caught herself in time. "That's okay. I hadn't planned on using them in the bar, anyway."

Rosy shrugged. "Still, it could be a conversation piece. Like Eddie and his family here."

Rosy ran her hand down the back of her latest creation, a quartet of frogs of varying sizes that she'd mounted around a lily-pad poker table. A fat bullfrog with bulging amber eyes and a flicking tongue was about to win the hand with a straight flush and lap up a fly at the same time.

Cleo was always a little icked out by dead stuffed things and figured she'd feel nearly the same about stuffed plastic ones. She didn't want that kind of conversation. Or the reminder of what'd happened. Even though she had no sentimental connection to the cows, it was still unsettling to know that someone might have done it to get back at her. That meant either Harmon or Lavinia.

Her money was on Lavinia.

There'd be an investigation, of course, but Cleo wasn't holding out hope that the police would actually be able to pin the vandalism on the woman. Too bad, because then Lavinia could be arrested, and it would get her out of Cleo's and the boys' hair. Out of Judd's, too.

Cleo hadn't meant for her sigh to be so loud, but Rosy noticed, and the woman looked at her. "Anything I can help with?" Rosy asked, her voice a whisper, probably so the boys wouldn't be able to hear.

"No." Cleo meant it, too, and that's why she was

surprised when she went closer to Rosy and added, "I just hate that Judd's gotten involved in this."

Rosy's sound of agreement only made Cleo feel worse. "Judd will be fine." But for once, she didn't sound so, well, rosy.

Cleo glanced back at Isaac and Leo to make sure they weren't listening. They weren't, so she continued and kept her voice low. "It's as if Judd's had to put his life on pause."

"You mean about Audrey?" Rosy asked.

Cleo suddenly felt like the bulging-eyed bullfrog, and she didn't want to admit it, but she had more curiosity than a dozen cats. "They were involved?" *Involved* was such a tidy word. Better than *boinking*.

Rosy made a check of the boys, too, then leaned in toward Cleo, as if telling a secret. "Audrey bakes him pies. *Pies*," Rosy said with emphasis, as if that was critical to this conversation, and it appeared to Rosy that Cleo would understand.

She didn't. "Pies?" Cleo asked.

Rosy gave a firm nod, complete with a tight, disapproving mouth. "When a woman bakes a man cookies, it's just flirting. I mean, she can hand him one, and he can eat it without even a napkin or anything. But a pie requires cutlery. Plates or saucers. It means sitting down and eating it." Rosy huffed. "Audrey might as well just strip off naked and jiggle her boobies in front of him."

Cleo was certain the stare she gave Rosy was a blank one. "Do, uh, other baked goods cross such lines?"

Rosy shrugged. "Muffins are fine. Cupcakes, too, but cake can be flirty since you can't eat some varieties with your hands. Too messy unless it's pound cake or coffee cake. Of course, it could be just showing off, too, if it's one of the fancy ones with icing roses and such. But showing off could be like proposing marriage."

Cleo had no idea that Rosy had so many opinions about the connection of baked goods and the subtleties of a courtship.

"Don't get me wrong. I don't dislike Audrey," Rosy went on. "But she's after Judd."

Cleo hated the pang of jealousy she felt about that. "And she'd be a good catch."

Rosy looked at her. "If she was, Judd would have already caught her. Something to think about."

Something else replaced the jealousy—the heat she felt for Judd. Of course, it didn't take much to stir that.

"Still, Audrey's not giving up," Rosy added a moment later. "Her uncle, Marvin, owns the Gray Mare Saloon, and now that he's found the 'love of his life,' he wants to get a partner to help him run it so he'll have more free time. Her name is Bambi, and she works at a 'nightclub' in San Antonio. According to what I've heard, her specialty is a 'slap and tickle' lap dance."

Cleo wasn't exactly sure what that was, but she now understood Marvin's urgency in finding a business partner for the Gray Mare.

"Marvin wants Audrey to buy part ownership of

it so it'll stay in the family," Rosy went on. "And she's got plenty of money to do that, but Audrey won't because of Judd's drinking problem." Rosy lowered her voice even more on those last two words.

And there came the jealousy again, and this time it was mixed with lots of other feelings. Including guilt. Audrey had avoided putting a liquor-lined path between Judd and her, and here Cleo owned the Angry Angus.

Rosy cleared her throat when Leo rushed back over to them, and it was a signal that the talk about pies, bars, boobies and such had to end.

"Eddie and crew will be even better when I get the sound and motion effects working," Rosy said as she turned her attention back to the frogs. She was fiddling with some kind of speaker contraption with a switch.

Cleo wasn't sure about the "better" part, but Rosy hadn't had any trouble shifting to a different conversational gear. Plus, she seemed to be enjoying what she was doing.

While Isaac spooned the batter into the muffin tin, Cleo glanced out the back window to check on Beckham again. He was where she'd last seen him— in the corral, grooming Judd's horses. Obviously, he was taking his job very seriously since it was only 8:00 a.m., and he'd already been out there over an hour. For a teenage boy, voluntarily getting up that early on a weekend was somewhat of a miracle.

After Cleo put the muffins in the oven, Isaac

and she walked to the window and looked out at his brother. "You think Mr. Judd could give me some work, too?" Isaac asked. "You know, just in case."

She did know, and it twisted at her to think that the boys felt as if they needed money stashed away. "He might. You can talk to him about it."

It would twist at Judd, too, but what was a little twisting if it gave the boys some security? After everything they'd been through, they deserved a little peace of mind.

"If Judd doesn't have something for you, maybe I can come up with an extra chore," she offered.

Isaac stunned Cleo when he hugged her, and just like that, her tears threatened. To an outsider, it would have seemed like such a small gesture, but she knew just how big it was.

Cleo would have definitely tried to hang on to that hug a while longer if there hadn't been a knock at the door. She glanced at Rosy to see if she was expecting someone at this early hour, but the woman only shook her head.

"I'll answer it," Cleo volunteered.

Her first thought was this was Lavinia. That's why Cleo had worked herself into a scowling bad mood by the time she reached the door and threw it open. But it wasn't Lavinia. Cleo didn't know who was more surprised—her or the tall brunette in a gray suit and heels.

"I'm Nicole Gateman," she said, flashing some kind of credentials. "I'm from CPS, and I'm here to do a home check. An unannounced one," she added, though that wasn't necessary. "I need to speak with Kace Laramie and then chat with Beckham, Isaac and Leo."

Cleo tried not to seem overly concerned about this, but of course, she was. Anything not up to CPS's liking could cause them to lose the temporary custody.

"Kace is at work, but I can text him," Cleo offered. "It'll only take him a few minutes to get here." She hoped. She wasn't certain of Kace's work schedule.

"Please do that." The woman's voice was as crispy as a fresh potato chip.

Cleo nodded, and Mrs. Gateman stared at her while she texted Kace. It wasn't a friendly stare, either. Her mouth pursed into a tight, disapproving bud.

"You're Cleo Delaney," she said when Cleo had finished the text. That also sounded like disapproval.

Cleo nodded again and moved back so the woman could come in, and so Cleo could keep watch for Kace. "I'm babysitting the boys this morning."

Mrs. Gateman made a sound that could have meant anything, and when she stepped in, she gave the house the same look of disdain that she'd given Cleo.

"You're alone here with the boys?" the woman asked.

Cleo tried not to give her any stink eye. "No. Rosy McCall is here. Her husband, Buck, is in his workshop just at the back of the house. Would you like for me to get them?"

Apparently answering that required her to take in a long breath. "No. I need to talk to you first. I'm well aware of who you are, and you should know there's been a complaint about you."

Like the stink eye, Cleo tried to bite off the profanity, too. "From Lavinia Mercer?"

"I'm not at liberty to say who made the complaint, but I'm required to investigate it. You have a police record," she added without pausing. "You work at a bar, and while under normal circumstances, that's a perfectly acceptable occupation, I'm concerned about these photos that were sent to me."

Cleo went stiff as Mrs. Gateman took out some hard copies from her bag. Groaning soon followed because it was a photo of Harry and his naked cowboy butt being ushered into the bar by Tiffany and Monica. The next photos were of the plastic cows strewn around in their Jell-O bath.

"I don't suppose you'll tell me who took these?" Cleo asked, but she quickly waved that off. Of course this woman wasn't going to rat out her source, though Cleo was more certain than ever that Lavinia was behind not only the vandalism, but also the photos. No one else would have anything to gain by giving CPS this kind of mud.

"I have to question if you're a suitable person to be around such impressionable young boys," the woman continued.

"Their mother thought I was," Cleo snapped. The

cocktail of emotions hit her at once. The grief over Miranda's death, the anger over what Lavinia was trying to pull and the snotty attitude of this prissy woman, who didn't know and probably wouldn't care that Cleo loved the boys as if they were her own.

"The boys' mother is no longer around to make critical decisions for them," the woman argued.

And Cleo was just as quick to argue back, "No, but it's what Miranda wanted. Since I didn't qualify by your standards, I'm not the boys' foster parent. Kace Laramie is."

"Then, why are you here? Because according to my source, you're actually living here at the ranch." Even though Mrs. Gateman hadn't asked that last part as a question, Cleo knew it was one.

Well, crap. Now it was Cleo who needed to take a deep breath, but she didn't have to answer because of the truck that came to a stop in front of the house. Not Kace, but Judd.

"Sorry," Judd said, coming straight into the house. "Kace is tied up with a domestic dispute right now so I came." He extended his hand to the social worker. "I'm Deputy Judd Laramie."

Apparently, the woman didn't approve of Judd any more than she did Cleo, because she gave him the same cool look. Well, coolish that turned hotish in a hurry. Mrs. Gateman did have more of a normal female reaction when she combed her gaze over Judd's face, then his body.

Cleo wanted to smack her. Not a very rational

adult response, but Cleo didn't appreciate her doing any cowboy admiring when her coming here would likely stir up more trouble.

"I'm Nicole Gateman." The woman shook his hand. "When will your brother be here?"

"Half hour, maybe less."

The woman didn't seem to approve of that, either, and sighed when she checked the time, as if a half hour would be a huge inconvenience. "Let me go ahead and see the boys, and then I'll have questions for both of you."

Judd and Cleo exchanged a look, part dread with a smidge of fear, and Cleo motioned for Mrs. Gateman to have a seat in the living room. "I'll get the boys."

Mrs. Gateman didn't stay in the living room, though. She followed Cleo, her heels pattering on the wood floor, and the first thing they saw when they reached the kitchen was Leo with the mixing bowl on his head. What was left of the batter was dripping on his face and shoulders while he licked as much of it as he could. There was a piece of a blueberry on the tip of his nose.

Popsicle was licking, too. The kitten was coiled around Leo's legs, lapping up the batter splatters.

Before anyone could say anything, the room erupted with sounds. Not sounds that Cleo had expected to hear, either. Mechanical belches, croaks and possibly farts. That was mixed with grinding gears and nearly maniacal laughter from Rosy. The poker-playing frogs were twitching while their lily pad undulated and quivered like a wave of slime.

"Eddie and crew are working," Rosy proudly announced, causing Isaac and Leo to run toward her at the table.

Probably because of the bowl on his head, Leo smacked into Isaac before he then rammed into a chair. Cleo hurried to him to make sure he was all right. He wasn't.

Leo hollered, "There's gunk in my eye."

There was. Lots of it. Cleo grabbed a handful of paper towels and started wiping. When Leo continued to protest, she lifted him to the sink and started flushing out his eyes with water. All while the frog noise continued.

"Oh, sorry," Rosy said. At least that's what Cleo thought she'd said. It was hard to tell with the other sounds, but Rosy was flipping the switch to get it to stop. Judd finally went to her and took out the batteries.

And the silence came.

Cleo gave Leo's face a wipe with the paper towels and eased him to the floor. There wasn't much she could do about the batter in his hair, but she did pluck the blueberry from his nose and tossed it into the sink.

Mrs. Gateman just stared at them.

"They're dead," Isaac said, and it took Cleo a moment to realize he was talking about the frogs that had snagged Mrs. Gateman's attention. "Miss Rosy stuffs dead things, and she's going to teach me how."

Cleo was about to explain that the stuffing hadn't happened on the kitchen table, but what would be the point? Mrs. Gateman had likely already decided that they were off their rockers.

"Boys, I'm Mrs. Gateman," the woman greeted. "You must be Isaac and you must be Leo."

"Must I be?" Leo queried. Of course, it sounded rude, but Cleo figured he hadn't meant it that way. He probably hadn't understood the stiff way Mrs. Gateman had put that.

"Where's the other boy, Beckham?" she asked, volleying glances at all five of them.

"I'll get him," Isaac volunteered, but he gave Cleo an uneasy look. She hoped the look she gave him back was a reassuring one, but she'd probably failed at that.

"Are you a babysitter?" Leo asked her.

Mrs. Gateman shook her head and stooped down so that her face would be closer to his. "No. I'm a social worker. I'm here to make sure you're in a good home with responsible, caring people. If not, then it's my job to find the right place for you and your brothers."

Cleo figured that explanation was way over a five-year-old's head, even a head coated with gunk, but Leo's face bunched up, and he squinted one eye at her. Cleo didn't think that was a reaction to the batter, either.

"You gonna take us?" Leo asked.

Mrs. Gateman smiled in probably what she thought was a reassuring way. "If necessary."

"Does that mean 'yeah'?" Leo persisted.

"It does."

While Mrs. Gateman kept smiling, Leo's mood went in the other direction. He balled up his little fists. "No!" Again, it was a holler.

And he punched the woman in her thigh.

That took care of the smile, and Mrs. Gateman did some hollering of her own. "You hit me," she snarled, rubbing her thigh.

Horrified, Cleo rushed to Leo, scooping him up to stop him from doing it again. "Leo," she said in a scolding tone, and that's the best she could manage because the boy was obviously in a fighting kind of mood.

"You're not gonna take us," Leo howled. "I like it here, and I got stars. I got three jail cards."

Of course, the woman wasn't going to understand that, either. Mrs. Gateman probably didn't play the BS—best scenario—game and probably thought they locked up the boys.

"May I speak to you in private?" Mrs. Gateman aimed the question at Cleo, and she spoke through clenched teeth.

"Of course." Cleo kissed Leo, whispered to him that she wouldn't be long and passed him off to Rosy.

When Cleo went into the living room, Judd came, too. "The boys have a good home here," Judd insisted. "They're adjusting and they're happy."

Mrs. Gateman rubbed her thigh again. "That might be, but I'm not seeing it right now. Once Sheriff Laramie is here, I'll sit down and have a long chat with him and all three of the boys, but I can tell you right now, there'll need to be some changes."

Yeah, definitely not a BS kind of person. "What kind of changes?" Cleo asked.

The woman took another long breath, and some of the disdain eased from her face. However, Cleo didn't like the expression that replaced it. It was one she recognized—she'd used it herself when she'd had to fire a nice person who just wasn't working out on the job.

"You can't live here with the boys," Mrs. Gateman said, looking directly at Cleo. "It's good that they have help with the McCalls, and their records are clean." She frowned a little, though, when her gaze drifted back to the kitchen. Maybe because she was thinking of the frog family.

"You're not asking me to stay away from them, are you?" Cleo didn't wait for an answer. "Because I can't. That wasn't what their mother wanted. Before she died, she asked me to watch after them."

"And you can do that, watch after them," the woman said to clarify. "But you can't live here." She sighed. "Sheriff Laramie's foster arrangement is temporary, but I understand he wants to make that permanent."

"He does," Judd quickly confirmed.

Mrs. Gateman nodded. "Then, don't do anything to compromise that. *Anything*," she instructed.

"We won't," Judd assured her. His jaw was drum-tight when he looked down at Cleo. "You'll be moving in with me."

CHAPTER FIFTEEN

JUDD DIDN'T HAVE to ask himself if this was a mistake. He knew that it was.

Cleo and he shouldn't be sleeping under the same roof, period. Still, other than her pitching a tent or staying in the barn, he couldn't think of another way around her being at the ranch while not actually living with Buck, Rosy, Kace and the boys.

"I won't be here every night," Cleo assured Judd as they hauled in her suitcases. Since it was a variation of something she'd already told him in the past twenty-four hours, since Mrs. Gateman's visit, Judd figured her nerves were playing into this.

His own nerves certainly were.

"Probably just once or twice a week," Cleo added. "On the nights that I stay until the bar closes, I'll crash at my apartment and then drive back here early the next morning before the kids get up."

That wouldn't be ideal, but the boys wouldn't be left alone. Buck and Rosy would be there, and the spreadsheets had been adjusted so that all times were covered. Again, they'd left off Judd's name.

Cleo put the suitcase she was holding next to the sofa and glanced around, as if looking at the place for the first time. Glancing didn't take long, though, because there wasn't much to see, and it was no doubt a reminder that they would be on top of each other.

Maybe literally.

Judd just didn't see how he was going to be able to keep his hands, and the rest of him, off her, when she'd be in his line of sight no matter which way he turned. Of course, he had plenty on his mind that might cool the heat. Kace could lose the boys, and if that happened, they'd go into the system.

"This has to make things right with the social worker and CPS," Cleo added, but it, too, was a variation of what she'd already said a couple of times.

Judd wanted to assure her that it would indeed fix the problem, but he wanted to keep his lies and bullshit to a minimum. Truth was, he didn't have a lot of faith in the foster system. He'd been in some bad homes and knew that Nico and Callen had been in even worse. Not every kid could get a foster dad as good as Buck.

And that brought him back to the promise Judd had made to Beckham.

He'd told the boy that he wouldn't let them be separated, and he had to follow through on that. Maybe not the way Beckham wanted, though. Judd wouldn't run with the kids, but he might be able to convince CPS to turn over the fostership to, well, him. Maybe even Kace and him together. If that didn't work, then he'd need to find someone acceptable to take the boys to.

"I need to talk to Audrey as backup," Judd said. He hadn't actually meant to say that aloud, and after seeing the surprised look on Cleo's face, he probably should have kept it to himself.

"Dr. Holcomb?"

He nodded. "If I ask her, she might do a report that could sway CPS in Kace's favor."

Cleo stayed quiet a moment. "Would that cost you?"

Again, going with the nonbullshit route, Judd didn't pretend that he didn't know what she meant. Audrey would likely do this as a personal favor to him. Emphasis on the personal. And while she wouldn't put any kind of pressure on him, he'd feel obligated to pay her back. That would be personal, too.

"Yeah, it would probably cost me," he admitted.

Cleo pinched her lips together a moment, then let out a long breath. "I wish I could insist that you not go that route, but…" She left it at that, and Judd was okay with it.

"I know what's at stake here."

That only tensed her expression even more, and she looked to be on the verge of apologizing—yet something else she'd been doing a lot of in the past twenty-four hours—but she stopped when her attention went to the window. Judd glanced over and saw Kace and the boys making their way to Kace's cruiser, which was parked in front of Buck's home. Neither the boys nor Kace looked especially happy.

"Something's wrong," Cleo muttered, and she hurried out the door. Judd was right behind her.

"CPS arranged for us to speak to a therapist," Kace volunteered.

"On a Sunday?" Cleo asked.

"They thought it would work better than the boys having to miss school. Donna Ezell agreed to do it at her office today."

Cleo looked at Judd, and even though she didn't ask, he figured she wanted to know if he knew this therapist. He did. "She's a guidance counselor at the middle school, but she also has a private practice."

Such that it was. Other than Gopher Tate, there wasn't a high demand for therapists in Coldwater. Folks who needed counseling usually went into San Antonio for that so that no one would see them coming and going from Donna's office. That would set the gossips' tongues wagging.

"Should I go with you to the appointment?" Cleo asked.

Kace shook his head so fast that he'd obviously already considered and then dismissed that idea. "No. I don't think it'd be a good idea for your name to be in the report, and Donna will have to send a summary to CPS."

Cleo smiled, but Judd knew it was forced. It was for the boys' benefit.

"We gotta talk to another lady," Leo mumbled. He had his hands shoved in his jeans pockets, and there wasn't much left of his usual sunny expression. Of course, the sunniness had diminished some after Mrs. Gateman's visit.

"I don't want to talk to her." That from Beckham. "I don't want to talk to any-damn-body."

Kace gave a frustrated sigh that let Judd know he'd been on the receiving end of all the boys' sour moods and that he didn't approve of the profanity.

"Could I talk to Beckham a moment?" Cleo asked Kace. "Do you have time?"

Kace checked his watch. "We've got about five minutes." He leaned against his cruiser while Cleo walked a few feet away with Beckham. Not far enough, though, because Judd could still hear her.

"Please keep it together for your brothers," Cleo told him. "*Please*. I really need you to do this."

"What if none of this helps?" Beckham snarled. "What if they try to take us?"

That was obviously Kace's cue to get Isaac and Leo interested in something else. He moved them into the cruiser, putting Leo in the front seat so he could play with the police radio.

"Seeing this therapist is the way to stop CPS from taking you," Cleo insisted. "Follow the rules and do as they say. Please," she repeated.

"The rules." Beckham spat out the words as if they were a profanity. "That's why you moved in with Judd."

"It is," she admitted, "but it's a small price to pay." She shrugged. "Well, for me, anyway. Judd probably isn't fond of sharing his space."

Beckham looked at Judd, and since the boy

seemed to be waiting on some kind of answer, Judd just shrugged, too. It was the truth. He wasn't fond of space-sharing, but it was only temporary.

"I don't like this," Beckham went on. "I don't like any of it."

Cleo ran her hand down his arm. "I know." She paused. "What about the letter from your mom? Did it help?"

Even with everything else going on, Judd hadn't forgotten about Cleo giving him that letter in the barn. He'd worried about how Beckham was going to deal with it.

"I didn't read it." Beckham looked away from Cleo.

"Why not?" Cleo asked.

Beckham still didn't look at her. The ground held his attention, and he took his time answering. "Because it'll be like a real goodbye. The last one from my mom."

"Oh, Beckham." Cleo reached for the boy, but he sidestepped her and shook his head.

"If I don't open the letter," he added, "she can't say goodbye." And with that, Beckham moved away from Cleo as if he'd just been scalded, and he hurried to the cruiser.

Ah, hell.

Cleo had tears in her eyes, and that couldn't be a good send-off for Beckham, either. Still, that five minutes was probably up, and Kace wouldn't want them late for the appointment. Cleo and Judd stood there and watched Kace drive away.

Cleo kept blinking hard, no doubt fighting those tears, and Judd finally put his arm around her and led her toward the cabin. "I'm really screwing this up." Her voice cracked over the words.

"No, you're not." Judd kept her moving and got her inside. "You're just trying to make the best of a bad situation."

Frowning, she looked up at him as if to see if he meant it. He did. Of course, words weren't going to fix things, but he thought of something that might.

"While we wait for Kace to get back, I can offer you ice cream. Your favorite, Rocky Road. Or at least way back when, it was your favorite. Mine, too."

Until he had told her the flavor, there'd been no sign whatsoever in her eyes that she was in an ice-cream kind of mood. "When we were sixteen, neither of us had a 'get out of jail free' card so you sneaked me some from the freezer after everyone had gone to bed."

"It was a teenage boy's version of candlelight and roses."

"Better than candlelight and roses." She gave him a dreamy smile, and their gazes held.

And there it was.

That heat that hooked him right around the neck and pulled him right toward her. Or at least it would have if Judd hadn't forced himself to look away.

"You get us some spoons. I'll get the ice cream," he said.

He went into the kitchen before he could change

his mind about that look, but Judd hadn't thought of the logistics of two people being in the small space at the same time. Cleo's hip brushed against his as she reached for the drawer next to the sink. For such a small touch, it packed a wallop. However, Judd hadn't been expecting Cleo's reaction.

She screamed, bolted back into the living room and screamed again.

Everything inside him went on instant alert, and Judd reached for the weapon that he kept in the high cabinet above the fridge. He stopped, though, when he saw what had caused her scream and what was causing her to bobble around on her toes and point at the drawer.

"Snake!" she shrieked.

Judd tried to tamp down the jolt of adrenaline he'd just gotten, and he took the snake from the drawer so he could hold it up for Cleo to get a better look at it. That clearly wasn't the right way to handle this because she shrieked even louder and backed up against the wall.

"It's not real," he assured her. He knocked on the coiled rattler's head with his fist so she could see there were no signs of life or sounds. "It's one of Rosy's taxidermy critters. She named it Sweetcakes, and, no, I don't know what made her come up with that name."

He'd hoped that Sweetcakes would get Cleo's plastered back away from the wall, but she didn't budge. "Why the heck would you have something like that in your kitchen drawer?" she demanded.

This was not going to be an easy or fun explanation, but going with his recent no-bullshit rule, he told her the truth. "It's my distraction. Sort of a focal point similar to what women in labor use to get their minds off the pain."

The blank look she gave him told him that his explanation was somewhat lacking.

"It's something my sponsor came up with," he went on. "If I get the urge to drink, I'm supposed to take this out of the drawer and stare at it while repeating a mantra of sorts. Safe words," he added in a mumble.

That finally got Cleo moving from the wall, but she didn't exactly move closer to him. She kept as much distance between them as she could manage in the small space. "And that works?"

He lifted his shoulder. "So far, though I can promise that I was just as skeptical as you are when Mercy suggested it. Mercy Marlow is my sponsor," he explained.

Since she was still eyeing the snake as if it might come to life, Judd shoved it back in the drawer. He took out the ice cream and got two spoons.

"Safe words?" she asked. "You mean like sex stuff?"

If only. "Mercy prefers the term 'safe word' over code. In this case, neither really applies." He debated a lie, but since this seemed to be amusing her, he went with the truth. "Dick inches. Those are my safe words."

Her mouth quivered a little. "So, when you get

the urge to drink you stare at a stuffed rattler named Sweetcakes while repeating 'dick inches'?"

"Yep. Mercy has this bizarre belief that it's okay to poke fun at AA and men in general. Did I mention she's a former porn star who's now a phone-sex operator?"

Now she laughed, and it was so good to hear it—and not see tears threatening in her eyes—that Judd figured it had been worth a little humiliation over telling her about his coping mechanisms.

"Considering Mercy's, uh, background, I'm surprised she'd suggest a snake," Cleo commented.

"Oh, that wasn't her first choice. I nixed a cock ring, a nipple clamp and a pair of edible panties. At least I can take the snake out in mixed company."

He sat on the couch, opened the pint of ice cream and handed her a spoon. Still smiling, she sat beside him and made a *mmm* sound when she took a bite. "How long has Mercy been your sponsor?"

"A little over a year." Judd wasn't sure how much Cleo knew about his drinking or if she could do the math, so he filled her in. "I haven't had a drink since Mercy agreed to take me on." To keep himself from babbling more, he had a bite of the ice cream and fed Cleo one.

"Then the unconventional Mercy deserves a huge thank-you," Cleo concluded.

Yes, she did.

Cleo dug in for more ice cream and probably didn't know that she now had chocolate smeared on her bottom lip. But Judd knew. And he felt his body do some clenching and begging to kiss it off. He wondered if distractions and safe words would work at keeping his hands off her.

"You don't have to tell me," she said, licking the spoon and giving his body another tug. "But did something bad happen to you when you were at Austin PD?"

Judd had a quick debate with what and how much to say. There was a simple answer here, and he gave it to her. "Yeah, something bad did. I became a drunk."

"There's not more to it than that?"

Obviously, she'd heard gossip. Hard not to, in Coldwater. But he doubted the gossips had gotten this one right.

"That's enough," he assured her. "I gave in to the flashbacks and the old stuff and stupidly decided to try to use whiskey to fix it."

"Judd, I'm sorry," she blurted out when he shifted. "I didn't mean to pry."

Cleo took hold of his arm as if she'd expected him to move away from her, but he had only been turning in her direction. He wasn't going anywhere. Well, not too far, anyway.

Part of him considered that one way to end this uncomfortable conversation would be to kiss her. It'd do double duty of also getting that chocolate off her mouth—though that was a very minor reason. The biggest reason was that he was just plain tired of resisting her.

Judd leaned in and kissed at the exact moment

that Cleo leaned into him. They nearly collided. It didn't help that she still had the spoon in the vicinity of her mouth and that he was holding the tub of ice cream.

There were some small sounds of pain and some adjusting before they sort of leaped at each other. The spoons and ice cream clattered to the floor, but Judd didn't care where they landed. At the moment, his mind was focused on just one thing.

Get Cleo naked now.

CHAPTER SIXTEEN

CLEO KNEW SOMETHING for certain—Judd tasted better than Rocky Road ice cream, and his taste was only one awesome thing about him. There were plenty of other parts other than his mouth that she planned on exploring.

Of course, Judd had kissed her before, but she could feel the difference between this one and the one in her car. That one had been a firecracker compared to this "stick of dynamite" one he was giving her now. There was a scalding urgency and the best part of all...

An erection.

She found this out almost by accident when she crawled into his lap, and the center of her body met the center of his. Hers was all soft, which made it somewhat easier to feel the long hard length of him. Apparently, that was all she needed to kick up her own need many, many notches.

Judd did even more notch-jumping by spreading his kisses down to the side of her neck, her ear and to the top of her breasts. Cleo definitely wanted more of that and worked her hands between them so she could unbutton her shirt. While she was there, she unbuttoned his, too, and got an instant treat when she ran her fingers over all those taut muscles in his chest.

The man was built. Really built. And she was going to enjoy every minute of the hard work he'd put into getting this body.

"Are we really going to do this?" she asked just to make sure. She didn't want to strip if he was having second thoughts.

He didn't answer, but he did move, causing her to curse herself for giving him an out and putting a possible halt to this.

"To heck with second thoughts," she said, though the words came out garbled because at that exact moment when she'd tried to speak, he took those scorcher kisses back to her mouth.

Judd also took *her*. Slinging his arm around her butt to keep her anchored against him, he stood. Not easily. With her still groping him, he got a little off-balanced and staggered. Cleo wanted him to stagger enough so that he'd drop back down on the sofa with her, but then she realized where he was going.

To the front door.

Either they were about to surprise Buck, Rosy, and the livestock and chickens by going outside, or... It was the *or*. Judd locked the door, something she was glad he had remembered because she certainly hadn't.

The kissing raged on as they staggered and groped their way back across the room. Not to the sofa, though. He took her to the bed and dropped her on the feather mattress. It swelled up around her, burrowing her even deeper when she pulled Judd down on top of her.

This was the same cabin, the same bed, where she lost her virginity, but Cleo knew there was one huge difference. She didn't have a boy in her arms. She had a man, and she was reasonably sure that was going to make this even more enjoyable.

Judd levered himself up, causing her to whimper in protest and reach for him, but he staved her off when he put his knee right between her legs. He probably hadn't intended to create some nice pressure there while he stripped off her shirt, but it was enough that Cleo just lay back and enjoyed the ride that had already started.

She didn't want to mention that Judd had gotten very good at undressing a woman. Definitely no fumbling, as he had when they'd been sixteen. He flicked open the front clasp of her bra, pushing aside both cups at the same time with a sweeping motion of his hands. Then he went after her breasts as if he planned on licking her to an orgasm.

Which much to Cleo's alarm, just might happen.

Apparently, she hadn't built up much of a resistance to Judd, and since she didn't want to go all quick-draw alone, she did something to up his own urgency. She caught onto him and flipped him on his back. Once she had him pinned, she licked her way down his chest and to his stomach.

His muscles tightened and quivered, but he wasn't giving off that high-intensity urgency of now, now,

now. So, Cleo unzipped him, freed him from his boxers and put her tongue to good use.

Now there was urgency.

Judd had no dick-inch issues at all. There was plenty of him for her to tease and torture.

He cursed her. Judd called her a really bad name that had her laughing, and she made sure there was plenty of breath mixed with it, too. It didn't do a darn thing to cool down her own body, but at least Judd and she were now on the same hot page. Both were needy and raring to finish this so they'd get some relief from the pressure cookers ready to go off inside them.

Still cursing her—and, yes, gritting his teeth—Judd took hold of her shoulders and dragged her back up his body. Then he turned her, reversing their positions so that he was on top of her again. Cleo nearly protested the halt to her tongue game, but he was out of his boxers now, and she could feel him hard as stone and ready…right between her thighs.

Not a bad place to be.

Judd got to work on her jeans, proving that his undressing skills were just as adept below the waist as they were above it. Adept, and he was able to multitask. He reached over to the nightstand, took out a condom and pressed it into her hand.

"Get this on me." His voice was smoke, heat and man. It went well with the rough, hurried hands he was sliding over her body as he peeled off her jeans and panties. Those two items landed on the bed next to her.

Apparently, she hadn't learned as much as Judd had about sexual finesse because Cleo fumbled with the condom. Still, she managed. Good thing, too, because Judd's kisses and touches had her right at the breaking point. She wanted to break all right but not without him inside her. And then that's exactly where he was.

Judd shoved into her.

Oh, my. That was so good. The pleasure hit her every place at once. She saw gold stars and heard music. At least she thought it was music, but when Judd cursed again, she realized it was her phone ringing. And his.

Who the heck was calling them now? Cleo was so caught up in the pleasure-hitting that she wanted to tune it out, but then she remembered the boys. Judd must have, too, because without moving off her, he took out his phone from his pocket. That caused Cleo to curse, but she took her cell out from her jeans.

"Darrell," he mumbled when he looked at his phone screen. "A cop friend." He didn't answer it.

"Daisy," she said when she looked at hers.

It couldn't be good that both would call at the same time, and Cleo volleyed glances at her phone and Judd while she tried to figure out how to handle this. Maybe a text to ask...

Or not.

With his phone still in his hand, Judd thrust into her. Hard and fast. Then harder and faster. It didn't take much at all because she was already primed and hot. Already needing to get to the breaking point. Judd fixed her up. He broke her, sent her flying and made her forget all about ringing phones as the orgasm rippled through her.

Even with the rippling, though, she was aware that Judd stopped. He definitely hadn't *broken* with her but instead he answered his phone.

"What?" he snarled to his cop friend.

Since he'd managed to get to his phone, Cleo answered hers, too, except she had to hit Redial since Daisy had already ended the call. Daisy answered right away.

"Cleo, I hate to bother you, but I just got a call from the cops," Daisy blurted out. "There's been more trouble at the bar."

IT TOOK CLEO a moment to fight through the postorgasmic haze and hear what Daisy was saying.

"What kind of trouble?" Cleo asked. "It's Sunday, and the bar's closed."

She couldn't hear what Darrell had told Judd, but whatever it was, it caused Judd to get off the bed—and off her. He gathered up his clothes and headed to the bathroom.

"I don't have all the details, but apparently it's something to do with Lavinia," Daisy said.

Cleo now had proof that even an orgasm thanks to Judd couldn't erase the irritation that she was feeling. Something she hadn't thought possible. There'd been no time to enjoy what he'd done to her. Heck, there'd been no time for her to do to him what he'd done to her. That's because once again she was having to put out a fire caused by Lavinia.

The woman was an emotional arsonist.

"What did Lavinia do?" Cleo asked. She also got up, and with the phone sandwiched against her shoulder and ear, she started to dress.

"I'm not sure, but the cop who called mentioned her name. I'll get there as soon as I can arrange a sitter for Mandy Rose."

Cleo was about to tell Daisy to stay put and spend the rest of her day off with her little girl, that she would handle it, but she couldn't. If the cops were involved, then as the legal owner, Daisy had to be involved, too.

"I'll leave now and should be there in under an hour," Cleo assured her and ended the call.

Judd was dressed when he came out of the bathroom. "Lavinia showed up at the bar and got in a fight with someone." When he snatched up his keys and headed out the door, she followed him.

Cleo suddenly had a string of questions pop into her head. "A fight? Who was Lavinia fighting? And why would the cops have called Daisy and you if the fight happened outside the bar? My God, did Lavinia break into the place?"

Judd didn't get a chance to answer any of that because when he threw open the door, Audrey was standing there. Her right hand was lifted as if she'd been about to knock, and she was balancing something on her left palm.

A pie.

Peach, judging from the color of the filling that was seeping through the golden-brown lattice-top crust. It looked perfect, like something made for a glossy food magazine.

"Oh," Audrey said, clearly startled that Judd and Cleo had nearly run right into her. Probably some of that startling was simply because Cleo was there— and was still buttoning her shirt. "Oh," Audrey repeated, the disappointment and hurt sliding through her eyes.

Cleo tried not to look as if she'd just had an orgasm, which wasn't hard to do, what with the irritation she was feeling about Lavinia.

"Audrey," Judd greeted. He definitely didn't have orgasm face. He was harried, annoyed and probably wondering why the heck his life had gone from pie offerings to mad dashes to San Antonio to deal with another of Cleo's problems.

"Uh, I can handle this by myself," Cleo offered, fishing out her car keys from her purse, which she'd grabbed on the rush to the door.

"No. I'll go." He looked at Audrey. "I'm sorry, but this is police business."

"Oh." Audrey again, and this time there was some flirty hope in her voice. She was probably rationalizing that sex hadn't just happened and that she still stood a chance with Judd. "Then I won't keep you." She thrust the pie at him—which was right in front of her boobs. In fact, for him to take the pie, his fingers just might graze a nipple or two.

Maybe Rosy had been right about her culinary-relationship observations after all.

"Thanks. I'll have some later." Judd snatched the pie from Audrey, put it on the foyer table and stepped out onto the porch. Since it seemed as if he wanted to say something else to Audrey, Cleo left them alone and went to her car.

And Cleo cursed. Because this wasn't a mere flitter of jealousy. It was a full-fledged smack of it upside the head.

Thankfully, she had a crisis to divert her attention. Lavinia and whatever havoc she'd created. Still, Cleo's attention drifted to the side mirror, where she had a perfectly framed view of Judd and Audrey. Judd was turned sideways, his legs apart as if ready to run, but he wasn't running. And Audrey had her hand on his arm.

For the first time in her life, Cleo wished she had lip-reading skills—and the ability to bake an incredible pie.

"Oh, God." She realized the words had come from her. It wasn't like the "oh, God" that she'd groaned out when Judd and she had been having sex. This one carried "pit of despair" emotion because it wasn't just jealousy she was feeling for Judd. Nor was it just sex.

She was falling in love with him.

Well, wasn't this just a kick in the teeth? Falling in love. With Judd. If she had to come up with a top-ten list of men who wouldn't be able to commit, *ever*, who wouldn't be able to love her in return, *ever*, he might not be at the very top, but his ranking would be pretty darn high.

Judd finally hurried off the porch, leaving Audrey standing there, watching him. Maybe it was because of Cleo's own self-revelation of falling in love, but she wondered if Audrey was feeling the same thing. If so, Audrey was one good catch, at least on paper, anyway, and since Judd wasn't stupid, he might soon figure that out.

The moment Judd was in the car with her, Cleo took off, hoping that Judd would launch into an explanation as to what Darrell had told him. He didn't.

"Stop the car," Judd insisted.

Cleo did because she was certain he had seen something wrong in maybe the pasture or the grounds. But once she'd stopped, he caught onto her chin and turned her to look at him. Their gazes collided, and it was as if he'd stripped away all layers and walls that separated the truth from what she wanted him to see.

"Well, shit," he mumbled.

Cleo eyed him and stayed quiet because a "well, shit" could cover a multitude of sins, and it probably didn't have anything to do with pie envy or falling for someone who was high on a hypothetical list.

"I knew it," he went on a moment later. "Having sex with me is messing with your head."

All right, so it did cover the falling for someone, but Cleo wasn't going to jump headfirst into a conversation this deep right now. "Actually, it messed with my body, in a really good way." She smiled, hoping it would cause him to do the same.

It didn't.

And that's when she knew that Judd would use every ounce of willpower he had not to touch her again.

Part of her wanted to believe that was a good thing because of her bad showing on paper and because she was an emotional drain on him right now. She wasn't fixing him prize-winning peach pies. She was dragging him into what would no doubt be another legal mess, one that might spill over to her other legal mess of the boys' custody.

"What'd Darrell tell you?" she asked and held her breath that he would indeed answer and not continue with details of why sex with him equaled head-messing.

She kept her eyes on the road, but Cleo could feel him staring at her. Could hear the debate going on in his head, but he finally answered. "Lavinia didn't break into the bar, but she was outside your place when she got into a fight. More of a shoving match," Judd explained.

It was hard for Cleo to muster up any sympathy for the woman or the person involved in the shoving match, but she had to shake her head. "Then why did the cops call Daisy?"

"Because there was still some goop on the sidewalk from the cows, and Lavinia fell in the scuffle. She's blaming you for not doing a proper cleanup, and she wants to sue."

Cleo groaned. Definitely no sympathy, not even if Lavinia was truly hurt. Which Cleo doubted she was.

"The reason Daisy got called in was because there was some damage to the bar. Right before Lavinia fell, she pushed someone into the front window, and when it broke, it set off the security alarm."

None of this was good news, but Cleo relaxed a little. A window could be fixed, and if Lavinia sued, then she had insurance. But Judd wasn't relaxing.

"Harmon was the person who got involved in a shoving match with Lavinia," Judd added. "The cops haven't taken his statement yet because he's getting stitched up in the ER. He got hit with flying glass when the window broke."

Cleo felt the next groan rumble in her chest. "Harmon was involved in this?"

But she waved off any answer Judd might have given her and pressed the button on her steering wheel, then gave the voice command to make a call to Harmon. Several moments later, Harmon's voice came pouring through her speakers.

"Cleo, I was about to call you," he said, and she didn't think it was her imagination that he sounded cheerful. "I was just leaving the ER and am on my way to the police station. Did you hear what happened?"

"I'd like to hear it from you," Cleo insisted.

"Yes, it's better coming from me, anyway. You know how things can get skewed. When I drove past your bar, I saw the woman lurking in the alley again. The smoking one who doesn't wear a bra."

"Why were you at the bar?" Cleo asked when Harmon paused.

Silence. For a long time. "Because you used to catch up on paperwork on Sunday afternoons, and I thought you'd be there. Cleo, I needed to see you. I can't sleep. I can't eat—"

"Tell me what happened between you and Lavinia," Cleo interrupted. No groan this time but a huff because once again Harmon had been stalking her.

"Well, like I said, I saw her hanging around the bar and figured she wasn't supposed to be there so I stopped to make sure she wasn't causing more trouble. I knew you'd thank me for that."

Well, she wasn't thanking him just yet. "You got into a shoving match with her?"

"No. Not a shoving match." Now there was insult in his voice. "Sheez, Louise, Cleo, I'm a grown man. I don't shove, but when I *verbally* confronted Lavinia about why she was there, she told me to mind my own business. Except she added a lot of curse words."

"Yeah, I'll bet she did. So, you didn't push her back or hit her?" Cleo persisted.

"No, but she knocked me into a window, and it broke. I have stitches, Cleo, and the nurse said I'd need pain meds, that I might need them for a couple of days."

Now, Cleo mustered up sympathy, though it was

possible Harmon was exaggerating this. "I'm sorry you were hurt."

"Where's Lavinia now?" That came from Judd, who clearly was in a no-sympathy kind of mood for this.

"Is that the deputy?" Harmon asked.

"It is," Judd revealed. "Now answer my question."

Harmon didn't. "Cleo, could you please tell the deputy to move away from the phone, that this is a private conversation between you and me?"

Since she wanted to hear what Harmon had to say and because arguing with him could put him in a snit, one that would silence him, Cleo went with some deception. She gave Judd's arm a nudge, moving him a fraction.

"Okay, Judd moved," Cleo told Harmon. "Now finish telling me about Lavinia."

"All right. Sure." He sounded a little perky. "About the time she pushed me into the window, a cop showed up. I guess somebody called them when they heard Lavinia and me yelling. Anyway, they hauled her off and took me to the ER."

"So, Lavinia is still at the police station?"

"Maybe. The cop said something about me needing to file charges against her for assault." He paused again. "But I'm not sure that's the way to go here, Cleo."

Cleo didn't like the sound of that. Judging from Judd's mumbled cursing, he didn't, either.

"What do you mean?" Cleo asked Harmon.

"Well, while I was waiting to get stitched up, I

had some time to think, and if I file charges against her, it might make Lavinia come after you and Miranda's sons."

"She's already coming after us," Cleo pointed out.

"Yes, but this could rile her so that she pushes even harder. I don't think filing charges is the best way to go about it." His next pause was long enough to have had an entire conversation, and she glanced at Judd to see how he was holding up.

If his jaw muscles got any tighter, Judd might crack some teeth.

"I came up with an idea," Harmon went on, "but just hear it all the way through before you say no." She heard the deep breath he took. "I can become the foster father to Miranda's sons. I have plenty of room, and they can live here. You could see them anytime you want. *Anytime*. Then you wouldn't have to keep driving back and forth between the bar and Coldwater."

"No," Cleo said, and she didn't think about it as Harmon had asked. "This sounds like an excuse to try to get us back together."

Judd mumbled a barely audible "Damn right."

But Harmon put his own spin on that. "It's what's right for the boys." Harmon said it so fast that it made her wonder if he'd rehearsed this part. "I co-own a reputable business, I'm comfortable with my finances and I don't have a police record."

No record. Something that hadn't been true for

her since she was a teenager. Cleo had never regretted that more than right now.

"Plus, the signs are here," Harmon went on. "Even you can't deny that."

"What signs?" Judd snapped.

"Why is he listening again?" Harmon said angrily. "Well, it doesn't matter," he continued before Cleo or Judd could say anything. "He can hear this, too. There are signs that Cleo and I are supposed to get back together. It hasn't rained in two weeks. Blood was spilled. And Cleo has experienced conflicted pleasure. I didn't know what the last part meant, but I understand it now. She was conflicted about the boys but is now pleased that I'll take them."

Judd gave her a blank stare.

"Harmon visited a fortune-teller in Wrangler's Creek, and she told him these things," Cleo explained.

"I know what you're thinking," Harmon went on, talking right over her. "You're dismissing her, but lots of people use psychics and fortune-tellers. But it's not something I'd tell Child Protective Services. I just pointed out the signs to you so that you'd understand this is something that should happen."

Cleo took her own deep breath, ready to tell Harmon that no matter what a fortune-teller said, she wasn't getting back together with him. But again, Harmon just kept on talking.

"You need to let me handle this," Harmon said. "Let me just get all of this out there, and I'll hang up so you can have some time to let it all sink in. Take twenty-four hours to consider everything I'm telling you, and you'll see this is the right thing for all of us." Another deep breath. "I'm going to Lavinia and will tell her I won't file charges if she backs off and leaves me, you and the boys alone."

"What?" Cleo snapped, but Harmon ignored her.

"The only thing you have to do in return is accept what I'm offering you," Harmon insisted. "And what I'm offering you, Cleo, is *me*."

CHAPTER SEVENTEEN

"DICKHEAD," JUDD MUTTERED as Cleo and he drove back to Coldwater. "Asshole."

Judd had already used every relevant curse word in his vocabulary. He was pretty sure he'd already repeated "dickhead" and "asshole" several times, but they were fitting for someone like Harmon.

Cleo was not going to go back to that twit. Or at least Judd hoped like hell she wasn't. Within seconds after Harmon had ended his call, she'd said his offer was out, that there was no way she would accept it. But Judd was worried that Cleo might cave if Lavinia continued to put on the pressure. After all, Cleo didn't have a lot of fixes available if Kace's temporary custody didn't hold.

For now, though, they were in a holding pattern because Lavinia hadn't even been at the police station when Cleo and Judd had gotten there. The cops had already released her when Harmon had told them he wouldn't be filing assault charges. The dickhead had even paid for the window repair, but he had likely only done that because he thought it would set things right with Cleo.

It wouldn't.

Even though she wasn't cussing and swearing, that wasn't a look of surrender on her face. Just the opposite. She was tired and pissed, not a good combination.

What they saw when they pulled into the driveway of the ranch likely wouldn't improve things, either. The boys were there, all of them leaning in various poses against Kace's cruiser. If there'd been a picture in the dictionary of unhappy kids, this would have been the shot. Even the kitten at Leo's feet looked as if it was sulking.

Kace was on the porch, talking to Rosy and the sitter, Lissy, but when Kace saw Cleo's car, he came toward them, reaching them before Cleo or Judd could even get out.

"Just a heads-up," Kace said. "The therapy session didn't go well when Donna brought up the possibility of them having to leave."

Cleo's shoulders dropped. "Leo didn't punch her, did he?" she asked.

"No. Just the opposite." Kace tipped his head to them. "They've been like this since then."

Judd recognized the surly signs because he'd had practice with this when he'd been a kid. Put up big ornery shields and folks were likely to give you a wide berth while you sulked and stewed about whatever the hell was bothering you. In their case, it was likely fear and the uncertainty that was driving this.

"I need to get back to the office," Kace said, checking the time. "But I can stay and try to handle this first."

Cleo shook her head. "No, I'll deal with it." She got out and eyed the trio. "Probably best to do this separately, though. I'll take Beckham first while Lissy's inside with Isaac and Leo."

Judd had a quick debate with himself. "I'll talk to Beckham. You take the other two."

Cleo opened her mouth, closed it and then repeated the process until he was about to joke that she looked like a landed fish. Judd understood her hesitation, too. She didn't want to put this kind of pressure on him, but the pressure was there. And it would be worse if he didn't do something to help.

"I'll talk to Beckham," Judd repeated, and he headed in the boys' direction before Cleo could argue.

As Judd approached, Leo broke from the pack and came toward him. Popsicle was right on his heels. "How much longer we gotta be mad?" Leo asked.

Judd was glad he didn't have a fast, easy smile because he wouldn't have wanted Leo to think he was making fun or light of this. "How much longer do you want to be mad?"

Leo made an uneasy glance back at the house. "Not long enough to miss chocolate chip cookies. Miss Rosy said when we got back, we could have cookies."

Judd couldn't fault the kid's priorities. Rosy's chocolate chip cookies were worth curtailing a bad mood even when the mood was warranted. He ruffled the boy's hair and shifted his attention to Beckham, hiking his thumb in the direction of the cabin.

"You're with me," Judd told the boy.

Beckham couldn't have made it more obvious that talking to Judd was something he didn't want to do, but with a huff, he pushed himself away from the cruiser and shuffled after Judd. At the rate he was moving, there wouldn't be a cookie crumb left since Cleo had already gotten the other two boys in the house.

If Judd had thought a chocolate chip bribe would have worked on Beckham, he would have tried it, but baked goods weren't going to fix what ailed this kid.

"Don't tell me that everything's going to be all right," Beckham snarled when he finally made it to Judd on the front porch of the cabin. "You said it yourself. Sometimes, shit can't be fixed."

"Okay. Everything isn't going to be all right. Your life is crappy, and it might continue to be that way for a while."

Beckham scowled, but his eyes glinted with suspicion.

"Hey, I'm not here to coddle you," Judd went on. "You should have figured that out by now."

"Adults are supposed to fix shit like this," Beckham growled. He jammed his hands into his jeans pockets.

"My motto in life is that sometimes shit can't be fixed. Your mom couldn't be and neither can Lavinia."

"The piss witch," Beckham amended.

Judd considered doing the adult thing and re-minding Beckham not to use profanity, but in the grand scheme of things, that just didn't seem im-portant right now. What was important, especially to Beckham, was keeping his brothers with him in a safe place. Judd got that.

Man, did he.

But he couldn't paint a rosy picture of how all this custody would play out. He couldn't lie to this boy. Maybe, though, he could let him know that he would survive whatever future shit came his way.

"Lavinia was a lot like my own mother," Judd said. "Except mine was a junkie, and instead of hit-ting me and my brothers, she just didn't take care of us. That's how we ended up in foster care."

Now Judd needed to take a deep breath, and he silently cursed the memories that just wouldn't go away. Hell, he was a grown man. Why couldn't this just go away?

"Some bad stuff happened to you, didn't it?" Beckham asked.

Judd nodded, not trusting his voice, and he cleared his throat. "Bad stuff," he confirmed and then looked at Beckham. "But I promised you I wouldn't let something that bad happen to you and your brothers. You probably don't believe that."

Beckham lifted his shoulder and leaned against the porch railing. "I figure you'll try. You're scary sometimes, but I think you'd try."

"Scary, huh?" Judd said. "I'll let you in on a secret. Sometimes, I scare myself."

Beckham gave him another of those skeptical looks.

"I'm an alcoholic," Judd went on. "That's why I didn't foster you and your brothers. I didn't feel I was the right person to help take care of you."

The boy stayed quiet a moment. "I've never seen you drink," Beckham pointed out.

"Hopefully, you won't. If I do, it means I've screwed up so bad that I might not come back from it. I've been sober a year. Not nearly enough time for me to start thinking it's no longer a problem."

"Why are you telling me this crap?" Beckham asked.

Good question, and Judd hoped this wasn't a bad answer. "Because you need to know that what's happening to you now can stay with you. If you allow it to happen, it can make you mean and bitter and make you believe that nothing will ever be good again. Don't do that. Don't feel that way. I'm your cautionary tale about that. Understand?"

"Yeah, you don't want me to turn out like you." Beckham met his gaze for a second, then glanced away. "But you're…okay."

Judd thought that might be one of the biggest compliments he'd ever gotten.

"Aunt Cleo talked to Mom about you," Beckham went on. He looked at Judd. "She never said anything about you being an alcoholic. It was all good stuff about how you looked after her when she was living here."

"I beat up some guy at school who was giving her trouble," Judd admitted. "I should probably tell you that was wrong, that I should have figured out a more peaceful way to resolve things, but the guy was a dick."

Which made Judd think of another dick—Harmon. Soon, he'd need to deal with that clown, but it wouldn't involve punching him.

Well, hopefully not.

Beckham's smile came and went fast. "I overheard Aunt Cleo tell Mom you were Judd the Stud."

Well, that was something he wished Beckham hadn't been privy to, but it made him wonder just how much Cleo had talked to Miranda about him. And why. Had it been just girl talk or had his name come up when they'd been discussing custody possibilities for the boys?

Beckham took out his hands from his pockets, but his right one wasn't empty. He was holding a folded-up letter. "It's the letter from my mom," he said.

Judd nodded. "I remember. You read it yet?"

"No." He flipped it over, studying it and running his thumb over the sealed flap on the back.

"You want me to read it to you?" Judd offered.

Beckham shook his head, dragged in a long breath and opened it. When the boy unfolded it, Judd could see that it was just one page with some handwriting and a picture.

"Mom was good at drawing," Beckham mumbled, his voice cracking. He turned the page and showed Judd the picture of the dog that his mother had sketched.

"Yeah, she was good at it. Was that your dog?" Judd asked.

"No." Beckham turned the letter back toward him. "We had one when I was a little kid, but it died. I wanted another one, but my dad died, too. Then Mom said we'd have to wait for things to settle down some before we could get one." He paused. "Things didn't settle down."

No, and it was possible that wouldn't happen for a long time.

"'Dear son,'" Beckham began, reading aloud. "'I'm not sure I can say anything to make this better so I drew you a picture instead.'" His hand was trembling now. "'When you get down and sad, look at it and remember that one day you'll have that dog you've always wanted. One day, you'll be happy again. One day, you'll forgive me for leaving you. Love and hugs, Mom.'"

Beckham stared at it, the moments dragging by. "She said goodbye." Beckham's voice was a broken sob. "My mom said goodbye."

Judd hated that he'd been right. Sometimes, shit just couldn't be fixed, so Judd pulled Beckham into his arms and let the boy cry his heart out.

CLEO GAVE ISAAC and Leo a quick hug and left them with Lissy so she could hurry across the yard to Judd's cabin. She'd talked to the boys for a half hour and expected that Judd would still be neck-deep in "conversation" with Beckham.

Judd was there, sitting on the top step, but Beckham wasn't.

One look at Judd's tired eyes and weary expression, and she knew she'd made the wrong call about leaving him to talk to Beckham.

"How did it go?" she asked, bracing herself for the answer.

He looked up at her, shrugged. "Okay enough."

Cleo frowned. "That's not an 'okay enough' look on your face."

Judd paused, stood. "Beckham read the letter from his mom. He cried."

Well, crap. Yes, she'd definitely made the wrong call about which kids to talk to. "Where is he? I need to go to him."

"He took one of the horses out for a ride. Said he wanted some time alone. He's not suicidal or anything," Judd quickly added. "After he finished crying, we talked some more, and he's dealing. He'll be okay."

If this had been anyone else, she likely wouldn't have taken that as gospel, but Judd had plenty of experience dealing with emotional and often bad family situations.

"How'd it go with Isaac and Leo?" he asked.

"We talked, but it wasn't anything like what you went through with Beckham. Isaac and Leo are at the age where cookies and hugs cure plenty of ills."

They stepped into the cabin, their attention first

going to the ice-cream carton on the floor. A reminder that they'd dropped it there before kissing
and groping their way to the bed. But the ice cream
wasn't the only sugary reminder of what had gone
on earlier. Audrey's peach pie was on the foyer table.

"It's nookie pie," Cleo commented.

Judd's eyebrow came up. "Excuse me?"

"Audrey's trying to lure you into bed."

He certainly didn't deny that, and since Judd was
a smart man, it wasn't a revelation to him. "She'd
stand a better chance of doing that with ice cream.
I'm not a pie kind of guy."

Cleo smiled because she knew that. The smile
went south in a hurry, though, when her attention
landed on his bed and the rumpled covers. She'd
never felt so guilty over an orgasm. The guilt went
up another notch when she glanced at her suitcases
that were tucked on the side of the sofa. Talk about
upending Judd's life, and now she'd invaded his
meager space. She really had to do something to
fix the problems she'd caused by trying to fix the
problem of fostering the boys.

Cleo turned toward him. "Look, I'm really sorry
about what I've put you through."

His eyebrow rose again, and this time it was coupled with a puzzled look. "Does this have to do with
sex, Harmon or the boys?"

Cleo was sure that now she was the puzzled one.
She got the references to sex and the boys. But not
the other one. "No. Why would it have anything to
do with Harmon?"

Judd shrugged and went to the kitchen. He was gathering up cleaning supplies, she realized, and she went to help him. "Well, because you might be regretting that you didn't go to Harmon first with the foster plan," he said. "Less complicated."

"No," she repeated, and she couldn't say that fast enough. "There's no way I'd consider Harmon as a foster father. I'm done with him, and I won't let him blackmail me into getting back together with him."

Sheez. Hadn't Judd been able to tell that from her reaction? Maybe not. She had been putting off a lot of gloomy vibes, and maybe he thought she'd considered Harmon an option instead of a pain in the butt.

Joining Judd on the floor, she got down on her knees, took some paper towels and started cleaning. The Rocky Road no longer looked appetizing with its marshmallow blobs floating on the chocolate puddle-goo.

"And as for the boys," Cleo went on, "I shouldn't have put that kind of pressure on you."

"What about the sex?" he asked.

Cleo knew what he meant. She hadn't forgotten his thread of conversation when he'd asked her if her apology had been for the sex. Like the other two topics—Harmon and the boys—this one wasn't so easy to explain.

"That probably put a different kind of pressure on you," she muttered.

She would have groaned at her own namby-pamby response if Judd hadn't kissed her. It wasn't just a peck, either. It was a full-blown kiss, with his tongue crossing her lips and going in for something long, deep and incredibly arousing.

Cleo lost track of time. It could have lasted thirty seconds or days, but when he pulled back from her, she had no doubts that she'd been thoroughly kissed by someone who knew exactly how to do it.

"Answer the question again now," he said. "Did you apologize for having sex with me?"

Somewhere in the back of her mind—yes, the very mind that'd just lost track of time and space— Cleo thought that maybe the kiss had been a dirty tactic to get her to start babbling. If so, it worked.

"No. I'm not sorry about that," she admitted. She huffed. "But then you finished me off. I didn't do the same for you."

He lifted his shoulder, and as if he hadn't just caused her hormones to fire on all cylinders, he went back to cleaning. "This is probably my dick talking, but I say we don't lump sex together with anything else that's going on, that we have sex just for fun—rec sex—and to heck with the consequences."

Judd paused, frowned. "Yeah, that's my dick talking."

Cleo laughed before she could stop herself. "Well, it sounded sensible to me. Of course, with the brain cells you just melted with that kiss, I'm probably not the voice of reason right now. Rec sex, huh?"

"It's the wiser way to go when it comes to me," he assured her.

He was close enough for her to dive right in and kiss him again, and he smelled great. The man scents mixed with the Rocky Road. Cleo thought that maybe this was how fetishes started. But kissing would lead to sex, and while her body was all for that, it wasn't a good idea.

"Beckham should be back soon, and I'll need to talk to him," she reminded Judd.

Other reminders came, too, and these weren't of hot kisses, sex with Judd or Rocky Road. It was that this was her life now. Trying to patch up three kids who'd had life dumped on them, and while she wanted to help them—desperately wanted that—she was beginning to have her doubts.

"I've been toying with the idea of selling the bar," she said.

Judd had just rested his head against the back of the sofa, but that got him shifting toward her again. He didn't tell her that was unnecessary or that she was jumping the gun. He just sat there, waiting her out. His silence was as effective as his kiss at pushing her babble button.

"Not having the bar would give me some flexibility," she went on. And it'd stop the stupid pranks and calls from the cops.

"What's this really about?" Judd finally said.

Cleo took a few seconds to try to boil it down. "I've always fixed things for myself. Well, except for Simon Peterson," she added when the image of him popped into her head. "You did me a huge favor and took care of that for me in high school by kicking his butt."

"That wasn't a favor. More like a civic duty." He

paused. "Is that why you asked me to have sex with you, because I stood up for you?"

"No. I asked because you were hot and I was in love with you. Not actually in-love love," she quickly added when she saw his face go blank. "Teenage-girl love." Which, of course, he wasn't going to get since he'd been a teenage boy. "Think of it like the smallest frog on Rosy's stuffed lily pad," she explained.

Okay, he really wasn't going to get it now.

"Rosy is doing her taxidermist thing on a passel of frogs," Cleo said. "One is clearly the alpha frog, and that's the adult version of being in love. He has layers, warts and stuff, and he's about to win the poker hand and catch a fly at the same time. A layered multitasker. But the little frog is just sitting there, taking it all in, and that's teen love."

He stared at her, smiled just for a moment and pushed a strand of hair off her cheek. It was a simple but intimate gesture. Not quite a little frog but close, and it was something that could lead to bigger frogs. And sex. That's why Cleo looked away and stood.

"I'd better watch for Beckham," she said. "If he comes back upset, I want to talk to him right away."

She'd also probably stay the night in the ranch house. It wasn't something the social worker would approve of, but Cleo wanted to be near the boys after the emotional day they'd had.

Judd didn't go with her to the window. He stayed there, sitting on the floor and looking like the very hot alpha cowboy that he was.

"So, before we got on the subject of frogs, teen love and Simon Peterson, you were talking about always fixing things yourself," he reminded her.

Yes, and she'd been trying to make a point. A serious one. It was hard to believe she'd gotten so far off track.

"I was leading up to where I went wrong," she explained. "I didn't do right by Miranda. I haven't fulfilled her dying wish." And if that wasn't a kick in the teeth, Cleo didn't know what was.

Judd made a sound of disagreement. "I don't see how you had a way around this. You couldn't get custody of the boys on your own."

"No, but I should have fixed it before it became a problem. If I'd thought to push Miranda sooner to do those custody papers, then maybe no one would have challenged that."

"True, but you said there wasn't time, that she died only a couple of weeks after she got sick."

"Yes, but I still should have thought of it, and because I didn't, I'm a step behind," Cleo added.

And because she'd gotten behind, her suitcase was next to Judd's sofa, Harmon was trying to blackmail her and she had to worry about where Lavinia would pop up next.

Judd's phone rang, and Cleo immediately looked in his direction to see if it was bad news. For a person who normally had a sunny disposition, she hated that "bad news" was her go-to response.

Since Judd didn't put the call on speaker, she stayed put and tried not to listen. After all, it could be Audrey with more nookie pie offers. Cleo suddenly felt as green as the stuffed frog she'd used in her teen-love metaphor.

Judd didn't say anything, but he did grunt twice, and that could have been in response to whatever the caller said. He finished the conversation with a "yeah."

"That was Kace," Judd told her when he ended the call. "Mrs. Gateman called him." His gaze locked with hers. "She'll be making another visit to the ranch, but she wanted him to know that things aren't looking good."

That took most of the air out of the room. "What does that mean?"

A muscle flickered in Judd's jaw. "Mrs. Gateman's going to recommend that the boys go to a different foster home."

CHAPTER EIGHTEEN

JUDD LOOKED AROUND his cabin and cursed. He didn't aim his profanity at anything in particular, but he should have directed it at himself. There was nothing wrong with his cabin. It was just as it'd always been.

He was as he'd always been.

So, why did the place feel empty? And why did he feel so restless?

He cursed the answers that came to mind. Well, one answer, anyway. Cleo. She wasn't there, wasn't in his bed, and while that was probably a good thing, it sure as hell didn't feel like it at the moment.

She'd stayed the night at Buck's. Again, that was a good thing. Beckham had been shaken up, and Cleo had needed to be close, to be there if the boy wanted to talk. In other words, she wasn't being as selfish as he was by wanting her in his bed.

While he was at it, he doled out some more profanity for the social worker and the system that was threatening to suck up the boys. Those kids didn't need the system, not when they had Cleo and everyone else who'd stepped up to help. Yet, the boys might lose Cleo because of an old police record and her less-than-savory occupation.

He finished his coffee when he heard the sound of the approaching school bus. It was right on time at seven forty-five. Judd went to the window and spotted not only the bus, but also Lissy, who was already there, waiting in her car for Beckham. Judd had glanced at the spreadsheet schedule and knew that she was on duty to drive Beckham to the high school.

Judd watched as Leo and Isaac came out of the house. Leo was running and carrying a backpack that seemed nearly as big as he was. There was a big grin on his face, but Isaac was less than enthusiastic and trailed along behind him. "Monday mornings suck" was written all over Isaac's mopey, tired face.

Cleo came out onto the porch, waving at them as they filed onto the bus, and as soon as it'd lumbered away, Beckham came out of the house. His expression mirrored Isaac's, and he didn't even look up from the ground as he made his way to Lissy's car. Once the sitter drove away, Cleo turned in Judd's direction, and as if she'd known all along that he was there watching, their gazes met through the window.

She was barefoot, a pair of sandals dangling from her left hand, and she was wearing a dress the color of ripe peaches. It skimmed along her body, reminding Judd that his hands itched to do some skimming. The other time they'd had sex, he hadn't gotten to do enough of that. Of course, hours might not be enough.

Her hair was loose today, those dark brown curls falling on her shoulders and haloing around her face. If she'd had a rough night with the boys, it certainly didn't show.

Man, she looked good.

Of course, she always did, and he suspected she looked even better today because of his whole "getting her in his bed" thing. He either needed to go ahead and have sex with her, or spell out the ground rules of why that couldn't happen and then stick to them. Judd suspected he knew how this would go.

Smiling at him, Cleo put on her shoes and started across the yard toward him. Judd dragged in a long breath that he was sure he would need and met her at the door. Yeah, he needed that breath all right because Cleo looked even better up close than she had from a distance.

"You look…" She stopped, chuckled. "I'm not sure I should finish that."

Wise woman, because Judd was certain he wasn't doing a good job of hiding his itching hands or the sudden urge he had to haul her into his arms. Since that wasn't a smart choice right now, Judd made sure there was at least a couple of inches between them. Still, he caught her scent. Peaches, like the dress.

"How's Beckham this morning?" he asked. It wasn't just a "making conversation" question to get his mind off Cleo and her fruity scent. He was worried about the kid.

"Okay, I guess. He showed me the letter from his mom."

Judd nearly asked if Beckham had cried again, but that might not be something the boy would want Judd to know.

"Anyway, I think he's as fine as he can be, considering." She pushed her hair from her face, her fingers brushing against the earrings that dangled from her ears.

He frowned when he saw they were armadillos. Not ones etched in precious or shiny metals. These were gray and bumpy like a real armadillo's hide. He hoped to hell that hide wasn't real.

"Oh," Cleo said when she'd noticed what he was staring at. "They were a gift from Rosy. They're replicas of Billy."

Judd would never understand Rosy's fascination with the critter, but they still managed to look as good as they possibly could on Cleo. He was pretty sure that was dick talk, though. Not an exaggeration like dick inches, but he figured the lust was playing into everything he saw and felt about her right now.

"Kace said you didn't have to be at work until eleven," she continued. "I'm on for a full shift at the bar starting at one and until closing at midnight so I'll be staying in San Antonio tonight. But for now, I was hoping you'd run an errand with me. It won't take long."

Judd tried not to react to the punch of disappointment that she wasn't there to hop into his bed and likely wouldn't be coming back to Coldwater tonight.

"What errand?" he asked.

Smiling, she caught onto his hand. "I need to see Audrey's mother."

Judd didn't have to give this any thought—he definitely didn't want to go there, and he couldn't imagine why Cleo would, either. "Uh, I was hoping to discourage more nookie pie." Along with coming up with a different name for it. There was no way to say it without feeling stupid.

"Come on." She pulled him out onto the porch. "This isn't about pie."

Yeah, but it'd be "pie once removed" since Audrey and her mom were close. Definitely not how he wanted to spend his morning off, but Cleo seemed set on this. Whatever *this* was.

"Why are we going to Mrs. Holcomb's?" He heard his grouchy tone but got in the car with Cleo, anyway.

"Lissy said Audrey's mom had a puppy. A golden-Lab mix. It's the last of a litter that she rescued, and she hasn't managed to find a home for it yet." Her smile was a little tentative now as she drove away from Buck's. "I want to get the puppy for Beckham."

It took Judd a moment to connect the dots, to remember that Beckham's mother had drawn the picture of the dog on his letter and hoped that he would get one soon. A dog was good for a kid to have, to teach responsibility and such, but Judd immediately saw one big flaw with this plan.

"You think this is a good idea, what with custody being so unsettled?" he asked. "What if the boys can't stay here?"

Her smile wasn't just tentative now. It was downright shaky. "That could be a problem," Cleo admitted. "But I think it'll give Beckham something to latch onto. Something that can give him hope and connect him with the good memories of his mother and his childhood. There were good memories," she insisted. "Unlike our childhoods."

Yeah, that was indeed something Cleo and he had in common. Instant empathy. That's why Judd felt so bad for the boys, but he still wasn't sure that getting a dog was the way to go.

"What if Beckham gets attached to the dog and then has to leave it?" Judd persisted, though it was making him feel crappy to play out these worst-case scenarios.

"I spoke to Buck, and he agreed he could fill in as dog sitter if it comes down to that." She paused, drew in a breath that was as thin and shaky as what was left of her smile. "Maybe it won't come down to that."

Yeah, maybe. But Judd was more comfortable with considering fixes if the worst case happened than he was trying to glitter this up with denial. Still, he didn't try to talk Cleo out of doing this. He'd just wait and see how this played out, and if necessary he could do a spreadsheet for taking care of the dog.

"Because of Popsicle, the puppy won't have free rein of the house," Cleo went on. "Not at first, anyway, but Rosy said if the two get along, she's okay with it. For the first night or two, though, he'll be in a crate. Maybe even the barn. That shouldn't be a problem, though, because Mrs. Holcomb has been keeping him in her barn."

So, Cleo had it all worked out. Judd still wasn't convinced, but he tamped down his doubts as Cleo pulled in front of the little house that sat just on the edge of town.

Despite the big barn in the back, he'd always thought the place looked frilly with its pale blue paint, ornate white shutters, and lattices threaded with roses and vines. Surprising since Mrs. Blanche Holcomb wasn't the frilly sort. Until recently, she'd worked at the Gray Mare Saloon that her brother owned, and in her younger days she had done bouncing duties herself whenever it'd been required.

Judd knew that firsthand.

And her *bouncing* technique wasn't exactly the standard.

When he'd been twenty-one and stupid, Judd had gone to the Gray Mare and gotten drunk enough and mean enough to get into a fight with Arnie Smelton. One that Blanche had promptly broken up and then shoved them out the door. Then, she'd flung a bottle of Pretty Polly perfume on Judd. It was a cheap, highly saturated sugary scent meant for eight-year-old girls that Blanche apparently bought in bulk and used for her bouncer duties.

It was hard to stay drunk and mean when you smelled like strawberry shortcake.

"Uh, there's not bad blood between you and Mrs. Holcomb, is there?" Cleo asked.

"No." But there was a history between them. Some good, some bad. She'd cleared the path for him to come back to Coldwater and become a deputy. That was the good. The bar incident wasn't. He was going to keep his eyes open for a Pretty Polly bottle. It'd taken him days to get that scent off him the last time, and he didn't want any repeats.

Before Cleo and Judd were even out of the car, Blanche came walking around the house from the backyard, and she peered at them from under the brim of a massive straw sun hat. The wriggling puppy she carried like a football was anything but puppy size. He was already a good thirty pounds, and judging from the size of his feet, he was going to get a whole lot bigger.

"Judd," Blanche greeted, but she didn't exactly have a friendly tone. Her eyes went from Cleo to him and kept on shifting until she reached them. "I didn't know you'd be coming."

That didn't sound friendly, either. More like some kind of unspoken judgment call. *Why are you here with another woman and not my daughter?* Judd would have preferred the nookie pie to this. But not the Pretty Polly.

"Judd came as a favor to me," Cleo said. "Thank you so much for this. Beckham's going to be over the moon." Her attention wasn't on the cool-eyed Blanche but rather the puppy. It zipped toward Cleo the moment Blanche put him on the ground.

While Cleo dropped to her knees, giggled and wrestled with the giant bundle of fur, Judd kept his attention on Blanche. Even though he still thought this puppy for Beckham was a bad idea, he didn't want Blanche reneging on it because she didn't approve of him being with Cleo.

"Audrey said you'd been busy," Blanche remarked.

Most people would have just nodded, especially since it was the truth, but Judd knew there was more judgment that went along with that comment, and he just shrugged. "No busier than usual. So, you're giving away the puppy?" he asked to change the subject.

Blanche hesitated a moment. "Yes, he's the last of a litter that got dumped at the gas station by some asshole. He's in good shape, but he's got a vet appointment this morning. Just a checkup and his final round of shots. I was about to leave for that now, but I can drop him off at Buck's afterward if that's okay."

"That's fine," Cleo said. She was sitting on the ground now with the puppy jumping up in her lap and trying to lick her face. "You can just have the vet send the bill to me."

"At Judd's," Blanche concluded. It wasn't a question.

Obviously, Blanche and he had some air-clearing to do. "Cleo, would you excuse us a second?" He didn't wait for her to answer, and using two fingers, he motioned for Blanche to follow him to the porch.

"Don't get your balls in a twist," Blanche muttered to him. "You think I'm being bitch-faced because of Audrey. Well, I'm not. Audrey can catch a man just fine without her mama running interference for her."

"Then why the attitude?" Judd asked.

Blanche managed to give him an amused look that he doubted had an ounce of genuine amusement in it. "Because of you, knot-head. There's a lot of pressure that comes with raising three kids, and yes, I know you're not actually 'raising them.'"

Judd huffed, put his hands on his hips. Hell. He hadn't wanted gossip about there being anything hinky going on with the foster stuff. "Is there some point you're trying to make?"

She stared him down while she continued. "The point is I like you, Judd. Always have, and I don't want to see you go under again because that would be a damn shame. I sure as heck don't want you showing up drunk again at the Gray Mare, or anywhere else for that matter."

Obviously, she knew about his drinking problem. Maybe because Audrey had told her, or perhaps she'd just figured it out herself. He wanted to fling off her attempt at sympathy, if that's what it was, but he really didn't want bad blood between him and an unpredictable, perfume-tossing woman who might indeed have his best interest at heart.

"You like me?" he challenged, but Judd kept it as light as he could manage.

"Hey, that bottle of Pretty Polly cost me ten bucks. You think I'd throw that on just anybody? FYI, I didn't get a drop of it on Arnie Smelton." She gave him a "playful" punch on the arm that packed a bit of a wallop. "Don't take off your floaties and get yourself in a fix again."

"Floaties?" he asked.

"Those plastic things kids put on their arms in a swimming pool so they don't drown. Keep your floaties as long as you need them, and unless you're as sure as hogs are made of bacon, don't take them off. Not for Audrey or anyone else."

By anyone else, she meant Cleo and the boys. Judd could see that side of it. It was the safe path that he'd been taking to stay sober. Safe by not putting himself out there and not taking any risks. The exact opposite of what Cleo was doing. Her entire life right now was one big risk.

He looked at her, and while she was still playing with the dog, Cleo was also keeping an eye on him, apparently making sure he wasn't getting in some kind of verbal tussle with Audrey's mom. When they got back in the car, she'd no doubt apologize for insisting that he come along for this.

"I know that look," Blanche said, drawing his attention back to her. "Do you have the hots or nots for her?"

Judd had to give her a blank stare.

"Hots is just lust," Blanche explained a moment and an eye roll later. "Nots is a whole lot more."

He was pretty sure the answer was only the hots. But maybe with a side order of nots thrown in. "Cleo's a good person," he said blandly. Which, of course, wasn't what Blanche had been asking.

The silence held between them for a few more seconds before Blanche looked at her watch and muttered some profanity. "Gotta get to the vet." She hurried off the porch and went to the puppy to scoop him up. "I'll get this little guy over to Buck's as soon as we're done," she told Cleo. "It was nice seeing both of you."

Cleo echoed something similar, and they watched Blanche drive away. "I'm sorry," Cleo told him as they got back in her car. "I shouldn't have asked you to come here."

Judd smiled. He'd been right about the apology and the speed of it. Even though there was no way Cleo would understand why he was smiling or what he was about to do, he hooked his arm around her neck, pulled her to him and kissed her. Considering they were sitting there where anyone could see them, it was a little too long and a whole lot too hot.

He pulled back to give her some air and stared at her. Not especially wise since along with her looking amazing, she now looked aroused. Still, he'd given up on being wise when it came to Cleo. Even with all his walls and missteps, he still wanted her, and that apparently wasn't going away anytime soon.

"I think this is a good thing you're doing for Beckham," Judd said as Cleo started the drive back to the ranch.

She glanced at him, studying his face as if trying to suss out if he was telling the truth. He was. Well, it was truth with an asterisk. It was a good thing even though training the puppy would be a pain in the ass. It would be many steps beyond PITA if Beckham had to leave and couldn't take the dog with him. Still, this was a shot in the dark for all the right reasons.

"So, should I ask what Blanche and you talked about?" she asked after several long moments.

"Old times." Again, that was the truth.

"You didn't talk about Audrey and her pie-making attempts?" she persisted.

"Only in a general kind of way." He wanted to groan when Cleo quit pressing because he figured she was filling in the blanks with the wrong info. Wrong info about Blanche trying to push Audrey and him to be together. "Blanche and I have a history that doesn't involve Audrey."

Judd didn't bother wishing that he hadn't brought that up, but he was sorry he hadn't worded it better because it caused Cleo to give him a funny look. Hell. Was she thinking he'd had sex with Audrey's mom? Good grief.

"Not that kind of history," he amended as fast as he could. The next part didn't come so fast, though. "She knows about my drinking problem, knows that I did some stupid things when I was younger, and she's always been fair with me."

But that didn't include tact and the kid-glove treatment. Still, fair was fine with him and better than he got from a lot of people.

"She was on the city council when Kace approached them about hiring me," Judd went on. "Technically, he didn't need their permission, but since I'm his brother, he didn't want to be accused of nepotism. Blanche stood up for me, squelching any arguments that the other council members had. She fought to make sure I got the job."

Cleo stayed quiet, maybe processing that, when she pulled to a stop in front of his cabin. "I hate not to give her the benefit of the doubt, but she could have wanted you back here for her daughter. Maybe that played into it. Even if Blanche had reservations about you, she knows that Audrey cares for you, and she might have wanted to see her daughter happy."

Since that was as much conversation as he wanted to have about Audrey and her mother, Judd went in for another kiss. He caught her little sound of surprise with his mouth. Ditto for her sound of pleasure that followed.

Cleo kissed like the way she did everything else in life. No floaties for her. She just slipped right into that kiss, adding a nice touch of her own when she nipped his bottom lip with her teeth.

"Better than peach pie," he drawled.

"You don't like pie," she pointed out.

"Better than Rocky Road," he amended.

She made a sound as if impressed and pleased. "Since that's the second time in the past fifteen minutes that you've kissed me and now you're flattering me with chocolate comparisons, I'm detecting something." She slid her hand over the front of his jeans. "Yep, it's something all right."

His eyes crossed, and he went hard as steel. Maybe he wasn't a "no floaties" kind of guy, but that little hand maneuver of hers had him ditching any concerns or doubts he had about diving in headfirst with Cleo.

"If you want to get lucky, and I'm reasonably sure you do, then we'll have to make it inside your cabin without someone seeing us," she said. "Think we can manage that?"

Probably not. He figured Rosy or Buck had noticed them drive up, but Judd pushed aside that thought, kissed Cleo again so it'd keep the heat simmering and threw open the car door. Hurrying with a hard-on wasn't easy, but he managed it. He caught onto Cleo's hand, and the moment they reached his front door, he practically pushed her in.

Cleo did some pushing of her own. Proving that she, too, had some immediate lust issues that needed tending. She backed him against the door, and her mouth took his. It was another scalding kiss that didn't stay a single shot. She went after his neck all the while her breasts pressed against his chest.

Judd figured they were in for some body-hardening foreplay, but Cleo proved him wrong about that. Breaking the neck kiss, she caught onto a handful of his shirt, locked the door and dragged him across the room.

"This time you're getting off," she insisted.

Judd just held up his hands. Sex with Cleo might turn out to be a stupid mistake, but he wasn't a stupid man. He wanted off. He especially wanted off with her.

Cleo shoved him back onto the bed. Clearly a woman on a mission because she dragged her dress off over her head and sent it flying. Her underwear was lacy and tiny, just the way he liked it. Of course, as hard as he was right now, he would have approved of flannel long johns as long as he could get them off her.

He got these off her with little effort.

Cleo just let him have his way with the underwear removal because she continued her own mission by unbuttoning his shirt. She left it on him, though, and went after his jeans.

"This time, I'm not going to be gentle with you," she insisted. Cleo said it like some kind of warning instead of the really good suggestion that it was, and she unzipped him.

"No floaties," he mumbled.

She gave him only a split-second confused look that he hoped hadn't killed the mood. It didn't. Cleo went after his mouth again.

Sensing that her good suggestion was going to move even faster, Judd fished out a condom, got it on and then flipped her so that he was on top of her. Cleo flipped, too, somehow managing to put him on his back. In the same motion, she pinned his hands to the bed.

And she took him inside her.

Apparently, her previous orgasm had only whetted her appetite for him because her hips pistoned, pumping him, driving herself against him until he felt the new climax ripple through her. Even then, she didn't stop moving.

Cleo had been right about two things. He got off, and this time she wasn't gentle.

CHAPTER NINETEEN

That thing you told me about—well, it wasn't really a secret, was it?

Let's just do this sex tape. No one will ever see It, promise.

Your ass is a lot bigger than my other girl-friend's.

"THAT LAST ONE started a fight," Tiny pointed out to Cleo as she was reading it.

Cleo was betting it had, but she turned her attention away from the Stupid Sh*t Men Say board to Tiny, who was behind the bar shelving some liquor bottles.

"A bad fight?" she asked.

"Naw, the lady just threw her Squirrelly Spider at the guy, and he left."

Cleo hoped that was the name of a new cocktail and not an actual critter, but even if it had been, at least the fight hadn't been rowdy enough that the cops were called. It was somewhat depressing that

the lack of police involvement was now her bench-
mark for what she considered a good night.

Well, lack of police involvement that didn't include Judd, that is.

He had certainly given her a good morning. Her
body was still tingling from the climax he'd given
her just hours earlier. Like a buzz that no cocktail
could have ever managed. The buzz came with incredible memories, too, of his naked body.

"Your ass is a lot better than my last boyfriend's"—she could have written the words on the
Stupid Sh*t Women Say board, but it wouldn't have
been shit. It was the truth.

She wanted to be in Judd's bed again, wanted to
keep playing with fire, wanted to believe that nothing could go wrong with this. Which made her a
candidate for even more entries on the board.

It's just sex.

No chance of a broken heart.

But, of course, there was a chance of that. *Her*
broken heart. Judd would probably never let himself
take a leap and fall that hard, but Cleo could already
feel herself leaping and falling.

Pushing that aside, Cleo went to her office and
was surprised to see Daisy there at her desk. "I came
up for an hour or so to catch up on things," Daisy
explained. "Just processed the final payment for that
graduation party we have booked..."

Daisy stopped and practically did a double take when she lifted her head and looked at Cleo. A slow smile curved her lips. "You had sex with Judd."

Cleo glanced down at her dress to make sure it wasn't inside out or there wasn't stray underwear or a condom wrapper clinging to it.

Nope.

No signs of sex, and she'd already made sure there weren't any visible hickeys, either. However, there was one on top of her left breast, and she checked now to be certain that it wasn't showing. It wasn't unless Daisy purposely looked past the scooped neckline, which she couldn't have done since she was sitting down.

"How'd you know I had sex?" Cleo asked. "Please don't tell me I'm glowing or anything." Though maybe tingling could produce a glow.

Daisy shrugged. "No glow. I just knew there'd be no way you could hold out against Judd the Stud." She paused, stared at Cleo. "Did something go wrong?"

"Not with the sex," Cleo assured her, but she sighed when she looked at the stack of folders, each of which would hold contracts that needed to be reviewed, invoices and such. She knew there'd be plenty more on her computer. "When I first bought the bar, the paperwork felt more like paper than work," she added in a mumble.

With her gaze still fixed on Cleo, Daisy slowly got to her feet. "What happened? What's wrong?"

Cleo wished there was an easy answer to that.

Maybe it was the fatigue just below the tingle or the fact that she'd been going nonstop in dealing with problems with both the boys and the bar. Heck, maybe it was the sex, and her body was shoving another round with Judd to the top of the list of things it wanted. But she knew bone-deep that it was more than that.

"This place just doesn't feel as important to me as it once did," Cleo admitted, and then she silently cursed when she saw the alarm that put on Daisy's face. "I'm not sure it's what I want."

Daisy came out from the desk, taking hold of Cleo's arms. Daisy didn't say anything, didn't press for her to launch into a blathering explanation of something she couldn't explain. She just waited Cleo out.

"I'm sorry," Cleo finally said. "I talked you into this arrangement, and you've been pouring yourself into making the bar a success."

She was disgusted with herself when she felt the tears sting her eyes. Talk about overreacting, and it wasn't an overreaction she cared to have. Cleo waved off her comment, squared her shoulders and stepped back from Daisy.

"Everything's fine," Cleo assured her. "I'll be fine."

Cleo probably would have added a whole bunch more to that, perhaps even some semi-untrue reassurances, but she heard the footsteps in the hall. For some reason her brain went into fantasy mode, and she imagined Judd striding in to rid her of all doubts and give her another orgasm or two. But it wasn't Judd.

"Cleo?" someone called out.

"Harmon," Cleo groaned, and she said it in a tone that suggested she had a persistent toenail fungus. Definitely nowhere near her fantasy realm.

"You want me to kick his ass, Cleo?" Tiny called out.

She stepped into the hall to tell Tiny no and to tell Harmon to get lost, but she hesitated for a moment when she saw the objects Harmon was holding. At first she thought it was some kind of club in his right hand, but when he held it up, she realized it was a plastic cow leg.

"Someone left this on my doorstep this morning." His tone wasn't exactly pleasant or welcoming, either. She couldn't blame him. The leg was splotched with red gelatin. "And this," he added when he lifted his other hand.

Even after carefully looking at it, Cleo had no idea what it was. Potatoes, maybe?

"Bull balls," Daisy said, peering over Cleo's shoulder. "Tiny said when they collected all the parts that they were missing two sets of balls."

Good grief. She didn't want to know why Lavinia had kept those. Or where the other set of them would turn up. Cleo didn't like to toss *ewww*'s around, but this situation seemed to call for it.

Tiny must have sensed a butt kicking wouldn't be required because he headed back toward the bar.

"I took pictures, and I'm letting the cops know,"

Harmon went on, anger in his voice now. "My agreement with Lavinia was that I wouldn't press charges if she left me, you and the boys alone. This is obviously harassment. Maybe even a threat."

He waited as if he expected Cleo to give him a rousing reply of agreement, but the best she could muster up was a nod. "Handle it as you see fit," she added when he just stared at her.

"I thought you'd be upset. I thought you'd be on my side," he complained.

Mentally repeating what she'd said earlier about the bar, this just no longer seemed important to her, and it definitely wasn't what she wanted, Cleo steeled herself and put on a metaphorical pair of those balls so she could put an end to this once and for all.

"Harmon, I'm sorry you're going through this feud with Lavinia, but I don't want to see you."

He tucked the cow leg under his arm, nodded and then shook his head. "I know. I really blew things the last time we spoke and I offered to take custody of the boys. You probably thought I was saying that so you'd get back together with me."

"Yes, actually, I did think that."

Another nod. "I just wasn't ready to say goodbye. I'm still not, Cleo. The signs—"

"Don't matter," she interrupted. She might not be certain of what she wanted, but Cleo was crystal clear about what she didn't want, and Harmon was in that "didn't" column.

"Harmon, it's over," she said, looking him directly in the eye. "And as for Lavinia, the best way to get her off your scent is to quit having any kind of connection with me. No more calls, visits or signs."

"But I wanted to help you keep Lavinia away from Miranda's sons," Harmon protested.

She heard what he said over the ringing of her phone, and the moment Cleo saw Judd's name on the screen, she knew it was a call she had to take.

"Goodbye, Harmon," she said, hitting the answer button as she stepped back into her office. "Hello, Judd."

She was about to hold her breath and brace herself for whatever bad news he was about to give her, but she could have sworn she heard Judd laugh.

"Is everything okay?" she asked.

"Fine. I'm sending you a picture. A selfie," he added, and yes, it was definitely a laugh.

A horrible thought popped into her head, and she hoped Judd hadn't been drinking. Cleo was about to jump to so many bad conclusions when her phone dinged with the photo. Not the image of a drunk man. It was an off-centered, somewhat blurry shot of Judd, Isaac, Leo, Beckham and the puppy.

"I picked up the boys from school. It's their lunch break so they're not missing any classes," Judd explained. "I knew you'd be late getting back so I thought you'd like to see their reaction when they met the dog."

Cleo saw it all right. She saw four very happy guys and a puppy who'd leaped up to lick Beckham's face just as the group selfie had been snapped. Leo's head was thrown back in laughter, and Isaac was grinning. Judd was the only one who was looking at the camera, probably because he'd been the one taking the picture, but there was a grin on his face, too.

"Thanks, Aunt Cleo," Beckham called out. The other boys echoed the same.

"Beckham's naming him Mango," Judd told her. "More details to follow, but I gotta go. I need to get them to school so I can get back to work. Later."

Even though Judd ended the call, Cleo just stood there, her gaze nailed to the photo that was still on her screen.

Finally, she had an answer to her question.

That was what she wanted.

EVEN THOUGH JUDD wasn't sure what was going on, he didn't have to guess that this was *not* something he wanted. He was tired all the way to his bones and would have given a week's pay just to crash in bed.

But bed and crashing were clearly going to have to wait.

Mercy, his sponsor, was leaning against the side of his truck in the parking lot of the police station. She was wearing a nun's habit. Not an understated outfit, either, but one with a hat the size of a truck tire. Had it been sunny, she could have provided shade for a family of five under that brim.

Judd quickly shifted his attention from the clothes to the woman. She was crying. Correction: Mercy was sobbing with wet, loud wails. Despite the bulky outfit, Judd could see her chest heaving beneath the black fabric.

It was going on midnight, but there were enough streetlights for him to see her and vice versa. Which meant there was enough light for someone else to have seen her, too. There'd be gossip, but he didn't give a rat's ass about that now. Mercy wasn't much of a crier so something bad must have happened for her to be like this and have come to Coldwater.

She looked at him, paused only a second and then went back to wailing again. "Pudge broke up with me," she said, her voice hiccuping.

Judd muttered more profanity as he walked toward her. He'd never met Pudge but knew from the way Mercy had talked about him, she cared a lot about the guy. Judd also recalled her saying that Pudge was a former wrestler who was hung like a horse with jackhammer moves. But the thousand-pound gorilla in this mix was that Mercy had been in love with the guy.

Mercy continued to sob. "I really thought he was the one."

Because he didn't know what else to do, Judd went closer and put his arm around her. His Stetson collided with her nun's hat. "I'm sorry. Want me to kick his ass for you?" It wasn't a particularly good or adult solution, but it seemed to be his go-to response. Probably not wise in this case, though, because of Pudge's former profession.

Her head whipped up as if she was considering that. "No," she said on a heavy sigh. "Maybe," she amended. "No," Mercy concluded several moments later. "He broke up with me while we were at the costume party at his friend's apartment in San Antonio."

Well, that explained the outfit, though he'd never actually believed that she would have checked into a nunnery.

"Pudge hooked up with a fairy princess," Mercy went on. "Perky little boobs, tight ass." Her tone wasn't so sobby right now and had taken on a jealous edge. He hoped Mercy didn't want him to beat up the fairy princess instead of Pudge. He'd have to draw the line on that.

"You want to go somewhere so we can talk about it?" he asked.

"No." She didn't hesitate, either. "I have Wild Turkey in here." She patted the area between her huge breasts.

Since he'd been listening carefully, he noted that she hadn't said "a" wild turkey, which meant she was talking about bourbon. The tension in his gut popped like a rubber band.

"Why do you have liquor in your bra?" Judd asked.

"It's not the actual liquor." The crying picked up again, and when she wiped the back of her nose with her hand, Judd took out his handkerchief and gave it to her. "It's a picture that I took. It was in the window of a liquor store."

She reached down into the habit and came out

with her phone. There was indeed a picture of a bottle of Wild Turkey.

Judd sighed. "Why'd you get that close to a liquor store?"

"Well, I didn't start there, and I didn't go in. It was on the way between the party and where I was parked. Before I took the picture, I tried to stop myself. I started saying my safe word."

"Bat-shit," he said, causing her to nod.

"When that didn't work, I used your safe word," she went on, "and then I took out my distraction. I always carry it in my purse."

"A strap-on dildo," Judd said. A disturbingly large hot-pink one with vibrating balls.

Another nod from Mercy. "FYI, it's not a good idea to be pacing in front of a liquor store while dressed as a nun, carrying a dildo and muttering 'bat-shit' and 'dick inches.'"

"Yeah, I could see that alarming somebody." His grip tightened on her. "You didn't get arrested, did you?"

"No." She huffed, and he got a whiff of her breath. No booze on it, thank God. "But nothing was working so I took the picture of the Wild Turkey." She made it sound as if it'd been a big-assed failure instead of just a little backslide. "Then I got in my car and came here."

Judd didn't want to get on her for the things she'd done right—not going into the liquor store and especially not drinking. Actually, that was what mattered most, but Mercy hadn't taken her own advice—advice that had worked for him since she'd been his sponsor. And that's what he wanted to get on her about.

"You should have called me when you started spiraling down," Judd reminded her. "You should have especially called me when the safe words and distraction didn't help."

She bobbed her head in a nod. "I considered it, but I know how much you've got weighing on you."

"Well, hell." Silently, he belted out some harder profanity. Judd didn't want Mercy thinking like that. "What's weighing on me isn't enough for you to hold off calling me when you need it."

"You're not my sponsor," she mumbled, but like his reminder, there was no bite in it. "I didn't call him because my actual sponsor's having business troubles. I didn't want to put this on him and having him get down."

"So, you thought of everyone but yourself." Now, there was a bite, and he thumped her on the arm. Hard enough to get her attention. "Don't do that again. Call me and we'll talk it through."

Mercy seemed to consider that, but then she shook her head. "I shouldn't have come here. You've been working all day, and now you probably have to get home to check on those kids, huh?"

"No. My brother Callen and his wife are on kid duty."

Which meant he didn't have anything to worry about. Well, not immediately, anyway. There was another visit from the social worker that was coming up in a few days, and that was weighing on him. For the moment, though, what troubled him most was Mercy.

"Do you remember what you always tell me?" he asked.

Her forehead bunched up, and she made another effort to wipe away her tears. "That you need a nubile young woman who'll lick you in places you've never been licked?"

Judd frowned. Well, she had indeed told him that. "I was thinking something more specific to what's happening right now." And since he didn't want her to keep tossing things around, he spelled it out for her. "When you need help, ask for it. Help is my middle name."

Her mouth quivered a little. "That's a stupid middle name. Say, what did the toilet say to the septic tank?" she asked, moving right into one of her really bad jokes.

"You're full of shit?" Judd said.

Despite his getting the punch line, Mercy laughed like a loon, and it did him good to hear it. Still, Judd didn't think it was all smoothed over just yet.

"You want to come to my place for a while?" he asked.

She looked up at him, frowned. "A hot guy finally asks me to his place. I've got a dildo, some cherry-flavored condoms and I gotta say no. I'm not the woman who should be licking you, cowboy."

Even though he knew she'd meant that as a continuation of the joke, Judd immediately thought of

Cleo and some licking that had gone on just that morning. An image of her flashed through his head. Of Cleo naked. And since that wouldn't help his focus on this conversation, he pushed it aside.

Judd tapped the picture of the Wild Turkey on her phone screen. "You want to delete this, or should I?"

"I'll do it." She hit the delete button and groaned when the next photo automatically popped up. "Pudge," she snarled.

Mercy hit the button again but not before Judd got a glimpse of the guy. Yeah, he was thankful Mercy hadn't asked him to attempt a butt whipping on him. Pudge looked like a cyborg wrestler.

Judd nearly suggested that she put a picture of her distraction on her phone, but since a strap-on probably wasn't the best image to carry around for possible viewing by others, he took out his own cell and showed her the group selfie he'd taken with the boys and the puppy.

Mercy leaned in for a close look. "Well, now that's worth at least a dozen or so words." But she didn't say what words those were.

Judd studied it, too, and just seeing it again brought back that moment. Of course, that's what pictures did. They brought back the good and the bad. In this case, it was both. The boys were so damn happy. Ditto for the puppy. And there'd been a smile on Judd's face, too, but now, like then, he was still tamping down the concerns.

"There's a lot of uncertainty about their future," Judd muttered.

Mercy adjusted her leaning so that she was staring at him. "Well, duh. Only a shit for brains would think the future was *certain.*"

Judd frowned at what were surprisingly wise words. He opened his mouth to try to justify his comment by using a different angle. Something along the lines that there were a lot more obstacles for these kids than the norm, but that only made Mercy's words even truer.

Mercy pushed herself away from his truck and patted his back. "You know, Judd, maybe it's time you pulled some tags off mattresses."

Whenever he had a conversation with Mercy, there were also some blank looks involved. Like now. "Excuse me?"

"Those tags always say don't remove them, but that's poo-poo nonsense. I mean, why not rip it right off? But people don't because the tag says not to. Well, I'm telling you to start pulling and see what happens."

He tried to work his way through that metaphor, but his brain was just too tired to figure it out. "You want me to drive you home?" he asked.

"No. I'm fine, really. All cried out and everything." She thumped his arm as he'd done to her, and in the same motion, she snapped a picture of them. "There. Now that's a screen saver if I ever saw one."

She held out the photo for him to see. Her nun's hat took up 90 percent of the shot, but he could still see Mercy's bright smile. And his puzzled expression. For them, that was the norm so he supposed it did indeed make it a keeper.

"Text me when you get home," he instructed, "and call me if and when you get the urge to stroll in front of any more liquor stores or take that strap-on out of your purse."

"Words of wisdom," she declared, tapping her heart with her hand in an exaggerated patter. "I will call you. Promise." Mercy moved in for a kiss on the cheek, but she damn near put out his eye with her hat.

Blinking hard and rubbing his eye, Judd watched as Mercy went to her car. "Hey, Judd," she called out. "What do you call a blubbering sister? A cri*sis*," she answered, without waiting for him to guess. She cackled with laughter.

Mercy's god-awful joke and her laugh eased some of the tension inside him. Apparently, when Mercy had a personal emotional crisis, crying it out and conversation worked. He'd have to remember that.

Judd waited until she was in her car and had driven away before he headed home. Another wave of fatigue hit him hard, a reminder that he hadn't been sleeping well, followed by a reminder that he'd agreed to take a morning shift for one of the other deputies who had a doctor's appointment. Falling face-first on the bed was a strong possibility.

Or not.

He quickly changed his mind about sleep when he stepped into his cabin and spotted Cleo. She was sitting up in his bed. And she was naked. Or at least she was from the waist up because the sheet she was holding in front of her had dipped down on one side to reveal her breasts. Apparently, Cleo's nipple was a cure for exhaustion.

"Want to get lucky tonight?" she asked.

She smiled, and Judd quickly realized he was smiling, too. Now, here was a mattress tag that he wouldn't mind pulling.

CHAPTER TWENTY

PULLING THE PILLOW over her head, Cleo slapped at the buzzing sound to make it stop. She froze when her hand didn't come in contact with a fly or some other critter, but rather warm, hard flesh.

That got her awake.

Since she wasn't accustomed to waking up in bed with anyone, it took her a moment to piece everything together. Judd was next to her. He was on his stomach and was also swatting at the buzzing sound, which she also figured out. It was the alarm on his phone.

Cleo reached across him, turned it off and started to give him a shake to get him awake. One look at him, though, and she decided on something better.

He was naked, only his butt and legs covered by the bedsheet. She remedied that by sliding it off him and biting his right butt cheek. It was way more effective than an alarm because he scrambled around, his hand going to his backside while his cop's eyes fired over the room. Well, they fired until they landed on her.

She smiled.

He blinked, stared at her. "Did you bite my ass?"

"I did." Now, she moved in for a kiss, and what the heck—she made it French. A nice way to start the morning and clear out the sleep from her head. Of course, the sleep quickly got replaced by a sizable dose of lust.

"Why do men usually wake up with these?" she asked, sliding her hand over his erection.

He grunted, a manly sound of pleasure to compliment the manly way his body shifted to pull her to him. "We have an eternal hope that we'll get lucky and want to be prepared if that lucky situation arises."

She settled side by side against him, trapping that morning wood between them. Since it was there, she bit his neck, too.

His next grunt was even huskier, and Judd slid his hand into her hair, cupping the back of her head to ease her in for a long, slow kiss. There was no urgency in it, considering he was obviously primed and ready to go.

Cleo went in the long, slow mode, too, figuring that they had at least a half hour before he had to rush out for work. Since Lissy would be getting the boys off to school, she had some time, too.

"You dreamed about mattress tags," she said while she nibbled her way from his neck to his chest. That required some sliding down the bed, and Cleo made sure she touched as much of him as possible on her journey.

"Really?" he asked.

"Yes, you talk in your sleep."

She definitely hadn't meant for that to alarm him, but Judd leaned over to the nightstand and checked his phone. Cleo felt him relax as fast as the tension had come. "Just making sure my sponsor didn't text or call when I was asleep. She's going through sort of a rough time. She texted me last night when she got home and said she was feeling better, but her mood could have changed between now and then."

Cleo stopped, and she lifted her head to meet his gaze. The heat was stirring and rising inside her, but he so seldom mentioned AA or his sponsor that she gave him a moment to add something. He only gave her a lazy smile and lowered her head back to his chest.

"You should invite your sponsor over here," Cleo said. Going with her morning theme, she bit his chest, licked it and then blew her breath over it. Her version of a non-BJ BJ.

"Uh, Mercy isn't exactly the inviting-over sort."

Intrigued, she lifted her head again. "Some people say that about me, but she might enjoy meeting the boys, Buck and Rosy. I'd certainly enjoy meeting her."

When he didn't say anything, she left it at that, but Cleo made a mental note to remind him that they were both off on Saturday. No pressure. However, Judd was obviously concerned about the woman or else he wouldn't have checked his phone for messages.

"You're a good person," he finally said.

She smiled. "You're a good person, too."

Judd didn't give her a chance to add more to that because he hauled her back up his body and flipped Cleo onto her back. Maybe it was momentum or merely the slick move on his part, but he landed on top of her with his erection pressing right in the V of her thighs.

Oh, yes. Now there was some urgency.

Apparently, the urgency was mutual because he slid right into her, one long, hard, amazing stroke that caused her toes to curl. It was possible Judd's toes curled, too, because he cursed, but if so, it was not the right kind of curling.

Still cursing, he pulled back and started fumbling around the nightstand again. Cleo wanted no part in him moving away from her, and she was just heated up enough that it took her a moment to realize what he was doing.

Putting on a condom.

Well, at least one of them could think smart at this hour of the morning. And multitask. He tore off the wrapper and moved straight back into a sizzling kiss while he got on the condom.

"Show me just how good you are," Cleo insisted.

And much to her delight, Judd did.

CLEO WALKED INTO smelly chaos that looked more like a bizarre crime scene than the living room at Buck's. The floor and all the furniture were littered with shredded toilet paper, and there was a puddle of red liquid and some disturbing-looking green stuff.

The TP was probably Popsicle's doing. The kitten loved tearing it up. The red liquid appeared to be spilled juice. Likely a Leo accident. But she didn't have a clue who or what was responsible for the green and wasn't even sure what it was.

She felt her stomach turn a little when she spotted a frog leg and what was left of the lily pad that had once been part of Rosy's taxidermic masterpiece. Crap on a Christmas cracker. The motion mechanism was still working, sort of, because the bottom part of the bullfrog was jigging his headless butt back and forth.

The social worker shouldn't see something like this. It probably wouldn't cause Kace to lose custody on the spot, but it certainly wouldn't leave a good impression, either.

That sent some panic through her that she tried to tamp down. Kace was depending on her to make this right, and the making right would have to happen without him since he was in the ER. Cleo hadn't gotten the whole story, but according to Kace's quick phone call, he needed stitches because of a poodle and some mascara. At least Cleo thought he'd said mascara, but she'd probably misunderstood him.

Other than making sure that Kace was okay—which he claimed he was—the only other thing Cleo had gotten from Kace's call was that Judd had gotten tied up with an incident at the nursing home. No details on that one. But Kace had asked her to make sure the house and the boys were as cleaned up as they could be, that he'd be there as soon as he could make it.

Cleo hadn't bothered trying to get in touch with anyone else on the spreadsheet schedule. Even if the social worker had warned her about living at the house, the boys were hers, and that meant this problem was, too. A problem Cleo would have to handle delicately since she'd need to let Mrs. Gateman know that she was merely filling in for Kace. Of course, if Kace showed up in time, it'd be a moot point. The house and boys would be cleaned and ready, and Cleo could step back and let him do what he'd agreed to do on paper.

Kace probably hadn't thought that "paper agreement" would eat up this much of his time.

That's why Cleo had to do whatever she could do. After getting Kace's call, Cleo had immediately gotten Tiny to cover for her at the bar, had jumped in her car and had driven back to Coldwater.

However, Cleo hadn't expected to face this.

Realizing that the TP and frog massacre weren't the only issues, Cleo lifted her head and sniffed, but her sniffing didn't have to be too deep for her to detect something she hadn't wanted to smell. Burned chocolate with the underlying aroma of puppy pee.

The pee wasn't a surprise. Rosy and Buck had insisted that the puppy stay inside and had even installed a doggie door for him. The little guy had gotten the hang of the door but he'd had more accidents than hits. No one seemed to mind, especially Beckham, who'd taken to the puppy just as Cleo had hoped. She just wished Mango had taken to potty training today of all days.

She checked the time. Almost four. The traffic coming out of San Antonio had been heavy due to road construction so it'd taken her longer than expected to get back from the bar. Still, she should have time to clean up and get ready for Mrs. Gateman's visit in an hour.

Except it wasn't just a visit.

It was an inspection. Mrs. Gateman was going to come in here and likely nitpick, and anything she saw that she didn't like would go in her dreaded report. That included the social worker still believing that Cleo lived there.

Picking up some of the toilet paper along the way, Cleo made her way to the kitchen, expecting to find Rosy, Lissy and the boys. Maybe Buck. But it was empty, and she soon saw the source of the bad smell. There were either hockey pucks or severely burned cookies on a baking sheet. Another frog leg sat ominously in front of the still-warm oven.

Good God, what had gone on here?

Her first thought was there'd been some kind of medical emergency, and everyone had had to rush to the hospital. Maybe because of the cancer treatments Buck had recently completed. Or perhaps one of the boys had gotten hurt, which would have caused a hospital rush, too.

That sent her running upstairs. No one. And her heart was all the way to her kneecaps when she finally heard something. Leo yelling. That caused her to sprint back downstairs. She hurdled over the debris and raced out the back door, bracing herself to see blood or something.

And what Cleo saw was a woman.

A large-breasted woman in a pink leather jumpsuit. Her red hair pointed up like a traffic cone. She wasn't alone. She was sitting in a chair beneath the shade tree sipping what appeared to be lemonade. Rosy was seated next to her.

Cleo glanced around, and the relief flooded through her when she soon spotted Mango chasing Leo and Popsicle by the barn. Buck, Beckham and Isaac were at the corral fence, and they were watching Nico ride a horse and put it through some fancy steps and moves. So, no medical emergency. No trips to the hospital. However, the boys did look a little on the grimy side, which meant they could all do with baths.

Other than the woman, there was nothing out of the ordinary. Nothing to explain the mess in the house.

The woman got to her feet when Cleo approached, and she spoke before Cleo could say anything. "Why did the golfer buy a single doughnut?" she immediately asked. "Because he wanted a hole in one." She hooted with laughter and slapped herself on her thigh.

"Cleo," Rosy said, standing as well. "You're home." Her "discussing the weather" tone made it seem as if there was nothing to be the least bit concerned about. Clearly, Rosy hadn't noticed the semi-panicked way Cleo had come rushing into the yard. "This is Mercy Marlow…a friend of Judd's."

Cleo tamped down the adrenaline that was still zinging through her and stared at the woman. Mercy wasn't just a friend. This was Judd's sponsor.

"Good to meet ya," Mercy greeted. "Judd said you wanted to invite me over this weekend, but my schedule's tight so I decided to drop by."

Normally, Cleo would have been pleased about that, especially since Judd had mentioned that the woman was going through a tough time, but this wasn't the best day for a visit.

"It's great to meet you, too," Cleo said, shaking Mercy's hand, and then she practically snapped toward Rosy. "Mrs. Gateman will be here in about forty-five minutes or so."

Rosy was smiling before Cleo reminded her of that, and she continued to smile afterward. "Yes. Everything is ready for her. Well, except for the cookies. Mercy and I got to talking, and I burned the darn things, but I'll clean up before she gets here. Lissy was going to do it, but then her mom called and asked her to pick up some meds."

So, Rosy didn't know about the other mess, and Cleo didn't get to tell her because Mercy continued where Rosy had left off.

"Rosy and I hit it off," Mercy explained. "So much to talk about, what with you and Judd."

Cleo had already opened her mouth but closed it a moment to figure out how to respond to that. She decided not to even address it.

"Uh, there's a problem with the frog family." Cleo added another "uh," then added, "It's been torn to bits."

Now Rosy finally quit smiling. "Oh, dear," she said after a long pause and started for the house.

"Please excuse us," Cleo said to Mercy, and because she didn't know how long it would take to deal with the mess, she called out to the boys. "Beckham, Isaac and Leo, make sure you're cleaned up for Mrs. Gateman's visit."

That got expected responses, mainly grumbles and complaints, because they obviously didn't want to end their fun time with Nico.

"Mango must have gotten in when we weren't looking," Rosy mumbled as she hurried to the house. "But I'm sure it's no big deal. I'll be able to fix it..." Her words trailed off after she opened the kitchen door and looked inside. Then, there was a string of "oh, dears."

"I'm so sorry," Cleo said, knowing it wouldn't help. Rosy had likely put hours of work into the bizarre project. Now, it made even a more bizarre mess that would probably make Rosy sad.

Cleo grabbed several plastic grocery bags, some paper towels and cleaner. "I'll collect the frog parts for you," she told Rosy. "And as soon as the social worker leaves, I'll help you put it back together." Of course, that might take a couple of years, but Cleo kept that to herself.

Since the juice and a pee puddle were near a couple of frog parts, Cleo tackled all of those at once.

She glanced up when she heard an odd sound and realized it was coming from Mercy. The woman's jumpsuit gave a slippery squeak whenever she bent down to pick up the debris. Later, she would owe Mercy a huge thanks.

The boys came running in with Nico and Mango right behind them. Talking all at once, they headed up the stairs, where Cleo hoped they'd clean up to make themselves presentable. She didn't want to beat them over the heads with how important this visit was. No. They were already feeling the pressure.

Once they had collected the frog parts, Cleo and Mercy followed Rosy into the kitchen, where they dumped the pieces on the kitchen table. Cleo checked her watch. Still a half hour. Plenty of time—

Someone knocked on the front door, cutting off Cleo's assurance of the "plenty" thought. She considered asking Rosy to answer the door while she hurried to Judd's to freshen up, but Rosy was already caught up in the frog repair. Sighing, Cleo went to the door and opened it. Not Mrs. Gateman.

Audrey.

Cleo felt a moment of relief, followed by anything but relief when Audrey blurted out, "Can we talk?"

"It's not a good time. The social worker is due soon."

Audrey nodded. "I won't keep you." She moved as if to step in, but she stopped when her attention landed on Mercy and Rosy. "I only need a minute,"

Audrey added, and she motioned for Cleo to come out on the porch with her.

Great. Cleo debated her options and decided it would be better and maybe faster to give Audrey that "minute." It might take longer than that just to put off the woman, and it was best to go ahead and get this cleared up.

"Is this about the boys?" Cleo asked as she closed the front door behind her. "Or Judd?"

Audrey blinked as if surprised that Cleo had been so direct. "Both. I've been worried about Judd, about the stress he's under because of the boys."

"Have you talked to Judd about that?" Cleo winced when she heard her "mean girl" tone. That wasn't like her, especially since Audrey almost certainly had Judd's best interest at heart.

"I've tried to talk to him," Audrey answered, "but it's as if he's shut down."

Cleo hadn't seen any signs of that. Just the opposite, and she remembered the photo Judd had taken with the puppy and the boys. And the way he'd looked earlier that week, when they'd had morning sex.

That was an especially nice memory.

But Cleo also remembered something else. Maybe Audrey was the safe choice for Judd. Safe, and someone who could help make sure Judd didn't hit a stress level so high that he turned back to drinking. It was something she had to consider. But not now.

Since the minutes were ticking away, Cleo decided it was time to wrap up this conversation. "Are you asking me to try to steer Judd toward you?" Cleo asked, and she prepared herself to hear some hemming, possibly some hawing from Audrey.

But there wasn't any. "No." Audrey drew in a long breath. "I'm here to give you an option if you end up staying here with the boys."

That got Cleo's attention despite the fact that she saw Mrs. Gateman's car turn into the driveway. "What option?"

"The Gray Mare." Again, no hesitation on Audrey's part. "My uncle is looking for someone to buy half the saloon, and if you're interested, I could loan you the money."

Cleo stared at her, shook her head. "Why would you do something like that?"

"For Judd. I'm in love with him," Audrey admitted. "I'm sure that won't come as a surprise to you." Now she paused. "But what might surprise you is that if Judd isn't already in love with you, he soon will be. I'll do this for you because even if he'll never love me, I want to make sure he's happy."

Cleo blurted out a garbled sound and felt her mouth fall open. Not exactly a flattering expression as Mrs. Gateman approached the porch. The social worker spared Cleo a glance before her attention settled on Audrey.

"Dr. Holcomb," Mrs. Gateman greeted. "It's good to see you again."

Cleo hadn't known the women had met, but

maybe Audrey had delivered her medical report in person.

"Is everything okay?" the social worker asked.

"Yes," Audrey quickly answered. "I was just chatting with Cleo, but I need to be going. You'll let me know about the business we discussed?" Audrey added and strolled away.

"I got Sheriff Laramie's message to say that he'd be late," Mrs. Gateman said as they watched Audrey leave.

Cleo nodded and considered pointing out that there was plenty of babysitting help for situations just like this, but because Cleo was supposed to be part of that "help," she just gathered her breath and opened the front door. She also added a silent prayer for a miracle.

And she got one.

The boys were all seated on the sofa. Clean, and the clean applied to them as well as the rest of the room. No trace of clutter, TP or bad smells other than a faint whiff of the burned cookies.

As if he was actually capable of being still, Mango had his head resting on his paws and was lying at Beckham's feet. Popsicle was sitting obediently in Leo's arms. With placid expressions all around, Cleo thought they looked drugged. Or threatened into being on their best behavior during this visit. Judging from the way Beckham was eyeing his brothers, the threat had come from him.

Nico was across from them, lounging in a chair. He tipped his Stetson in greeting at the social worker and flashed her one of those smiles that had charmed more women than Nico could probably count. And he wasn't the only one smiling. Despite Rosy having a handful of frog parts, she was, too. Mercy didn't exactly fit into the serene family scene, but she also looked happy.

"I sorry for punching you, Mrs. Ga-man," Leo said after Isaac gave him a nudge with his elbow.

"He got a time-out in his room and had to use all of his 'get out of jail free' cards to make up for it," Rosy added.

"The cards are a way of giving the boys a clean slate," Cleo explained. "And they have to do extra chores or get good grades to get the cards."

"He won't do it again," Beckham insisted, and while he wasn't smiling, he looked one or two notches up from his usual surly self.

Mrs. Gateman nodded and seemed pleased about that, and the woman's positive reaction was Cleo's cue to leave.

"I'll just be next door while you visit with the boys," Cleo said to her.

However, Mrs. Gateman stopped Cleo before she could leave, and she motioned for Cleo to follow her back to the porch. The woman didn't say anything until they were outside and the door was closed. Apparently, today was the day for porch chats.

"Look, I don't personally have anything against you, Miss Delaney. I can see you love the boys, and I can also see that Sheriff Laramie and his family care for them, as well."

"But?" Cleo prompted when she didn't continue.

The woman gave a confirming nod that there was indeed a "but." "You know there are things that count against this placement. Mr. McCall's recent fight with cancer. His and his wife's age." She motioned toward the living room. "The flux of caregivers for the boys."

"*Good* caregivers," Cleo reminded her. "All of Kace's siblings have stepped in to help. Especially Judd. He's really been a big help with Beckham, but all the boys seem to connect with him."

"So I've heard. When I last talked to the children, each of them mentioned Judd, and it was all positive."

Cleo held back her huff. However, there was another "but" in Mrs. Gateman's tone.

"Still, the ideal would be for the boys to be part of a stable, two-parent household," the woman explained. "One that could lead to a permanent placement."

"I can't give them ideal," Cleo admitted. "No one can. They've lost their mother and have been uprooted. But I can give them love. So can Kace, Judd and his family."

"I don't doubt that, but they can possibly have love and that stable two-parent foster family. I'm working on getting them just that."

Everything inside Cleo went still, and since she didn't trust her voice, she just waited for Mrs. Gateman to continue.

"It's too soon to give details," the social worker

went on, "but I think you should prepare yourself in case it all works out. It's possible I can have the boys in a new foster home by the end of the month."

HELL. HELL. HELL.

And if Judd had thought saying it more times would have helped, he would have kept on mentally repeating it. He'd had his share of bad days, but this was one coupled with god-awful timing, what with his being late, the social worker's visit and with Kace getting injured. Now he was about to add another heaping pile of crap onto that bad timing.

A longhorn was blocking the road. Yes, the very road that Judd needed to get to the ranch. The bull was holding up traffic again—something it did on a regular basis whenever it broke fence. Today, it'd also dropped a big pile of shit, so big that Judd wondered if there were intestinal issues involved.

There were at least a half-dozen folks out of their vehicles, all fanning their hands in front of their faces to disperse the stench from the fresh crap. Even the longhorn had moved a distance away from it, but it hadn't moseyed nearly far enough to the side to allow traffic to get by.

There were hoots, hollers and frustrated oaths from the onlookers, who were trying their best to shoo the bull along by flapping various things, from handkerchiefs to a bag of microwave popcorn. But one of those folks was doing the flapping and hooting while wearing only a raincoat, tighty-whities and black socks under a pair of flip-flops.

Gopher.

Today, the man had a green ribbon tied around his cotton-covered junk, and while the man's junk wasn't exactly what Judd would call prominent, it still fell in the indecent category. And Gopher knew it.

Sighing and cursing at the same time, Judd grabbed the canned air horn from his glove compartment and got out of his cruiser.

"About time you got here," Miss Pettymyers *greeted* him. The woman was eighty if she was a day and had likely been in a sour mood for at least seventy-nine and a half of those years. "You'd darn sure better be here to arrest him."

Judd hoped the woman meant for him to arrest Gopher and not the longhorn. Either way, he was going to have to do something about both of them.

"You," Judd snarled, aiming his index finger at Gopher. "Get in the back seat of the cruiser. You're under arrest."

Gopher glanced down at his underwear and the satin bow as if seeing them both for the first time. Strange, since he seemed to enjoy letting everyone get a look at them.

"I was just trying to help," Gopher mumbled and, frowning, he headed toward the cruiser.

"Next time get dressed before you help," Judd warned him, and he charged forward to deal with the longhorn. "Back up," he told the others, "and don't step in that shit."

Too late. Miss Pettymyers stepped in it, and Judd

was sure he hadn't heard the last of it. She'd likely file a complaint and threaten to sue, which would in turn tie him up even more. For now, he drowned out whatever fuss she made by sounding the air horn. Or rather trying it. Obviously, it was running out of air because it sounded more like a series of belches rather than a blast of noise. Amazingly, though, it was enough to get the bull moving.

All the onlookers except Miss Pettymyers and Gopher cheered Judd, and he didn't wait around to hear the rest of what the woman had to say. He hurried back to his cruiser and sped off. Not heading toward the police station, though. Judd went in the direction of the ranch.

"Thought you were gonna arrest me," Gopher said.

"I am, but I've got an errand to run first."

It was hardly standard procedure for a cop to go to a personal meeting with a prisoner in tow, but Judd didn't want Cleo to have to deal with the social worker. Mrs. Gateman had already made it clear that she didn't find Cleo *suitable*, and Judd didn't think that would be a good thing to have playing into whatever report the woman made about this visit. Of course, Cleo was involved all the way up to her pretty eyeballs, but there was no sense driving that point home to CPS.

As Judd approached the turn to the ranch, he saw a car leaving. Audrey's. And he muttered another string of those "hells." He very much wanted to know what she was doing there, but like Gopher, she'd have to wait. Judd just gave Audrey a quick nod and kept on going.

Judd parked under one of the many shade trees on the grounds, and he lowered the windows so Gopher wouldn't get overheated. "You stay put," Judd warned him. "So help me if you leave and I have to hunt for you. You will pay. Got that?"

His lecture would have been a whole lot more effective if Gopher hadn't already fallen asleep. His head was tilted back, his mouth was wide-open and he was snoring. Judd considered waking him up just to repeat his order to stay put, but he didn't want to waste any more time. He got out and hurried into the house. Where he got another surprise.

Mercy was on the living room sofa having what appeared to be tea with Rosy.

What kind of new level of hell was this? First Audrey, now Mercy. Was there some kind of get-together that Judd hadn't heard about?

Without explaining why she was there and as if her presence was the most natural thing in the world, Mercy fluttered her fingers in the direction of the kitchen. "The kiddos are back there with Mrs. Gateman," she said in a whisper. "But your brother Nico had to leave to talk to someone about important rodeo business. He's sure a cutie-pie."

Judd ignored that and turned to Rosy. "Where's Cleo?"

"Outside." Rosy whispered that, as well. "Poor thing. You can tell she's all upset."

Mercy made a concurring sound of agreement

and gulped down some tea. Hell. If Cleo was upset, then the meeting hadn't gone well.

"How's Kace?" Rosy asked. "Did he really have to go to the ER?"

Judd nodded. "He's fine." And he kept it at that.

He didn't want to get into a long explanation about Silla Sweeny dropping her purse outside the inn and having Estelle Robbin's poodle, Puffakins, clamp down on some pricey eye-gunk stuff that'd rolled out of the purse. Silla had thrown a hissy fit and Puffakins had bolted, which had started a foot chase down Main Street. A chase that had ended with Kace getting bitten when he tried to stop Puffakins.

Dragging in a long breath, Judd went to the kitchen to find out what was wrong. After the other things that'd gone on—Kace's injury, the longhorn and Gopher—Judd steeled himself for the worst. But there was no worst going on.

The boys were all seated at the table having cookies and milk. Mrs. Gateman was chowing down with them, and someone must have said something funny because they broke out into laughter. Well, all but Beckham, but even he wasn't scowling as hard as usual, though he had his phone under the table and appeared to be texting someone.

Judd cleared his throat, causing all of them to look in his direction. That included Mango and Popsicle, who were sitting on the floor as if they were the calmest, best trained pets in the state.

"Leo told us a knock-knock joke," Mrs. Gateman said to explain the laughter.

Judd was glad Leo had managed to pull that off, and he winked at the boy to let him know he approved. "Kace sends his apologies for being late," Judd told the woman. "He's at the ER getting stitches. Nothing serious," he added when he saw the alarm in Isaac's eyes, and hers. "He should be here soon."

"Good. I do need to talk to him." Mrs. Gateman checked her watch. "Could I have a moment with you first, and then I'll visit with the boys while we wait for the sheriff?"

When she glanced around as if searching for a place for them to go, Judd motioned for her to follow him to the back porch. The moment they were outside, he glanced around for Cleo and saw her peering out the cabin window. She quickly ducked out of sight.

Since Judd figured Mrs. Gateman was about to dress him down over Kace's absence, he put his hands on his hips and got started with whatever amount of groveling he had to do.

"I'm sorry Kace isn't here," Judd said. "Sorry that I didn't make it here in time, either. But I want you to know that the boys are always supervised."

She nodded and, judging from her slightly bunched-up forehead, his comment had surprised her. "Yes, your other brother Nico gave me a copy of the schedule spreadsheet before he left. I think you've all done a good job of pitching in, and that'll go in the report."

Judd felt his own forehead do some bunching. "But?" he persisted.

Mrs. Gateman sighed. "You know it's not a slam dunk for your brother Kace to get custody, so we need to try to address any questions that could come up. I'll include the schedule spreadsheet in my report, but I think it'd also be a good idea to have a statement from you saying that you'll back up your brother in situations just like this one today. I'd like ones from Nico, Callen and his wife, as well."

Judd couldn't see a problem with any of them giving a statement since they were already filling in when needed. However, he did find this somewhat confusing.

"This sounds as if you're on Kace's side," Judd said. "As if you actually believe he should get permanent custody. But you didn't seem to feel that way with your other visit."

She didn't jump to confirm that. "The boys should stay together. None of us dispute that. And right now, there just aren't a lot of options for that, so I want Kace to keep temporary custody until something permanent is in place for them. I don't think it would benefit the kids to be moved to another temporary home, but rest assured when something more suitable is arranged, the boys will be leaving here."

He wanted to argue with that. Heck, he wanted to argue for Cleo to get the kids, just as Miranda had wanted, but that ship had sailed. Now he'd do a statement or whatever the hell else it took to make sure this worked out for the boys while he also tried to work out a way for them to stay permanently.

"You really think you'd find a better place than this for them?" Judd asked.

"Maybe." She opened her mouth as if to say more but then closed it. "Maybe," she repeated, and then quickly added, "I should get back inside and talk some more with the boys." Mrs. Gateman stepped around him to go back in the house.

Judd stood there a moment, replaying what the social worker had just said. And what she hadn't said. The *maybe* was puzzling and made him think she had someone specific in mind. Someone more *qualified*.

Someone who could take the boys from Cleo.

Well, hell. That put a knot right back in Judd's stomach. Worse, Cleo was at the window again, and she was clearly waiting for an update. Judd started toward the cabin, and he glanced at his cruiser to make sure Gopher had stayed put.

And Judd practically skidded to a stop.

Mercy was at the back window of the cruiser, and she was leaning in. Judd didn't have to guess what she was doing because everything in her body language said she was flirting with Gopher. Judd nearly hurried to them to stop it, but then he shrugged. If there was anyone who could accept a ribbon-wearing flasher, it was Mercy. Instead, Judd went to the cabin, and the moment he opened the door, Cleo pulled him inside.

"Did Mrs. Gateman tell you?" Cleo immediately asked.

"You mean about CPS finding a permanent place. Yes, she did. But that could be a long way off. Right now, we just need to focus on making sure Kace keeps temporary custody."

She was blinking hard when her eyes met his. "Beckham texted me to tell me what they've been talking about in the kitchen." Cleo's bottom lip trembled a little. "He thinks Mrs. Gateman and her husband might want to foster all three boys."

Well, hell. The social worker hadn't volunteered that, but it was likely what those *maybe*s were about.

"God, Judd," Cleo said, going into his arms. "I'm going to lose them."

CHAPTER TWENTY-ONE

JUDD FROWNED WHEN his phone rang, and he saw the caller ID on his screen. Not the social worker, as he'd hoped. And it wasn't Cleo, who'd be checking in to see if there'd been a call from Mrs. Gateman. And it wasn't Kace, who might have filled him in had there indeed been a call about the kids' possible new foster home.

Instead, it was Mercy.

Since Liberty was still in the squad room and her desk was just across from Judd's, he didn't put the call on speaker. He hit the save button on the report he'd been writing and took the call.

"Did you hear the one about the blind hooker?" Mercy asked the moment he answered. As usual, she didn't wait for the punch line. "You've got to hand it to her." She cackled with laughter. "Get it? Hand *it* to her."

"Yeah, I got it," Judd answered, and while she wouldn't have been able to see it, he didn't dare crack a smile. She might sense any form of amusement, and he didn't want to encourage it. At least not until she got some better jokes.

"You're sure you don't mind me seeing Gopher?"

Mercy asked a moment later. "Because I gotta say, you looked mighty pissed off when you saw me talking to him when he was in your cruiser."

That image was still crystal clear in his head even though it'd happened two days ago. "Not pissed off. Confused as to why you'd want to spend time with a man who accessorizes his dick and gave himself a rodent nickname."

"Dick accessories are a personal favorite of mine. Besides, Gopher's a fun guy."

Obviously, Mercy and he had a different definition of what constituted fun, and Judd didn't even want to consider that Mercy's comment about Gopher could be sexual. The only sex images he wanted in his head right now were of a naked Cleo. Thankfully, his head cooperated with that just fine because at any moment of the day, the sight of her bare ass in his bed popped into his mind. With their crazy work schedules, though, he'd had to do with just the images and not the real deal.

"Gopher's what I call a misunderstood man," Mercy went on. "He's lonely, that's all."

"A lonely pervert," Judd amended. "I've arrested him plenty of times." And since maybe Mercy had some insight into this particular problem, he added, "Any idea what the deal is with him tying up his junk like that?"

"His late wife," she answered without hesitation. "It was something he did on Christmas morning, birthdays, holidays and such. You know, sort of like a joke."

Judd frowned and was sorry he'd asked. It was both pitiful and disturbing. Disturbing because again it was likely sexual. Pitiful because maybe Gopher was flashing as some sort of coping behavior.

Well, shit.

Judd hadn't had a clue about that, and he'd known Gopher for a good chunk of his life. Leave it to an alcoholic former porn star to suss that out. "Do me a favor and try to convince Gopher to get some counseling for that," he told Mercy.

"I'll try, but I've told him if he wants to flash his dick around that he should flash it to me. He's got my number in case he wants to send pictures."

Judd bit off the groan and squeezed his eyes shut a moment, hoping that image didn't appear in his head. Shit. Too late. It was there. Too bad there wasn't mental bleach for crap like that.

"Anything yet from that social worker?" Mercy asked, pulling Judd's attention back to her and onto a subject he preferred over discussing Gopher's junk.

He'd told Mercy the bare bones of the situation. That Mrs. Gateman might or might not want to foster the boys. According to Beckham, she did indeed want that, though the woman hadn't actually come out and said that when she'd chatted with them in the kitchen. According to Mrs. Gateman, she was "considering all options."

It twisted at Judd to think that one of those options could cut Cleo to the bone if she lost the boys. It twisted more that it might have a negative effect on the boys. Beckham had seemed to make a breakthrough with the addition of the puppy, and Judd didn't want him doing any backsliding. Since he was a backsliding expert, Judd knew what a dark hole that could be.

"Are you okay?" he asked Mercy. Because the image of her crying was crystal clear, too.

"Sure. I'm right as rain now. That other time, you just caught me on the downswing after the breakup with Pudge."

Yeah, and Judd was troubled that another breakup could do the same. Or worse. Even a "breakup" with Gopher might trigger it. Of course, he couldn't see Gopher breaking up with a woman. Any woman.

"You do know you can do better than the likes of Gopher?" Judd suggested.

Mercy giggled like a schoolgirl. "Well, I think that's the nicest thing you've ever said to me."

Judd hoped not, but in case it was, he made a mental note to say nice things more often. "Just take care of yourself," Judd added.

"Right back at you. Hey, what did the dick say to the condom?" Mercy asked. "Cover me. I'm going in." The last thing Judd heard before she ended the call was Mercy's earsplitting belly laugh.

Judd put his phone away and finished the report. Since his shift was long over, he was about to head out when his phone rang again. Not Mercy this time, but it was a name he recognized. Crawford Banning. The reporter that Lavinia had been trying to prod into stirring up trouble. Judd might have answered it, just to tell the guy to fuck off, but he let it go to voice mail as the front door opened. Again, it wasn't anyone he wanted to see since it wasn't Cleo or the social worker.

It was Audrey.

She gave him a tentative smile, her gaze sliding to Liberty and then to Kace's office, which was empty. "Kace is with the kids?" she asked.

Judd nodded and was thankful that Audrey didn't know that firsthand because it would have meant she'd been at the ranch again. Cleo was at work so she wouldn't have had to deal with Audrey, but Judd felt uncomfortable with the way the woman just kept showing up. Maybe she'd always done that. In hindsight, he remembered other times like this when Audrey had just popped in. Other times, like now, when she held up a pink box from Patty Cake's bakery.

"Chocolate chip cookies," Audrey explained, giving the box a little rattle. For such a little wiggle of a gesture, it sure seemed to carry lots of weight.

It was like the nookie pie all over again.

Dragging in a heavy breath, Judd collected his things and was about to lead Audrey outside so he could go about setting up some ground rules, but Liberty must have realized what was going on because she mumbled something about the bathroom and the deputy hurried off fast, as if her panties had suddenly caught fire.

"Audrey," Judd began, but that was as far as he got before her eyes widened, and she shook her head.

"Well, this was a mistake," she murmured. "I

guess since you're a cop, you didn't have any trouble seeing through the thin cookie disguise." She said it with some dry amusement in her tone, but there was enough quiver in her voice that he knew this hurt her.

And Judd hated that. "Audrey—"

But again, she interrupted him. "I had to try. I had to make sure I didn't have a shot with you. I can see that I don't. Are you already in love with Cleo?" she asked but then waved that off before he could answer.

Not that Judd would have answered, but the wave gave him a chance to jump into the conversation. "We don't have a shot," he said. Part of him wished he'd put some kid gloves on it, but Audrey would have likely taken that as an opening—yet something else she'd been doing for a while now.

"Well." There was the dry amusement again. "I see." She set the box of cookies on the dispatch counter. "I said this to...well, that doesn't matter, but I'll say it to you now. I wish you only the best."

"Thanks for that. I feel the same way about you." He was sincere but it probably felt like a jab, something along the lines of "we'll always be friends."

Audrey folded her arms over her chest and glanced away from him. "This won't interfere with Cleo and the Gray Mare," she said.

If Audrey had been looking at him, Judd was certain that she would have seen his blank, confused stare. "Excuse me?"

"The Gray Mare." She waved that off, too, but

then kept talking. "If Cleo is interested in buying it, my feelings for you won't get in the way."

That statement didn't do away with his blank stare, but he decided this was a conversation he'd best have with Cleo and not a woman who was currently blinking back tears.

Well, crap. He'd hurt Audrey. Not intentionally. But, yeah, he'd hurt her.

Swiping at one of those tears, Audrey walked out, leaving Judd to curse himself and wish for a rock that he could use to hit himself on the head. This was why he put up walls and shut people out, but apparently his wall-building skills were seriously lacking.

"Is the coast clear?" Liberty asked, coming back from her bathroom break. "Yum, cookies," she added when she peered into the box.

"Help yourself," Judd offered. "I'm heading home."

Liberty wasted no time biting into one of the failed nookie bribes. "Wait. Did you get the letter that came for you?" Liberty asked.

Judd had already reached for the door, but that stopped him. "What letter?"

Clamping the cookie in between her teeth, Liberty riffled through the inbox on Ginger's desk and came up with a letter in a plain white envelope. Judd took it, his attention immediately going to the return address.

Shit.

CLEO TURNED OFF her headlights as she approached
the ranch. Since it was nearly 2:00 a.m. on a school
night, she didn't want to wake the boys or anyone
else in the house. She parked outside Judd's cabin,
frowning when there were no lights on inside. Not
that she'd expected him to be up, but it didn't feel
right just creeping in like this. That was yet another reminder that she needed to make better arrangements.

Being in Judd's bed had some incredible bene-
fits—sex and the amazing view of having him naked
next to her—but she needed her own place. Judd
was already doing so much to help with the boys,
and she didn't want him to start feeling as if this
had all been crammed down his throat. First thing
in the morning, she would need to press the Realtor
again to come up with a rental for her.

She dragged herself from her car and felt her feet
and calves groan in protest. Normally, wearing heels
didn't bother her, but she'd ended up having to tend
the bar after Tiny had come down with stomach flu.

Cleo pulled off the shoes when she reached the
porch and eased open the cabin door. She hadn't
been wrong about no lights being on inside. It was
pitch-dark, so she waited a moment for her eyes to
adjust.

That's when she saw, and heard, Judd.

"Dick inches," he mumbled.

Wearing only a pair of boxers, Judd was sitting on
the sofa, and he had the stuffed rattlesnake, Sweetcakes, positioned on the coffee table directly in front

of him. Cleo figured that would have caused anyone to be alarmed, but she knew what the snake meant. It was his distraction, a focal point, and coupled with his safe words, Judd was trying to stave off his need for a drink.

She froze, not sure what she should do. Judd didn't give her any clues about that. He just kept saying "Dick inches."

"Bad night?" she asked. Turning on a lamp, she went closer and sank down on the table across from him. That put her right next to the snake. Judd probably didn't know that doing it had taken some effort on her part. The snake creeped her out, but that seemed very small potatoes compared to what Judd was going through.

"I'm okay," he insisted.

Maybe. There weren't any signs of liquor around, and he clearly wasn't dressed to go out and buy some.

"We can work this three ways," she said. "I can call Mercy or—"

"No." Judd shook his head, plowed his hands through his hair.

"We can work this two ways," Cleo amended. "You can tell me to get lost or—"

"No," he interrupted.

"Okay, that makes it really easy." Well, it did if he went with option three, which she was still sort of formulating in her mind. "You tell me what's wrong, and we talk this out."

Silence. But at least it wasn't a "no."

"And then we can have sex," she added to sweeten the pot. "Dirty sex," she amended.

It had the intended effect. Judd not only looked at her, but he also gave a little flat chuckle that was totally half-hearted, but it was better than dick inches and rattlesnake staring.

She hoped.

Judd still didn't say anything, but he took something from off the sofa and tossed it onto her lap. It was a letter, and while the envelope had obviously been opened, she didn't take it out and read it. However, she did look at the return address, and bells the size of Texas started to clang in her head when she saw the name. A name she recognized.

"Avis Odell," Cleo commented. "The man who hurt Nico and Callen." And she began to come up with all sorts of stinky scenarios. Maybe Avis was threatening Judd or poking at old memories. Maybe the guy was just being a bastard.

With his hands still in his hair, Judd groaned and leaned back on the sofa. "Avis is in some twelve-step program, and he wants to apologize. To make amends. He says now that he's clean and sober he knows what he did was unforgivable but that he hopes I can find it in my heart to get past what he did."

Cleo took a moment to let that sink in. "The asshole."

Judd looked at her. "That was my reaction, too."

She nodded. "Anything he could say would take a poke at you and stir up old memories. But now he wants you to clear his conscience. Even if he's being sincere, it's still an asshole thing to do."

Of course, if Avis did nothing at all, she'd still put him in that category. Basically, he was going to carry that label no matter what.

Judd nodded. "I think it's supposed to feel petty if I don't forgive him."

"Do you want to forgive him?" Cleo asked.

"No." He groaned. "Maybe. I would if I thought it'd make this all go away." He tapped his head.

Cleo leaned in so their gazes would connect, and she, too, gave him a head tap. "I don't think that's going away. It's made you who you are, and it isn't the sex talking when I tell you that you're a good man."

He stared at her. "A man who won't forgive a sonofabitch."

"A man who doesn't *have* to forgive a sonofabitch," she amended. "Just because Avis wants this from you, it doesn't mean you have to give it to him. One letter doesn't clean up the stench of a bad asshole."

She frowned at that and bit back the "ewww" that formed in her throat. Judd smiled, causing that "ewww" to ease up some. Apparently, icky humor was the way to go here to lighten his dark mood.

"What does a receptionist at a sperm bank say as clients leave?" Judd asked her, but he didn't wait even a second before he continued. "Thanks for coming."

Now she smiled. "A Mercy joke?"

He nodded, reached out and pushed a strand of hair from her cheek. He didn't pull back, though. He let the curl wrap around his finger. It was a simple gesture, but it sent a really loud signal to her. Then again, Judd just being Judd sent signals that caused the heat to stir inside her. She considered telling the heat to knock it off, that Judd might need to keep talking this through.

But Cleo thought of something else that might work.

Of course, she was pretty sure the heat had been the one to come up with the idea. Still, as ideas went, it wasn't an awful one.

"For the next fifteen minutes or so," she said, "let me be your distraction and your safe words."

He raised an eyebrow. "Dick inches and a stuffed snake?"

"Not quite."

She scooted to the edge of the coffee table, dragged Judd to her and she kissed him. Because this was a test to see if this idea sucked or not, she carefully noted his reaction. And it was a good one. He made a husky sound of pleasure, maybe mixed with some surprise, but he slid right into the kiss.

"For the next fifteen minutes or so, I want to make you forget," she whispered against his mouth.

"Fifteen minutes?" Judd hooked his arm around her and hauled her into his lap. "Let's go for thirty."

CHAPTER TWENTY-TWO

JUDD STOOD IN the shower, his hands braced against the tiles and his head down while the scalding hot water hit the back of his neck. Despite the late-night sex with Cleo that had lasted well past the thirty minutes, he still felt the tension in nearly every muscle of his body.

Nearly.

His dick still seemed content that it'd gotten lucky, but he rarely put much stock in that brainless part of himself. It didn't take into account things like emotional baggage, reality or limitations of a hard-on. Thirty minutes was a long time to last with Cleo and her clever arsenal of sex tricks. The woman certainly knew how to take him all in.

Since the reminder of that snagged the interest of his dick again, Judd pushed aside the thought and went back to the emotional baggage/reality that the brainless wonder had dismissed. He needed to deal with the tension, with those tight neck muscles and with the dick punch he'd felt when he'd gotten that letter from Avis.

He didn't want to give Avis any kind of power over him like this. Even if the man had changed his ways, he would always be a piece of shit in Judd's mind. Maybe it wasn't mature to hang on to that, but Judd just didn't see a way of letting it go. Not yet, anyway. Maybe not ever, and he'd have to live with that. No way could he let asshole Avis twist him up again and cause him to risk his sobriety.

Behind him, the shower door opened, and he felt the warm slide of the front of Cleo's body against the back of his. Her nipples rubbed against him in the best kind of massage. Now that was better than hot water for relaxing all muscles but his dick.

"This is nice," he said, reaching around to grab her ass cheek, "but we'll have to be quiet so we don't wake Cleo."

She bit him on his shoulder. "Don't worry. Cleo's a heavy sleeper. She'll never have to know. But you'll know," she assured him. Her tone was both playful and slick with heat.

And speaking of slick, that applied to her wet hands, too, because she skimmed them over his butt, around his hips and to the front of him.

"I've never had you in the shower," she said. She had a condom and immediately started rolling it on him. "Are you better here than in the bed or on the couch?"

"Here."

It was all bravado, of course. The shower was small and slippery, which would not only limit movement, but it would also possibly result in injury, scalding or death. His dick dismissed those concerns and declared this the greatest idea ever by getting harder than stone.

"I do my best work on the floor, though," he assured her, turning so he could capture her mouth with his. It was a good capture, all right. She tasted like mint toothpaste and sin, and that combo was apparently some potent foreplay.

"You'll have to prove that to me later." She licked his neck, flicking her tongue over his earlobe. "And I'll prove I do my best work on the seat of your truck."

Judd hadn't thought he could get even harder, but that comment proved him wrong. Which was crazy since truck sex would give him even less maneuvering room than this shower, and the last time he'd tried it, when he'd been eighteen or so, he'd bruised his kidney on the gear stick. Still, he rather liked the idea of nailing Cleo in as many locations as possible.

She continued with the licks and tongue flicks as Judd hoisted her up so she could wrap her legs around his waist. The injuries started almost immediately. Her elbow banged against the door. The faucet that had seemingly gotten razor-sharp dug into his hip bone. Pain, though, wasn't much of a deterrent because the moment the centers of their bodies were all lined up, Judd pushed inside her.

And everything but Cleo vanished.

Tight, wet and, well, perfect. Of course, that was his dick talking again, but his brain thought that maybe this one time the dick had it right. It was perfect. Well, if you totally discounted the pain.

Cleo yelped when her knee accidentally nudged the faucet so that the water spray turned to icicles. Without breaking the rhythm of the thrusts, Judd fixed the temp and shifted them so that Cleo's back went against the shower door. That would have been a clever idea if the door had been fully closed.

It wasn't.

They tumbled backward, and it was only through luck and his leg muscles that they didn't fall on their asses.

With Cleo laughing like a loon and with her legs still hooked around him, he lowered them to the floor. Half of their bodies were still in the shower and the water was spewing out all over the room. Those weren't concerns, though, for a dick on his mission. And his definitely had a mission, one as timeless as sex itself.

To get Cleo off so he could then do the same.

Cleo's laughter died down when Judd got serious about the getting off. That was the thing about going deeper, faster and harder—everything pinpointed to finishing this and finding that "pot of gold" release at the end of the thrusting rainbow.

Cleo and he had only been together a handful of times, but he could tell when he had her close to a climax. It went against everything his hard-on was demanding, but Judd slowed a little, to draw it out a few more seconds. And he used those seconds to clear his vision and watch her face.

Amazing. So beautiful.

At least that's what his mind was thinking. His

hard-on had moved back to its original train of thought. "Nail her now" started to repeat with each new thrust. Unfortunately, he was a guy, through and through, and therefore powerless to resist it. Judd nailed her, feeling her body squeeze around him like a greedy fist. He was powerless against greedy fists, too, because he finished like a double-engine rocket right behind her.

There was also a problem with finishing like that. It drained him of any energy he could have used to get them off the now sopping wet bathroom floor. In the back of his mind, he figured it had to be worse for Cleo, since she was lying in at least an inch of water that was quickly turning cold. Still, she managed a very smug and not the least bit uncomfortable smile when she looked up at him.

"You're right." Her voice was a slack purr now, and her eyes were glazed with the aftershocks of the climax. "You *do* do your best work on the floor."

He smiled with her. Kissed her. And probably would have just collapsed on her if she hadn't taken his face in her hands.

Cleo looked him straight in the eyes. "Judd, I'm in love with you."

CLEO WATCHED JUDD FREEZE. Maybe time did, as well. In fact, the only thing that didn't seem to be in freeze mode was Cleo herself.

She laughed, but it wasn't the ha-ha "got you with a joke, didn't I?" kind of laughter. Though Judd probably would have preferred that. In fact, he likely wanted her to jump back in a time machine and have a do-over, where those words didn't even pop into her head much less come out of her mouth. But she had said them. And she meant them.

She was in love with him.

It was a strong, strange mix of feelings. Like an incredible emotional orgasm that had built, then soared, then skyrocketed and finally slammed through her with pleasure and relief.

Yes, relief.

Until the moment she'd said the words, she hadn't known what she was going to do with all the stuff that she felt for him. She hadn't really had a handle on just how deep all the feelings could go. But the handle was there now, and it would change her life forever.

Cleo was pretty sure it would change Judd, too, but maybe not in the heart-bursting way it had her. He'd be scared, she knew, and she could practically hear all those doubts galloping through his head right now. He would consider himself a planet-sized emotional risk. Someone incapable of anything more than recreational sex, but Cleo hoped to change his mind about that. And if she didn't…

Well, Judd Laramie was certainly worth a broken heart.

It would sound mushy if she said it aloud—and could possibly send Judd into cardiac arrest if he wasn't already—but even if her love for him stayed one-sided, that was enough.

Judd didn't say anything. He just lay there, staring at her, but she saw in his eyes the moment that changed. He was about to attempt to talk her out of what she'd said. Maybe even rationalize it away as the side effect of the orgasm. That was her cue to get out of there and give him some time.

Unlike Judd, she could move. Perhaps because the water beneath her acted like a lubricant. She shimmied and wiggled until she was out from under him, and she stood, the water sliding down her body and plopping in fat drops onto him.

She leaned down long enough to smack a kiss on his stunned mouth before she grabbed a towel and walked out. Of course, that meant giving him a view of her bare ass—which he would have almost certainly noticed if his brain had been able to register more than just surprise.

Still buzzing from the sex and falling in love, Cleo dried off and got dressed. It had been Lissy's day to get the boys off to school, and before Cleo had slipped into the shower with Judd, she'd gone over to the house to say goodbye to them and wish them a good day. She'd gotten hugs from Isaac and Leo and enthusiastic licks from Mango and Popsicle.

There'd been nothing enthusiastic about Beckham's mood, but that'd been the norm since they'd found out that Mrs. Gateman was looking into fostering them herself. Cleo didn't have any doubts as to what she felt for Judd, but she had plenty of both doubts and concerns about the social worker taking the kids. Unfortunately, some of those concerns were selfish ones on Cleo's part.

She could lose them.

That pierced her heart in the total opposite way that falling in love had. Plain and simple, it sucked. She loved the kids and wanted to raise them. Having them had messed up everything and made it better at the same time.

Actually, that was an apt description of falling in love, too.

Judd probably didn't feel that way about the "made it better," and that was probably why she'd yet to hear him stir around in the bathroom. Considering that he might be waiting for her to leave so he could have some breathing space, Cleo finished dressing so she could pop over to the main house and have a quick cup of coffee with Rosy before she headed into work at the bar. But before Cleo could even make it to the door, she heard a car approaching.

Her first thought was that it was maybe a visit from Mrs. Gateman, but when Cleo opened the door, she spotted a man getting out of an SUV. A redhaired stranger who was so skinny that she wondered why his clothes didn't just slide right off him.

"Miss Delaney," he greeted as he approached her. "I'm Crawford Banning."

There was instant name recognition, but because she knew who he was, it pretty much shot down what was left of her sex buzz. It was the reporter who was "friends" with Lavinia.

"What do you want?" Cleo asked.

His sigh let her know that he'd picked up on her hostile tone. "We need to talk."

She shook her head. "I don't think so. If you're working with Lavinia, then you and I have nothing to say."

"But we do," he argued, catching onto the door when she tried to close it. "Lavinia has found some things that could cause lots and lots of trouble."

MAYBE HE'D MISUNDERSTOOD CLEO.

Yeah, that had to be it, Judd decided as he hauled himself off the bathroom floor and to his feet. He'd misunderstood her or else she had truly meant it as a joke. But what if it wasn't? What if she'd meant it?

Judd, I'm in love with you.

Well, fuck, fuck, fuck.

That wasn't good. Falling in love with him was the highest ladder rung of things not to do. It would mess up everything. Including sex. And while sex wasn't his top concern right now, it wasn't something he wanted to mess up with her.

Still cursing, Judd turned off the shower, cleaned up and got dressed. He didn't hurry because he was trying damn hard to figure out how to go about handling this. Cleo would probably want to talk it out, might even want to plead her case for why she'd done something so stupid as fall in love with him. He only hoped she wouldn't want to do any case-pleading while she was naked. He already had strong evidence that her nakedness didn't give him a good foundation for thinking straight.

Judd steeled himself, took a couple of deep breaths and came out of the bathroom. Much to his relief and to his dick's disgust, Cleo was fully dressed. But she wasn't alone. She was at the door and was talking to some guy. A tall lanky man with ginger hair and a pinched face. And she definitely wasn't smiling now, something that put Judd on full alert.

"Judd," Cleo said on a rise of breath. "This is Crawford Banning."

Even though Judd had never met the guy, he knew exactly who he was. "Lavinia's pissant reporter." And, no, Judd didn't bother to tone down his scowl or sound even remotely pleasant. "Fuck off," he added since that was what he'd been wanting to tell the guy.

Crawford held up his hands when Judd went to shut the door in his face. "I need to talk to you. You should hear what's going on."

That stopped Judd, temporarily, anyway, from slamming the door, but he kept his hand in place in case this idiot said something he didn't want to hear. Since he was in cahoots with Lavinia, there was a good chance of that happening.

"First of all, I'm not Lavinia's reporter," Crawford insisted. "Yes, she came to me to find dirt on you two. I had some time, thought it could have an interesting angle if I pulled up something."

"You have a grudge against cops," Judd snarled. "Because you got arrested for trespassing when you were trying to chase down a story."

Crawford acknowledged that with a nod. "It started out as a grudge. Sort of. Coupled with Lavinia making me believe that the two of you were trying to screw her over. But then I found plenty of dirt on Lavinia herself."

Judd's grip on the door didn't relax, but he gave the guy a nod to signal him to keep going.

Crawford took some folded-up papers from his pocket and handed them to Judd. "It's a report about the dirt I found on her. I believe Lavinia's the one responsible for destroying some plastic cows at the Angry Angus," Crawford revealed, causing both Cleo and Judd to give him a flat look. "And I believe she vandalized the sign so that it read 'Anus' instead of 'Angus.'"

More flat looks from Cleo and Judd. Obviously, this guy wasn't giving them any news flashes.

"Lavinia's been calling CPS to pressure them into taking the Morrelli children, her grandchildren," Crawford went on, "and putting them into another foster home, one that has no association with either of you."

Since Judd couldn't flatten his look any more without his face imploding, he started to shut the door.

"And Lavinia's going to feed some avocados to some chickens and set them loose in the bar," Crawford blurted out. His words were a lot faster now. "Apparently, chickens get severe intestinal problems after eating avocados, and she wants them to crap all over the place and stink it up. She plans to sneak them in through the back door just before closing so that no one will notice them until it's too late."

The reporter stopped, maybe surprised when he finally got reactions from Cleo and Judd. Definitely not flat any longer. Cleo now had a similar expression as to when she'd made the asshole reference. An "ewww." Judd just wondered if he should introduce Lavinia to Mercy so that Mercy could flatten her.

"I've installed some extra security at the bar, and she won't be able to get in through the back door without a security code," Cleo informed him. "But don't tell her that. I'd like for the chickens to stink up her car while she's trying to get inside."

That was almost as good as having Mercy punch her lights out. Well, not good for the chickens.

"There's more," Crawford went on. "Lavinia asked me to dig into both your backgrounds." He shifted his attention to Judd. "She thought there might be some dirt connected to your transfer out of Austin PD."

Judd went with a glare this time. It was his favorite way to neither confirm nor deny a vague shit-fling like that while sending a strong signal that this was none of the reporter's damn business.

After some moments of silence crawled on, Crawford turned to Cleo. "I don't know how Lavinia found out, but I didn't tell her," the reporter said.

"Found out what?" Cleo snapped, and she sounded about as pissed off with this conversation as Judd was.

Maybe it was Judd's intensified glare or Cleo's

narrowed eyes, but Crawford made an audible gulp before he continued. "That you actually own the Angry Angus. I'm sorry, Miss Delaney, but I think Lavinia plans to use that to cause some trouble for you. She says she's going to tell the cops."

Since Judd had already cursed enough this morning, he didn't add any more "shits," "damns" or "hells." He just stood there, shoulder-to-shoulder with Cleo, and watched the reporter hurry back to his SUV and drive away.

"I'll make some calls to my cop friends," Judd volunteered. "If all the paperwork for the sale of the bar was legit, then you should be okay." And he hated that he had to qualify that with the "should."

Cleo stayed quiet.

"I'll also try to touch base with Mrs. Gateman today," he went on when her quietness continued. "Or I'll have Kace do it." He was hoping by now the social worker had come to her senses and had decided to leave the boys at the ranch, but that was a mighty big hope. One that Cleo probably didn't buy into.

"Thanks," Cleo finally said. She turned toward him, their gazes meeting.

Judd went through another steeling up, figuring it was now time for them to have that talk about why she couldn't be in love with him. But it wasn't a talk look she gave him. Nor was there any gloom in her expression.

She smiled, and it wasn't one of reassurance. Nope. It had a naughty edge to it with her teeth clamping over the side of her bottom lip. And—what the hell?—that glimmer in her gaze was an eye fuck. One that made his body wish they were right back on the bathroom floor again.

She fisted a handful of his shirt, pulled him down to her and kissed him. "Accept it, Judd. I'm still in love with you."

CHAPTER TWENTY-THREE

CLEO HADN'T WANTED to have this conversation with Daisy over the phone while she was driving to San Antonio, but she couldn't put it off any longer. With Daisy's and her work schedules, there just hadn't been a lot of opportunities for face-to-face conversations. Heck, there hadn't been time for a lot of things.

Well, other than telling Judd that she loved him.

That had been pretty monumental. Along with hearing from the reporter that Lavinia might cause a stink about the bar—both literally and legally.

Both Cleo's declaration of love and Lavinia's plan had been important in their own way, but Cleo figured there was little she could do about either of them. The balls were in Judd's and Lavinia's courts now. Judd could either accept that she loved him or erect walls to keep them apart. Of course, in an ideal world, Judd would fall in love with her, too, but Cleo wondered if his past had already messed things up for his future. That's what he thought, anyway, and it was why he'd wanted only rec sex from her, had a stuffed rattler and went all mantra with "dick inches."

The ball was a little easier to decipher in Lavinia's case. The woman would continue to spew her venom, period, and if she couldn't do that by using the bar, she'd likely just find some other way. That's why Cleo had to prepare Daisy for the storm that could be coming.

It was still early, barely 9:00 a.m., but if Daisy was on schedule, she would have already gotten her daughter off to preschool. Cleo got confirmation of that when Daisy answered on the first ring.

"I was about to call you," Daisy said. "Lavinia came by this morning to gloat about how she's going to bring down you and the bar. Can she do that?" Daisy asked after a pause.

"Not really. I paid for the bar and put it in your name." It didn't matter, she hoped, that she'd done that only so there wouldn't be any hitches with a liquor license—something that had seemed so important just several months ago.

Apparently, some monumental things didn't stay so monumental.

"I'm on my way to see Lavinia now," Cleo explained. "I want one last chance to reason with her."

"You can't. She's not a reasonable woman."

The understatement of all understatements. But Cleo needed to try to get the woman off Judd's back. Cleo didn't know what had gone on in Austin to make him transfer, but if Lavinia had found some dirt, Cleo couldn't have her using that against Judd. The memory of his near meltdown was much too fresh for him to be put through anything else like that.

"Isn't there still a restraining order against Lavinia?" Daisy asked.

"Yes, but that's so she can't come to the ranch and get anywhere near the boys. I can still go to her house and get some things straight."

Daisy's huff was easy to hear. "You'd have more success just putting a voodoo spell on her."

"I'll keep that as an option," Cleo said dryly.

"You should." And Daisy wasn't in the dry-tone mode. "It works. Power of suggestion and all that. Just say 'I curse you' three times and fling an imaginary wand at her. If you believe it hard enough, it'll happen."

Cleo really hoped it didn't come to that. She equally hoped that her desperation level wouldn't hit so high that she started to believe malarkey like that would work.

"What could you possibly say to Lavinia that would make her change her mind about anything?" Daisy persisted.

Well, Cleo did have an approach in mind, but it was one that Daisy might not like. Since there was no way to soften this, Cleo just blurted it out. "I want to sell the bar." And she held her breath, waiting for Daisy's reaction.

"Uh." And that's all Daisy said for several seconds. "So you can be closer to the boys and won't have to drive back and forth?" Daisy asked. Cleo couldn't tell from her tone if she was upset or just shocked.

"That's part of it. A big part," Cleo added. "There's a chance the boys might not be able to stay in Coldwater, and I want to be able to move wherever they are. I don't want to skimp on my promise to Miranda."

"No," Daisy quietly agreed.

"And I'd like a fresh start to do things the right way. If I buy another bar or have another business, I want everything out in the open. I want my name on the ownership papers. Then no one, including Lavinia, will have anything they can hold over my head."

Cleo did more breath holding and waited for Daisy. She hoped her friend wouldn't be so upset—

"Good," Daisy said, interrupting Cleo's mental trip down a worst-case-scenario lane. "I can tell you're not enjoying this as much as you should be, and that means I'm not enjoying it, either."

"I'm sorry," Cleo said with a wince.

"No. Don't be. You bought this place before Miranda got sick, and you had no idea what was going to happen. It's just too much for you with the boys there and the bar here. Plus, I get the feeling you'd like to be closer to Judd."

Yes, in more ways than one. But Cleo stayed quiet about that because there was a possibility that her being closer to Judd might not make things better for him.

"That's why I have a business proposition for you," Daisy went on a moment later. "Tiny and I could buy the bar together, and we'd both run it." Daisy's explanation came so fast that Tiny and she must have discussed it. "Tiny wants to change the name to the Pissed-Off Cow."

Yes, definitely a discussion had gone on, and while Cleo didn't exactly approve of the name change, she was glad that neither Tiny nor Daisy were the ones pissed off about this.

"My mom said she'd lend me the money for my half," Daisy went on, "and then she could take care of doing some of the books and paperwork."

Cleo felt as if she'd just had a massive weight taken off her shoulders. A weight that returned when Lavinia's house came into view. Maybe this visit would go as well as the chat with Daisy had.

"Thanks for this," Cleo told her. "Once I've chatted with Lavinia, I'll come into the bar, and we can talk some more about this."

"Why don't you take the day off instead?" Daisy suggested. "You'll need some downtime after you deal with Lavinia."

Maybe, but Cleo was going to think positive about this. She ended the call and was about to get out of her car when she spotted the truck pulling up behind her. Judd. She hadn't mentioned coming here, but maybe he'd followed her. Or else he wanted his own version of a showdown.

Both Judd and she got out of their vehicles at the same time, and at the same time said, "I'll handle this."

They stopped, stared at each other. "You're here to try to stop her from screwing me over," Judd concluded.

Cleo only lifted an eyebrow to let him know that she was aware he was there to prevent the same for her. Apparently, screwing each other had spurred him to protect her.

"And you're here to stop Lavinia from messing me over," Cleo replied.

"She can't do that. Not over the bar, anyway. SAPD won't go after you for buying the bar and putting it in Daisy's name."

"Really?" Cleo asked.

"Really," he assured her. He paused. "Sorry about that," Judd said, tipping his head toward her. It took Cleo a moment to realize he was motioning toward her neck, which, of course, she couldn't see. "A love bite," he explained.

Oh. "I missed that when I was getting dressed. There's another one." She touched the top of her right breast and expected him to babble another apology or at least show some regret. But no.

There was heat in his cool brown eyes.

Heat that caused her to smile, and since she thought they could use some levity, she nudged him with her elbow. "You know, if you ever want your own personal suck mark, then all you have to do is ask."

He glanced away, taking that heat from her, and he cursed. "I'd let you give me a thousand hickeys if it'd make you stop thinking you're in love with me." He stopped, frowned. "Guess that wouldn't be the best way to prove that."

"Probably not," she agreed.

It was somewhat evil of her to enjoy watching Judd squirm. Of course, Cleo had to admit that her enjoyment was probably because of the tingle and tug he sparked inside her. The man could make her body burn. And she could apparently make him curse because that's what he did when he started walking toward Lavinia's front door.

Cleo had to hurry to catch up with him. "Are you going to threaten to shank Lavinia or something?" she asked.

"Possibly. As a backup." Judd said it with a straight face, too, and while he seemed calm enough, Cleo knew the woman was an expert button pusher.

"My backup is a voodoo curse with a pretend wand." She shrugged when he stared at her. Apparently, it didn't sound any better coming from her than it had Daisy. "Just use your code words if things get tense. Dick inches," she mumbled just as Lavinia opened the door.

For some reason, Cleo's voice carried as if she'd shouted it.

Obviously, this visit wasn't off to a good start, and Lavinia's sneer confirmed it. Cleo hadn't thought it possible for the woman to look more disheveled than usual, but she was wrong about that. Her hair was ratted up like a nest on one side of her head. Still no bra, and one of the holes in her gown lined up with her sagging right boob. The bottom edge of her nipple peeked out from that hole.

Judd handed Lavinia a paper, and Cleo quickly realized it was a copy of the report that Crawford had given them. "SAPD has that, and if you don't back off of Cleo, I'll have you arrested for each and every thing on that list."

That didn't tame Lavinia's sneer any, and if Judd's tone and body language hadn't managed it, Cleo doubted she stood much of a chance. Still, she'd try.

"Miranda would be happy to know that her sons are doing so well," Cleo said. "There's no need for you to keep taking swipes at Judd and me because the boys are all settled in with Sheriff Laramie."

Lavinia sneered, smirked and smiled all at the same time. It wasn't pretty. "Mrs. Gateman just called me," the woman said.

Cleo figured she shouldn't be surprised by that since Lavinia was the boys' grandmother, but Lavinia's smugness was skyrocketing with each passing second. It caused Cleo's stomach to plummet to her ankles. Even if Lavinia had changed her mind about getting custody, there was no way CPS would give the kids to her.

"You can't be thinking about going after the boys again," Cleo insisted.

"Not me." Butter wouldn't have melted in her unbrushed, unflossed mouth. "Mrs. Gateman's going after them. She said her husband and her want to foster the boys, and they just started the paperwork to make that happen."

JUDD WANTED TO tell Cleo that what she was doing wasn't working. Since they'd left Lavinia's and arrived back at the ranch, she'd gone from a depressed, almost catatonic state to repeating "I curse you" while flicking her hand in the air. Probably a gesture for that imaginary wand she'd mentioned earlier.

But wands and curses weren't going to fix this.

Before he'd jumped to the "doom and gloom" mode, Judd had called Mrs. Gateman to make sure Lavinia hadn't lied to them. She hadn't. The social worker and her husband had indeed decided to foster the boys, and Judd figured CPS wasn't going to turn them down. A married couple with their credentials would stack up pretty damn well against a sheriff with family backup.

According to the social worker, the boys needed a permanent, stable home now, and she was certain she'd be able to convince her superiors of that. Even though it was rare for a social worker to foster or adopt children from their own agency, it could be done in extreme cases. Mrs. Gateman considered this situation extreme since it would be next to impossible to keep the boys together otherwise.

Judd didn't flick anything, but he was back to mumbling "shit" and other assorted profanities. Of course, that would have to stop once the boys got home from school. Then, he'd have to keep his mumbled "shits" in his head while he tried to figure out a way to fix this.

Judging from Cleo's intense expression, she wasn't in "figuring out" mode, either, but if she'd come up with anything better than a voodoo curse, she wasn't passing that info along to Judd. Like him, she was sitting on the cabin porch, waiting for inspiration, which had better hit in the next hour before the boys got home.

"I screwed up," she said. She quit flicking and exchanged the nervous gesture for pacing across his porch. "I should have prepared the boys better for something like this." She paused. "Or maybe I shouldn't have insisted they be on their best behavior around Mrs. Gateman. If they'd acted out, she might not have wanted to foster them."

Judd had gone through the same things, and he had "bonus points" for promising Beckham that he'd make sure that he, Isaac and Leo stayed together. It was looking as if that's the way things were leaning, but it was possible that Mrs. Gateman would cherry-pick and decide against taking the surly teenager.

When her pacing ran its course, Cleo dropped back down beside him, and that's when he noticed the hickey again. Definitely not one of his better lover moments to mark her up like that.

"What?" she said, following his gaze, and she slapped her hand over her neck. "Oh, that. I'll put some makeup on it before they get home so they won't see it."

Good idea, but Judd was reasonably sure that out of sight was not going to equal out of mind for him. The memory of him neck kissing her was like X-ray vision. He'd still see the hickey, and, worse, he'd want to do things with her that had the potential to create more hickeys.

Since that was giving him stirrings in a place that shouldn't be stirred, Judd did a shift in thoughts and went with one of the other many things they could be talking about.

"You're really considering buying the Gray Mare?" he asked.

Cleo lifted her shoulder. "I've been approached about doing that. In fact, Audrey's uncle Marvin asked to meet with me tomorrow to discuss it. He's calling himself a motivated seller who'd be willing to provide financing."

"Yeah, that has something to do with a nightclub dancer named Bambi that he met online. She wants him to move to San Antonio."

"The one whose specialty is a 'slap and tickle' lap dance," Cleo mumbled.

He wasn't surprised that particular detail had made it to the gossip mill. Judd probably should have felt some concern over a sixty-something-year-old man he knew well falling for a stripper with a fondness for ass slaps, but considering he'd found his solace in a bottle of eighty proof, he wasn't one to judge.

"What exactly does get tickled in a slap and tickle?" she asked.

He smiled before he could stop himself. "I'm not an expert, but I think that's optional. The idea is just to keep it playful."

She smiled, too, and poked him with her elbow. "Want me to give you a slap and tickle?"

More than his next breath. That was the sudden and intense reaction that went through him, but even with the dick-twitching her question caused, he managed to give a noncommittal grunt. Then he shifted the conversation away from what would earn him an erection and another hickey for Cleo.

"You want to hold off on making a decision about the Gray Mare until you see what happens with the boys?" he asked.

"In part," she readily admitted.

Judd pressed some more. "You're holding off because you're in love with an alcoholic."

"Yes."

He frowned because he hadn't expected her to just admit it. Not without putting on kid gloves first.

"I'm already putting pressure on you," she went on. "First by asking you to help with the boys. Then by practically moving in with you. By the way, the Realtor did find me a rental house, but that's on the back burner, too, right now."

Judd thought about that a moment. He hadn't heard about the rental, but he'd figured something would come up sooner or later. "You didn't put pressure on me."

"Sure I did, and I added even more when I told you I was in love with you. I'm not taking that back," she quickly added, "but I feel guilty that I didn't spell out that you're not responsible for my feelings." Cleo shrugged. "Well, you are partly responsible because you're a hot, decent guy who's good in bed, but that doesn't mean you have to do anything about me being in love with you. You don't have to feel anything other than what you already feel."

Maybe not, but it sure as hell felt that way—especially since she thought he was hot, decent and a good lay. And now he was feeling guilty because Cleo was hot, decent and equally good in bed. Or on the bathroom floor.

"Careful with those compliments or you'll end up with another hickey," Judd joked.

It had the exact effect he wanted. Cleo smiled. She turned to him, their gazes connecting and holding. He knew what she said wasn't lip service. Cleo did believe he didn't have to do anything about that dose of "I love you" that she'd given him, along with the other "good in bed" stuff.

But Judd sure felt as if he owed her something.

"There was nothing bad for Lavinia or the reporter to find in my transfer records," he said, knowing that the abrupt shift in conversation would get her complete attention. It did.

She shook her head, maybe about to let him know that wasn't what the gossips were saying. Her eyes combed over him, searching his face, but she stayed quiet. Ironically, it was her quietness, her no-pressure approach, that made him keep on talking.

"There was a DS. A domestic situation," he said to clarify. "A man had gotten drunk, had an argument with his pregnant wife, and when she'd told him she was going to leave him, he took her hostage. He did that to prove to her how much he loved her."

Judd couldn't have kept the sarcasm out of that if he'd tried.

"I responded to the scene because I was in the neighborhood," he went on. "The front door was open, and I could see the asshole standing there wearing just his boxers. He had his terrified pregnant wife in a choke hold and was holding a paintball gun. It was one of the smaller ones that he probably could have shot with just one hand. It wouldn't have killed her, but it could have put her eye out."

"God." Cleo pressed her fingers to her mouth.

"Don't worry. This has a happy ending. While I was waiting for backup and the hostage negotiator, I talked the guy into putting down the gun and coming out so I could arrest him."

She kept staring at him. "How?" Her question was tentative, as if she might not want to hear the answer.

"Not exactly standard procedure, but I told the guy I was going to shoot his dick off if he didn't let go of her. And I reminded him that my gun had real bullets and that I was pissed off that a shithead like him would threaten to hurt a woman half his size just because he was pissed off. He put down the gun and let her go." Judd paused. "Things went right that day. Not because of anything I did. It just went right. And that's when I realized that I didn't need to be there in Austin to try to outrun my past."

Cleo probably wouldn't be able to see the connection, and it was the reason he never discussed it. But he'd gone into work that day and put in his transfer papers.

"A moment of reckoning," she said. "Like the one I had on the bathroom floor with you. What happened to the woman?" she asked before he could say anything about the reckoning. Not that Judd knew what to say about that, anyway.

Had an orgasm really been responsible for her falling in love with him? If so, that sure put a lot of pressure on the future orgasms he had planned for her.

So he could answer her question about the woman, he took out his phone and scrolled through until he found the picture of the wrinkled newborn baby, who, in Judd's mind, resembled a pissed-off Hobbit. "She divorced the guy, gave birth to this kid that she named after me—Judd Lee O'Leary—and she applied to the academy so she could become a cop. The next time some guy tries to mess with her, she can handle it herself."

Cleo smiled when she looked at the baby. "Yes, a happy ending."

Of course, Cleo hadn't meant that as some kind of code for the happy ending she wished for him and her. Cleo didn't play word games like that. But still that didn't mean it wasn't what she wanted.

Well, hell.

Did she want that? Better yet, did *he* want it?

Judd looked at her again, trying to tamp down his tornado thoughts and any equally tornado words that might come out of his mouth before he could think this through. That's why the relief jolted through him when his phone rang and he realized he had a reprieve.

Neither the relief nor the reprieve lasted when he saw Kace's name on the screen.

"I got a call from Mrs. Gateman," Kace said the moment Judd answered the call. "And she's on her way to the ranch. I figured one of us would need to talk to the boys about that so I went by the schools to pick them up early. They're gone, Judd. All three of them are missing."

CHAPTER TWENTY-FOUR

Because Cleo was right next to Judd, she had no trouble hearing what Kace had just said. The boys were missing.

"How long have they been gone?" Judd asked, already on his feet and heading for his truck. Cleo was up as well and hurrying after him, and even though she didn't hear Kace's response, she could see and feel the urgency in Judd.

"Cleo and I are leaving now to look for them," he added to his brother before he ended the call. The moment he had the truck started, he drove away.

"How long?" she asked.

Judd's weary breath told her she wasn't going to like his answer. "None of them even went to class. Lissy dropped them off," he quickly explained, "but the boys weren't there when attendance was taken."

Hours ago. God, hours. They could be anywhere by now.

"Kace called Buck first," Judd added. "Neither Rosy nor he has seen them since Lissy picked them up for school, but Rosy said there's some food missing from the pantry."

Judd didn't hesitate when he reached the end of

the ranch road. He headed toward the elementary school. "I found Beckham down here once before. He might have come back."

Good. That was a start, though Judd didn't sound especially hopeful. Neither was Cleo. Beckham had talked his brothers into running because they hadn't wanted to leave the ranch and go with Mrs. Gateman.

"I should have guessed something like this would happen." But even as Cleo admitted that, she had to tamp down the fear.

The boys had run, and now they could be in danger.

She willed herself to think, to try to put all the pieces together. Beckham probably had a little money that he'd saved from working the part-time job that Judd had given him. And Beckham had perhaps even called one of his friends from San Antonio so they could get a ride. Not that most of his friends had their driver's licenses, but it was possible there was an older sibling who could be talked into doing this.

But a ride to where?

"Would they try to go back to the place where they lived when their mom was alive?" Judd asked.

"Possibly. It was a rental, and they hadn't lived there very long, but they might go there."

She took out her phone to text both Tiny and Daisy so they could check at Miranda's old house, Cleo's apartment and also the bar. The kids had never been to the Angry Angus, but the address would have been easy enough to find, and if they made it to her apartment, they could have possibly talked the super into letting them in.

Judd pulled off the road near a cluster of trees, and he muttered some profanity when he looked around. "This is where Beckham was last time he ran off, but they're not here."

No. There was no sign of them, and since Beckham had likely figured out that they'd look here, this was probably the last place they would have come.

Judd's phone rang, and she saw Kace's name pop up on the screen. She held her breath as Judd answered it and put the call on speaker.

"They didn't go to Shelby and Callen's," Kace said. "I had Callen check his office in town, too. They're not there."

Cleo had to play another round of mental Whac-A-Mole with her own panic because she knew that would only get in the way of her thinking straight. "Maybe they'd go to Audrey at the hospital?" Cleo suggested.

"I'll check," Kace volunteered before he hung up.

"And I'll check with Mercy." Judd immediately texted his sponsor. "I don't think she had a lot of interaction with the boys when she was at the ranch, but it's possible she told them where she lived."

Cleo considered that. Yes, it was something Mercy could have done, but it didn't feel right. In fact, nothing about this did.

"Where are Popsicle and Mango?" Cleo asked.

Judd's gaze snapped to her and, cursing, he

snatched up his phone again. This time, he called Buck, and Judd did a U-turn in the road as Buck answered.

"The boys aren't in the pasture," Buck immediately said—again, Cleo could hear. "I've been riding out here checking for them."

"What about the cat and puppy?" Judd asked.

"You know, I haven't seen them all morning. I just figured Lissy or Rosy was taking care of them."

"Ask them for me, will you, and then let me know?" Judd ended the call the moment Buck assured him that he would, and he hit the accelerator.

Since Judd was heading back to the ranch, they were obviously on the same page, and Cleo could have kicked herself for not considering it sooner. Leo wouldn't have left Popsicle, and Beckham probably wouldn't have left Mango. That meant they were likely somewhere on the grounds.

Cleo said a prayer when Judd braked to a stop outside his cabin, and they hurried out, both of them running to the barn. Judd took the right stalls. Cleo, the left. They ran the length of the barn and came up empty.

And that's when Cleo heard the sound.

A muffled bark, followed by what appeared to be muffled voices. Sounds all coming from the hayloft. The relief came. It came like a flood. But the dread quickly followed. Cleo prayed that they weren't hurt and that they'd see how dangerous it was for them to do something like this.

Judd put his hands on his hips and glared up at

the opening of the hayloft. "They pulled up the ladder," he growled. "Get down here now," he called out to the boys.

There were more muffled voices and one not-so-quiet bark from Mango. It was the dog who trotted to the opening above them and looked at them. He wagged his tail in greeting even as someone—Beckham, probably—tried to pull him back.

"We know you're up there," Judd added.

"No, we're not" was the response. Leo. As expected, his brothers gave him a whispered scolding.

Several moments later and after what sounded to be a tense discussion, the ladder appeared in the opening and slowly lowered to the ground. Judd set it in place and motioned for them to get moving. They did, at a snail's pace, and Cleo soon realized that it must have taken some effort for them to get up there.

Isaac came down first. He had a bulging backpack over his shoulder and Popsicle tucked in the crook of his arm. Once he was halfway down, he tipped his head to Leo, who started down the rungs. Not exactly risk-free, since Leo still could have fallen, but Isaac was clearly ready in case that happened.

Judd stepped in, taking Popsicle and passing the kitten to Cleo before he hauled down both Isaac and Leo the rest of the way. Then Judd went up the ladder to get Mango. The kitten and puppy were obviously unaware of the looming trouble because they launched right into "let's party" mode.

After Beckham was down, the boys stood in front of them as if they were in a police lineup. Isaac suddenly became riveted with the barn floor since he didn't take his eyes off it. Though practically at attention, Leo giggled at Popsicle when he swatted Cleo's earring. Beckham met their gazes head-on, giving them a decent defiant stare.

The silence came, dragging on except for Mango's squeaky puppy bark. Cleo used the time to fire off some "we found them" texts to the people who were looking for the boys. Kace, Rosy, Buck, Callen, Shelby, Daisy and Tiny. She suspected there were others out there searching, maybe even the entire police department, so she added a request for Shelby to spread the word.

"Do we gotta go to jail?" Leo finally asked. And he took out a "get out of jail free" card to hand it to Judd.

Despite being furious with them for scaring her, Cleo nearly laughed. Probably not the most mature reaction for someone who should be doling out some punishment right about now.

"Is this how you see yourself taking care of your brothers?" Judd asked—the question was definitely aimed at Beckham, where he'd fixed his cop's glare.

Beckham was glaring, too, and he was almost as good at it as Judd. "Yeah, because we're not going with Mrs. Gateman."

"And you think this is the way to fix that, by hiding in the hayloft?" Judd added.

"It was better than what you were doing, which was nothing," Beckham snapped.

Cleo wasn't sure if the boy actually believed that or if it was the anger talking. Maybe both.

With possibly the worst timing in the history of bad timing, Cleo saw the car pull up in front of the main house. Mrs. Gateman, and she wasn't alone. Cleo guessed that the tall blond man with her was her husband. Hopefully, they'd come just to visit and weren't going to try to take the boys on the spot.

The muscles in Judd's jaw went to war with each other when he spotted the Gatemans, and he looked at Cleo as if trying to decide what to do. She wasn't sure there was a "right" way to go with this, but it was probably best if Beckham didn't confront the Gatemans right now.

"Why don't you take Leo and Isaac inside?" Cleo suggested. "Beckham and I can talk." Though she suspected she'd be the only participant in a chat. Beckham had already gone into his "pissed off at the world" mode, but one way or the other he was going to listen.

"Do we get cookies in jail?" Leo asked Judd.

"You're not going to jail, but if you tell Mrs. Rosy you're sorry for scaring her, you might get some from her kitchen." She hadn't thought it possible, but Judd's jaw was battling even more. "Come on." He scooped up the kitten in one arm, the puppy in the other and motioned for Isaac and Leo to follow him.

"We maybe get to have cookies," Leo whispered to Isaac, and the boy was obviously no longer concerned about incarceration. Leo skipped his way to the house.

"Go ahead," Beckham snarled. "Yell at me and tell me how stupid and wrong I was to try to protect my brothers."

Cleo frowned. Hard to reply with the way Beckham had framed it, but Cleo went with it. "You were stupid and wrong."

His narrowed gaze whipped up, zooming in on her. Obviously, he hadn't been prepared to hear the truth. Or the partial truth, anyway. Cleo sighed and went to him.

"You were stupid and wrong, but I understand why you did it," she amended. "Partly understand, anyway. What exactly were you planning on doing? Staying in the hayloft until you turned eighteen?" But then it hit her. The real plan. "Or staying here until Mrs. Gateman realized the three of you were too much trouble for her to want to foster?"

That didn't get his eyes unnarrowed, which was just as good as Beckham giving her a resounding yes on her theory. So Cleo continued to fill in the blanks.

"After Lissy dropped you all off at school, you didn't go inside. Instead, you met somewhere and told Isaac and Leo to go and then you came back here. How'd you manage to get Popsicle and Mango out of the house without Rosy or Buck seeing?"

Beckham lifted his shoulder and dodged her gaze, which meant he wasn't proud or comfortable with what he'd done. "I sneaked into the house and

got them after I had Leo and Isaac up in the hayloft." He paused. "You didn't give me a choice about
doing this."

"No. Because I didn't have a choice," Cleo
snapped. "I've got a police record and I own a bar.
In the eyes of CPS, that makes me unfit. That means
someone without a record and with a more suitable
job can swoop in and try to give you and your brothers a good home."

Beckham kicked at a clump of hay, and since it
seemed to ease some of his anger, Cleo tried it, too.
Unfortunately, the clump she chose had some horse-
shit under it, and she ended up kicking that. Her
misfortune made Beckham smile, for a nanosecond,
anyway, and it made her wonder if she could find
more shit to kick. The flicker of a smile was a start
to breaking this iceberg between them.

From the corner of her eye, she saw Buck approaching, but the man stopped. Probably because
he picked up on the fact that a serious conversation
was underway. He gave her a nod and led his horse
back toward the corral.

"You were doing an okay job of giving us an all
right home here at the ranch," Beckham mumbled.

That was high praise coming from a disgruntled
teenager so she hooked her arm around his neck and
yanked him in for a cheek kiss that he obviously
didn't want. But he didn't fight it, either. In fact, he
stayed there, his head pressing against her.

"So, what do I do—just give up?" he asked but

didn't wait for her to answer. "Do I just go with the Gatemans and pretend that my life isn't effed up?"

Even though her last "Honest Abe" answer hadn't gone over too well, she went with more truth. "I don't know. I wish I did have a fix for this, but I don't. I can talk to the Gatemans and plead your case to stay here. I can remind them that your mother wanted you to be with me. I can cry." She stopped, looked at him. "You think crying would help?"

His mouth tightened in a scowl but the tough expression didn't make it to his eyes. There was some softness there now. Some pain. Some hurt. And, yes, even some tears that he was blinking back. Beckham would rather sit on a cactus than cry in front of her.

"So, you'll talk to them?" Beckham asked, and she could see him trying to man up.

Cleo nodded. "No crying, but there might be begging involved. You think begging will work?"

Beckham didn't smile, not even close, but his muscles loosened just a little. Or rather they did until his attention landed on her neck. "Did Judd give you that love bite?"

Only then did she remember she hadn't put on that makeup after all. Mainly because she didn't want to make up a story about hitting her neck on a door, she just nodded.

"Does that mean you two will be getting together?" Beckham persisted.

She didn't want to make up a story about that, either. "No."

Cleo hadn't expected that to upset Beckham, but

this time it was anger that flashed through his eyes. "He'd better not hurt you or I'll kick his ass."

It took her a moment to gather enough breath to speak, and she had to do her own hard blinking to ward off the tears. "I think that's the nicest thing anyone's ever said to me. I love you, Beckham." And because she thought they could both use it, she kissed his cheek again.

Later, though, she'd remind him not to use the word *ass*. Or *effed up*.

She stood there several more moments, ones that she was certain she'd remember for the rest of her life. Holding him. Loving him. Wishing that love would go all magical on them and fix everything.

"Are you ready to go in and listen to me beg?" Cleo finally asked him.

Beckham nodded, wiped his nose with the back of his hand, and let her lead him out of the barn and back to the house. Since Cleo wasn't sure what to expect once they got inside, she gave Beckham's hand a gentle squeeze and stepped in. They were all there in the living room. The Gatemans, Kace, Rosy, Buck, Judd, Isaac and Leo. Even the puppy and kitten were sprawled out on the floor.

Whatever conversation had been going on came to an abrupt halt, and that was Cleo's cue to launch into the beg mode. However, Judd spoke before she could even gather her breath.

"The boys were hiding out because they don't want to go with you," Judd told the Gatemans. He sank down on the sofa next to Leo. "They want to stay here."

That earned him some nods and mumbled agreement from all the humans except for the Gatemans. "The children need stability," Mrs. Gateman said.

"And they can have that here," Judd went on.

Mr. Gateman shook his head. "They need family."

"They have that here, too, in Coldwater." Judd, again. "I'm not talking about being just fostered, either. Even though a lot of that has gone on here, and it's helped plenty of kids. Including me and my brothers."

Everything inside Cleo went still, and she walked closer, her attention nailed to Judd. Where was he going with this? Cleo didn't have to wait long to find out.

"I want the boys to stay," Judd insisted. "I don't mean I just want to foster them. I want to adopt them."

CHAPTER TWENTY-FIVE

WHAT HAD COME out of Judd's mouth hadn't been a surprise to him, but judging from the reactions of everyone else, they hadn't had a clue what he'd been about to say. Nine sets of eyes were on him now. Eleven if he counted Popsicle and Mango.

"Adoption?" Mrs. Gateman said.

"Yeah," Judd confirmed, and he meant it, too. Of course, he hadn't had a lot of time to come to this decision. Basically, it'd happened in the one-minute walk from the barn to the house, but it felt right.

God, he hoped it *was* right.

He'd screwed up plenty of things, and he didn't want to add these kids to any sort of shit list. Still, it wouldn't be a piece of cake. His alcoholism wasn't part of any official records, but he'd have to disclose it along with getting statements from Mercy and Kace that he'd stayed sober. If that wasn't enough, Judd would get recommendations from every cop he'd ever worked with. Buck, too. And anyone else he could think of.

His being single wouldn't be a plus for him, but in Texas he couldn't legally be denied adoption based on his marital status. If and when the subject came up, he'd bring in that same hoard of cops, family members and friends to convince whoever needed convincing that he could do this.

He figured it would help that he had a steady job, solid finances and plenty of people who would help him with this. He also figured that he could nip in the bud any future claims on the boys from Lavinia by documenting all the stupid and hateful things she'd done. That would mean getting more statements from the boys and a detailed medical report from Audrey to document the abuse. Judd wouldn't let anything slip through the cracks that would allow the woman back in the boys' lives.

"I don't want the boys moving to another foster home," Judd went on. "Not even your foster home," he added to the Gatemans. "I'll go see a lawyer today and get the paperwork started."

Judd glanced around the room to see if there were any objections to that, but everyone was still in gob-smacked mode. Everyone but Leo, that is.

"What's adoption?" Leo asked no one in particular.

"Judd would be our dad," Isaac explained.

Leo considered that for even less time than Judd had. Five seconds tops. Then he beamed a big old smile, then scrambled to get to his knees and threw his arm around Judd's neck. "I like that. Can we have a cookie now?"

In the grand scheme of things, that was a pretty darn good response. Judd felt relief. Then warmth.

Then love. Of course, Leo was the easiest of this group to convince.

"Well, I think that's a fine idea," Rosy said, getting to her feet. "Both the adoption and the cookie. Boys, would you like to come to the kitchen? I've got some fresh snickerdoodles."

Leo bolted off the sofa to follow her. Isaac moved a little slower, but he got up. "I'd like you being my dad, too," Isaac declared, and Judd got a dose of gobsmacking when Isaac hugged him.

Beckham kept his gaze on his brothers and Rosy until they were out of sight, and then he turned to Judd. "You really mean this?"

Judd nodded, and while he didn't exactly get a dad endorsement, Beckham didn't snarl at it. At least he didn't snarl at Judd, but he did have a steely expression when he snapped toward the Gatemans.

"You're not going to fight this, are you?" Beckham demanded. "You're not going to keep sticking your nose in and messing things up for us, are you?" They weren't exactly questions. Judd had heard threats from hardened criminals that'd sounded friendlier.

The Gatemans looked at each other. Then at Judd and Beckham. What they didn't do was give a clear answer that they were backing off.

"Judd and the boys could move permanently in here," Buck suggested. "It's a big place, and they're already at home here. I'd already talked this over with Rosy, and we'd agreed that we'd be signing over the ranch to Judd, anyway."

Judd was sure he blinked, and later he'd tell Buck that wasn't necessary. Though he did appreciate Buck allowing him to move in, Judd would later give him an out on the offer. An out that Judd was positive that Buck and Rosy wouldn't accept. No. Because in every way that mattered, Buck was his father, and he would want the same for Judd.

"I'll still be around to help Judd," Kace insisted. "My whole family will."

"I see," Mrs. Gateman said after a long pause. "This is really what you want?" she asked, her attention sliding from Beckham to Judd. Then to Cleo.

Judd certainly hadn't forgotten about Cleo, but since she was standing behind the sofa, he couldn't see her expression. Still, he doubted she'd fight anything that kept the boys here together. Well, she wouldn't unless she thought it would add more of that pressure on him she'd talked about.

Hell.

He hoped she wouldn't see it that way.

"It's what I want," Judd told her.

Beckham nodded. "Me, too." Unlike Isaac and Leo, he didn't hug Judd, but the glare in the boy's eyes dissolved when he looked at Judd. "Thanks, man," he mumbled.

That gave Judd another shot of that warmth, followed by more love. It was almost enough to make him forget that he could screw this all up.

"All right." Mrs. Gateman got to her feet, her husband standing along with her. "You said you'd be starting the paperwork right away?" she added.

"Today," Judd confirmed.

That seemed to be the right thing to say because the Gatemans gave more nods and headed for the door.

"By the way, you're grounded for skipping school," Judd told Beckham.

Beckham's jaw set, and he looked ready to launch into an automatic protest. One that never materialized. "For how long?" Beckham asked.

"A week." Judd wished, though, that he'd added more time to that because Beckham seemed far too relieved with the seven-day sentence.

Kace smiled, but he didn't let Beckham see it. "And speaking of school," Kace said, "I'll drive you and your brothers back to school so you can apologize to the principals and pick up the work you missed."

Good idea, and Judd was glad he hadn't had to come up with it. That was the nice thing about having backup. He didn't have to come up with all the good ideas himself.

Kace started rounding up the boys, but Beckham stayed put. "If you hurt Cleo, I'll kick your…butt," Beckham whispered to Judd. "Got that?"

Somehow, it was easier to agree to the adoption that would change every aspect of his life than it was to assure Beckham that there'd be no hurting when it came to Cleo. That's because there very well could be. That whole "Judd, I'm in love with you" was still looming over them like a tornado ready to drop.

Judd waited until Kace had the boys out of the

house before he turned to Cleo. She still hadn't moved, and she was sort of leaning forward as if her feet had been cemented to the floor.

"You don't have to remind me about the pressure," Judd said as a preemptive strike. "Or how hard this'll be. And maybe hold off on telling me that I've lost my fucking mind."

Her eyes stayed connected with his, and she moved then, walking toward him. Cleo's expression gave away nothing about how she was feeling. Not until the slow smile spread across her mouth. She took hold of his arm, leaning in until her mouth was right against his ear.

"No lectures." Her voice was a whispery breath that hit against his skin.

Judd waited for whatever profound words she was about to say. But Cleo pulled him to her, drawing him into a slow, thorough kiss. And that, he decided, was the best kind of endorsement she could have given him.

JUDD STEPPED OUT of the lawyer's office and looked around Main Street. Everything here was so etched in his brain that he could have described every detail with his eyes closed. But he looked now, carefully, as if he expected to see some kind of change.

Nope.

Everything was the same. Including the fact that the longhorn was obstructing traffic yet once again. But Judd felt different. Scared shitless was the first label that came to mind. Stupid was a close runner-up.

But the most surprising difference was that he felt, well, content.

Not a jolt like scratching off a winning lottery ticket but something that stirred through him like a gentle whisper. A whisper telling him that he was doing the right thing. And he hoped like hell he wasn't going to have to explain that aloud to anyone.

Judd was about to head across the street to get his air horn to deal with the longhorn when he spotted Cleo's car parked in front of the Gray Mare. He checked the time. It was still well over an hour before the boys would be getting home from school, so Judd went to the saloon to see what was up. Since the place wasn't open yet, he hadn't expected to walk into what appeared to be a party.

"Did you get the paperwork started with the lawyer?" someone immediately asked him. Not Cleo. The question had come from Audrey, who was at the bar with her mom, her uncle Marvin and a very busty redhead that Judd assumed was Marvin's girlfriend, Bambi.

Well, that explained the permanent smile that'd been on Marvin's face for the past couple of months. Judd figured his smile was somewhat similar when his attention landed on Cleo. Just looking at her could sucker punch him with yet more emotions that he hoped he never had to explain.

"I did the paperwork," Judd answered, and he

spent a couple of seconds studying Audrey's expression to see if that bothered her.

It did. But maybe she felt that way because it was tied up with the "eye fuck" look he'd just given Cleo. There was no assurance he could give Audrey, but he sincerely hoped that she found someone who'd give her one of those looks and that she'd then feel the unmentionable mush all the way to the toes.

"Cleo's agreed to buy half the place so I can take a whole lot more time off," Marvin announced. That apparently pleased his girlfriend because she squeaked with delight, clapped her hands and bobbled on her toes so much that Judd was surprised the movement of her boobs didn't off-balance her.

"We've already put in the boards," Blanche said, and she pointed to the Stupid Sh*t Men Say chalkboard. Next to it was one for Stupid Sh*t Women Say. They were both blank now, but Judd suspected once the booze started flowing, then so would the chalked gems.

"You're okay with this?" Audrey asked him. She didn't know that Cleo had asked him something similar about adopting the boys. He'd said a very truthful yes to that, and he said another one now.

Audrey smiled, and Judd didn't press to see if it was a genuine one.

"Well, I'll be going," Audrey said, smiling at Cleo, too. "Congrats on buying half the Gray Mare." She added a muttered "good luck" and headed out.

"She'll be fine," Blanche said to him. "Bambi here is going to introduce Audrey to her brother."

Blanche winked at Judd, brushed a kiss on his cheek and added her congrats to Cleo before she headed out.

Blanche's departure possibly spurred Marvin and Bambi to leave as well, but Judd thought that had more to do with Marvin sliding his hand over Bambi's rather curvy ass. Apparently, Marvin was going to start putting his time off to good use right now.

After Marvin and Bambi were gone, Judd stood there and stared at Cleo. She was still smiling, but he didn't go to her. Instead, he went to the Stupid Sh*t Men Say board, picked up some chalk and started writing.

I'd let you give me a thousand hickeys if it'd make you stop thinking you're in love with me.

Cleo's smile widened, and she went to the women's board.

What exactly does get tickled in a slap and tickle?

Their mutual nods indicated they were both good ones.

Now she came to him, and as if she'd stolen a page from Bambi's book, she slid her hand over his ass. "Still feel that way?" Cleo asked, tipping her head to what he'd written on the board.

"No. But we could do the hickeys on their own

and not tie them to the whole 'declaration of love' thing."

"You are such a romantic." Cleo leaned in and kissed him. And Judd kissed her right back, sliding against her and making the kiss long, deep and full-bodied.

"But about that whole love thing, the rec sex and the pressure," Judd went on with his mouth still against hers. "I want all three of those."

"You could add the hickeys to that want list," she reminded him.

He could almost taste the smile that curved her mouth. "Four then. Hickeys, rec sex, pressure—and I'm in love with you, Cleo."

She eased back, and yeah, the smile made it to her eyes. "Judd Laramie, you are so getting lucky tonight."

Judd didn't have to wait for the night for that. He'd already gotten lucky, and he pulled Cleo back to him to show her just how much.

* * * * *

Look for more books from
USA TODAY *bestselling author Delores Fossen,*
available from both HQN Books and
Harlequin Intrigue, later in 2019!

Unfairly labeled by his family's dark reputation, brooding rancher Levi Tucker is done playing by the rules. He demands a new mansion designed by famous architect Faith Grayson, an innocent beauty he would only corrupt...but he must *have her.*

Read on for a sneak peek at
Need Me, Cowboy
by New York Times *bestselling author Maisey Yates!*

Faith had designed buildings that had changed skylines, and she'd done homes for the rich and the famous.

Levi Tucker was something else. He was infamous.

The self-made millionaire who had spent the past five years in prison and was now digging his way back...

He wanted her. And yeah, it interested her.

She let out a long, slow breath as she rounded the final curve on the mountain driveway, the vacant lot coming into view. But it wasn't the lot, or the scenery surrounding it, that stood out in her vision first and foremost. No, it was the man, with his hands shoved into the pockets of his battered jeans, worn cowboy boots on his feet. He had on a black T-shirt, in spite of the morning chill, and a black cowboy hat was pressed firmly on his head.

She had researched him, obviously. She knew what he looked like, but she supposed she hadn't had a sense of…the scale of him.

Strange, because she was usually pretty good at picking up on those kinds of things in photographs.

And yet, she had not been able to accurately form a picture of the man in her mind. And when she got out of the car, she was struck by the way he seemed to fill this vast, empty space.

That also didn't make any sense.

He was big. Over six feet and with broad shoulders, but he didn't fill this space. Not literally.

But she could feel his presence as soon as the cold air wrapped itself around her body upon exiting the car.

And when his ice-blue eyes connected with hers, she drew in a breath. She was certain he filled her lungs, too.

Because that air no longer felt cold. It felt hot. Impossibly so.

Because those blue eyes burned with something.

Rage. Anger.

Not at her—in fact, his expression seemed almost friendly.

But there was something simmering beneath the surface…and it had touched her already.

Don't miss what happens next!
Need Me, Cowboy
by New York Times *bestselling author Maisey Yates.*

Available April 2019 wherever
Harlequin® Desire books and ebooks are sold.

www.Harlequin.com

HARLEQUIN® Desire

Sensual dramas starring powerful heroes, scandalous secrets…and burning desires.

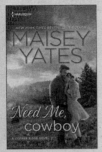

Save **$1.00**

on the purchase of ANY Harlequin® Desire book.

Available wherever books are sold, including most bookstores, supermarkets, drugstores and discount stores.

Save $1.00

on the purchase of any Harlequin® Desire book.

Coupon valid until June 30, 2019.
Redeemable at participating outlets in the U.S. and Canada only.
Not redeemable at Barnes & Noble stores. Limit one coupon per customer.

52616323

Canadian Retailers: Harlequin Enterprises Limited will pay the face value of this coupon plus 10.25¢ if submitted by customer for this product only. Any other use constitutes fraud. Coupon is nonassignable. Void if taxed, prohibited or restricted by law. Consumer must pay any government taxes. Void if copied. Inmar Promotional Services ("IPS") customers submit coupons and proof of sales to Harlequin Enterprises Limited, P.O. Box 31000, Scarborough, ON M1R 0E7, Canada. Non-IPS retailer—for reimbursement submit coupons and proof of sales directly to Harlequin Enterprises Limited, Retail Marketing Department, Bay Adelaide Centre, East Tower, 22 Adelaide Street West, 40th Floor, Toronto, Ontario M5H 4E3, Canada.

U.S. Retailers: Harlequin Enterprises Limited will pay the face value of this coupon plus 8¢ if submitted by customer for this product only. Any other use constitutes fraud. Coupon is nonassignable. Void if taxed, prohibited or restricted by law. Consumer must pay any government taxes. Void if copied. For reimbursement submit coupons and proof of sales directly to Harlequin Enterprises, Ltd 482, NCH Marketing Services, P.O. Box 880001, El Paso, TX 88588-0001, U.S.A. Cash value 1/100 cents.

5 65373 00076 2   (8100)0 12416

® and ™ are trademarks owned and used by the trademark owner and/or its licensee.

© 2019 Harlequin Enterprises Limited

HDCOUP0419

Get 4 FREE REWARDS!

We'll send you 2 FREE Books plus 2 FREE Mystery Gifts.

FREE Value Over **$20**

Both the **Romance** and **Suspense** collections feature compelling novels written by many of today's best-selling authors.

YES! Please send me 2 FREE novels from the Essential Romance or Essential Suspense Collection and my 2 FREE gifts (gifts are worth about $10 retail). After receiving them, if I don't wish to receive any more books, I can return the shipping statement marked "cancel." If I don't cancel, I will receive 4 brand-new novels every month and be billed just $6.74 each in the U.S. or $7.24 each in Canada. That's a savings of at least 16% off the cover price. It's quite a bargain! Shipping and handling is just 50¢ per book in the U.S. and 75¢ per book in Canada.* I understand that accepting the 2 free books and gifts places me under no obligation to buy anything. I can always return a shipment and cancel at any time. The free books and gifts are mine to keep no matter what I decide.

Choose one: ☐ **Essential Romance** (194/394 MDN GMY7) ☐ **Essential Suspense** (191/391 MDN GMY7)

Name (please print)

Address   Apt. #

City   State/Province   Zip/Postal Code

Mail to the **Reader Service:**
IN U.S.A.: P.O. Box 1341, Buffalo, NY 14240-8531
IN CANADA: P.O. Box 603, Fort Erie, Ontario L2A 5X3

Want to try 2 free books from another series? Call 1-800-873-8635 or visit www.ReaderService.com.

*Terms and prices subject to change without notice. Prices do not include sales taxes, which will be charged (if applicable) based on your state or country of residence. Canadian residents will be charged applicable taxes. Offer not valid in Quebec. This offer is limited to one order per household. Books received may not be as shown. Not valid for current subscribers to the Essential Romance or Essential Suspense Collection. All orders subject to approval. Credit or debit balances in a customer's account(s) may be offset by any other outstanding balance owed by or to the customer. Please allow 4 to 6 weeks for delivery. Offer available while quantities last.

Your Privacy—The Reader Service is committed to protecting your privacy. Our Privacy Policy is available online at www.ReaderService.com or upon request from the Reader Service. We make a portion of our mailing list available to reputable third parties that offer products we believe may interest you. If you prefer that we not exchange your name with third parties, or if you wish to clarify or modify your communication preferences, please visit us at www.ReaderService.com/consumerschoice or write to us at Reader Service Preference Service, P.O. Box 9062, Buffalo, NY 14240-9062. Include your complete name and address.

STRS19R